THE HEIDI
CONUNDRUM

THE HEIDI
CONUNDRUM

KEVIN READ

Copyright © 2022 by Kevin Read.

Library of Congress Control Number:		2022907712
ISBN:	Hardcover	978-1-6698-8807-9
	Softcover	978-1-6698-8806-2
	eBook	978-1-6698-8805-5

All rights reserved. No part of this book may be reproduced or transmitted in any form or by any means, electronic or mechanical, including photocopying, recording, or by any information storage and retrieval system, without permission in writing from the copyright owner.

Any people depicted in stock imagery provided by Getty Images are models, and such images are being used for illustrative purposes only.
Certain stock imagery © Getty Images.

Print information available on the last page.

Rev. date: 08/11/2022

To order additional copies of this book, contact:
Xlibris
AU TFN: 1 800 844 927 (Toll Free inside Australia)
AU Local: (02) 8310 8187 (+61 2 8310 8187 from outside Australia)
www.Xlibris.com.au
Orders@Xlibris.com.au
839240

ACKNOWLEDGEMENTS

Thanks to my daughter, Katrina, who was always there to assist with my technical issues. What a life saver!

My long- time mate, Terry Belleville, who resides in Canada, and inspired me to write a novel one day. Terry, thanks for your great friendship and support in Heidi finally being published.

Mike Andrews, my friend and relative for his ongoing encouragement and contribution.

And my cousin, Julie, who worked tirelessly with me in writing The Seduction of Min Xie, my first novel (unpublished), which inspired my two novels about Heidi.

Final thanks to my old mate Tony Cashmore for allowing me to use his name.

CHAPTER 1

The brilliant red Jaguar turns right onto the South Gippsland Highway north of Cranbourne. The Eagles' *Hell Freezes Over* DVD pounds in Mathew's eardrums; subconsciously, his left foot taps to the beat while he meditates on Min Xie and what might have been. He blinks, knowing she'll appear on his eyelids; it agitates his angst, but what can he do? He's in love, but she's gone.

Invasively, his mobile phone interrupts the rampant introspections; and as its early days since the end of his affair, they readily recycle to taunt and tease. He answers without pulling over, adjusting the radio volume as Milly's sing-song voice titillates. 'How are you today, Mathew? Been golfing, I assume?'

'Yeah, g'day, Milly. You sound bright and chirpy on this blustery day. What are you up to?'

'Golf tomorrow at Cowes but Park's crook. Any chance you might make up the four?'

He muses at her utilisation of the colloquialism, wondering why a Chinese chick will use crook instead of ill or simply not well. 'What time are you hitting off?'

'At 11.36.'

'I'm down by myself this weekend. It's about time we had a hit.'

How opportune. Strike one. she counts. *Be bold. Go for strike two.*

'How about dinner in Cowes tonight, my shout?'

'You're on. I'm a great believer that the flavour of the feast is considerably enhanced when seasoned by someone else's money. Name the time and place.'

The mirth in her voice traverses the mystic distance. 'The Mediterranean, it's on the main drag but after your last comment, we'll go to Macca's.'

He laughs softly and counters, 'No, we won't. There isn't one in town.'

'Very perceptive. See you at seven thirty, okay?'

'Too right. Drive carefully.'

Strike two. Milly congratulates herself. *How bloody easy was that?'* She punches Park's speed dial number into her phone, intent on pursuing an extremely delicate favour.

Mathew declines to shut the phone off and settles it beside Michael Dobbs' book *Winston's War*. He is heavily involved in the spellbinding storyline of fact and fable and it's his intention to complete it this weekend. The artful contrivance of Milly's telephone call will put paid to that agenda; still, it seems appropriate to pursue her offer of golf and dinner as the intent is surely innocent. However, Milly remains a character of interest – intelligent and humorous, tall for a Chinese with long shapely legs, with distinctive cheekbones set high on the typical round flat face, framed by a short haircut, bobbed at the back and sides with the obligatory long fringe, sitting on manicured eyebrows and like Min Xie, her lips are bold and perfectly shaped.

Is this planned? He questions, recalling the Christmas party where she was upfront about being single. His egotistical contemplation is disturbed by the throbbing music; adjusting the volume, he marshals concentration. *There's something askew in her relationship with Peter Lee. She's too bloody smart, too much the mover and shaker yet, by purpose, remains in the background. Maybe she wants to discuss the Adderley Street project, where Peter is failing in the provision of pre-development input. Regardless, they must appreciate, this is an important project with early sales in a tightening market, key to the development and my bloody success.*

A police car suddenly swerves out and passes just one car and then eases back into the stream of traffic. The unusual manner catches Mathew's eye in the rear-vision mirror; automatically, he checks his speed as a flash of adrenaline courses through his veins. The cruise control is set exactly on 100 kilometres per hour, then reality hits home – he's being followed again. *Don't those bastards ever quit?* He scratches his stubbly chin. *But why so bloody obvious, passing for no apparent reason and using a marked car?* His head nods in beat with the music, and his left foot taps in time. *Bugger, I'm becoming paranoid. I'll pull off at Tooradin and see what they do.*

Thoughts drift back to Milly. *I don't know much about her history except she came to Australia from Hong Kong, plays golf at Eagle Ridge, and works as Peter Lee's personal assistant at Jefferson Wright Estate Agents in the city.*

Reflections return to the Christmas party, where private invitations were covertly conveyed to several select business associates for supper. Spice, surreptitiously added to the occasion when Mathew extended invitations to the stunning Milly and the equally beautiful Mandy. The combination turned out to be compelling; they acted like a professional comedy duo, captivating the guests, ensuring the night would be discussed at other festive functions – the Milly and Mandy show. He recalls Mandy's lingering kiss, licks his lips to test the taste, and smiles. *Silly old bugger! But what's tonight all about? Dinner with friends, golf tomorrow to strengthen the ties that bind, surely orchestrated by Peter, trying to suss out my marketing intentions for the Adderley project.*

The single lane of traffic progresses through the Five Ways. Mathew looks to the left and marvels at the market gardens, deemed to be set out by theodolite and survey. Symmetrical straight lines of vegetables. almost ready to be harvested for market and cannery. In a moment of imaginary innovation, he crunches into a fresh carrot, a pod of peas and a crisp celery stick; the fantasy fades and reality returns to the initial proposition. *It's a bloody set-up. That little shit Peter has sooled her onto me. I need to be sharp, ready for the affray.*

But Mathew is wrong.

The radio knocks out 'The Girl from Yesterday'. *Yeah*, he groans, *That'd be bloody right!* Thus, without premeditation or deliberate intention, contemplations drift on the breeze like scarlet oak leaves as the season turns to Min Xie. With his eyes shut for one second, her face appears on his eyelids, tarrying in sublime recollection, like an enchanted autumn morning.

It's two wretched months since their last meeting, that fateful Sunday evening when Vincent finally demanded the relationship end. *The nerve of the bastard demanding we cannot see each other. I should have gone to his house, emptied my bucket to his wife, found him, and beat the shit out of him.*

Mathew's gut twists in anger while he rants and raves about the little prick, whom he hates with an abiding passion. In a sudden fit, he bangs the steering wheel with his hand and cries out, 'You bloody bastard, your time will come! One day I'm going to stick it where it hurts, your ego.'

The rear-vision mirror paints a grim picture; the police car remains in the ruck. Mathew takes a reassuring deep breath and returns to the reminiscing. *Settle down. The pain is diminishing. I often go some hours without thinking about her, when I'm busy, that is. But when the quiet times come, so does Min Xie to my mind, my heart, and my soul. God, I love her so. But it's over. I have to accept she's gone, committed to Vincent. I had my chance. I held the winning ticket to her life, our lives together, but I threw it away, electing not to battle the problems of my complicated property holdings intertwined with my foxy accountant's contrivance and, stirred by my own meddling, seeking taxation relief and manipulative opportunity amongst the family. Of course, deep down, I never once imagined she'd leave. Such arrogance. Such stupidity!*

Tooradin sits at the north end of Western Port Bay between Sawtells and Evans Inlets, comprising a dozen streets of mixed housing and vacant building lots. A landmark hotel dominates the sweep in the highway, adjacent to which, whether by clever planning or the pub's luck, resides the obligatory small-town football, cricket, and tennis clubs. He crosses the bridge, flicks the indicator on, and pulls into the service road as the police car cruises past, without a sideways glance from either officer.

The radio is directed to the sports station. Mathew decides it's time to mull over the Aussie rules football season, as the opener is just around the corner. *See how the experts predict the season.* He manages a smile. *I'm trying to move my thoughts from Min Xie to footy, understanding unreservedly there's no comparison, Your Honour.*

The police car fails to reappear; he concludes it's a false alarm but cognisant of the fact as long as he's involved with Horace the Horse, dodgy Brian and the faceless men in Sydney, the risk of constantly being under surveillance remains a prospect. He reaffirms his decision to keep his nose clean, no tricky deals, nothing to precipitate the Real Estate Institute or the law to instigate any investigation. Worry lines make waves across his brown forehead, inciting a frown and rightly so approaching the South Gippsland turn-off, he spots the police car, almost hidden in a copse of scrubby ti trees. When it fails to follow, he decides it has been just an erroneous perception; still, nagging thoughts remain and a worry worm churns his gut.

CHAPTER 2

It had commenced as a typical autumn day, crispy and misty, tempered by a gentle breeze that became gusty, eventually blustery. Mathew reflects on his golf game, replaying each hole as this is standard procedure after playing particularly well. He crosses the bridge at San Remo, noting the white caps out in Bass Strait and trusts it might just be one of those fronts, that come and go within twelve hours.

From Smiths Beach Road, he steers through the rickety old timber gate into his unkempt yard, the sunburnt country parched and brown. He's surprised someone has used the mower but the edges have been left rough, like the garden beds. His son's car is parked under the deck. Mathew wonders why, understanding he inherits the house this weekend and that is of no concern, except if he intends on keeping the old man company at golf tomorrow; a problem arises.

Mathew removes the basket of kitchen goodies from the boot and motions for the front door. Andrew greets him on the veranda and offers his hand. Mathew gathers a fatherly sense of pride, taking in the handsome slender man grinning happily as his large blue eyes sparkle. His brown hair is spiked up in the current fashion, reflecting 'disheveled' yet sort of in place, fitting the casual nature of the person.

'Heard the car pull up. How are you, mate?'

'This is a nice surprise.'

'Last-minute decision. Sandy is with friends over in Rhyll, they have a house on Reid Bight. Thought I'd pop over and say g'day.'

'The friends must be into fishing. They're obviously not into surfing with a house there,' Mathew adds in his often unthinking, arrogant manner.

Sandy is Andrew's latest young lady on his calendar of events. *Nice calendar, nice event*, Mathew muses, recalling he's only met her once, recognising a Miss Personality type on the surface; then as the evening wore on, both he and Hope determined she is, in fact, quite shallow and singularly one-dimensional in general conversation. Still, if looks counts, she rates up there.

'Been for a surf?'

'No, it looked a bit choppy. Then the wind picked up, so I gave it a miss and mowed the estate. How about a beer in the hot tub? I turned it on to your favoured forty degrees.'

They chew the fat about common interests but as always, conversation drifts robotically to Mathew's business. Andrew is continually and relentlessly in pursuit of the happenings with existing developments, new innovations, new clients, changing economic signals, problems in planning or construction and how they are resolved – all the nitty-gritty stuff which Mathew understands is part of the game, a way of maintaining dialogue with the old man.

'I'm going to Cowes for dinner with one of my city agents, want to join us?' Mathew asks.

'No thanks, mate. I'm booked in for dinner too,' he reminds him.

Another cold stubby slips down and conversation returns to Mathew's business as Andrew delves deeper into his stock control.

Later, Andrew barrels Mathew in the kitchen. 'Strewth, you look a bit swish. Male or female client?'

'Female and friends. I'll be home before you though.'

He is often wrong.

CHAPTER 3

Patting his ruffled head, Mathew pushes his way through the frosted glass doors, decorated in a tacky marine theme. The wind has whistled up Phillip Island Road, encouraging ice cream and chocolate bar wrappers, plastic soft drink tops and early autumn leaves to race and run in willy-nilly fashion, disturbing the normally pristine streetscape and Mathew's hair.

The minimalist dining room is only partly full. Purposely, he searches for Milly and friends on a table of four; instead, she approaches from the bar like a vision splendid, all frocked up in a long black number draped elegantly over one shoulder. A stunning strand of pearls decorate her elegant long neck; teardrop earrings studded with three small pearls complement both. *Why dress upmarket for a seaside restaurant?* he wonders and then notices the guys along the bar watching her walk, svelte, slinky, gliding with class.

'Good evening, Mathew. My, you look handsome. Nice jacket.' The linen coat over his heart is gently patted as she leans over and kisses him on the cheek. 'Shall we have a drink first?'

Without waiting for his planned comment of 'My, and don't you look bloody terrific', Milly turns and returns to the far end of the bar. Mathew ogles the long slit in the dress cut to the hip and her bum moving rhythmically, as a small grin creases his mouth. He raises an eyebrow to the boys at the bar, acknowledging what's attracting their attention, the statuesque, shapely Chinese siren whose dress has purposely been designed to fit firmly around her rear end.

The quiet end of the bar is secured; privacy a premium as if by purpose. 'Pleasant atmosphere. I haven't been here before. You?'

'Just once. We spend most weekends on the Peninsula.'

'Of course, playing Eagle Ridge. Shall we kick off with a glass of champagne?'

'Perfect. We decided this weekend to have a shift in venues. We do occasionally as it's a challenge to play other courses. Helen and Kim are life partners and Park, our Korean mate, makes up the four but he's crook, so it gave me the opportunity to call you. I hope you don't mind.

'Of course not. I understood I had the house to myself. I intended on curling up with my book, then cut the heads off the weeds tomorrow. Instead, I discovered my son was in occupancy and had mowed the estate, so we sat in the hot tub and split a couple of beers.'

'Are you always by yourself?'

Mathew wonders if Milly is opening cans; regardless, for some unknown reason, he tells it the way it is and asks, 'Is the Peninsula your escape place?'

'Yes, Kim and Helen own a small holiday house at Tootga-bloody-rook, three bedrooms, one bathroom unfortunately.' Her nose wrinkles as she grins. 'Not very private at times.'

'Better than nothing and when I was a late teenybopper, we'd slick our hair back and terrorise the rock dance at Tootgarook. If we couldn't crack a sheila, we'd brush our hair to the side and rush back to Rosebud and the jazz club.' He hesitates; a memory flashes. 'I particularly enjoyed Lazy Ade Monsbourgh's band.'

Mathew appreciated her politeness when there is no pursuit of 'who?' as the tune of 'Sweet Patootie' did the full lap of honour around the grey matter, only for him to realise it was the signature tune of the Red Onions.

'Ah.' She laughs. 'We have lots of fun. It's a very basic little house in a natural ti tree setting. No garden, therefore no work, except mow occasionally, if we can start the machine.'

Mathew imagines the scene; his grin widens.

'It suits us down to the ground. We love to play at being Aussie, swigging on a stubby, watching the grass grow, have another beer, then light the barbie and have another beer, look at the mower and reckon it's too hot or the grass too short, so we have another beer and say, she'll be right, mate.' Milly claps her hands loudly. 'Life can be fun just doing nothing.'

And so, the evening commences. They are in no hurry. Just as well, Milly's planned a long one.

The dinner table is located in a quiet corner; Mathew perceives if he'd been planning a night of intimacy and seduction, it follows the stratagem he'd have probably concocted. In a manner which he deems surreptitious, he gives Milly the once-over while she studies the menu. Confusing inappropriate visions emerge; however, unbeknown to Mathew, Milly's intention tonight is purely business. Seduction isn't on her mind; the opportunity to entice, she trusts, will occur at another time.

Conversation revolves around her friends, yet no offer's advanced on why the others haven't joined them and Mathew determines, it isn't for him to pursue.

'May I comment on your ring?' Milly suddenly asks.

'Of course.'

'Quite stunning, very Chinese, may I venture.' She offers that look women are so good at, half-smiling, enquiring, wanting to know but not desirous of being too obvious; and Milly, like a well-trained dog, chases the ball. 'Obviously very expensive if it's old English gold.'

Mathew declines to play ball and shuffles the subject back to what's easy. 'Tell me about the golf trips.'

Milly recognises the deliberate change in tack; being a clever skipper, she sniffs the wind and elects to follow in the wake, knowing there will always be time to revisit unanswered questions. 'Every so often, we take a long weekend to experience other places, discover diverse, vibrant Victoria, surveying new courses, ferreting out unexplored towns, enjoying the fellowship. We travel well together.'

Mathew decides he can play games too. 'Are you and Park an item?'

The look is quizzical; then she laughs. 'No, romance is not a consideration, just close friends.' She giggles, obviously tickled by the intimation.

After lengthy general conversation of a little of this, a little of that, which Mathew recognises Min Xie would refer to as 'rubbish' while he understands it to mean 'breaking the ice', finally, Milly arrives at the decisive exploratory question. 'So, what is it exactly you do Mathew, in detail if you may? Enlighten the uneducated in the ways of your world.'

Clarification involves a detailed explanation of how he acts for people seeking to invest in property but who don't have the time, the inclination, or the expertise to do all the investigative research, the often-tedious groundwork and demanding analysis. 'I do the sourcing and checking, making appropriate recommendation, often liaising with the client's accountants, bankers and or investment advisors.'

Milly delves and probes explanation and elaboration specifically in relation to the process of planning and permit obtaining, project design, construction, marketing and sales programs. Ordinarily, Mathew wouldn't dwell on his business; however, tonight he chooses to steer a different course as Milly represents the marketing and sales arm of a client who'll shortly be selling the Adderley Street project. Or that's what he assumes she's on about. He has the paddle; it's just that he's up the wrong creek, again.

Spotlights are activated; fascination commands centre stage and Milly acts brazenly, climbing into his brain, plumbing and probing, pursuing each answer, gently demanding clarification then soliciting additional explanation of the responses proffered.

Suspicion is reconfirmed, the assertion assured. *She's on a job for Peter, picking my brains. Maybe they're considering setting up a copycat style of business. Why am I here by myself? Why does she so openly dress to impress like a sultry Asian temptress when she's supposedly golfing in a casual holiday environment?*

Mathew is intrigued, amused at her game, and he decides to play along yet struggles to come to grips with whether he's batting or bowling, serving or receiving.

The process of securitization escalates. Milly pursues supplementary information on projects currently in planning or under construction, which automatically usher's interrogation directly to how much stock he controls. Mathew, by now, is totally losing the perspective of where's she coming from, let alone which game they are playing. And in regard to the stock, he has no secrets; they're not going to snip anything. So he sets the rudder and steers the good ship of possibility on a short cruise around the cargo he's carrying and totally empties his bucket, concluding with the Murray River project of some 150 villa and townhouse units, plus a boutique hotel which may see 20 to 100 suites sold off for investment purposes.

Milly is ecstatic. *Hooly dooly, around thirty-six residential suburban units, plus the Murray River project and to top it off, sixteen office suite investment units in suburban Sydney. All up, stock under control must amount to around 200 investment properties.* Then she sums it up. 'Great mix, Mathew – city fringe Melbourne and Sydney, Melbourne suburbia and the Murray River tourist track. You've done well.'

There is no need to comment. He isn't being arrogant; it's just the way it is.

Milly conducts him down the market track, questioning sales projections and the impact interest rates might have on residential multi-unit properties, particularly those dependent on 'off the plan' contracts. Might construction slow and developers disappear interstate, may end buyers dry up and will the role of investment advisers take over from, or seriously impinge on the traditional estate agent? Milly truly is into unearthing the nitty-gritty and Mathew reckons her investigation is exemplary.

Dinner is well and truly over before Milly stops and they pause for a breather. Mathew is under no illusion; she is after something. It's all too encompassing and too bloody specific. *I've been set on a definitive course, yet the destination beggar's my discovery.*

Milly strives to restrain her growing excitement. *Wowee, if we'd have conjured this up in Sydney, I'd have jumped off the bridge in delight. My star signs have been positive, promising a great year, new wealth, new business, new men – plural, I like that. New friends, travel and sporting opportunities increase. Wow. And here it is, sitting in front of me like a newborn baby. So, I'm committed. He has to hear my story, and then the plan will be exposed – well, part of it.*

'Do you fancy sweets, Mathew?'

'No, the flounder filled me up, but you go ahead. Enjoy.'

In manner conspiratorial, she leans towards him. 'I'm with you, full up.'

Mathew realises, *There has to be more than food to that sly look.*

'So, might I have tweaked your imagination? We need to have a very private business talk. Will you come back to my apartment, share a coffee and listen to my story?'

Inspired for no other reason than to discover what in the hell this is all about, Mathew simply nods. It will prove to be an eventful decision. How strange, life turns on questions and little whims, but most importantly, it's the yeses that open and close every sale, the crux crucial to adding another layer to life's fortune.

CHAPTER 4

Seconded in the living room of the Bay Beach Apartments, with the wind rattling a loosely fitting balcony door, Milly prepares coffee and readies to partly empty her bucket. Mathew relaxes, oblivious of how the story about to unfold will change his life, leading him into a future unimaginable. If he could have related the wicked twist, he's conjured up about *Winston's War* to his life going forward, he might have sought counselling as another chapter in the never-ending saga of truth being stranger than fiction, is about to be played out, in his very own life.

'There's obviously a reason for me delving so deeply into your business life, another side to my examination but where to start?'

'Try the start.'

'That's right.' She nods in confirmation. 'To appreciate the business opportunity, you have to know me and what has driven me to be here tonight. It'll take a while. It's a long story as I am obliged to commence at the start as you say.'

A Winstonism occurs to Mathew as he sips the strong, sweet coffee. *I understand the end of the end will not be played out tonight. Neither might I arrive at the beginning of the end, but it may just be the end of the beginning.* Grinning, he recycles the obiter dictum.

And Milly places Mathew's bike on the road to his destiny.

CHAPTER 5

'MY HERITAGE IS A SMALL town in rural China and reflecting on the time, it symbolised peace and tranquility in a little backwater. The communists were all powerful, the takeover well and truly completed but the community suffered no obvious excesses. My parents, like all the farmers, participated in the rural agricultural joint socialist state-operated farms. To survive, they nurtured small patches of vegetable gardens for their own sustenance, bartering excess produce to add a little cream to the very small cake, you might say. Life respected and even appreciated the ideology of struggle. It husbanded survival, chaperoned by antiquity, the genetic strength to go on. Existence was tough, often traumatic yet relatively untroubled, then the Cultural Revolution shook the very foundations of the nation. It took some years before our town was besieged by forced city labour, driven to work the farms by hard-nosed, brutal cadres whose humanities centred on increased production for the state and they discarded totally the ancient rural reverences, to heritage and community. Ultimately, the cadres seized control of the town by over throwing the local communist committee. My father sat on such a committee, representing the farmers but the new members set about radical change – out with the old, in with the new with absolutely no compromise and no disagreement. Failure to act on the committee's instructions often resulted in death and ultimately the execution of my father. When my inconsolable mother confronted the committee, she was taken out and shot like a crazed dog as an example to the peasants. I was made to watch her cold-blooded, callous murder.'

Milly places her hands at each ear and pulls them apart, exclaiming quietly, 'I can still see her head exploding.'

Mathew grasps the horror sweeping across her face and rushes to her side, holding her close as she shudders.

'Ha, so sorry. For a little girl, it was quite inconceivable to comprehend. Even today, the recollection rattles the roots of my soul. Thank you, I'm all right.'

He returns to the chair, adrenaline coursing as he replays the descriptive, theatrical use of her hands, evidencing death and murder most ghastly.

Milly gathers the strength to carry on, taking a deliberate deep breath to unfold the saga. 'My elder sister and two brothers were taken away. I've never seen or heard from them since. I was moved to a nearby town and became the slave of the cadre leader. Luckily, I was too young to be a sex slave, in that regard propitious, no doubt, through his cunning not because of any benevolent trait. A virgin has a value, a marketable commodity. At the time, I didn't appreciate 'beauty'. The Cultural Revolution wasn't time to take stock in such bourgeoisie contemplation. However, Cadre Fung suggested often I'd grow to become very attractive and one day he will sell me for lots of yuan. In the meantime, he kept up my schooling, pushing me to become proficient in reading, writing and coming to grips with my numbers. Such a lonely time. I'd lost my whole family, all my friends, all my relatives. I knew no one, a sad miserable period and I cried every night for what seemed like a year. The death of my poor father bad enough but to be made to behold my own mother's murder, impossible to bear, and now I relied on the butcher to survive, making it even more obscene. No one loved me. No one cared for me except Cadre Fung, whose only concern involved a perceived future monetary value.'

Milly grins, trying to lighten the moment. 'Today you'd say he was playing the futures market.'

Mathew agrees and returns to his cup.

'Anyway, school and drudgery dragged on year after year and then a wonderful thing happened. A school teacher took me under her wing. She'd been banished from Peking to teach against her will in the countryside. I discovered later that her children had been sequestered and sent far into the desperate depths of the country, placed without care or concern with people who would hopefully look after them, more likely to treat them as slaves. To suffer such a travesty, she must have done something very, very wrong or upset someone in a very, very high place. Her circumstance often mystified me as she was intelligent, extraordinarily creative and courageous. Thus, by mutual deception, I became her daughter, a clandestine arrangement we had to be so careful as even one of the children could dob us in to Cadre Fung. I didn't know it at the time but teacher, Miss Lee-Sang, proved to be shrewd, cunning, a very clever person with another side, which I didn't perceive, until it was time to show her true colours. Harboured in her bosom, invested a heart corrupted and twisted into a burning hate for the regime, which confiscated her children and banished her to a town of peasants and uneducated scum. Being of the ilk who had been trained or who just had the nous to plan and act for future eventualities. Miss Lee-Sang came prepared for the worst, she'd seen her fate coming and planned accordingly, drawing on the hate to strengthen and feed her resolution and resolve. A brother lived in the north of the country, beneficiary of a government contract to sail bimonthly to Hong Kong, delivering and returning with trade. Miss Lee-Sang ensured before banishment, whether by sufficient influence or nerve or nous, to surreptitiously obtain several sets of travel documents that afforded train passage to Peking. The key was the papers granted the bearer rights to travel on any major line, beyond Peking to any city, which for her meant going onto Yingkou. She knew the trip would be fraught with danger as she'd have to train into Peking Central and then north to Shenyang, a trip of around 500 km, changing to go 150 km virtually backwards to Yingkou, which is at the head of the Gulf of Liaotung. She'd conjured up a plan, based simply around the concept, if life became difficult or dangerous, just skip one Friday night, trusting her disappearance wouldn't be noticed until Monday. Therefore, if luck her passenger, she'd be in and out of Peking before the alarm went up. As time went on, I became closer in her heart, of course, I didn't know this at the time. To implement part of her plan, Fung approved a school photo be taken and using a borrowed camera, she took extra shots of me which were used for my travel documents. I'm now 12 years, starting to take shape. I was tall for my age with long legs, developing hips and Fung said he would sell me soon for big money. I approached Miss Lee-Sang and sought information about my fate when Fung sold me for my virginity. I was disappointment she only asked to be kept informed and if I had prized possessions which might accompany me when I left. You know, Mathew, I never even thought to query what she meant by leaving, funny, hey? Anyway, one evening Fung came home quite drunk, accompanied by a revolting pig of a man. They made me strip naked. He knelt down, opened my bottom cheeks and looked at my anus, ran his hands up and down my legs and using his fat fingers opened my petal. I watched in desperation and loathing. He peered up at me with an evil smile and somehow, I found the courage to stare him in the eye. Then I was made to leave the room and I heard them arguing quite vehemently. Finally, it must have been agreed as I heard the spitting and hand slapping, signifying the sealing of the deal. Fung told me later, I would leave in two weeks. Next morning, I sought out Miss Lee-Sang and conveyed in abject despair the frightful news. Ha, yet she remained so calm. I will never forget her words. Child, I can only tell you once. Listen carefully, or we are both dead. I will go to Cadre Fung and arrange for you stay with me over the weekend to help with schoolwork and that is all you need to know. On Friday night, we went to the station and embarked on the weekly to Peking. The miss had papers prepared, they included my family Chinese name as hers. Therefore, we travelled as mother and daughter. The trip into Peking was uneventful. I didn't see much until the suburban lights started to amaze me. Am I boring you, Mathew?'

'Absolutely not. It's like a tale from a book, an adventure story.'

'Shall I make more coffee?'

'I'll make it. You continue. I'm fascinated.'

'When we disembarked, the station was inundated with soldiers and as we transferred to the platform for Shenyang, our travel papers were checked several times. I remember clearly the soldier's boots shone brightly in the station lights. Ha! Funny, the things you remember and I can still taste the bean curd we ate at a stall.'

Milly smiles faintly. Mathew assumes she's recalling the taste.

'For five hours, we waited for the train. I understood Mummy encapsulated the epitome of nervous. If the word's out we're on the run, Peking Central Station will be the obvious place to look. Mummy took me into a bathroom and with a pair of scissors, quickly cut off nearly all my hair. Strictly, she instructed me to walk like a man, take longer steps, slouch as I walk and swing my shoulders a little. The toilet block became a practice ground. Now I resembled a male, tall and skinny with baggy clothes that covered the little of my sex. Mummy went back into the toilet, cleaned up and changed the travel documents. I was now her son. Can you imagine, Mathew, how clever, what expertise or how experienced she has to manage this?'

Mathew nods, trying to imagine the danger surrounding them.

'I lay on the long seat and slept, entrenched in the adventure, not understanding the ramifications of discovery. Ultimately, the train arrived two hours before departure. The station starts to fill with police and more soldiers and the impending travellers. We were questioned on several occasions; Mummy believes the word is out. The hunt is on but they're looking for a lady and a young girl and intuitively or instinctively, she changes her voice and talks rough country, uneducated, not like a teacher. Our carriage is full to overflowing. Several people squat on bundles of belongings on the filthy floor. We are accompanied by ducks, chickens, puppies in cages and a small goat on a string tether. The smell becomes quite terrible. People hurry to push the windows down, which offers no respite as the smoke billows back. Ha, but that's aside to the story.'

'But it adds colour and flavour to your narration.'

Milly screws her nose up. 'Pity I cannot add the odour. With the dawn came departing. I was excited. The train huffed and puffed, jerked and jolted and the smelly smoke spewed in. Then people rushed to close the windows, which only encouraged the pong.'

Milly twitched her nose again, sipped the coffee and continued, 'I began to appreciate the size of the city, seemingly sprawling away forever, a sea of timber, brick and tin and a mass of wires. I'll never forget the tangle of overhead wires.' She shook her head in disbelief at what she'd witnessed.

'The suburbs faded away, and the wonderful countryside emerged. I sat at a dirty window, taking it all in as we travelled north at a steady rate through endless visions of rice paddies, vegetable and fruit gardens, meticulously set out fields often separated by mossy brick or dark stone walls or tall poplar trees swaying precariously in the wind. But what were we travelling to? I had no idea, Mathew. Miss Lee-Sang might have intended selling me as a sex slave. Still, it was the adventure I loved. I revelled in the excitement of the guards, the soldiers, the police all questioning and inspecting our papers and the fellow travellers. Ha, if I only had time to explain the sights and smells, and I was obviously ambivalent to the dangerous situation we were in.'

Milly hesitates as she takes to her coffee cup again. 'The train line returns to the coast at Shanhaiguan, which borders on the Gulfs of Chihli and Liaotung. A mandatory stop offered opportunity for the railway police to board and check our papers, before we could alight and stretch our legs. I'd curled up in a small space and slept on the floor, then woke sore and cramped. But poor auntie stayed awake, the protector of myself and our small bag of irrelevant valuables. Next morning, we arrived in Shenyang with a whole day to wait for the train to Yingkou. Miss Lee-Sang debated about going to a cheap railway hotel but declined the temptation, only more people to inspect our papers. Outside, we stumbled on a small park and a tiny eatery which allowed us to fill our tummies with rich, hot, thick vegetable rice soup. Auntie said she must sleep and I remember her stern, hard words of warning that if police or soldiers or anyone suspicious approached, I must wake her immediately. I took those instructions to heart and was so diligent she slept for so long, I began to wonder if she'd died.' Milly grins.

'We found a market but it stank, so shocking even for our Chinese noses. We stumbled out, gasping for fresh air, which in reality, I have to say, wasn't too fresh either as the station didn't reside in the most salubrious part of town. Anyway, we retreated to the park until evening and then returned to the station. Auntie kept reminding me to walk like a man, saying, 'You look like a man. No wonder this is working well. I think we are going to be okay.' Once as our documents were being checked, Auntie told a young soldier we'd run out of money and are destitute until we arrive at her sister's house in Foshan.

'Hey, hold on, you said they were going to her brother's in Yangow.'

'Ah, Mathew, your pronunciation is terrible but I'm impressed. You've been listening. Wise auntie said it purposely so if we were traced, the soldier under questioning would say, 'Yes, I saw them, and they went to Foshan.' Clever, hey? And how good is this? The soldier returned with two bowls of noodles. I am making this a long story. So sorry, anyway eventually, we reached our destination. Auntie sought directions and we arrived at her brother's house, where we were greeted with great excitement. Then I received my first big shock. Auntie started to teach me to speak English. I recall her words so clearly. 'This, child, is the language of your future. Mandarin the language of your heritage. You must be diligent like at real school. You must work hard. I have plans for you. I cannot make them work unless you give me the tool. The tool is your capacity to speak this new tongue.' I recall saying to her, I had no idea you can speak languages and she commented back wryly, there is much you do not nor ever will know about me, child and I believed her. So, Mathew, do you understand that sometimes in life, we have bad luck?'

'Yes', he replies and considers adding more but determines it isn't the right time.

'But isn't life wonderful? At times, it brings you good luck, yes?'

Again, he responds, 'Yes', simply adding, 'I have enjoyed much in my life.'

'Good. Then you appreciate the language comes easy to me, so easy, in fact, Uncle starts teaching me Cantonese at the same time. 'It is the language of Hong Kong.' Uncle took me to his ship. He called it a big ship, but even I knew it was too small to be called such. Regardless, it seemed to have an abundance of cargo room under deck with an expansive deck area for more storage. Uncle explained his small crew sails to Hong Kong via Qingdao, Shanghai, Wenzhou, Fuzhou, and Shantou. He portrayed himself as tough and savage with pockmarked skin like beaten leather, a legacy from the sea and the salt, I assumed, still he treated me kindly, almost with respect and I was allowed to explore the boat at will. One day mucking around in his office, which doubled as his sleeping quarters, I heard several people approaching. The proper course was that of discretion, so I took sanctuary in the map cupboard. Through a crack, I spied Auntie, Uncle and two men dressed like city people. Each placed on the large table a battered suitcase held together by thick leather straps and the older man said, 'Five million yuan in the suitcases and the machinery crates stored in the hold and added gruffly equal to US$500,00, and we'll accept the usual deal, $350,000 to the Hong Kong account.' Everything seemed friendly. I assumed this might be a regular occurrence. Then I had such a shock I nearly fell out of the cupboard as uncle said,

'We have developed a brainwave.' Then he laughed loudly. I remember Auntie didn't. He referred to me as having no family, no history, no records, yet they had deduced I was clever with a capacity to learn quickly and comprehend easily. Uncle proposed he ship us to Hong Kong. Auntie will be my governess and ensure I progress through school onto university, where I'm to study commerce, business management and ultimately into a bank for experience. Then to Australia or Canada or, worst case, New Zealand, where we were to be responsible for the investment of the secret funds directly into income-producing properties. He used the term *safe as the emperor's garden*. I thought it strange, China no longer having an emperor. Ha, I diverge again, sorry. Anyway, there was much excited conversation. The city men became enthusiastic. Finally, it was agreed and there was more excitement. I was excited too but didn't know why.' Milly laughs loudly.

Mathew turns the jug on, recognising it is indeed going to be a long night.

'Mirth and excitement suddenly evaporated when the men said they cannot provide international passes to travel to Hong Kong. I heard the word smuggle, I became frightened and cringed into the dark confines of the musty cupboard. Uncle and Auntie acknowledged the risk but agreed it would be worth it and the city men seemed buoyed and commented, the scheme was breathtaking in its scope to provide a future measured in secure, safe property. I'll try to abbreviate this, Mathew.'

Stirring the crystals into the dark brown beans, he comments forcefully, 'No way. It's like a novel. I'm right into it.'

'The next part of the adventure truly terrified me, yet typically, Auntie remained stoic and strong. Uncle taught us how to duck-dive first in the shallow bay, then in open water in the dark and finally under his boat. In the hull, a section about the size of three bodies had been built. It formed an air pocket. Two pairs of goggles with tiny air snorkels were attached to the wall by a clip. Uncle explained, if we were approached by the navy, we'd slip out through a door opening just over the waterline, dive and find the air pocket, slip on the goggles to save our eyes from stinging and that would help our concentration to breathe through our noses so as not to choke, cough and splutter in panic. We discovered arm hold bars and a strap for our feet to assist in buoyancy. Every day, often in the pitch of midnight, Uncle forced us to dive and bloody dive until it came easy, while in the daylight hours Auntie pounded me with English. Then it was time to set sail for Hong Kong and into my future. We were accompanied by two men who sailed as crew. They were good-natured people who respected us in what you might understand was tight circumstances. The weather was clement until we entered Pohai Strait and the big swell rolled in. I loved to stand on the bow and watch the boat dip and dive into the waves, marvelling as the bow reached over the horizon and then crashed back down again, often with the spray washing over me. Auntie begged Uncle to stop, it being too dangerous, so he asked if I was frightened. Knowing I'd be stopped yet wanting to challenge my fear, I lied, elaborating it was nothing like anything I'd experienced in my life, which indeed contained the truth. I'd not seen a sea, let alone sail on one. The trip was actually quite boring except in and out of harbours, but we had to remain reclusive, undetected by the coolies and the bosses. We were boarded once about 250 km from Hong Kong, the navy boat coming out of the harbour at Fuzhou. It meant panic stations for us as we slipped under the boat but the practice gave us the courage as the ship lurched in the swell, waiting to be boarded. Whispering encouragement, Auntie talked about the fabulous future in Hong Kong and then possibly Australia. I recall asking Auntie, where is Australia? We stayed under the boat for nearly an hour, the sailors not interested in the ship, wanting only coffee and a bottle of hard liquor and some chit-chat. The rendezvous was a regular occurrence. Uncle expected it and started preparing his bath, so he told the navy men. Later, when we emerged nearly frozen stiff, the bath was a lifesaver as it thawed our bones. Have you ever been on Hong Kong harbour at night, Mathew?'

'No, but I've flown in over the Peak. That's something else.'

'Well, we arrived just after dusk and sailed slowly up Tathong Channel and executed a hard-left-hand turn between Lei Yue Mun Point and Hong Kong Island, then the light show began. I'll never in my life forget that sight but it was punctured without warning, when a jet airplane took off from Kai Tak Airport. God, Mathew, I thought the plane might take our heads off. The sound of thunder in the wildest storm coupled with the screaming of the engines and the smell of kerosene – it was all quite incredible. As the jet swept over us, the crew waved and smiled at me. I must have expressed the most amazing look of astonishment on my face. Slowly, we steamed down Victoria Harbour. I marvelled at the amazing spectacle of the towering buildings, all the lights and my head was on a swivel, turning repeatedly, searching the shores for more exciting sights. It seemed quite unbelievable, yet I discerned the place suffered a distinct odour, failing to live up to the name Fragrant Harbour. We dodged our way around dozens of huge ships seemingly anchored at random, with no sense of design or purpose. Many were surrounded by a multitude of lighters swinging peacefully on the millstone while frantic workers, like frenzied ants, rushed willy-nilly under the ship's lighting system and the relentless mass of walla-wallas bobbed their way around us, the lighters, the ferries and the ships.'

Milly smiles and sips her refreshed coffee. 'Finally, we anchored just before the typhoon shelter south of Kowloon and the cross-harbour ferry terminal. The typhoon shelter's a permanent place for small boats to dock, which is also home to thousands of people. Auntie and I lived on one of those boats for the next eleven years. As uncle expressed to the men that day in his cabin, my life developed into schooling and studying. I had little outside life. Still, I was happy and free. I perceived a future and each year I understood more as slowly, they explained my role in the scheme of things. With maturity came Auntie's lectures. She was a good teacher, very explicit, knowledgeable, and obviously experienced. I enjoyed her sex lectures as my body sought an excuse to have my own adventures, to discover my sexuality. Auntie made it sound so exciting, something to relish and enjoy, to please and be pleasured in turn. I qualified for uni at the international school, which arrived with a bonus. I met kids from all over the world. My lecturer in business banking became my sex educator and my study guru. I spent all my spare time with Michael, studying both BB and the human body and what makes it tick sexually. If you have enjoyed sex that is so special, you often cannot believe it. That's what Michael and I shared.'

Mathew smiles, which isn't picked up on.

'I graduated from university third in the class but I had little to celebrate. Michael left me pregnant and flew home to Canada. Auntie understood my predicament. 'One of the catches of being sexually active,' she espoused. But Uncle was furious and threatened the Number Eight Toe Clan will find him, break a knee, or snip a toe or two off. Initially, I struggled to cope with the seriousness of the threat and then gathered from Auntie, Uncle never offered a casual comment when it came to the clan, so I pictured Michael in Vancouver or Toronto with a limp. In my fifth month, Typhoon Nellie hit. I was late leaving the bank. I expected to be safe. However, I'd never experienced such winds that were far too strong for my skinny frame. I stumbled in the dark, fell over the gutter and tumbled down the road until two policemen caught me. I lost the baby.'

Her eyes close and lips tighten, but before Mathew could comment, she blinks and continues, 'You understand, Mathew, we Chinese have a different attitude to time. When they signed the Treaty of Nanking in 1842 with the British for the island and then the New Territories in 1898 for ninety-nine years, the future of Hong Kong predicated on 1997, when reversion to China was destined. Can you imagine an investment lasting 100 years?'

Not waiting for an answer, Milly proceeds, 'Of course not. Frankly, from what I discover about Aussie investors, five years is a long time. Anyway, the old Chinese were happy to let the British have the harbour for 100-plus years because in that time they would know everything the British knew, 'pick their pockets' as they liked to say, plus what might they finish up with. At that stage, who knows? Still, it had to be so much better. What I'm saying is we think very long term, and Uncle, in conducting his currency deals, took a medium-term investment, being prefaced on a very specific sunset clause, the first of July 1997. The top echelon of bureaucracy was smuggling money out of China, but they only had yuan, the mainland China local currency. It needed to be converted into hard currency to invest overseas, so Uncle and his bank associates took the yuan, discounted it by 30 per cent and transferred the equivalent into a US dollar account. Uncle made 30 per cent in yuan on every trip, investing in Hong Kong on the twofold presumption property values will only rise and probably boom after takeover and then his yuan will rank equally with the mainland. He was in that win-win Chinese love. My time at the bank allowed me to learn all about international currency trading, the how and where to shuffle money internationally. Then Auntie and I moved to Melbourne on visitor's visas. I recall them arguing about permanent residency. He kept saying, 'Don't worry, the clan has contacts and will use *h'yeung yau*.' You understand fragrant grease, Mathew?'

'Yeah, sort of.'

'Auntie kept saying, you better. Uncle encouraged me to enroll into a full-time real estate licensing course, which I passed in just one year. Then I worked for twelve months with a St Kilda Road branch office of Carters. They no longer exist, taken over by someone. I forget. Doesn't matter, hey? Uncle, through contacts, steered me into the position of assistant to Peter Lee and my real estate experience helped me settle into the firm quickly and productively. Our fortune was made in the halcyon years leading up to 1997, when the money poured out of Hong Kong. So, Mathew, you know where Peter Lee's success comes from?'

'I think I have heard enough, but you're going to tell me.'

'It comes from me. Every month on average, I give him two sales from clients emanating from the Tiger Commercial Trust Bank as it transfers directly or authorises funds to be moved from other banks located in countries offering convenience to the use of secret accounts et cetera. These funds satisfy the purchase of very select properties which I source, vet and make appropriate recommendations to the bank which controls it all. So, Mathew Allen here is the crux of tonight. What the preamble has been all about, Uncle and I want more of the pie. Peter pays us only 1 per cent of each sale. Our average investment per month is $750,000 Aussie. That's just $7,500 to us, and frankly, we think it's chicken feed. We want to work with you, place our investment dollars into your stock. It's quite a simple plan. You have the stock. We have the money. And with respect, you're in a changing, probably declining, market, whereas my money supply market is about to boom. Money will start pouring out of Hong Kong. The flight of the yuan will increase out of China as the upper middle class seeks safety and security. We have opened up a channel out of Taiwan, another place where people are making millions. Now they also seek safety and security and Uncle's very secret contacts in Pyongyang remain intact and active.

'You see, Mathew, we do what you do. We source and recommend investments for our clients, hold their hands and maintain control like clever you. Our projections show at least a million a month and we envisage it being worth $30,000 a month minimum to us. It may be more if interest rates rise and the market suffers a correction. Your clients will then love our cash flow and they will pay for it accordingly but the bonus is no marketing costs, so we believe we are very democratic in our demands.'

Mathew glances at his watch. 'Crikey, it's late.'

'Well that's about the story anyway. What do you think?'

'I think you are a very adventurous bugger and Auntie sounds like a character I have to meet.'

'Ah, so sorry. She had cancer. It was not discovered until too late. I lost her last year. I miss her so.'

'Oh, sorry for your loss. I appreciate she meant much too you. As to the business, it's a lot to take in. Can we talk more next week?'

'Of course. See you at golf and by the way, my friends know nothing of my story. I trust it remains our secret.'

Mathew racks the possibilities for the future. A strange feeling of excited contentment settles over him, until he turns into the driveway of his house, where the lights burn bright. *Strewth, how do I explain this?*

'Hey, mate, a big date, a long night. Hey, didn't know any of the eateries over the other side would be open this late.'

Andrew laughs with a wide smile. 'So, what's it worth to keep mum?' The wink is slow, sly and questioning.

'Yeah, good one. When you have time, you should hear this story. It's a beauty. In fact, it'd make a good book.' Mathew deliberately offers his serious face.

'Really, just business?'

'Of course, you silly bugger. Can you see me having a fling? However, she's Chinese, tall, slender, beautiful body, mature, smart. Now you see why I'm late and yes, mum is the word. Anyway, goodnight, mate. Need to be at the track at eleven. Thanks for mowing the estate but next time, tidy the edges. It finishes the job.'

Milly stretches out on the couch, sipping a final tea. *Well, Comrade Keng, we've designed the kite. Without being unduly coy, I believe I floated it temptingly into the wind. Let us pray it soars and sails majestically. In the meantime, I'm going to call it strike three and you're in.* She laughs out loud and in animation almost spills the tea and admonishes herself. 'Patience, silly girl, but how exciting. I can't wait to read the tea leaves.'

CHAPTER 6

For Milly, golf has been a day of frustration. Patiently, she waited for Mathew to convey a signal of intent but when none eventuated, she was left to add patience to determination.

Back at his house, Mathew discovers Andrew has whipper-snipped the garden edges and he smiles. Inside, he finds a hastily scribbled note, 'Gone to Inverloch, visiting friends then back to the smoke.'

Finding solace in the hot tub, accompanied by a cold beer he contemplates the story of Milly and ponders the secrets that lie hidden in people's lives. How shocking the experience of her childhood, yet how obvious the love of adventure, contributing to the person she is today and what a godsend she might be to his business. Mathew is convinced the reserve bank will kill the investment property market. The fear of more interest rate rises, continually talked up by the press and the so-called experts, will eventually stuff the market. But it will be good news for the stock market and he decides, it might be a good time to invest more money into blue chips and hold. Then he ranges over current projects, worrying firstly about Sydney as their property market's looking particularly weak; consistent sales into the near future will be of concern. Now Brian talks of no union concerns at the Murray River project and if that carries right through to completion, margins will be maintained, but where will sales come from? Milly and her investors might just be the backup to a slowing market. So, at his next meeting with Brian, he proposes to introduce her as it's suddenly timely. And in conjunction with the Milly deal, he retains in the back of his mind Brian and the group might well be the saviors of the total Murray project. The lack of end retail sales will stuff cash flow; the sale of the super lot will be insufficient to even fund completion of the clubhouse, let alone the golf course. Corporate success is in danger. Steady land sales are vital. If Milly's investors can be encouraged, to participate in single lot land purchases for capital gain, then the construction of a house for income, via the project rental plan, might be an option for long-term retirement. Mathew slowly chews on the hypothesis's bone. *Is it a condiment or the whole course? I'll gnaw on the piquancy of the predilection.*

His grin widens as acceptance of his clever deliberation settles in. Then the penny dreadful explodes. *Is this part of the plan? After so many years in planning and preparation, Milly and her controllers will have considered every contingency, scrutinised every possible angle and arrived at a road map that must include all the potential initiatives incorporated into the travel guide to Successville, whatever I come up with must marry or complement plans in place. Like, if I curry favour with Brian, may well his builder venture into home construction? Hmm, it's like an intricate puzzle, if only the pieces might tie together flawlessly.*

Thus, regardless of the market, Mathew garners confidence in the plan and Milly extenuates the determination until he realises, *It's just like a bloody sale with a nasty catch in the conditions, the proviso so pertinent. Milly herself must accept the potential for her people to invest in the project.* Mathew clearly understands the Sydney and Melbourne projects are perfect investment vehicles for the long term. *But bugger it, I cannot sanction the snipping of the jewels, abandoning the dregs, to be worked over like a famished dog worrying over a dry bone. Therefore, the trick is her commitment to the stock; it must be all or nothing and that prospect, affords minuscule enhancement to my bloody poor bargaining position.* Like water in the tub, it swirls, bubbles, expands and explodes as his exciting contemplations mesh and mash.

CHAPTER 7

Monday morning, Mathew dwells on the furthering of Milly's proposals. He decides a definitive resolution is required and as such, he works through the issues, utilising his infallible debit and credit system. The process protracts until lunchtime as he continually has to deal with numerous phone calls, most of which require immediate follow-up or a resolution to be initiated.

When solace prevails, he directs his intellect to changing the strategy and simply confirms that which has been obvious – there is no downside except if the market contracts, vendors will be under pressure and Milly might seek to increase the commission. *And I can live with that as long as the unforeseen costs are in the budget.* He nods in confirmation.

At reception, Mandy greets Mathew with a wide smile; he recognises her hair's been cut and, emboldened, comments, 'I prefer it long.'

'Yeah, that's all very well for you blokes but it really is a bugger, when you're naturally straight. At it every day, sometimes twice, if the evening offer is worthwhile.' A wink accompanies the warm smile. 'We must golf. When are you inviting me out to Springy?'

'Up to you. Name the day. Tuesdays are good, no competitions and if there's no trade day, the course will be quiet.'

'Great, I'll check my diary. In the meantime, Brian's asked me to sit in today.'

Mathew smiles and reckons, *Golf and Mandy, all about her checking the diary.*

Brucella is welcoming in his usual effusive manner and the conversation evolves, initially as Mathew has imagined, around the ongoing projects. Previously, Mathew has alerted Brucella to the soil contamination problem at Adderley Street by using the bad-news-good-news principle. He instructed the architect Bruce-Smith to come up with a plan to utilise the excavations as underground car parking, creating a small precinct of party wall condos involving the parking. The results are tabled today; Brian baulks at the extra cost, so patiently, Mathew waits for the diatribe to cease and then counters by offsetting cost against an increased density of four units due to the cluster arrangement, coupled with moving on ground garaging underground.

'You have all the answers, but one day I'm going to catch you out.' A small grin gathers around Brian's mouth as he looks at Mandy but addresses the question to Mathew. 'So, what's this new marketing strategy?'

Mathew talks about the market, where he sees it going, time frames and how Sydney and the Murray project will be affected by declining sales. He discusses the implication on cash for future projects, then imparts the Milly manifesto, cleverly coupling it with the original kite he's flown and Horace picked up on, he'll become the controlling sales agent for the Murray project.

Brian confirms the proposal; he's anxious to get on with an idea they have been working on. It melds perfectly with Mathew's thoughts.

'Slip on your big-picture hat. How might we go about acquiring the whole project, the whole bloody shooting works?' Brucella leans forward to emphasise the proposition, holds Mathew's eyes and steeples his fingers.

'Well, I reckon the vendor's vulnerable. Residential lot sales have dried up, so obviously has cash flow.'

'Then if we pursued a takeover, linking it with your new sales plan, we'd be in a winning position?'

'Absolutely.'

Mandy poses, 'How can you be so sure when we've only just thrown this at you?'

He grins. 'Because I've always had it in the back of the filing cabinet.'

Mandy looks at Brian; they both peer at Mathew and burst out laughing. 'You're a bloody classic. We thought we'd surprise you. Then you walk in with Milly's plan, which makes it more of an opportunity at the right price,' Mandy gushes.

'What price have you come up with?'

Brain nods to Mandy, who opens a file that has lain on the coffee table. 'There are 108 lots unsold at $20,000 each in globo and I estimated $40,000 per lot development costs. Add 25 per cent profit, ten large in selling and admin costs and I arrived at a selling price of $85,000. I'm possibly a bit low on raw land cost but we face an uncertain market so I decided to be cautious. The golf course valuation came in at $6.5 million, which includes a completion component of $1 million and another half a million in machinery and maintenance first year. The clubhouse, our builder estimates, is $3 million in construction costs expended, so I arrived at a nice round $8 million.

'What about memberships?'

Brucella answers, 'I don't imagine we'll sell a lot at ten grand a clip and frankly under that. It's not worth the marketing cost nor the admin hassle.'

'So?' Mandy asks.

'I think you're $2 million short and that is simply reflected in the number you plugged in for raw lot value. My numbers are double that and there's your extra $2 million. The new cat amongst the pigeons is Milly. If she produces, each sale will automatically attach a golf course membership, so that bird just escaped the bunker. Plus, you've forgotten the eleven residential lots we talked about and to give comfort to your numbers, I'll contract now to buy the lot at $1.54 million, no commission.' Mathew allows an instant for it to sink home and changes tack. 'Regardless, you're driving the ship, you structure an offer and I'll go to bat for you. However, let me pursue Milly first. I'll be more comfortable in the numbers once I possess her absolute commitment.'

'You're right. Still, can you at least open the door and pick Nigel's brains?'

'You bet. Now back to my proposal. I'll take over the sales agency provided you agree with the margins incorporated in the Milly deal.'

'We talked about this when Horace was around. He sends his regards by the way. We thought it had merit then and I think this new sales plan you propose ensures we will almost certainly agree. Just don't go overboard on the incentive program.'

'OK and following on with the Milly plan, I think you should have a long talk with your solicitor. Her current sales have been made from completed stock, here we are envisaging a lot of off the plan contracts. Our mutual security is a ten percent deposit and what happens if the world changes and international transferring of funds is suspended, the overseas bank goes belly up or the purchaser goes broke or pulls out. We will all be up that smelly creek.'

Brian and Mandy both stare at each other until Brian says, 'Bloody good point, Mandy will you phone Marion at Swisser's office and get the ball rolling.' Then he utters a last query. 'Where in the world would you go, first choice, if the magic fairy arrived?'

'Hmm, I'm due for an overseas adventure and I've have been debating a Rhine cruise or first class over the Canadian Rockies.' Mathew mulls the proffered choices, the purpose of the question and arrives at a resolution. 'The Rhine.'

'We are very pleased with you Mathew. Put this deal with Milly to bed, lock in a forward commitment for her to place at least three properties per month and we'll throw you two first-class tickets to take that trip.'

'That's a great incentive. Thanks, and changing the subject, where are you at with the builder for Adderley Street?'

'All screwed down like the snake box in the pet shop. General Constructions received the nod. Their contract price fell safely within the guidelines of the turnkey projections and we're given comfort, by the sales prices provided by your good self with Steve Lowry's input. This creates a tight tie-up, enabling us to apply tough penalties for late completion and stringent contract provisions to ensure they'll not go overboard on contingencies. I am confident this project will be completed on time and on budget.'

'You're very brave, all bloody union jobs,' Mathew quips.

Brucella doesn't smile. 'With no variations, unless driven by us, I don't think I'm at risk.'

'But all your eggs are in one union's basket.'

'True and all our own men, occupy the secretary and organisers role of that union.'

Brucella nods and raises his eyebrows to make emphasis and Mathew decides it's time to quit. *I'm obviously playing in the wrong league.*

Mandy conducts Mathew to the elevator. 'Tell me when you want to golf, Mandy.'

'Stuff the golf. You go and put that bloody deal together because I'm the second ticket down the Rhine, mate.' She grins widely, gently punches his arm, turns and simply walks away.

Mathew questions if there's more of a flagrant swish in her hips; is that a bounce in her step and is it the bounce in the flounce or the poignancy in the proposition that tickles him? Whatever the portent, it rides in the elevator to the lobby and arrives to the smell of freshly ground coffee; Mathew follows the invasive intoxication into the café, orders a double-shot latte, shovels in three sugars and contemplates the meeting. He dwells on how best to calculate an incentive program, that will enhance Milly's perceptions but quickly realises he's got the cart before the horse again. Surely, first-hand discovery of the project's potentialities is the priority; sniff the fresh air and listen to the peaceful possibilities. Clearly, it must extenuate her enthusiasm. In appreciation at the necessity of closing Milly's commitment, he calls her mobile but receiving no answer, leaves a message. Then in reaffirmation at the opportunity created, he rationalises the importance of the visit. *It's key to the whole shooting works. I'd better have my dancing shoes on. I may not manage a second shot and I trust the legal eagle comes up with an appropriate idea that Milly must be happy with.*

Contemplation turns, with a second coffee, to Mandy. *What did she mean? Might she be for real? Would I? Should I? Why not? Imagine cruising the Old World with Miss New World. I can see us now posing on the promenade deck, sipping a glass of crisp, fruity Moselle as the panorama of the Rhine Valley slips peacefully past. But where in the scheme of things might Mandy see herself fitting in?* Then a small bombshell hits. *Is this Brucella inspired? If so, what are the implications and most importantly, what are the long-term ramifications? And what about Horace? I liked his upfront personality and he was on my side. Perjury, relating to the Woods enquiry, what does that mean if found guilty?*

The tall bloke in the black tracksuit makes his move, heads for the unmarked Falcon, and carefully eases into the traffic, keeping the unmistakable Jaguar in sight. Mathew drives home, unaware of being tailed. The Falcon driver cleverly elects not to turn into Mathew's small street, knowing his presence will be too obvious. Besides, the driver knows he's home and turns back, deciding, *More wasted time, but I'll keep digging. Something will turn up.* He laughs. *Like the new bloke with his Chinese pussy and he's already moved in. Next surprise, I'll catch Daisy with the accountant but so bloody what? Gossip is good but I can't hang my hat on it to prove anything against Allen.*

Mathew checks what he's previously allowed in the file for the Murray project and concludes he's right. They are at least $2 million light. He telephones Nigel. 'Need to meet. Any chance early tomorrow?'

The commission and bonus program for the Murray project becomes the next game. Mathew eventually decides to split the holdings into three groups and deal with each individually to arrive at the commission percentages firstly by bundling condos, hotel suites, vacant allotments and house and land deals into one encompassing package, cunningly leaving the eleven lot sales unaccounted for as they are part of a more devious plan he retains up his sleeve. Sydney ranks next due to the city's slowing market and the final plan relates to Adderley Street, together with the other small projects, where he'll be the least generous.

For some reason, his attention turns to his uncle Andrew, who first alerted him to a career in real estate so many years past, yet he'd made his money in the insurance industry.

'*What did he appreciate about that industry. Of course, annual renewal commissions.*' Mathew claps his hands. *Bloody brilliant. I'll structure in an annual fee for all buyers who list on the project rental plan to receive a commission for, say, three years and instead of paying myself the commission, I'll pay it to Milly. As the management company will collect 7 to 15 per cent of all rental commissions, surely, I can flick 3 per cent, even if I have to subsidise a bit and all she has to do is sign the investors up to the, in house, property management scheme.*

Mathew determines, *Might be a big deal for Milly. If she produces enough sales, I'll encourage her to calculate the reward. She'll be surprised, yes, very surprised.*

He grins at his inventiveness and acknowledges Andrew. 'Thanks, Unc. You always were a good bloke.'

CHAPTER 8

M ATHEW'S REFLECTIONS WANDER TO MIN Xie; he tries to conspire another east or west in his brain, still unable to truly admit she's gone. A relentless battle evolves with his ego, trying to be the man he isn't. *Admit it and move on or wallow in despair for the rest of my life.* Undaunted, he contemplates the unanswered questions remaining from the bonfire. *It's been over two months. Was it lust and sex or truly love, or did I simply seek something else from my life? Could it have been as simple as excitement? Min Xie came along at the right time and reignited my fire as life had steadily become bloody boring.*

Lines came from a favourite poem, one he had Min Xie commit to memory. 'What is love? 'tis not hereafter; Present mirth has present laughter.' Immersed into the words he took them personally, analysing the way Shakespeare utilised the verbiage. *What is the Bard trying to tell me, that love is not hereafter? It's now? Today is the time to laugh.* He reflected long and slowly, trawling the depths of his soul. Suddenly, the blinding inquisitorial light wrought the night into day.

I should have left Hope! I will leave Hope. There is no one in my life. I can, this time, be honest. Yes, this is just about me, what I want out of the rest of my life. Bugger, what do I want? I'll never find another Min Xie. I'll find another lady perhaps but will I find the adventure that came in her package? Probably not, yet does it matter? If it doesn't matter, why leave Hope? Because at least I want to try. I feel better about this now and I don't care about the bloody asset split. I have ample commission and fees outstanding, which with Brian's contrivance I might manoeuvre to a nefarious account.

'What's to come is still unsure: In delay there lies no plenty.'

So that's it. Here I go again, another meeting with Hope, but this time, I have to be ready, to move immediately as, truly, 'In delay there lies no plenty.' I need to plan perfectly and the first contention is, where will I move to? Originally, the beach as I'd be close to Min Xie and our golf courses. How about the city instead? Maybe that works. All my business is city or fringe. Why not a nice high-rise with a pool and a gym? The south side seems perfect. I can use the freeway to access my golf club, maybe a twenty-minute drive and I can handle that. I'll rent first, cash flow's no problem and I don't have to worry about financing, in what might become a falling market. This time, I'll talk to Andrew. Mum's the word, mate, just for the moment. I was his mum and dad when he was little. That may count. Regardless, I will not play on it. Then it's resolved and if I was this committed previously, I'd be with Min Xie. But this is different. I have a singular mindset. This is right. There is no one else involved.

Milly thanks him for being considerate about the time to meet. In the usual manner of backwards and forwards, they resolve to meet after hours and Mathew suggests, 'I owe you a meal. Let's talk over dinner?'

'Thanks, but another time. I don't want to be seen with you at this stage. Just my bloody luck Peter or one of the partners walks in and springs us. How about my apartment tomorrow night?'

'Yep, that's okay.'

'May I just ask one question?'

'Sure.'

'Are we heading in the right direction?'

'Absolutely and it's not tricky. If you're committed, I'll seal the deal for you.'

'Great, how about seven? Will you share my Chinese cooking?' He can tell she's grinning.

As soon as the receiver goes down, Milly dances a jig in unadulterated excitement around her kitchen, through the lounge room and finishes unintentionally in the bedroom, stopping in front of the bed. *And, Mathew Allen, we'll play the business and pleasure game with scheming, sharp stratagem and sex intermingled. I intend to gladden and gratify you in reward for acquiescing and according me unfettered, unrestricted opportunity to secure my financial future and to favour me with much face amongst my Asian associates.'*

CHAPTER 9

The conversation with Nigel revolves singularly around the opportunity to acquire the Murray River project. Mathew grasps the fact Nigel remains a valued consultant and gravitates to the awkward conclusion, he's placed him in the invidious position of inevitable conflict of interest. Nigel, in turn, realises, *Position profound, I understand the project is in financial trouble. My resultant loyalty to the original client causes hesitancy in discussing the drama openly.*

Mathew plays the 'pry the lid open' game by emptying his bucket, encouraging Nigel to agree, without openly divulging that which he is privy too. As such, Nigel is left with a negotiating brief; Mathew departs, happy in the knowledge, conflict has been circumvented surreptitiously.

With the planning permit issued for the Adderley project, the builder locked in, the marketing ready and the printing underway, it's time for Mathew to chew the fat with Steve. 'Where are you at with your potential super lot buyer?' Mathew prods at their next meeting.

'Proceeding steadily. They're well into due diligence and frankly, without being over-optimistic, I can't see any problems.'

'I can. It's quite likely the buyer might have to lock into a construction contract with the vendor's own builder.'

'Strewth, that's a bit rough.'

'Maybe not. Consider this. One builder over the whole project equals an economy of scale. How about tough completion dates, no harsh penalties and an onside union?'

'See what you mean. When will I know? I shouldn't be pushing until I've more information but I need sales. You know the story when you have an overbearing banker.'

Mathew nods in sympathy. 'Let's mull over the price and the structure of the terms you've come up with.'

As Steve assembles the information, Mathew studies him closely, recognising the build as typical of one who has trampled the hell out of the opposition, up and down the rugby paddocks. With broad shoulders and a strong upper torso shaped into the waist, his heavy hips and powerful thighs contribute to his long hitting on the golf course. Mathew speculates at the stories conveyed of Steve smacking six after six when motivated by mouth, incurring sledge or scurrilous slight on the cricket pitch and owning a tendency to trust the tales about his capacity to swing the ball both ways, when trundling them down as a strong first change bowler. *Once he slows down from concentrating on business and turns his energies more to golf, he'll finish up a single figure player. I envy his potential.* His thoughts are interrupted.

'I put the condo lots at $100K each. I had to start somewhere. I think they'll come in more around $80K. I floated a 20 to 25 per cent down with up to six months to complete. How sure are you of the council's conduciveness to issue the permits?'

'Application for our current plan has gone particularly smoothly. Nigel's been the driver. Don't hesitate to talk to him. We're all mates in this game.'

'What do you reckon about price and the terms?'

'Mate, you keep knitting. I'll stitch up the price.'

Steve smiles broadly. Mathew's comment hits home; he contemplates the monthly commission ledger being sent to his business banker. *'It might shut the wanker up for a while.'*

Mathew retains the Milly plan up his sleeve, recognising the opportunity for another commission override once Steve arrives at the 'selling off the plan' station. *'Shifty prick'*, he concludes. *'Another 1 per cent for Mathew.'*

'Change the subject. What's happened to twilight golf and the next Triple C golf day?'

'Don't know. May hasn't been in touch for ages. I think she's pissed off because I didn't attend her charity day.'

'No, it's because you keep knocking her back.'

They look at each other and laugh.

'And the lovely Min Xie?'

'Don't know. No correspondence, Your Honour.'

Steve opens his diary. 'Let's call May and see what's going on.'

'Hey, May, it's Steve. I have Mathew with me. We're wondering what we have done to be in your bad books. No twilight golf day invites?'

Mathew listens to Steve's response. 'Then it's our turn to play host. I apologise and extend an invite to you and

Min Xie. Friday week at my club, nice talking to you too, okey-dokey.'

'She has a habit or a love for that saying.'

'I assume you know what that was all about. It's our fault.'

'Can't be. We played at Springy last.'

'Who cares? Upshot is May will call Min Xie and phone me back.'

Mathew left the meeting wondering what excuse Min Xie will offer, knowing the penny will drop with May sooner or later.

Dinner with Milly requires explanation to Hope. Mathew decides to keep it simple. 'Meeting a lady client.'

The reply was frank. 'Anywhere special?'

The answer was explicit. 'No.'

Milly conjures up a lumpy, meaty stir-fry, hot and spicy. Mathew contrives to arrive accompanied by a bottle of champagne and then suffers second thoughts, wondering whether it's appropriate, deciding in the negative. The bottle remains on the back seat of the car.

Their conversation centres on business, resulting in Mathew committing to the commission arrangement, conditional on the Murray River project being involved as part of the overall package. Milly isn't the least concerned.

'The bank has trust in me. I, in turn, rely on my inner-city-oriented nous to select properties beneficial to their investment strategy. I must have credence with your recommendations, so I ask you seriously, will these investments benefit the bank's clients?'

'Absolutely, but Brian's solicitor has raised several issues relating to off the plan sales. Mandy will send you written details but here are the bones. Mathew explains the problems he had originally perceived and adds. 'Brian's solicitor will open a second Trust Account into which your people will pay the whole purchase price and you will sign an account sale providing for twenty five percent to be transferred when requested, the balance will remain in trust until settlement can be effected.' Mathew grins, 'And here's the kicker for you, the commission will be increased to four percent of which half will be paid out on account sales.' He nods in confirmation as her grin expands and he adds, 'Will Uncle go along with it?'

'Yes, and so will my Hong Kong associates as they really do not have a choice. This is very clever Mathew and you'd best ask Brian to send me this in writing ASAP.'

'I'll check it first and now before we go too far, I prefer you take in the scene personally, experience the opportunity so you are totally committed. We can be up and back in one day. How about next Sunday?'

'Ah, priorities, Mathew. I'll miss my golf?' She leaves it hanging.

'We all have priorities. Mine's business, so let's go Saturday and I'll not golf.' He smiles, hoping she'll interpret the message.

'Sorry, not trying to be difficult, let's go Saturday and I'll invite you to my club on Sunday?'

'You're good, Milly. You think quick. I appreciate someone who knows how to negotiate. I'll be here at eight o'clock on the nose.'

Intent on being shifty, Mathew keeps the commission for referring her clients to the management program up his sleeve. As Mathew leaves the building, the man in a blue Falcon yawns and stretches. *'Thank goodness, now I can quit.'* He wonders how he'll write up the report. *Did they have drinks, dinner, or sex?* The resolution was simple, reckoning sex was the answer Chief Inspector Robertson will prefer to hear.

Milly sprawls along the couch and pats the cushions. *I'm Chinese, patience, it will happen soon, you are ready, Mathew. I can see it in your eyes, and I don't think I'll rush into booking golf on Sunday.* Her grin widens as she gently rubs her hands together.

CHAPTER 10

Next morning, opening her car door, Hope, by chance, happens to look into Mathew's and notices the bottle of champagne on the seat. *Did he succeed without needing to crack it? Or is it a gift or maybe an inducement to a future rendezvous?*

Realising her marriage is on unstable ground, Hope wonders why last year, when he was committed, he decided not to leave without meaningful explanation. *I know the sexual closeness has gone, but then his indecisiveness suggests capriciousness and unpredictability. Maybe he's vacillating between what and what or who and who and I don't care. It will happen again. Why bother refloating a sinking ship by filling it with sexual ballast? Besides, whilst I don't want to be unduly hopeful, I'm reveling in the slow, quiet seduction being performed daily at the hospital.* Her toes curl up, her nipples harden and smiling, Hope allows a 'woo woo' to escape from her lips and that surprises her. She laughs loudly, then glances at the car in the next lane to see if she's been spotted, in her moment of mirth.

Steve telephones Mathew. 'May is a bit miffed. Min Xie turned her down on both evenings. Will you call her and find out what's going on?'

'Yeah, leave it to me.'

He phones May, asking straight out, 'What's the problem?'

'I have no idea. She was quite short with me, not like Min Xiela at all. I'll call her back. Maybe just a bad day, hey?'

'Okay and what about your next charity day? Must be coming up soon. Don't forget to invite us. I'll get Steve there this time and by the way, do you know Milly Cheong?'

'No. Should I?'

'Not necessarily. She works in property, well connected internationally. Her Asian friends golf at Eagle Ridge. Might be a good group to invite.'

'Can you fax me her information?'

'Yes, and may I suggest you invite her and her three friends?'

'Will do, but I'll have to give members first booking rights. Anyway, talk soon. Wonder what's wrong with Min. It's not okey-dokey.'

As they motor north, Min Xie keeps company in Mathew's head.

Conversation with Milly suffers extended moments of playing the no-talkies game; he's lost in the fond memories of this road and the bed it leads to – the last time with Min Xie, her first inspection of the Murray project. And they stayed overnight in their favourite king-sized bed. He recalls the words that drifted from under the sheets. *Can you find me?*

'You somewhere else today, or is it me?'

'Oh, sorry, Milly. I'm being rude. My apologies.'

'At your Christmas party, you were elsewhere. Even at supper, I knew you were with someone else . . . somewhere else.'

Mathew, not into emptying his bucket, waits.

'Is it that difficult?' she pushes on.

'Yes.'

'We all have a past. Sometimes it helps to just let it hang out.'

'Probably, but this is too recent, too close to the bone, the pain too intense.'

'A love affair or your marriage?'

She's persistent, he determines. *But bugger it, I've opened the door.* 'Both actually. I had an affair. It's over and I've decided to separate.'

'Which one pains you the most?'

Clever girl, he thinks. 'Both but the one that's gone uppermost.'

Peace reigns for a few moments.

'Did you bring your lady up here?'

'Yes, she's a golfer. It became a favourite escape place for the odd weekend, and she accompanied me when I first visited the project.'

'You stayed the night?'

'Yes.'

'And played golf?'

'Yes, Shepparton that time.' Mathew is filling in the bits; she has him going now.

'Why didn't you suggest we stay the night if your lover has gone and you are intending to separate?'

'You are very upfront, Milly.'

'Ha, you know I've had a tough life. I realised very early on if you want something, you have to ask. If that doesn't work, you go somewhere else or you just take it. Nothing has come to me easy except Auntie, Uncle, and languages. I look back at my bad luck in life, yet I have to realise I have been so lucky except in love. Ha, now I'm talking about me.'

Is this a game? Mathew poses, confident the answer isn't readily available. 'No, Milly, you are talking about yourself. We obviously have our own inner demons.' He continues to play.

'No, mine aren't demons, more like regrets. And your lost love is not demoniac. It's a lament. Did she fly or flee?'

Crikey, I don't want to expose all the dirty water. Still, I've gone too far now, so what the hell, Mathew reasons.

'Poor calculus, I left the door open for another man to take her away.'

'Redeemable?'

'No and unfortunately, that's a categorical no.' Mathew feels a tear well up; he looks straight ahead at the road, determined now to try to change the conversation, noticing she's not pursued the question 'Why didn't you ask me to stay?'

'Wanna stop for a coffee?'

'Ah, great idea, I'm a coffaholic.'

Mathew noses the car into the roadside service centre. The day is perfect, not a cloud to be seen; the project will present picture perfect. A successful reconnoiter of the development's progression, once undertaken, should highlight the overall potential and that's what it's about. But Mathew incurs no comprehension his concept of the future will soon be blown out of the water. However, he is sufficiently aware if Milly says yes to include the project into her sales basket, his immediate success is a given. Brian and his 'boys' are protected by having guaranteed contracts each month and with up to twelve months lead time to completion, each project will have sufficient sales to ensure a profitable outcome.

Waiting for coffee, Mathew concludes, *With my future finances secure, the asset problem that created the conundrum with my previously planned split will not eventuate. So, with them primarily in the kids' names and as they will, in all intents and purposes, finish up theirs one day anyway, who gives a shit?* He grins. *The split is on!*

Behind his sunglasses, Mathew takes full opportunity to take a long slow inspection of his guest. Milly has brushed on sufficient make-up to highlight her facial features –high cheekbones, pencil-thin shaped black eyebrows, faint notion of a shade under her eyes and similar to Min Xie wonderful, kissable lips. Her pale blue denim jeans are matched with a short denim jacket. In slow motion, Milly stands and removes the jacket. Mathew smiles; the man on the next table spills his coffee, suddenly discovering her white T-shirt and perfectly round breasts staring him straight in the eyes.

'Getting quite warm. Don't need it anymore,' she comments to no one in particular.

Mathew maintains the vigilance, taking in her shapely body and her face typical Asian, silky smooth and unlined except around the eyes, where little laugh lines appear fine and faint. The realisation he's looking at someone quite beautiful sinks in.

Milly thinks, *How bloody obvious, hiding behind the sunnies, giving me the once-over. I'll remove my jacket and let him have a real perv at real tits.*

Milly's sense of business moves her to seek more background information on the project, encouraging Mathew to slip back to reality. After completing their coffees, Mathew suggests he'll take one to go. Milly laughs. 'And I'd love one too. That was a good cup of joe.'

They hadn't driven far; Milly starts again. 'You haven't dodged my loaded question?'

'I knew you'd bring it up again, so if I'd suggested we stay the night, would you have agreed or told me where to go and take your business with you?'

'I would have agreed.'

'Really. Now I have to ask the why question.'

'Simple, for sex. You are an attractive man. I enjoy your company. Why not?'

It's an Asian thing. Milly is like Min Xie, no stuffing around.

'Do I not attract you, Mathew?'

'Of course, you're a very beautiful girl.'

'Then why not?'

Mathew struggles to retrieve information about Hope's itinerary, not recalling if she's gone to the island and it doesn't matter, all he has to say is he's dining with the chief council planner.

'Do you want to talk about the bird that flew away?' Milly asks.

'Not now, maybe one day.'

'We'll miss a game of golf. Next time, I'll bring my clubs.'

And how easy was that? Milly concedes.

CHAPTER 11

Upon arrival at the project, Mathew diligently executes show-and-tell using the maps and plans, explaining boundaries whilst pointing out the overall concept, which is becoming easier to delineate. They walk the fairways of the first and seventh holes. Mathew is impressed at how the Santa Ana couch has covered them since his last visit, spreading so evenly with another strong growing season; this time next year, it might be open. Milly comments on the two-tee arrangement, suggesting the club tee, which incorporates the ladies, being so long, offers flexibility to make each hole different by simply moving the markers. Mathew understands; that's the logic in the architect's plan and at least she's thinking positively.

Milly is enrapt in the day and demands to walk several of the second nine, intent on capturing the allure and essence of the beautiful scenery. In her mind, she plays the hole as she walks, encouraging club selection and imagining the shot. Returning to the car, she jokes, 'I like this course, it suits my game.'

Clubhouse construction has progressed; it's approaching lock-up stage. Milly studies the architect's facade drawings. 'Wow, the clubhouse will look grand, very Aussie in style. Would you call it a big Queenslander, Mathew?'

'Yeah, very much so. It fits the casual style of a destination resort. You don't want to go away and find the clubhouse like the one you left behind. The facility needs to be part of the escape. I think the architect's got it right.'

In traditional descriptive sign language, Mathew waves his arms, depicting the super lots and the hotel site. 'Picture the boutique hotel in a similar flavour to the clubhouse, which leaves the condos to add contrast in design style yet remaining in sympathy with the complex.' Mathew utilises the elevation concept plans prepared by Bruce to highlight and embellish his conceptual ramblings.

Milly suggests a walk around the total super lots site. Upon returning to the clubhouse, she concedes, 'I really like this, I can appreciate what you have portrayed. Now can we go into town? I'd like to throw confetti in the air, see where it falls. I want to be totally in control with the way I describe the local infrastructure, hospitals, schools, motels, et cetera, all the pigments painting the picture.'

Mathew wonders what it all means and then presumes in cinemascope what he envisages doesn't mean a fig; he's here, they are staying and he needs to contact Hope. With no answer on either of her phones, he leaves messages relating to his overnight intentions and tries Stephanie, again with the same result, so he takes the attitude that if daughter one fails, try number two. 'Hi, Daddy, shouldn't you be at golf?'

'You're right, but I'm up at the Murray River project. I'm going to stay the night. I need to let Hope know and I can't find her. You got any clues?'

'God, you two are weird. She's at the island this weekend with Andrew, and he's taken his new filly down. Have you two forgotten how to communicate? Like me to pass on a message?'

'Yeah, good on ya. Thanks, Tiff. And when are we seeing you?'

'Next weekend, we're all at the beach. Steph and I are taking golf lessons again.'

'Oh yeah, I remember last time.'

'I won't have a hangover this time.' She laughs.

'Okay, mate, nice talking. See you then.'

'Thanks, Daddy. Love you.' She'd hung up before he could say, 'Love you too.'

The football ground appears to be busy and Mathew assumes for the time of year that it has to be a practice game. 'Local footy, Milly, a big crowd for a scratch match. Nice to see the country game is alive and well. Do you support a football team in Melbourne?'

'You bet. I'm a Bulldog.'

'Really, how come?'

'Well, firstly, I like their red, white and blue colours. Secondly, they come from the tough side of town like me. Thirdly, I'm like a bulldog – tough, strong, determined; yet if you treat me right, I'll wag my tail, be faithful and lick you to death.'

The look expresses intent and purpose. Mathew catches the message and decides he's not going there – well, not yet anyway. 'Would you like to eat casual or in a nice restaurant?'

'A pub meal, mixed grill with an egg, chips, a crisp salad, and a cold beer', she replies.

'Are you sure you're not an Aussie?'

'I told you, we love to be Aussie when we go to Tootgarook. You must join us for a barbie. We have so much fun and it's special to have good friends around, when you play the fool.'

He isn't sure if it's a comment or a question, so when in doubt, he takes the safest way and agrees. Mathew senses he's warming to this girl; just as well, it's obvious he's sleeping with her tonight.

'Typical Australiana, Mathew. I love these two-storey old pubs with their wide lacy fretwork verandas. I've always had a hankering to stay in one, spend the night in the bar with the locals, stagger up the stairs, fall into a super-soft bed and wake up to a big breakfast.'

'And a hangover.'

She laughs. 'Probably, hey.'

The waitress arrives. 'Lucky the chef's friendly, or you'd be without lunch, love. We're runnin' a bit early today due to the footy.'

'Practice match?' Mathew questions.

'Yeah, well, sort of. The league calls it a scratch match, but as it's us versus them and we hate each other, it'll be a ding-dong beauty, so hurry up, mate. I've only got an hour before the seniors bounce.'

'Who are you playing?'

'Bloody Corowa!'

'Ah, that mob from over the border!' Mathew pretends he knows what he's talking about.'

'Yeah, bloody oath, mate. Bloody New South Wales poofters, so come on, mate. What'll it be?' She smiles at Milly.

'Mixed grill, a runny egg, and make the steak moo.'

The waitress looks at Mathew in the hope of a quick resolution. 'Same, hey, but bring the mooie medium.'

'Don't worry, love, I'll make sure he's dead.'

Milly salutes and clinks his glass. 'To us!'

'You bet.'

He takes a long swig and grins as Milly swallows half the glass in one long gulp. 'Beauty. I needed that.'

'You're full of bullshit, Milly. You're an Aussie.' Then rather than allow her to add fuel to the fire, he continues, 'When we drive into town, let's find the tourist information centre. You can put together a package of brochures highlighting the tourist trail and what's on around the joint, apart from footy.' Mathew changes tack, 'Have you been back to China?'

'No,' came without expression as she finishes the beer.

'Now it's open season. Don't you have any desire to go back to your birth town, maybe try to find your siblings?'

'I know it's difficult for westerners, who have everything, to try to comprehend life in China. If I'd have stayed, life would have been miserable, being the youngest girl, not wanted, unloved, my birth only causing more burden on my parents. I may have been lucky and managed four or even six years of grade school and then put to work in the fields all day every day in the heat and you cannot escape it. Then the cold and you cannot escape it either. It's very cold, all mud and slush. Every fibre chilled right to the bones. Or I might have gone into a sweat shop, slave twelve hours a day, go home and slave there as well. No fun, no participating in organised sport or playing anything. I harbour no happy memories of China except that amazing adventure with Auntie all the way to Hong Kong and my life changed. I'm like that strange animal. What's it called?'

'A chameleon.'

'Yes, one of those things. I change everything, so there is no China remaining. No need to return. If I was lucky and discover relatives, what can we talk about? Hooley dooly, can you imagine me in some humpty dumpty in the bloody boondocks of Cathay debating the failure of the current five-year plan and the direction of the Melbourne property market?'

Milly laughs lightly and returns to attack her lunch; chomping and chewing aggressively, she continues. 'I like you, Mathew. Respect emanates from that meeting with Peter when you presented the offer for the Adderley Street sites. You were on the money. He had another buyer, been on the go for weeks, hustling and haggling, trying to wear him and the vendor down. The end prize included a sole selling agency with a secret kicker for sales performance. The priority came easy – sell to them. Ha, I laugh up my sleeve the way you treat him – how you say? – caught him with his pants down. He lost face. Then you were particularly cunning. You gave face back. Regardless, he'll never forget a gweilo outsmarted and outmaneuvered him.'

'Is that why he's not participated in the broad-brush and subsequent meetings?' Mathew adds a chip and a bit of beetroot to the final piece of steak and waits for the reply.

'He resents you bettered him, threatened him, played the game, gave him a plan he had to follow and because of it, you won. Ha, you're so smart, you gained my respect from day one. I'd love to tell the story of those negotiations but cannot. Not good business to blab.'

Mathew cleans his plate with the remaining chunk of bread, wipes his mouth, reaches for the remains of the beer and pensively points out, 'I'm close to giving him the flick completely. Frankly, he's contributed nothing, whereas Steve Lowry has been working diligently with the architects.'

'He can see it eventuating. You'll make an enemy.'

'Will it hurt you, Milly?'

'No, because if we wrap this deal up, I'm out of there. I'll work from home. In fact, I'm thinking of going upmarket a little, trying to secure an extra room for an office. I'll work with you and your consultants, liaising with my contacts and life will change again.'

'Then you can play golf during the week.'

'You're right.' Her eyes light up. 'I'd thought about that but not at Rye, too far. I'll need a city club.'

Mathew recognises he's pried opened the can and decides he'd be wise not to pursue the contents at this stage.

She smiles, adding, 'I need another beer. Nothing like a draught out of the tap on a hot day.' Milly heads off for the toilet and the bar while Mathew relaxes, trying to come to grips with her openness.

Mathew takes in the busy street scene, then snaps back to reality as Milly returns with the beers and says, 'I said something before about respect. I also like you as a person and your persona depicts someone gentle, considerate, even though Peter may not think so, hey?' She laughs again. 'You have a certain manner of arriving at the point, no bullshit. I like that because I'm the same. I want to sleep with you, enjoy the sex, so I come out and say it.' A wide smile arrives with the question, 'So where shall we stay?'

'Frankly, my dear, I have no idea. Let's see what we discover as we drive the town and we must find the tourist centre.'

'Good idea. I can send two sets of information to my bank contacts. I'll ask them to pass one to Uncle on his next visit. Oh, I miss the dear old man so.'

'Why don't you go visit? Time it with his next trip. Take the brochures and project information with you.'

Silence like the spring springs eternally. Milly suddenly reaches across the Laminex table, clasps her hands over his ears, pulls him close, kisses him hard on the lips, clapping her hands as she sits down. 'Mathew Allen, I love the way you think. You'll come too. The icing on the bloody cake, my associates will love it, to actually meet the man.'

Her face beams, her eyes expand and she tilts forwards again. 'I can see it now; you can answer the banker's questions. Oh, this is brilliant. Why didn't I think of it earlier? I'm embarrassed, not quick think. Ha, that does not sound right, but you know what I mean. I'm so excited. I can't make the words come out correctly. I have my diary in the car, I can work the dates out and the best thing is we can make love in exotic, erotic Hong Kong.'

Whilst sex invites excitement, his first priority must be to conclude the deal for Brian, set up his future security and the big bonus close the Rhine cruise with Mandy. *But is she for real? Will she go? Will dream time become real time? And in the meantime, I'm going to make a fortune.* He grins. *And my philosophy in life is it's all about time.* Then he berates himself. *All very well, Milly saying she should have thought this out. I'm the one who could have been proactive, supposedly planning one of my strengths. The concept is breathtaking in its brilliance. The bankers greet and grill, question and quiz the master. I shut every door and the deal is done. Consummation complete to everyone's content. Yes, it really is a stunning scenario and I'll induce introduction to the inscrutable uncle.*

Whilst Mathew postulates about future directions, Milly wrestles with an idea that's been whirling like a crazed rota, swirling, twirling around in her head but it spins so fast, she's not able to grasp the handle.

'However, Milly, there's a problem,' he inserts a serious composure. 'What if we are not compatible in bed?'

Her grin spreads. 'I can guarantee you that will not be the case.' She gave him an intense stare, then she breaks out laughing. 'Let's go, Mathew Allen. We have an adventure to pursue and I'm so excited to see Uncle but before we go, I'm trying to come to grips with a revelation. One minute, hey? Let's see if I can spit it out.'

'Lucky it's not hydrochloric acid.'

'Sorry?'

'It's okay, I'm just being stupid.'

The look is piercing; concentration dominates her face. A small grin gathers at the corner of her mouth, her nostrils flare, her eyes open wide, the grin extends happily across her face and she claps her hands in obvious celebration, exclaiming, 'As we completed the site inspection, it came to me, yet I struggled to conjure up the reason.' With determined intent,

Milly hesitates, heightening his anticipation. 'What is the trick? What will encourage the bank's wealthy clients to invest here?' Milly waits, adding more tension.

Mathew declines to pursue, recognising this might be the missing crucial element, the lucky link elucidating the answer he believes she'll possess. *But if she's only just discovered it, who cares?* he concludes.

'So, Mathew, the answer is simple, stupid. The initial inclination materialised as I heard nothing, but the rowdy cacophony of the birdsongs on the wing, on the ground, up in the trees – ah, the trees – I envisaged the wattle in winter, other blossoms blooming in spring and the evergreen summer. I smelt the invigorating fresh air, accepted placidity at play, imagined the lifestyle – golf, tennis, lawn bowls and the club life. The clatter of mahjong tiles, cards being shuffled, all only minutes from hospitals and health care, peace and bloody serenity in the perfect climate. Fuck, Mathew, I'm so excited. Don't you get it? It's retirement!'

She claps her hands again and leans forwards to emphasise the point. 'Can you see the old chows with their elegant ladies or their young tai tais on their arms? God, it's perfect!'

Milly giggles, then laughs loudly and taking hostage of Mathew's arm encourages him with. 'Come, we have a fortune to make, cobber.'

They travel the tourist route, finding and photographing the important medical buildings, especially the hospital, remedial and rehabilitation centre as Milly is fascinated by the variety of specialists. She captures the images of their shiny brass nameplates. 'I'll put together a montage. It will enhance the professional services available.'

She takes shots of the dentist's opulent office, then expresses surprise at the impressive veterinarian set-up. 'That'd be right, bloody typical, animals receive superior treatment to humans.'

Ultimately, they stumble on the tourist centre, where the lady manager counts stitches instead of tourists. 'Ah, welcome, someone to talk to. It's been so quiet today. If I don't knit, I'm up to pussy's bow in boredom and to think I could have closed the joint and gone to the footy.'

Peggy, as her handwritten label announces, falls over herself to assist Milly, who finally manages to escape the almost overbearing offer of 'Take this and that and oh this is important.' They depart with four sets of comprehensive tourist information, accompanied by a recommendation to the Old Colonial Inn, located out the other side of town, which features spa rooms and king-sized beds. The latter stirs Mathew momentarily, wondering if Min Xie had known about the bed.

After settling in, Milly asks to go over all the maps and plans so everything will be stuck in her memory. Mathew appreciates the work ethic, acknowledging the thoroughness borne by her quick recognition in locating the main infrastructure facilities and features. After completing the journey of discovery, he admits she's on the right page and now is the time.

He rolls on his back and extends his left arm. Milly accepts the invitation and moves willingly to his side. They kiss for the first time.

It's like Min Xie when we kissed without passion, simply enjoyable. But Milly's different. She breaks the kiss and licks under his chin and around his neck, seeking deliberately by design or desire his ear, which she proceeds to make love to. Incessantly, she worries the appendage, nibbling, sucking, licking, breathing heavily into it and being one of Mathew's on buttons, he reacts immediately. His penis jumps. Her hand goes to his crotch. Her exploration is rewarded. 'Ooh my, you hot too.' The passion ignites.

Her wide, thick red lips return to his, but this kiss is different as mutually they insert the lust. Tongues engage for the first time and they play the game, like kids experimenting with holding hands for the first time. Mathew addresses her neck and an ear; her body levitates and lifts slightly off the floor as if searching for something. The kiss reignited, they roll on their sides and seek close contact of the intimate kind. Mathew pushes his penis onto her bone and grinds slowly, purposely as his right hand reaches for her hip and around the cheeks of her bottom.

Milly welcomes the grind with the irrefutable understanding lust has well and truly arrived responds accordingly, pushing back into him; knowingly, a smile is developing as he adjusts position. Milly opens her eyes. 'I'm hot for it, Mathew. Can we make tonight last? I'm not into a quick root and next thing I know, the man is snoring. I'll please you as long you reciprocate. Let's go soak in the spa, then make love in that magnificent bed.'

Yes, Mathew senses, *Of course you silly moo. Just like Min Xie, wash the day away, cuddle in the tub, and make love for hours.*

Milly rolls over on her back and Mathew offers that which he deems is appropriate. 'You are very beautiful, Milly.'

'Perfect timing. My sloppy sentimental side sought hope you'd utter something romantic. It may be just sex, yet to add some quixotic fondness inspires spice to tantalise the tease and in the wash-up, I wonder, is it more about bonding and not the bonking?'

Their kiss is long and slow like lovers. She wraps both arms over his shoulders, pulls him down, and grinds as their mouths mesh and meld. He opens his eyes to capture her face in full view and Milly recognises a crossroad has been reached.

'I'm of the mind, Milly, that with you and me, today, tonight is more about the bonding.'

Milly melts, the moment sublime but being prudent, she accepts the romance alluded to is unrealistic. Still, it doesn't matter. He has expressed the most important sensation of all, caring. Her pussy tingles; she's wet.

He holds the dark chocolates and seeing nothing, says, 'I'll go run the spa.'

Pausing at the door, he offers, 'Milly?'

'Yes.'

'I do care.'

Oh goodness gracious me, he's a mind reader too.

The spa is a jumbo beige standard corner unit with the shower above. Mathew likes the set-up; it's easy to wash the soapsuds off. He adjusts the taps, lays the bath mat and sets two towels on the side. Finding the bubbles packet, he rips open the tear top and pours all the ingredients into the water, allowing them to do their thing – make bubbles.

Milly is lying on the bed. *Comfier than the floor.* She holds out her arms. Mathew slips off his shoes and socks in one motion and slides onto the bed; with eyes locked open, they kiss. She snuggles close.

'You're nice to cuddle,' he confides in a soft voice.

'Will I feel better naked?' She continues looking into his eyes.

The urge is too strong. He laughs. 'Of course.'

'Can you imagine what I'll feel like? Can you imagine my breasts in your hands? Can you feel my nipples? Are they large or small, hard or soft? Can you imagine caressing my body? Is my tummy hard and flat? Can you feel my bottom in your hands? I think it will fit nicely. Can you smell me, taste me? Can you imagine entering me for the first time? Can you imagine my climax? Can you imagine all that, Mathew Allen and think we will not be compatible in bed?'

'I should be court-martialed and shot at dawn, Your Honour.'

Quickly, she removes her jeans, pushes her undies to her ankles, steps back, and kicks them off. 'If you're a tit man, you'll be disappointed. I'm typical Chinese, quite small.'

'But what you don't know is I love small breasts that fit into my hands.'

Milly giggles. 'Really, or you just say that to please me?'

'In delay there lies no plenty.'

'What's that mean?'

'It is a line from a poem. It seems appropriate.'

'There is more?'

'Yes, come kiss me, sweet and twenty, youth's a stuff will not endure.'

She reaches behind her back, unhooks her bra in a professional manner, covers her breasts as the bra falls to the floor, drops her arms and presents her perfect round breasts with perky nipples standing erect, like his penis.

'I am very horny, Mathew Allen. Might you be of a similar persuasion?'

'Yes.' His voice gives him away, arriving low and animalistic.

'Good because I'm going to make you suffer. Make me a coffee, black, one sugar.'

Her walk reminds him of Mandy and that sponsors the ironic realisation of the position he's in. The Rhine trip depends on Milly committing to the Murray project. His trip to Hong Kong will seal the deal, he reckons without a doubt. Then if Mandy is for real, it's them cruising. *I must be dreaming and isn't life amazing?* He grins to himself, recalling the lines 'Higomy hogamy. Man is monogamy. Monogamy minigamy. Woman is polygamy.'

With their toes playing touchy, the conversation moves to Hong Kong; Milly elaborates on her excitement to reunite with Uncle after so many years, the chance to discuss the developments and answer the banker's questions.

'And you're committing to the selling of all the projects?'

'Yes, but I haven't seen the Sydney project.'

'Why don't we tour the project and the surrounding infrastructure then fly to Honkers later in the day?'

'Will that work?' she queries.

'I'll check flights with our travel agent.'

'And I'll check Uncle's Hong Kong dates and we can commence planning?'

'No, Milly, we'll do that later.'

The reply comes attached with a wicked grin. 'Of course, what a silly Chinese sausage I am!'

They are hungry; food hasn't been on the evening's menu. Breakfast is devoured early, and they return to soak in the spa. The morning's completed in bed.

Arriving back at Milly's apartment mid-afternoon, she asks, 'Do you want to come up?'

Mathew declines; they kiss without passion.

Milly adds a single comment. 'Hong Kong, I can't wait.'

Mathew sends Brucella an email confirming Milly's commitment to bundling all the projects into her property basket and then adds the bonus. He is to accompany her to Hong Kong to consolidate the deal by meeting the players.

Mathew drives to the island after golf for the family dinner. He's a smidge peeved, immediately after coffee, the kids disappeared to various pubs and parties. By ten thirty on Sunday morning, none have surfaced; he decides to go back to Melbourne, wondering what happened to the twins' golf lesson.

CHAPTER 12

Mathew asks that the sales agreement be ready tomorrow. Mandy confirms she'll take it to golf. Brian phones to discuss the fax regarding the sales deal with Milly. 'Has an agreement been mandated, who directs sales to which property?'

'Good question. I've suggested, based on four sales a month, one to Sydney, one or two to Murray River Country Club, being one hotel or condo unit and a vacant lot. The other's allocation a Melbourne residential, depending on the price point. This qualifies them to receive 3 or 4 per cent commission. However, the total sales value of the four sales must be a minimum of $1.4 million.' He elects to change the subject. 'And have you closed the deal with General Constructions regarding the condo lots? I think we may have this buyer of Steve's close on super lot D. If we close, you'll have half your money back from one sale.'

'Less two first-class tickets to cruise the Rhine. Will the buyer go with our builder?'

'Hopefully if the contract contains all the tough clauses, particularly the completion date.'

'What if we guaranteed no rise in the contract price, no extras, no nothing unless requested by the client? Can we close at our price?'

'With 4.5 per cent commission?' Mathew pushes.

'Yes.'

'As we fudged $200,000 on top of the asking price, maybe we should discount it and be happy to have a sale in the bag.'

'Do your best. Don't lose him. In the meantime, when might you consider going to Europe?'

'Weather-wise, the best time of the year last week of August, first week of September.'

'Talk to me soon.' Brucella hangs up.

Mathew confirms coffee with Milly on Thursday to discuss travel plans and to discover when she'll leave Peter Lee, knowing it's like a sale – close all the doors.

May phones. 'Mathew, Min Xie has gone quite strange. Anything going on with you two that may have soured?'

'Not from my point of view.' And that's the truth. 'Tell you what, I'll bring Milly, the property girl I told you about. Good opportunity for you to meet her. Is Friday okay at Steve's club?'

'Have you been two-timing me, Mathew, taking another woman to the Murray?' Mandy questions with a lilt in her voice.

'If I have, pray tell, when was the first time?'

'You have an answer for everything.'

'Sorry, not trying to be smart.'

'But I was.'

'Shall I pick you up tomorrow?'

'Perfect. What time?'

'How about ten? You can sleep in.'

'Goodo and by the way, do you really expect Wonder Woman, to produce all this new business?' she asks.

'Yes, and sorry I have to rush, lots to do. I'm slacking off tomorrow, taking some bloody client to golf. Hooroo.'

'Silly bugger, see you at ten.' He can tell she's laughing; it's a nice, friendly, happy laugh but what does it all mean?

Mathew directs his call to her mobile. 'Can you talk, Milly?'

'Yes, nice to hear from you. Everything ready for Thursday and Friday?'

'All arranged but just a point. For what it's worth, one sale, just one sale, will help consolidate my agreements with the vendor client. I'm not being pushy, one sale in this deal is nothing and you'll understand one day, I'm dealing with people, who are not necessarily in the business of trust.'

'I appreciate where you're coming from and as I'm leaving Peter next week, I'll have transferred sufficient funds to cover two acquisitions. Bugger, I intended surprising you Thursday but clever Mathew pried it out of me, so will 650,000 pats pacify the dog?'

Mathew recognises the pleasure in the patter. 'You really are an Aussie, only one of us would use that saying.'

Waiting in a clearly marked No Parking zone, the blue Falcon sits patiently on Nepean Highway. The driver brushes his stubbled chin and glances again at the dashboard clock as he's becoming anxious; it's only twenty minutes before other duties call, but he's prepared to put all his plans on hold to find out more about one Mathew Allen. Then as if willed by necessity, the unmistakable Jaguar emerges from the side street and turns towards the city.

Mandy appears with her golf bag slung over one arm, her golf shoes in the other hand. She's dressed neatly, white slacks with a plain navy-blue golf shirt; a white casual jacket drapes casually over one shoulder, partly covering the matching handbag. Mathew places the clubs in the opened boot. Mandy waits at the car door; he returns to play gentleman.

'I think you owe me a kiss.' It's a demand.

He kisses her on the cheek; she doesn't move.

'Come on, you can do better than that.'

The next kiss is delivered, as requested, firmly on the lips; he receives a smile and a simple nod with raised eyebrows. A rush of lust envelopes him. He dwells on la dolce vita as he purposely licks his lips, testing the sweet, erotic flavour.

The driver of the Falcon smiles too; his camera clicks repeatedly, capturing the scene. *Christ, who is this bloke? He's been shacked up with Miss KL and visits Miss Hong Kong. Now he's golfing with Brucella's number one girl, and isn't she a honey? The chief will love this. At least one shot will show him licking his lips, but in the overall scheme of things, where does any of Mr. Allen's affairs fit in?*

Mathew decides Mandy has been practising; she cruises around the 6,161-metre course, twelve over. 'I like this track.

I can wind up and let 'em rip. I have a desire to get back into club golf. Will you nominate me?'

'Pleased to and the boys will thank me.'

'Just want me for my body.'

Mathew passes. 'Coffee or beer?'

'A heavy draught, seeing as you're driving. Thanks for the application forms. I'm going to put it on Brian to pay my annual fee and I'll use the course to entertain clients. Brian doesn't golf. I can be the man, if you know what I mean.'

'Mandy, without being overly smart, you'll never be the man.'

'Thank you, kind sir. You're always passing compliments even though you never cross the line and by now, I would have thought you might have suggested a romantic dinner. Is the lady you took to Sydney the one in your heart? Sorry, but you must be aware with us, there are no secrets. It's fundamental we know who our major people are dealing with – playing with, if you like. And as we consider you a 'major person', you and your consultants and contacts are important. Now this new deal involving Miss Cheong is exciting as long as she performs. Are we putting our stock into the right barrel?'

'That's a lot of questions, Mandy. Firstly, the lady whom I took to Sydney is in my heart. Sadly, she's not in my life, so can we leave that subject alone, please. As to dinner, I would love to take you out somewhere romantic. And as to Miss Cheong, will you be happy when two sales arrive on your desk next week to, as you might say, 'suggest good faith' and she'd say, 'pat the dog.'

'That is a lot of answers. Firstly, I'd welcome your romantic dinner invite. Secondly, sorry about your lady. Anything we can do?'

The thought comes instantaneously. *Yes, have Arsehole kneecapped.* But just as quickly, he acknowledges his nicer side. *No, that's not fair to Min Xie. If he is her man, I have to let it go.* 'No thanks.'

'Remember, if you need anything, see us. We look after our main people, understand?' She wags her head deliberately, emphasising the point. 'Finally, to Miss Cheong, if she brings in two sales immediately, your stocks will rise even further and that brings us to the Rhine cruise. I'm not talking out of school. You'll be rewarded beyond expectations if the current level of performance continues. Brian told me you've suggested late August, early September for the cruise, perfect time of the year. May I change the subject slightly?'

'Sure.'

'How about Mrs. Allen? Might I be so bold to enquire, what is your married status likely to be in the future? I am serious about going to Europe, provided you're comfortable with the arrangement. However, if you prefer to take your wife. . . I wonder, why a romantic dinner?'

Isn't it strange? Mathew thinks. *All our chats have been just chatting. Suddenly, it's all business, including very private business.* 'I've resolved to separate.' He allows the statement to sink in; why he's not quite sure. 'I need to find a future abode before I do the deed. I want to move immediately without dither and doubt.'

She grins openly. 'I like dither and doubt, very droll. Which suburbs are you considering?'

'Probably fringe city high-rise. I thought a pool with all the goodies, a sauna and spa and maybe a gym.'

'Will you buy?'

'Probably not. High-rise prices aren't going anywhere but down. Rents are relatively cheap, flexibility opportune with a lease and I thought down the track I might buy an Adderley penthouse unit and pop a hot tub on the deck.'

'We'd do a good deal. Offset some commission against the price. Anyway, I've a feeling one of our associates owns a vacant sub-penthouse in Southbank. I'll check it out for you.'

'Thanks. Another beer?'

'A latte would be nice.'

Waiting for coffee, Mathew runs the chat through his brain. *If the Rhine cruise is on and I've split, why not have Mandy with me. But same old question, why me? Anyway, who cares? If Brian is kosher, why not?*

'Let's resolve the Rhine trip. Frankly, I'd love to have you along. I might be an old male, but I have sufficient hormones, alive and kicking, that attract me to you. Therefore, the romantic dinner is appropriate and you know now I intend to separate.'

'The Rhine is a dream. To do it with you could be perfect.'

Mathew poses, 'Really? Perfect? How can it be perfect?'

'Can I talk openly, just you and me?'

'Of course.' *Here we go. She's opening the can.*

'I'm not up myself. I know I'm attractive. I've been the party girl in most great cities of the world, but I'm over it. I'm over the jocks and the jokers who only want to find a way to climb into my undies. You attract me in a fatherly manner. Please don't take it the wrong way. I'm seeing a level-headed, nice person whom I reckon I'd travel well with, whose company I'll enjoy, appreciate the arts and ancient history, going with the flow of the magical Rhine. Romance is an interesting concept but unnecessary. We don't have to fall in love. Let's see what happens.'

'Want to shake on it?'

'No, a nice kiss later will seal this deal.'

Mathew melts around the knees, recovering to add, 'I'm going to Hong Kong shortly with Miss Cheong. I want to meet the connections, source the money flow, and confirm arrangements. I floated the idea past Brian. I want you to know.'

'And I have another surprise. You're to book business class, take two suites at the Princess and utilise the hotel's Rolls whenever required. We agree it's imperative to check out the people and consolidate the deal. Book on your credit card, fax a receipt with a copy of the itinerary and I'll reciprocate with a cheque plus 2,000 cash in U.S. currency.'

Mandy rummages through her handbag and passes over a battered business card. 'Our travel agent. I've told her to expect your call.'

'You people are incredible.'

'Because of that trust word. Now the dark side.' In a clandestine manner, she leans forwards. 'Expect a visit from the law. There's no doubt you'll have been spotted with Horace. You'll be on file, in their records. You're an unconnected fish and may not come under scrutiny, but if you do, just tell it the way it's been. You were referred by an established client and you can name him. Sid is mum. Horace came seeking ways to invest personally, nothing else.'

Mathew feels a little shiver run through his bones. *The law and me. Shit, hope they don't come to the house. Oh well, I have nothing to hide.*

'Now more business. We need another site, something in the one-million-dollar range. Prefer a residential construct and move on. Project cost up to three million. Anything comes to mind?'

'Simple answer, no, but I'll get on my bike.'

'We know you will.'

Mandy's apartment is on the sixth floor. Mathew makes a mental comment. *Attractively decorated, nice furniture, quality stuff. Her knick-knacks reflect someone trying to hold on to memories.*

The coffee pot clicks on. He settles into a huge armchair, absorbing the rich aroma of expensive leather and that conveys him to another lounge room, but his reminiscences are cut short. Mandy hands him a particularly large coffee mug. 'If you're going to have a cup, have a real cup.'

Mandy wanders to the holiday. 'Modelling in Europe, I set my heart on a Rhine cruise. Somehow it never eventuated. I hope you don't mind me throwing myself at you. I can taste the river.'

Mathew laughs. 'You're like me. When I was a youngster, my uncle occasionally hired movies from the state film library. One night he showed a touristy-type colour doco on the Canadian Pacific Railway. I'll never forget it, and I promised myself, 'One day.' I've been to the States many times but never taken the trip.'

'I'll put that in the computer. Next time the boys want to reward you, I'll know exactly the trip, across the Rockies first class on the Mountaineer, a suite at Chateau Lake Louise and the Banff Springs Hotel.'

'Including you?'

Mandy deliberately, almost in slow motion, places her coffee mug on the side table and then as if stirred by a primal urge quickly sits on his lap. Exactly repeating her previous action, the kiss is slow; only the lips are involved. Finally, her mouth opens a little. Tongues arrive at the edge, passion ignites and they go for it, with Mandy running her fingers through his hair, grasping his whole head in her hands, pulling back, looking at him as a tiny grin creases the edge of her eyes.

'I can see us at Banff, peering down the fabulous Bow Valley, taking in the spectacular serenity. And changing the subject, I knew you'd be a great kisser. I just knew it. I love to kiss, Mathew. I can lie for hours in the right person's arms and play touchy-feely and kiss. But not today. The time has to be right. I'm in no hurry for us. Are you?'

'No, I've waited this long. I'm very patient.'

'What do you mean you've waited this long?'

Mathew decides, *I'm a weak bastard. Let's push the barrow.* 'I've had the hots since the first time we met.'

He pecks her still pursed lips. 'Really and you never once made a pass.'

'I assumed every man would make a move. I reckoned if it's going to happen, then time will show us the way.'

'Hmm, I'm going to contemplate that and roll the resolution around, as you might say, over time and I believe the right time will come for us. In the meantime, thanks for the day. Nice to chat and I can't wait for August.'

CHAPTER 13

Mathew decides to circulate the A-list of preferred estate agents, advising that the hunt is on for a site up to a million dollars, with plans and permits approved preferably.

A private meal, taken almost formally at the dining room table, creates the opportunity for Mathew to inform Hope of the impending trip, but he only fills in the basics. 'Hong Kong on business, up and back in five days. Give me a shopping list. Just don't hold your breath if it's long and complicated.'

Without comment, Hope changes the subject and coolly discusses the kids' impending visit to the island. Mathew suggests they include the old girls and have the family together, elaborating Andrew will have to sleep on the converter couch, while the twins share the second bedroom toping and tailing or rolling out the trundle, while the oldies share bedroom three with the twin king beds.

The 'oldies' jump at the chance of seeing everyone together and Mathew volunteers to collect the girls after golf. 'In that case, I'll go down Friday night after work,' Hope throws in.

'I'll arrive at around six o'clock. What shall we do for dinner? Go out, eat in or I'll do a barbie, except you'll have to chase the fish?'

'A barbecue sounds like fun. Let's see, we have four flounder and about six ling fillets in the freezer. I need about another dozen fillets. What shall I buy?' Hope poses.

'Flounder whole or fillets, King George, flatties, or you might be lucky and find some gars. Worst case, you can't go wrong with gummy shark fillets. I'll wrap them in foil with some seasoned butter and a drop of white wine mixed into a lemon squeeze.' Mathew grins as he imagines the taste.

On Wednesday morning, Mathew telephones Steve. 'Sorry to annoy you, but I'm off to golf. Where are we at?'

'Good timing. I finished with the boys at eleven thirty last night. I almost called you but thought more about Hope. She works. You only golf.' The laugh was more a grunt. 'We agreed the compromise price with 10 per cent down on the signing of the contract. I'm holding $20,000 on account. Settlement in six months or on the issuing of the building permit, whichever is later but not longer than six months from the date of the contract. The buyer approved the inclusion of the construction clauses in the contract or under a separate agreement. We'll let the legal eagles decide whichever is most appropriate. Finally, they prefer to use their own architect. Does that pose a problem? I thought we might be locked into Bruce-Smith.'

'Good on ya, mate. Well done. Firstly, the last bit, yes, we are locked into Bruce, so reduce the price by $25,000 on the understanding your client liaises with Bruce and springs him the twenty-five large for the pleasure of their input. As for the rest, I'll phone the vendor now and come straight back. Do not go out. Hooroo.'

Mathew hangs up and proceeds immediately to dial Brian. Mandy answers. 'Hi, Mandy. Thought I'd call and tell you I can still taste that kiss.'

'You are so full of it. If it was that good, you'd have been at my door this morning, waiting for another one.' A smile comes attached to the quip.

'Yeah, right, anyway, how about dinner Friday night?'

'You're on. I have a passion for Vietnamese or Thai. It can still be romantic because it's you and me.'

'Done. We'll go back to my favourite in Gardenvale, seven thirty at your pad.'

'In turn, done. And after you've successfully snowed me, I assume you really want Brian. I'll put you through. Is it good news?'

'Yes.'

'Great. Hooroo. Ha ha! Now you have me saying it.'

Brian ticks off on the super lot offer and instructs Mathew to pass the information to his solicitor. 'Ask them to prepare the contract including the specific construction and completion clauses and deal with the other parties' solicitors.'

Expecting that business matters have been completed, Mathew takes the opportunity to thank Brian for the Hong Kong offer. 'I don't mind putting my hand in my pocket, Brian.'

'Understand and by the way, I don't want to be out of school, which it isn't really. Are you comfortable, man to man, with Mandy going to Europe with you?'

'I'm okay. Are you all right?'

'No problems. She's entitled to holidays. Now back to business, we've decided to sell only one more super lot. We'll develop the remaining site ourselves. Don't despair, we'll pay you a commission as we transfer the site to another company.'

Mathew wonders how many clients might offer that deal and proceeds to another of his priorities. 'Hotel suite sales! Any closer to a final decision? And while I'm at it, Milly will have two deals next week, one at Preston as we only have one sale off the plan and I thought I might slip the second into a hotel suite to start the ball rolling.'

'Perfect. I like your selection. Now we've decided to go with 50 per cent hotel suite sales and our solicitors are working on a draft contract. Sales prices are up $5,500 on your suggested selling price. It's chicken feed in the overall scheme but it helps the bean counters, as we'll guarantee 6.35 per cent return for two years.'

'I'm going to enjoy golf on Friday but what's happened with Min Xie?' Steve asks, still grinning as he swallows the acceptance news.

'Not playing', Mathew replies in a casual manner. 'I've invited another Chinese, a lady friend of yours – Milly, Peter Lee's ex-PA.'

'What do you mean ex?'

'She's made the big move, gone out on her own. Invest some time with her. It might prove worthwhile.' Then he smiles all-knowingly. 'Well done on this sale, Steve. It's a real win right across the board, including your client. See you Friday.'

Mathew made Wednesday night 'call the kids' night, intent on catching up with their goings-on and confirming arrangements for Saturday at the island. His specific instructions were said clearly. 'It's a bloody family night, no parties!' Andrew catches the message, makes a phone call, and changes plans none too happily.

Poor Peter is fuming! Mathew grins, imagining he's been riding on Milly's back for years; now the freebie is over, and the gravy train's derailed. Without undue discussion, a resolution is quickly arrived at, which concludes their previous chat relating to how sales will be allocated to which particular project. Milly will make the recommendations directly to Mathew, who – once property selection is agreed – will make the appropriate applications to the Foreign Investment Review Board (FIRB) for each unit sale to be formally approved and referring a copy of all correspondence to Mandy. In conclusion, Milly announces, 'I'm on the hunt for a larger pad. I really need my own office space.'

'If you need access to my A-list agents, just ask,' Mathew volunteers and smiles internally, envisaging a commission split in the wind.

Mandy conveys details of the apartment at Southbank but it has a catch. It has three bedrooms, fully furnished.

'Excuse me, that's perfect. Bedroom three can be the spare. Now the real bad news, how much is the rent?'

'A thousand a week. However, because you are taking me on my fantasy Rhine cruise, we'll take it out of your fees and commission account at $4,300 a calendar month. Your accountant should like that.'

'Sounds great. When can I inspect?'

'Monday, straight after work.'

'Want a bite afterwards?'

'Are you for real? Why do you think I set the inspection for after hours?'

CHAPTER 14

Mathew makes a concerted effort to property-shop, utilising the Real Estate Institute's diary. Repetitiously, he phones agent after agent, eventually arriving at Gary Scullin, the agent involved in Sid's subdivision who, after listening to the preamble, poses, 'How about the beach?'

'Which bloody beach?'

'Rye! Walk to the RSL, the shops and the bay beach. Listen to the record. Position, position!'

'Yeah, location, location. Talk imperial, please.'

'Come on, Mathew, you're a New Age man. What's this persistent pursuit of the past?'

'It's easier for an old fart to think quickly in the old language.'

'Twenty-five thousand two hundred square feet, corner site totaling 180 feet by 140 feet, a standard easement traversing the long rear boundary, three old houses let at only $125 per week each. They're a bit of an eyesore.'

'So that's the good news. How bad is the bad?'

'Purchased three years ago, the owner tried to sell last year, a deal agreed at $510,000 or $85,000 a site based on six units. Unfortunately, the sale fell over. Now the market's slipped but he's stuck on $525,000 and here's the twist. The bank called me last week, seeking an updated current market appraisal. Being the bank, I hit 'em low at max $475,000.'

'Any peripheral work done?'

'Yeah, Rick Clarke, the surveyor at Rosebud, has shot the levels and completed a feature survey.'

Mathew pushes his luck. 'Any plans?'

'Hey, mate, you can't have everything.'

'Are the houses on leases?'

'No, all casual.'

'Leave it with me. I'll call you back. By the way, do you have any runners?'

'No, it's off the radar due to price.'

Mathew telephones Nigel, asking him to check the density as being a corner he schemes, if, with planning support, they might achieve seven units. Within the hour, Nigel returns the call. 'You might remember one of my old uni mates is Bicky Burkett. He heads up planning at council.'

No, he hadn't.

'He says, suddenly, there's a lot of interest in the site. He handled three over the counter enquiries in the last two weeks, plus the ANZ bank made an enquiry of the valuer's office. As to density, he'll support seven, providing the facade is in keeping with the beach scene, whatever that means. Give him prior input opportunity before any plans are lodged. Ball's in your court. Have you seen the site?'

'Not yet.'

'Bicky says it's a tip and being such a prominent position, council is anxious to see it redeveloped. Instruct your architect to pay him the compliment of a chat before he puts pen to paper. Going to save everyone a lot of time.'

'Great advice, Nige. Talk soon.'

Mathew immediately telephones Brian, quickly relays the story and is instructed to proceed to negotiate. Hanging up the phone, Mathew grins, wondering how good the trust is. Mathew's first question to Gary is, 'Do you still have the name and number of the guy at the bank?'

'Silly question. Of course.'

'You're right, silly question. Start writing, $475,000 and you can go another five, ninety days' settlement, unconditional with one proviso – the vendor pays for and delivers all the surveying work or authorises us to deal directly with Rick Clark once the deposit has been paid.'

'Vacant possession?'

'No, we'll take the rent for a while. Who's the managing agent?'

'Brown and Brown.'

'Sounds like the Dodgy brothers.'

'No, they are good blokes. And the bank?'

'Just phone the man as a matter of courtesy and casually drop the offer.'

'You are one foxy bastard, Mathew.'

'Talk tomorrow on both issues.'

Mathew relaxes with his feet up and considers all the irons in the various fires smoldering away, yet nothing is burning. His attention turns to next week and the inspection of a potential new place of abode; excitement runs high, yet he understands the implications of a successful viewing will dictate the timing of the vital talk with Hope. With Andrew at the island on the weekend, contrary to Mathew's previous expedition up this creek, he decides to front him, raise the subject and gauge a reaction.

CHAPTER 15

The water is cold, the swim chilling. Both Mathew and Woofy run up the beach, necessary to stimulate blood flow and then turn back south into the strong, icy wind. It makes Mathew wonder at the sense of pursuing the health kick. Trudging through the cold sand, he suffers one of his bad Min Xie moments. *God, how I'd love to talk to her, just to say hi, chit-chat about rubbish. I miss her little face, those red lips like sunset. Why can't I accept the sun has indeed set on us?*

A scam evolves in the dark recesses of his tricky mind. *I need May to believe Milly is my new lady. It'll filter back to Min Xie in a flash and then I'll connive to have May invite them to the next golf day. She might decline. Regardless, it's part of a new web I determine to weave.'*

Negotiations proceed backwards and forwards all morning over the Rye property. The final phone call conveys the news – the deal agreed at $490,000 with a seventy-five-day close.

'The trick the bank, they're about to move, the owner has slipped into default. Lucky Mathew struck at the right time.'

Yes, indeed, lucky Mathew recognises he's been in the right place at precisely the right time. Enthused, he changes the time to meet Milly and they head to Rye, with Mathew electing to enhance the experience by taking the scenic route.

'We don't come this way,' Milly offers in a questioning manner.

'Probably because you're intent on the destination, not the journey.'

Milly debates the answer and in time replies, 'It took me a minute to understand where you're coming from. Very perceptive, Mathew. It's about life, hey. Not enough time to smell the wattle?'

'It doesn't smell.'

'You know what I mean.'

'Keep your head down. Don't walk in the shit.' With Milly considering the reply, Mathew smiles. 'We make hurry to arrive, often missing the enjoyment of experiencing the experience, you might say.'

Milly persists in meditating the conversation. Mathew turns off Point Nepean Highway near the Rye Pier and readily discovers the site. 'A long drive, only to find it exactly as depicted. Still, I couldn't take the chance of buying a dud just because I didn't go the extra yard to suss it out.'

'Great position. Walk to everything, even the pub!' Milly excitedly exclaims.

'You're right, position A. Let's stop for a coffee and watch the seagulls soar, the boats rock at anchor and then we'll go play some golf.'

On the way-out Boneo Road, Mathew poses, 'So, Milly, possibly another seven units for your investors. Any chance you could angle this to possible end users because of its locale? I thought being equidistant to all the facilities and only ten minutes back to the Rosebud Hospital, it might ring the right bells.'

'Funny you say that. I'm trying to enhance the acceptance of the Murray River condos by pushing that barrow in Hong Kong. It's an angle to promote – rent out now, occupy later on.'

Mathew smiles, acknowledging she's right into the groove without having to over-advocate the proposition. He hates to be pushy; it rings the wrong bells.

Discovering Steve in the pro shop with May, Mathew conducts the introductions and notices May gives Milly the once-over. 'Are you single, Milly?'

'Very.'

'Haven't I told you, Mathew, not to invite number ten girls? How am I going to find a man when beauties like Milly show up?' Turning to Milly, she continues, 'My god, girl, you so tall and beautiful.'

'Thanks, and how are you Steve? Long time no see.'

'Very good, thanks, Milly. Mathew's bought me up to speed on your new move. Congratulations. Trust everything goes well.'

'I hope so. I know this evening is social. However, I have a time frame issue. Mathew and I are going to Hong Kong in two weeks, staying at the Princess, if you don't mind and I'm going to love swanning around in their Rolls. I need to have a quick business chat after golf.'

Oh, you sweetheart, Mathew thinks. *May will be on her mobile as soon as she drives out the gate.* 'Hey, Min Xiela, you should see Mathew's new lady. My god, what a beauty. He is *taking her to Hong Kong. They are staying at the Princess. Wow, she must be hot to stay there.'* But of course, it's all in his mind.

On the way out to the first tee, May comments, 'Normally, Mathew and I play as a team. Are you guys okay we maintain the tradition? I don't want to come between new lovers just for the sake of golf.'

And Milly falls in perfectly. 'No problem. Maybe I'll give Mathew the flick and chase Steve.' A big wink accompanies her knowing nod. Mathew successfully restrains the laugh.

After golf and the obligatory bathroom visit, the girls join the boys at the barbecue; the sizzling commences and conversation turns to Milly. May takes a particular interest in her occupation, driven by her perceived involvement with Mathew. The discussion becomes very business oriented as Milly's future plans are expanded on. May soaks up the comments on the wheeling and dealing, which ultimately includes comments on the previous poor performance of Peter Lee, leading her to pipe up, 'I know Peter. He is invited to our golf days but he never fronts, a bit like someone else I know.' She peers purposely at Steve, who sets off towards the bar, with Milly trailing behind.

Mathew understands her intention is to offer him the opportunity to act as property manager of all new sales. He wonders if Milly will allude to the fact that if Peter becomes difficult, she'll transfer every investment unit managed by Peter's company to Steve, or will that ace be kept up her sleeve?

Now alone, May comes right to the point. 'We have been friends for a long time. I know you were pursuing Min. Now she's given us both the flick. What's going on?'

'Make an effort and pop into her house without notice to visit one night. You might receive a shock to find out who's with her. This isn't about me, May. It's about Min Xie. I'm here. She's not, but I tell you what. Invite her to the next golf day and if the question is posed, simply fib, no, he's not playing.'

'That'll be a surprise.'

'You can see it all,' he jibes.

'Ha, not quite this time. I had her with you. I told her last year I knew who the new man in her life will be. I kept your name to myself because you were married. Are you still?'

'I'm separating as soon as I find new accommodation. I'm looking at a sub-penthouse in South Century City Monday night, so I might be by myself quite quickly.'

'Then you'll have a nice trip to Hong Kong?'

Mathew relishes the opportunity to add salt to the rub for Min Xie. 'Yeah, flying up first class.' He then suffers one tiny millisecond of recrimination for the exaggeration, yet revenge for the lingering hurt demands that he add, 'And in August, I'll be cruising the Rhine and the Danube via Vienna and Amsterdam.'

CHAPTER 16

The weekend is all about family, providing Mathew a quixotic opportunity to scrutinise the brood bundled together for what may be the last time in truce and tranquility. Through the looking glass, it creates a panoramic glimpse of kith and kin partitioned by imagination and determination; there's a better life on the other side.

Patiently, Mathew seeks a fortuitous opportunity to steer Andrew into a private chinwag out of earshot and without the sudden unwanted intervention into their powwow; when it arrives, he cuts straight to the chase. 'We need to have a man to man. What is said today must remain that way until I say otherwise. You understand?'

The answer comes concise and contrite. 'Yes and no.'

Mathew's not of the inclination to pussyfoot around, especially now he's mustered the courage to commence, knowing he can't stop. 'Hope and I have been having relationship problems. We've discussed separation on several occasions and I've always walked away from the final decision.

This time, I will not. I'm not seeking your comment, just telling you man to man. Life is going to change. It's simply about me, the way I foresee my future.'

'Is this why you were so late the other night? You were with her?'

Mathew actually laughs. 'No, that was truly all about business, which has eventuated in new directions sales-wise. And young man, you need to know there is no one else. I'm not moving in with someone and no one is moving in with me.'

'Well, Dad, I'm shocked. I had no idea. There's been no indication. You've never fought, yelled and screamed. I don't know what to say.'

'You don't have to say anything but keeping you right up to speed, I'm looking at a pad on Monday night. If it's acceptable, I'll go immediately as previously I never went, just wavered around.'

'Mum will be cut up and what about the oldies? I don't think the girls will like this. They'll be on Mum's side.'

'I trust this isn't about sides. It's Hope and I saying neither of us are happy. It's time to move on.'

'I understand, but I don't. If there's no one else, why?'

'I suppose because simply it's just life. I'm not happy and I'm not making Hope happy.'

'Are it's about sex?'

The drive back to Melbourne offers time for a final deliberation and Mathew questions for one last definitive time whether he really wants to separate. The resolution is conclusive; the die's cast, he's in the mood and trusts the apartment suits.

Information relevant to the Rye property is sent to each consultant, along with its normal operation procedure including designating time frames, which Mathew will demand they work to as the purpose is to move this project on quickly. Upon reflection, recognising draft sketches have to be completed by his return, he flips back to the list and under Architect and alters the schedule.

CHAPTER 17

The day is bleak and biting, exaggerated by a brisk breeze shuffling the drizzly rain willy-nilly all over the place. 'An early glimpse of winter?'

'You bet. Hop in, Milly. I'll deal with the luggage.'

'Bad timing. We'll get caught in peak traffic.'

'I didn't have a choice. Always a client to attend to and as long as there are no dramas, we'll be right.'

In the undercover long-term car park, Milly confirms the good planning. 'Okey-dokey, time to spare.'

Mathew has organised a taxi; the driver is provided with instructions to proceed directly to the Sydney site. It isn't long before he's up Mathew's nose. 'Usual Melbourne, wet and cold, beautiful here though.'

'You know, Milly, every time I come to Sydney, it's hot and sunny, whilst Melbourne's chilly and raining.'

Mathew doesn't have to wait long for the driver to bite. 'Yeah, that'd be right. You must travel up regularly, mate?'

'No, just once a year.'

The pacified driver parks under the canopy of a shady tree and opens the passenger door, seeking a breeze while they walk the entire perimeter. Mathew wonders at the driver's sense of humour, articulating, 'Up yours', as the door swings open.

Milly exercises her camera and brain, posing tricky questions. It's full-on business as her intention is to totally understand the site and floor plans, then the overall concept will fall into place. 'As good as the position of Adderley Street. I know where I'd invest my long-term money.'

Mathew sucks up to the petulant driver, drawing on his local knowledge to conjure up a few detours back to the airport, enabling Milly to photograph local infrastructure features. At Sydney International, with the flight not due until mid-afternoon, they suck on coffee and light pastries as Mathew assumes Skippy will serve a late lunch in business class. Milly climbs into his brain, reiterating the different types of investment units in the Sydney project, wanting to be doubly sure and Mathew acts as quizmaster, posing appropriate questions in relation to all the relevant projects, expanding and elaborating on the answers, being fussy and finicky, pushing the bar, expecting perfection. In complimentary conclusion, he notes she's top of the class and he's impressed.

Milly leans her head on his shoulder. 'I'm so excited. Meeting Uncle will be exhilarating but to bask in my associate's acclimation will enhance my face. Still, I must have humility.' She swivels her head and smiles directly at Mathew while sustaining the gaze.

'Uncle will be proud. Your maturity is apparent, the beauty evident, shining from within and I trust the associates recognise your adroitness and diligence. Rest assured, Milly, if opportunity occurs, I'll push your cart.'

'Oh, thank you, Mathew. I am so happy. This is you and me together. Ha, and you're the cherry on my pie. I tell you; my connections are confounded. You make the effort to visit when really, it's not necessary. Now I offer an insight, a tip, you say. If they invite you for dinner, be on your toes. Leave the dancing shoes at home.'

'I have to ask why.'

'They'll take you to a girly bar or restaurant and invite a beautiful temptress and if you succumb, they will hold something over you.'

He blinks, deciding, *This might be tricky.* 'I'll be careful. I'm going to see if I can sleep for a few hours.' But Mathew doesn't rest; the events of the last two weeks flood back.

The evening inspection of the sub-penthouse encompasses twilight, the setting sun spectacular; the sky converges into a conglomeration of tinges of fiery red with tints of soft pink and orange. Expansive living areas inspire imagination, aspects in winter peering into the swirling mist dense and deep; beneath his window, an urban white sea coalesces with the insipid pale sun like blancmange setting across Victoria Harbour while the heater toasts the toes. The main bedroom gifts an easterly aspect, perfect for sunrise; bedroom two commands a sweeping view around the southern bay suburbs and that will house the office, while bedroom three is set aside for guests.

'I like the furniture, Mathew, all the modern brown tones, clean-cut, simple lines. The word *minimalist* pops into mind but it's your house, what do you think?'

'Perfect comes to mind.' He saunters into the kitchen and adds all the extensive cooking gear to the appliance inventory, TVs in all bedrooms and a wall-mounted unit in the living area. The dining table will seat eight and the living area incorporates a gas burner pebble fireplace.

'But' – he stirs Mandy – 'it doesn't have a coffee machine.'

'Readily fixable, I'd have thought.' Mandy smiles and questions, 'Are you happy?'

'Too right. Still, I can't believe the rent. Who cooked the books?'

'Just accept it in the manner portrayed, a nice pad to rest your bones, until you decide if you want an Adderley penthouse or whatever. Let's go check out the recreational facilities?'

'It truly is ideal. I only have to bring my desks, filing cabinets and I'm set.'

'And your golf clubs.' Mandy nods.

His mind winds back to Hope, acknowledging the stoic manner in which the final decision had been accepted but it came with one telling comment. 'I knew you'd go. It only revolved around when.' The comment unsettled him, cutting to the core. The strength of the relationship was questioned as he understood he'd been the rock, she the moss. Instead of drama, he'd been confronted by a contrasting attitude, casting a new shadow on the safe, solid ground he always thought he stood on. It forced him to question, *Does she have another man in her life?* Has he been blinded by arrogance, blighted by determination to see the cup half full? Their discussion concluded on property settlements, the agreement to involve the kids resolved and Mathew, regardless of the undertaking, assumes there'll be a few family meetings this week.

Biting the bullet, he called a meeting with the twins and Andrew; he delivered the revelation over a commonly shared bowl of mixed fruits and frothy cappuccinos. He was immediately conscious Andrew had indeed kept mum and, in the time, it took to sip half a cup of froth, life changed. The girls were visibly shocked, crying as neither believed nor accepted there was no one else. Mathew clutched the short straw, accepting the no-win situation; only time will heal this wound. Upon finishing the coffee, grasping, he'd sucked the life out of the family; he threw a twenty-dollar note on the table, plucked the last strawberry from the dish and left them to meditate on the throwaway line 'I'm still Dad. I'm here for you. I'm not going anywhere. I've worked hard for a long time at being a dad, a husband and a provider. It's now Mathew time.'

After his timely escape, Tiffany said angrily, 'You know the old saying 'Once a parent, always a parent.' I thought marriage vows were the driver of 'Once a husband, always a husband.'

'Obviously, not anymore', Stephanie replied.

'Bloody bullshit. Let me tell you, when my turn comes, it'll be that way or he'll be carried out.'

Mathew simply wondered if they'd see him as just a selfish old prick and frankly, he preferred it not to be debated.

Stephanie telephoned to apologise for crying. 'I recognise you've not been close for some time, so in reality, it's not a surprise. Disappointed is more like it. Safe trip and good luck for the future. I'll be here for you, Daddy.'

Tiffany failed the test to connect.

Mathew's last morning at the beach was a moment of melancholy as he spotted Woofy appear through his gate and, with his tail in gyration, bounded across the sand, barking in what Mathew had always perceived was exhilaration. As Mathew swam, Woofy belted up and down the water's edge, terrifying the seagulls, adding mayhem as they rose and settled, only to be annoyed time and again. Then with his canine mate, Mathew jogged along the hard sand, talking to the dog like a best mate. 'I've enjoyed your company, Woofy. You're a great dog. Thanks for being a patient listener. Pity I never discovered your real name.'

The parting was difficult. Mathew took the dog's head in his hands and ruffled its soft ears as his big brown eyes acknowledged animal trust and the tongue huffed and puffed happiness. Mathew turned away, unable to look back; a solitary tear gathered in his eye. The dog loped away home, unaware sharing mornings with this human were over.

The law arrived as Mathew prepared to move out. The coincidence got his goat. 'Perfect bloody timing. It must look like I'm doing a runner.'

'Mathew Allen?'

'That's me.'

In plain clothes, the usual tuppence, old cop and young cop. After introductions, Mathew politely invited them in, offering coffee or tea; they declined gruffly and his goat became an angry billy as the interview took place in full sight of his neighbours. 'You've been recorded as having been in the company of one Horace George Smith. Do you recall this, Mr. Allen?' the senior policeman commenced efficaciously.

Mathew reckoned he was an overbearing bastard and simply answered yes, deciding to remain cool, letting them do the asking.

'Then you admit knowing Smith?'

'That's right.'

'In what capacity do you know him?'

'I'm a property investment adviser. I create and manage individuals' wealth. He was referred by a satisfied client.'

'Has Smith concluded any business with you?'

The truth was, as an individual, no, and that was the answer offered.

'Has Smith been in contact with you since he's been in custody?'

'Christ, no!'

The young officer jumped in, 'Why so positive?'

'Because there's no reason. Why would he want to contact me?'

'What types of investments did he enquire about?'

'Nothing specific. His attitude amused me.'

'Why?'

'Well, he had absolutely no idea. By that I mean he didn't seem to know which station to get on at nor his destination.' *I'll try to confuse 'em.*

The officers glanced at each other, the younger in pursuit of exclamation. 'What does that mean?'

Now I'll stick it up 'em. 'It's easy really. I gave him some homework to study and decide on, stuff like equity, cash flow in duopoly, financing by interest only, P and I or bills, negative gearing, amortisation, taxation implications, our own estoppel, all the tricky stuff. But he never came back. The test too tough, hey? Anyway, I don't chase business. C'est la vie.'

The older inspector changed his direction. 'A successful businessman then, Mr. Allen.'

His look was more a sneer, his answer direct. 'Might I offer a few referrals?'

'See you're moving.'

'My wife and I have separated. Do you require my new address?'

'Whose choice?'

'What business has that to do with you? I believe this interview is terminated.'

'We can take you down to the station.'

'Really, if you're going to waste everyone's time doing that, let me call my solicitor first.' Mathew reached into his pant pocket and grasped the mobile phone, trusting the bluff worked. He had no intention of involving his legal eagle at that stage.

'You are a smart-arse, Mr. Allen.'

Mathew's cranky cranked up, his dark side on display. 'No, you're the smart-arse. I have cooperated, answered every question, so you might treat me with a smidge of respect, not as a dickhead.'

'We'll be in touch.'

Suddenly, in appreciation of the win, he purposely pushed the point. 'Really, what about?' In recognition of the weakness in their questioning, Mathew, emboldened, took out his diary and deliberately noted their names and the license number of the car, ensuring his actions were noticed and then strutted arrogantly down the centre of the street, following the car, unconcerned at any witnessing neighbour.

Later that evening, when transferring his last load of gear, Hope accompanied him to visit his new home. Mathew assumed Andrew had been on the tom toms as he'd called in unexpectedly; still, it afforded opportunity to explain in a devious manner the unexpected visit of the constabulary, which Hope decided had nothing to do with her and commented instead, 'I can't believe you've moved into the city, so out of character but a wonderful apartment. I trust you find what you're looking for.'

With the city lights as a backdrop, they came together and hugged. Hope pecked him on the cheek. 'You've not been happy for a long time.'

Mathew was unable to decide if that was a question or a statement of fact, and that was not the time to become involved in complications; he just nodded.

'Last time, was anyone involved?'

'No, and this isn't about another woman.' But Mathew knew, with this woman, he hadn't been truthful for some time.

CHAPTER 18

The approach to the new airport is not as spectacular as flying into Kai Tak. The exciting, or terrifying, over-the-hill approach has been simply spectacular, provided a seat on the starboard side of the plane is occupied. The perception truly is one of reaching out and plucking clothes off the balconies of the apartments as they flash by, seemingly metres away.

Milly quickly spots the Princess Hotel driver in his immaculate light grey chauffeur uniform with the hotel's gold and green logo emblazoned boldly. An ostentatious gold-plated sign reminiscent of an ancient Roman standard-bearer displays his name. Mathew soaks up the opulence, indulging in the lap of luxury as the limousine floats along the new freeway. A glance at Milly catches the glimmer of a smile; he assumes it's a reflection of her contentment and expectation, whilst for him it's all about the latter.

The hotel greeting is professional and friendly; in no time, they are ushered to the elevator and whisked to the eleventh floor and their adjoining suites. Mathew tips the boys with Yankee dollars. Milly opens the connecting door and rushes into his arms.

'Welcome to my home of so many years.' She chuckles. 'It wasn't like this. I'll take you to the typhoon shelter, but I doubt you'll appreciate how we lived. Anyway, I truly hope you enjoy your stay and our business is memorable.' She puckers her lips and holds his eyes. 'In fact, Mathew Allen, I'm going to ensure the whole time is unforgettable.' She floats a kiss, flicks back her black locks, winks in a wanton way, kicks off a shoe and announces, 'I'm going to relax in the tub. Order supper to the suite. You will join me.'

Mathew takes it as a positive proclamation, knowing he enjoys being organised. Motionless, he appraises the panorama, the mass of illumination; some fixed, much twinkling, moving by land and water around the harbour and up the Peak, dazzling as ever. In an orderly fashion, he settles the toiletries around the handbasin and shaves long and close, recognising it to be a considerate decision.

A knock at the door disturbs an onset of lustful notions, quickly dispelled by the bellhop, who presents a silver tray containing a message sealed in an embossed hotel envelope. The illusion creates a sense of untainted, unread information; for all intents and purposes, who counts how many eyes have perused the contents before placing it into the paper shroud? Mathew delays opening the delivery and drifts into conspiracy country, recognising he is in the mystic realm of the master illusionists, where everything is a riddle with another reason, another meaning. The ancient art of duplicity, blackmail, treachery and plain-fashioned double dealing weaved indelibly into the intricacies of the Middle Kingdom. Emphasised emphatically by Milly's advanced warning, 'They will invite a temptress.' Purposefully, he ponders the secret in the shroud. How many nefarious hands have already shuffled it? What doors may it open or close, the machinations extended to the far edge of the fanciful horizon? Impulse driven, he rips it open; anxiously, his eyes rip into the vital communique. 'Be a good boy, behave yourself, save up for Vienna or the Rhine. Mandy.' He falls onto the bed, laughing hysterically at his ridiculous imagination.

An amazing night of eroticism commences in the tub, seduction in reverse. Milly performs the massage. Sleep approaches in a haze. Mathew reverts to conspiracy theories. *If they want to find out, they will. It's obvious even to blind Freddie. We've used massage oil, one bed not slept in, the sheet's a mess, only one bathroom used, and so on.*

The day dawns but not at sparrows; its eight thirty when the alarm breaks the peace and Milly's immediately up to the task with the right attitude. 'Have to prepare. Uncle at ten o'clock and we need sustenance.'

Mathew returns to his suite, attends to his ablutions and comments to the full-length mirror, 'At least both bathrooms have now been disturbed.'

Dress of the day is smart casual – Country Road beige slacks, Jaeger dress shirt and an Italian-styled but Chinese-made blue linen and poly jacket. Through the connecting door, he finds Milly in her underwear, applying make-up.

'You look particularly ravishing. Can we cancel Uncle until tomorrow?'

He kisses her neck; the subtle hint of Joy drifts delightfully and dwells in his nose.

'Why don't you go and have a cup of anti-horny coffee? I'll be there in around fifteen minutes.'

'I might be rude and eat without you.'

'That's fine. See you down there. Have I told you I'm excited?'

With a copy of the *South China Morning Post*, Mathew takes temporary occupancy of a quiet table. Breakfast is the choice of Asian or American buffet style, brilliantly presented and prolific. In typical Mathew fashion, he takes a small jug of fresh pineapple juice, pours it over a bowl of cornflakes and slices a banana into the mix, failing to notice the waitress, who gapes at the concoction. 'Ha, gweilos, nothing surprises me.'

He opens the paper, sports pages first, continuing to the business section featuring an article on China's booming economy, which in turn fuels the mining boom in Australia. It is a readable, quality piece of journalism. Mathew notes the writer's name. He isn't sure why.

Milly arrives, although Mathew determines she floats in – no, maybe it's gliding, whatever. She stops the room, he stands to hold her chair and she responds with a kiss on the cheek, offering one of those special smiles that photographers seek to discover on their models' faces. 'Milly, you look stunningly beautiful.'

'Thanks, and I see you've managed a coffee and some cereal. I trust the portion of anti-horny potion isn't too potent.'

After breakfast, Milly's morning is devoted to the reunion, the Uncle and Milly show. Mathew goes on a shopping expedition, circumnavigating his way around bustling Kowloon, searching for the bargains demanded by the family wish list and the more private little something for Mandy and May. He scores a classic pair of long gold earrings with a single pearl in the drop for Mandy. While for May, he stumbles across a Hermes silk scarf; because of the cost, he assumes quality, failing to recognise the brand name. In the essence of good business or great bargaining, the offer of a discounted second scarf creates opportunity to buy an additional one, knowing Mandy will love the bright, bold colours and concludes so will Milly, so he buys her one too and then realises, just his bloody luck, they'll turn up together in similar ensemble.

Not far away, a telephone call is made, destined to change his life. 'Heidi, good morning. You are well?'

'Ah, yes, good morning and thank you. Yourself in excellent health?'

'Very much so and my apologies, we haven't seen you of late and I regret the short notice I posed. Might you still be available to attend a special dinner tomorrow night?'

'Yes, of course, always for you and with respect, is it indeed a special occasion?'

'One of particular importance, my dear. Bring your property repertoire as company, you'll meet the new man from Melbourne.'

Heidi gently closes the phone, leans back and kicks her legs in the air. 'Exactly as expected. My spy's information was on the money. And Grandfather in heaven, if the rest of the intelligence stacks up, we might be in for an amazing adventure.' Her mouth widens as the grin spreads and eyes sparkle.

Amidst the frantic frenzy of Nathan Road, Mathew sips a particularly weak, insipid coffee and then receives the expected call. 'The foyer of the Harbour Plaza Hotel in twenty minutes.' It not being too distant, he decides to join the masses and meander rather than cab or swan up in the Rolls, although he contemplates the temptation.

It's a typical Hong Kong day for the northern hemisphere, relatively hot and humid. Mathew, with his jacket slung over a shoulder, appreciative of the short-sleeved shirt, strives to saunter casually but is carried along by the massing, milling throng that is Downtown Kowloon.

A wizened little man appearing a hundred years ancient is perched on the couch like a child; his feet swing clear of the floor. Milly is gushing and cooing in the introductions; Mathew offers a short bow in salutation, acknowledging respect; a gnarled hand and a warm smile are extended, the grip firm, a strong handshake that Mathew appreciates. There is nothing worse than a limp wrist welcome, but there is nothing weak about this vertically impaired person, medium build for his height, with strong arm muscles extending from his wide chest on which perches a bald head with only whiskers, a tiny David Niven moustache, which Mathew concludes looks out of place.

A chunky solid gold chain hangs around his neck; his wrist and two fingers on each hand exhibit wide gold bands.

Quite ostentatious, flashing one's savings, telling the world your worth. Mathew chuckles inwardly.

Tea and casual conversation commence. This is the old man of the sea. Mathew reckons if he was cheeky, he'd call him Salty. Uncle did the asking. Mathew spent most of the time in answer mode.

Overlooking the harbour, they settle at a table allocated against the dining room window. Mathew shakes his head in appreciation of the spectacle that is the harbour, knowing one never tires of the view. The conversation slowly turns to business; Milly takes it on herself to order lunch. Uncle becomes quite effusive, expressing appreciation for Mathew's assistance in establishing her new position and in the process, acknowledges her increased prestige within the bank. Salty smiles when he and Milly discuss the commission income to be derived from the new arrangement.

As agreed, Mathew pushes her barrow and asks Milly to pass on his personal dissertation. 'Milly should be highly commended. She conducts herself professionally with great business acumen. Her influence is immeasurable, encouraging me to offer up my property portfolio which will enable the bank's clients to invest for secure income and long-term stable growth. She has worked particularly diligently to bring this new commission arrangement to fruition. I'm only here because of her business and negotiation skills.' Then he wonders whether he's gone over the top.

Milly is lengthy in interpretation, and that results in Uncle smiling broadly, facial lines expanding with the grin. He bows from the waist, lets out a stream of Chinese verbalisation addressed to Mathew, and bows deeply on conclusion.

'I owe you one, Mathew. Uncle is taken by the compliments. The group now holds me in high regard for suggesting and carrying out the plan. He will reiterate your comments. Uncle asks me to warn you a honeypot will be dangled under your nose and that confirms my comment on the plane. I believe you have won a new friend as he is explicit, the bankers are relishing the opportunity to grill you personally, instead of doing business via fax and email.'

At the conclusion of lunch, Mathew suggests he leave them to reminisce. Milly's adamant uncle will pay the bill, but Mathew wins the reverse fumble. With time available, Mathew runs the projects through his brain. *If I'm going to be grilled, so be it. Confidence in my stock and industry knowledge affirms I can handle any barrage of detailed questioning. Still, I can't be overconfident. Humility and empathy towards their lack of understanding about Aussie ways and methods is paramount in achieving acceptance. I shouldn't become bogged down in detail nor waffle to expand on my own importance or to win a battle but lose the war. It's going to be an interesting lunch.*

Disturbed by a shuffle, he opens an eye, squints, and sights Milly removing a hotel robe, revealing her magnificent body poured into a pure white one-piece swimsuit. His other eye opens in admiration. *Well, might men rave at beautiful girls in tiny bikinis, the right girl with the right body in the right one-piece swimsuit will leave a bikini for dear, and isn't Milly the epitome of perfect in that hypothesis!* 'As always, you look absolutely stunning.'

'Good enough to eat?'

'Of course.'

'Good, let's go. Must be time to christen your suite.'

'I thought you came down for a swim.' It was a question, not a statement.

'Don't be silly. This swimsuit never gets wet.'

Dusk has drawn near; the window furnishings remain wide open. 'So, Milly, how is the reunion going?'

'Wonderful. If only auntie were here, it would be sublime. In her memory, Uncle has constructed a tiny contemplation corner of his garden, explaining he sits and talks to her, offering congratulations on the plan she dreamt up to escape from the village and China. My education, experience at the bank, then in Melbourne, her foresight to conjure up the investment scheme to utilise the illegal currency, locked away in the vaults of many banks. Uncle admits it was her brains, that encouraged him to find the right contact, to develop the scheme in Hong Kong. He has such admiration for her he says, 'If only she had written a book or at least written her story down.' Uncle only knows so much about her life. Now regrettably, it's gone and I learnt something today. He has always been in distress because Auntie lost her children, so many years ago, he sought help from the Beijing men to search the records, to trace what happened and you know what they find?'

'No.'

'Nothing.'

Mathew sits up in shock at the revelation. 'What do you mean nothing?'

'Auntie never existed – every trace, every record gone. Like a file in the computer, just click Delete, and it disappears.'

'How bloody strange. What does that mean, Milly?'

'He believes someone at the very top of government, a very powerful man or woman, decided to eliminate her and destroyed her records, including the children's. Now everything is gone. She was never born, she never lived, she never taught, no kids, no nothing. Uncle wonders at the plight of the children – no past, no records – and despairs Auntie will never have a history. Then she lived in Australia and he never saw her again, now she's gone. It's all just here.' Milly taps her head and her heart.

'We all know how tough life can be on some people. You epitomise that, Milly. You hold within your heart and soul the good and the bad.'

'And the lucky.'

'Like so many Chinese peasants and little people in history. In Australia, we call them the battlers. History rarely records their struggle.'

'True but not for us. We can record our own history for the future, have you?'

'No, have you?'

She turns her head and smiles. 'No.'

'Then you must. You have an amazing story to tell. Start writing it down before it runs away with the grains of time.'

They must have dozed off. Darkness has descended. Mathew stands at the hotel window, gazing at the stars, wondering at their glory, knowing in China they are everlasting ancient stars. But what about auntie, to whom credit is given for the life plan? What hasn't been explained is who set up the currency deal. Who is the brains? How did it come about with this particular bank? It will take a long time, with lots of water under the proverbial bridge, before he learns the full story.

Milly stirs. 'What's the time?'

'Eleven thirty.'

'I'm hungry. Feel like going out? Might be fun, hey.'

'Yeah, you bet and we'll make it fun. I bet you dinner I'll dress before you.' He jumps out of bed and dashes for his clothes with Milly after him, laughing.

'You funny man.'

He won. She paid.

Nathan Road at midnight acquaints to most Main and High Streets on Christmas Eve – frantic. They dine at a compact, cluttered family eatery in a side alley; it is noisy and untidy and he thinks better of inspecting the cooking facility, yet the fare is delicious and by choice, he remains unsure of what he's eaten, leaving the ordering to Milly.

Arm in arm, entertained by the bustling, boisterous crowd, they savour the moment – hot, humid, and exciting.

'Want to do something silly, a little crazy?'

'Tell first.'

'Let's go to Star Ferry, take a ride across the harbour and marvel at the light show.' She grins like a little girl. 'Can we?'

'Sure. You want to race?' Letting go, he makes out to run. Next thing, a tall Chinese streak bolts past, stops and questions, 'Are we racing?'

'No, just pulled a hammy!'

'What is a hammy?'

He explains.

'I've not seen my Bulldoggies since last year. We must go to the footy one day.' She will but not with Mathew.

Chapter 19

Mathew hears Milly in the bathroom, the clinking of china cups and the rustle of sugar packets. Stretching, he smiles and slips back under the doona. *How bloody good is this?*

Milly returns to bed while the coffee brews; they cuddle and kiss. 'Enjoyed last night?'

'Yes', she replies. 'It was fun going out late, crossing the harbour, seeing the lights, similar to a fairy tale. But now it's today. Important, hey and I'm sure you are up to it.'

In a stroke of extravagance, Mathew orders the Rolls-Royce to convey them to the meeting, recognising the exquisitely over-the-top move; but if the right people notice, he'll have made an impression. Milly suggests he dress exactly as yesterday, slacks with a casual dress shirt and jacket. She wears a cream dress, white high heels and a pale blue blouse cut low enough to exhibit the hint of the swell of her breasts and the frilly top of the matching blue bra. A cream jacket draped over a shoulder completes the ensemble.

'You look a million bucks, mate.'

She bows. 'Thank you, kind sir, all for you.'

No, Mathew understands, *for the boys.*

The silver Phantom whisks them to the hotel in no time. Mathew tips the driver in U.S. dollars, who hands over a business card. 'Call fifteen minutes before a proposed departure time and I'll meet you in the porte cochère.'

How bloody good is this. The driver has a business card! Mathew is flabbergasted.

Uncle and three elegantly dressed men stand waiting in the hotel lobby. Mathew reckons he has created the right impression by arriving in the Rolls. One Mister Soo conducts the introductions. Mathew, knowing he must commit the names to memory, repeats them silently. *Mr Soo Yoong So, Mr Basil Boxer Sun Xhu and Keng Xing Xiong.* Only later does Mathew discover Basil's father was contrived to be born in the year 1900; thus, he came tagged with the infamous rebellion of that year. Basil, being born in 1925, the year of the death of Sun Yat-Sen, inherited his father's name, together with the addition of Sun, in reverence to the father of modern China.

A hotel staff member speaks discreetly to Mr. Soo Yoong, who indicates they should follow. Mathew's maps and plans are fielded, quickly disappearing in the opposite direction. The plush timber-paneled private dining room offers no surprises; the harbour panorama is enchanting. A beautiful young lady, dressed in a tight-fitting cheongsam, welcomes them to the Golden Peacock private dining room.

A glass of what appears like fruit juice is delivered by two waiters. Soo Yoong has remained standing and in perfect proper English, welcomes Milly back to Hong Kong and he greets Mathew Allen by offering a short critique on the purpose of their gathering. Milly has suggested this type of salutation will take place; therefore, he stands and replies, thanking Mr. Soo Yoong and the others by name, expressing his humble gratitude for the friendly reception, adding, 'It has been many years since I was last here. I am very happy to be back in Xianggang and to be welcomed by such august personages. May I toast you for good health and good company?'

Mathew earnestly debates whether he has gone over the top again, but the doubt is discounted when they clap in what he deems to be a polite manner; he notes Uncle actually beams. Soo Yoong suggests they partake of a seafood lunch and then adjourn to the meeting room, where Mr. Allen can display the maps, plans and the other things he may need to refer to.

Lunch is conducted in an air of relaxed optimism, but as it moves on, Mathew detects the mood is tinged with a sniff of a primeval hunter and he wonders if it might have been like this at the Last Supper or worst. Is he to be drawn, quartered and served to the Chinese hordes? The three suits are sharpening their knives, whetting their appetites to practice on this humsup gweilo, then this is war, possibly one of many battles but all he has to do is win the important one.

Lunch is long. As is the tradition, many dishes are served. Mathew loses count and maybe this is the war – kill him with food. Yet he's surprised no wine or hard liquor is offered.

The meeting room features an oval-shaped oak European table ornately carved and set low so they can sink into the matching leather armchairs. Mathew notices his plans lying neatly arranged on the table. Soo Yoong commences by complimenting Milly on the professional manner she has conducted herself in Australia, acting unwaveringly on behalf of the investment group and then elaborates briefly on her move away from the relationship with Peter Lee to join Mr. Allen, whose company controls the stock to be discussed today. Milly shows no emotion, only bowing her head to Soo Yoong and the others.

Once proceedings commence, they develop into, as Mathew describes later, 'the proverbial bun fight', which ultimately deteriorates into the three suits jumping from project to project. Mathew twigs the planned strategy, an endeavour to try to confuse and create indecision, shaking his confidence. But as is his manner, he determines to become even more dedicated to the cause and focuses diligently at keeping his wits centred as the bastards come prepped and prepared. War has indeed been initiated and Mathew mans the battlements, relishing the repelling of each assault. Confidently, he answers every question. Not once does he fluster or become flummoxed; self-control is maintained as what they don't know is one of his natural skills is thinking quickly and communicating efficiently and, in this case, effectively.

Silly buggers trying to do battle on my turf, my subject, my experience. They don't have a chance, Your Honour. Regardless, I'm being particularly careful not to be arrogant or insert the sword to any of the soldiers. The battle rages for over an hour; Mathew is so pleased with his performance and struggles not to grin and laugh.

Sun Xhu thanks Mathew for a most informative meeting, congratulating him on his general and specific knowledge of the projects and the property industry, the local market and finally the Australian economy. Then in recognition of his business acumen and expertise, an invitation is extended to celebrate the business venture by joining them for dinner. Mathew offers a shallow bow expressing humility; Basil confirms he will be met at the hotel at nine o'clock.

Mathew uses his mobile phone to call the number on the driver's business card as Milly and Uncle enter into a separate conversation. Leaving, as is often the case, takes some time. Mathew is waylaid; the prices of Sydney residential waterfront properties are pursued. He offers a broad-brush picture and suggests if they seriously wish it to be specific, they should try the net or his contacts and he might source specialist agents. Yet Mathew's a little bemused, distinctly under the impression Keng is the kingpin, yet Soo Yoong seems to control the game and poses several last-minute questions related to inflation, how Mathew sees it materialising in Australia and its effect on the market in terms of rental values and sales. Mathew acknowledges privately, he's a clever bugger when the pressure's off, seeking to stick the knife in and see if he'll bleed. *Silly bastard, I never bleed in public.*

Milly notices the limousine parked under the elaborate veranda and Mathew, like a winning motorbike racer, runs a final lap of the bankers, shaking hands, remaining calm and composed in triumph, deliberately leaving Uncle last, who stands off to the side of the other men. He winks at Mathew, who offers a tiny smile and a nod, pondering briefly on the incredible human instinct to communicate when common language is unavailable.

Unable to trust the driver, no comment is made until they're back in his suite. 'Bloody hell, Milly, I need a beer but better not. I might have a few tonight so I can drink the boys under the table.'

'What if the drink of the night is brandy?'

'Brandy, can't stand the stuff.'

'If you do not drink, you lose face.'

'Oh, come on, Milly, I won the war today.'

'You won an important battle but the conflict is not over that will be won or lost tonight. Remember the strategy they will employ. Yes, you gained much face, much respect, handling the questions and their tactics beautifully. Maybe they will be easy, recognising you won.'

'I hope so.'

'Mathew, we are all winners today. The men left knowing you outsmarted them. Your knowledge establishes credibility and their confidence. Come, I'll make coffee. You fill the spa. We'll relax. Then I'll massage you in preparation for tonight.'

CHAPTER 20

It's that time of night; the foyer is frantic, with people hustling and bustling, coming and going. Mathew dodges around groups congregating and escapes through the giant revolving door and is welcomed outside by the scent of the East. It excites him. He looks both ways, appreciating So will not keep him waiting, oblivious to the life-changing moment about to reshape his life. It's cool; the humidity blown up over Nine Hills by the sea breeze adds a smidge of chill to the air.

The latest-model burgundy Rolls-Royce Phantom glides silently to a complete stop right in front of him. A stunning young lady alights from the front passenger seat, rushing to open the rear door, offering in perfect British English, 'Good evening, Mr. Allen, sir.'

Acting like a spotlight, the rear interior light is deliberately centred on Miss World, sitting angled by purpose in three-quarter facade. She introduces herself, 'Good evening, Mr. Allen. I'm Heidi.'

Stunned by her beauty, he blurts out, 'But Heidi is a typical Dutch name.'

And he thinks, *What a dork.*

Instantaneously, she captivates his heart and momentarily disrupts his common sense. 'My father came from Holland.' Her smile is imperious. She pours two glasses of Mumm champagne, offering one to Mathew as the intoxicating smell of rich new leather blends with her Poison perfume, making him for a nanosecond a little faint.

'You must have known, my favourite champers.'

'Quite fortuitous on such an occasion.'

Flustered by the serenity of the beauty in his company, he fails to query the comment, gathers his composure and salutes with the flute. 'Cheers, and my name is Mathew, no misters, no sirs.' Trying to recover from the clumsy start, he says, 'I suppose everyone comments on your name.' But he fails, fumbling verbally, struggling to come to grips with the pixel-perfect goddess framed in the picture.

'Yes, a common remark.'

Wow, if the boys are into gamesmanship, good on ya, mates. I'll play your game as it's the final battle and congratulations. I'll give it to you. You have chosen the most stunningly beautiful girl in the world to be the temptress. I can't take my eyes off her. This is the most gorgeous lady I've ever had the pleasure of laying my eyes on.

He knows he's staring yet unable to control his eyes as she offers that fateful combination of East and West. *Bloody perfect*, he recognises. *This is going to be some night.*

If only he knew.

Heidi is stunned, desperately trying to hide her shock. *It's him, the man of my dreams. This is impossible, yet it is he, here in the car and my task to seduce him. Oh my god, don't do this to me. It isn't fair. I have waited so long. Oh golly gosh, what do I do?*

Mathew continues to stare. Heidi stares too; he misunderstands her professional intention is quite evident. She misinterprets, taking it for lust, yet if she could have read him, she would have seen Cupid shooting an arrow and he hasn't realised what the sting is.

He gazes deeply at her perfectly shaped face framed on a distinct trace of black. Her hair is cut in a medium fringe, trimmed out to highlight the nose and her mouth and then angling back, with long strands falling over her shoulder with the odd wispy length falling to her breasts as if deliberately placed to tantalise and tease, encouraging the eyes to follow directions. And as instructed, his eyes keep falling to the flash of thigh erotically presented by the seductive split in her pure white and glittering gold cheongsam. Mathew imagines correctly her legs will be something to behold.

During the moments of mixed communication, Heidi grasps in anxiety at the man confronting her and Mathew at the magnificent personage in his presence. They pass a hotel he's previously stayed at; he's in Tsim Sha Tsui. The limousine stops in front of a brightly lit, highly decorated combination restaurant and bar. The young lady opens Mathew's door, the driver Heidi's.

Heidi takes his arm, before he contemplates offering his in the traditional, old-fashioned act of gallantry. She ushers him forwards to fate, which she has instantaneously decreed to determine somehow. He is seduced by her perfume; the rhythmical bump of her hip and the slight pressure of her right breast make love to his arm.

Mathew gawks at the consistent beauty of the women lining the bar, many in the company of businessmen dressed in suits and smart casual. His eyes roam unintentionally yet consciously soak up the scene; the interior mood drops from bright and garish to lavish and luxurious, the lighting reflecting an exaltation of expected excitement. Wending his way through the generously spaced tables, Mathew takes control and leads Heidi to the bar, orders a Foster's and carries it into the future.

The destination, an ornate and richly decorated private dining room, occupied by the bankers, accompanied by their beauties. Already, a bottle of Moët sits devoid of its distillation. Heidi stays close, almost clingy, but who's complaining? Mathew consents to his imagination. *If she is the femme fatale to tempt and trap, then simply, I should be so lucky.*

Introductions to the 'girls' are lengthy, with tedious, repetitive questions resulting in bouts of verbal diarrhea, otherwise known to Mathew as 'talking rubbish'. *And that's part of the game, mate. Patience. Forget who's on your arm for the moment.*

Another Foster's arrives deservedly as he's dry as a dead dingo's donger and he trusts they accept, this is his drink, an Aussie for an Aussie. He chugs on the stubby and then ashamedly remembers his companion. 'Strewth, sorry, Heidi. You don't have a drink.'

'I'm sure you'll attend to me after the other ladies.'

Christ, I've cocked this up nicely. If I'm going to make an impression, I'd better pick up my game. Mathew offered no thought of worrying about 'impression' when escorting a professional.

'Then champagne might be appropriate, Heidi?' His look cheeky; the returning smile so brilliant he wonders at the pixels in the picture.

'Perfect, thank you.' Her smile continues, her half bow acknowledged again as he offers his broadest grin.

Christine Lam takes it all in. *Ha, shuffling cards, their first moments together and that's exciting if the bells are ringing.*

The night develops in total contrast to the lunch meeting; it is all fun, laughter and sharing male drinking experiences. Men the same all over the world. When circumstances coexist and opportunity arises, male one-upmanship surfaces, particularly after a few brandies, bourbons or gins. Mathew relaxes as the suits fixedly chat to their lovely companions, whilst he strives diligently yet politely to encourage direct dialogue with the enchanting Heidi. He stares deeply into her dark brown eyes, like Old Gold chocolate and unwittingly licks his lips, the sensation recorded in his brain. The sweet delicacy of her lips sends an enchanting shiver, tingling his nerve ends.

Heidi stares too, seeking remedy to her condition. *I need to sit, relieve the stress on my weakening knees, sort my muddled min, and sieve the sweet sounds in my soul.* 'Shall we sit?'

Food arrives at regular intervals as do the drinks of their choice. Two girls start feeding Soo Yoong and Basil, whilst Keng remains, like at lunch, aloof yet polite and attentive to his lady, whom Mathew discovers later is one Christine Lam, much older than what her beauty depicts. If he might read the cards, he'd discover Heidi and Christine will intertwine with his family for life. And so, it is written, inscribed in the tea leaves, part of the joss and clever planning. The two entangled games of cat and mouse and chicken and duck have commenced.

The men drink copious amounts of alcohol, retaining a reasonable modicum of good grace and manners, whereas Uncle surprises by failing the sobriety test completely, drinking glass for glass with his very attractive companion, a waif of a girl, the particularly young Wei Li. And the drinks keep coming.

Mathew watches closely, noticing the girls appear to be drinking equal to the men. Mumm and Moët champagne arrive and as fast as one bottle empties, another magically appears to top up the delicate long-stemmed flutes. It encourages Mathew's paranoia; they've substituted bubbly water. The next time Heidi recharges her glass, he grasps the glass and sips. *'Well, fuck me dead,' said Foreskin Fred. It's the real deal. The Bastard from the Bush just duded me!*

Surprise spreads across his face; like the restaurant's exterior lights, it flashes brightly, knowing he has just lost face. And in that instant, Heidi realises he's been warned. Someone with malicious purpose has sprung the trap; she shall have to be careful and Keng appraises. *I'll tread on eggshells, but somehow, I must encourage Mathew to come in pursuit in the time remaining to let loose the worm of lust and desire in his heart. God, look at his face. What a profile. What a body, lean and athletic. What a mind, pleasing and expansive in his manner of communicating with me, enquiring, delving, probing as if already in chase. Might I be so lucky? Yes, it is my year. My lady of the future cards has been quite earnest. Be ready, Heidi. He is coming, travelling from a long way, tall and dark. Oh, it is all so propitious, once coupled with my spy's communications.*

Mathew, when invited, participates in the general conversation yet declines at every opportunity to tell drinking and party-type stories. Christine respects his gallantry. Of all of them, only Keng understands what is really going on. Basil has only Heidi in his mind. So wonders why a man declines to partake in the stories of life. Uncle realises he must act the drunken fool so Mathew picks up on the reality of being made look an idiot.

Heidi recognises her role to entrap is deleted from the game; she might only have one chance to discover the way to his heart. Mathew looks Heidi full in the face, unknowingly returning to the pursuit, breaking the ice, establishing rapport, still not cognisant of why. If he wants her, she'll be easy. He admits, *My god, another time, another place.* He relishes the studying, appreciating the perfection in her face, the cut of her hair, obviously professionally attended, with eyebrows shaped to suit her eyes, dark and deep. The cheongsam fits where one should, almost in a caressing manner, adding to the sculpture of her frame, more European than Asian, tall yet confusingly shaped, deceptive, almost diminutive.

Two people tickle Mathew's ego. Both Wei Li and Christine continually give him the once-over. When he makes eye contact with Wei Li, she offers the tiniest of smiles, whereas the demurer Christine quickly looks away. People shuffle places with the introduction of more food; some depart for the toilet and Basil for a smoke. Christine takes the opportunity to join them. Mathew notices her English, correct and proper and wonders if she'd been educated in the old Dart. An amazingly beautiful lady for her years, with an exquisite figure and delicate hands, dainty, elegant, never seen a day's work, with brilliant red nail polish matching the lipstick. He usually does not recognise the value or quality of ladies' clothing, yet with this particular lady, Mathew recognises the class that must cost some poor bugger dearly as diamonds flash and sparkle with the sapphires. Her conversation generally relates but not specifically to his business and the Melbourne lifestyle and innocently, she imparts the information her daughter a final-year student, 'doing a double commerce and law degree in Perth'.

Mathew is baffled at how Christine acknowledges Heidi with an unusual degree of respect, which is rightly returned. He perceives the tiniest of grins, just a wrinkle around the mouth, a secret signal conveying something mysterious, enigmatic. Twigging a moment of contemplation, he is interrupted by Keng, who is ranting on about the drip-feeding of donations via a Bangkok affiliate to the tsunami disaster.

Time moves on. Outside the private room, the joint's jumping. Mathew decides to check it out and excuses himself to go to the men's room. After pointing Percy at the porcelain, he returns to the bar and orders another Foster's and a black coffee. In no time, two long-legged beauties go into attack mode. 'Where are you from, man? You a Yankee?'

Mathew shakes his head and tugs on the beer.

'You must be Pommy, man.'

'Hey, no, he's drinking Foster's. Must be an Aussie. You a kangaroo, mate?'

He turns to answer, but Heidi appears and, without hesitation, blasts the girls in a fusillade of Cantonese. Meekly, they move away, leaving Heidi and her best smile to take ownership of his arm.

A moment of obmutescence hangs suspended. Contrasting colours, the brilliant blues and dark chocolate browns are steadfastly searching; both sending signals by stealth. Mathew's heart hammers out a missive. The noisy activity in the room fades and freezes. The world stops. His mind grasps to gather the meaning of the silent communiques.

Heidi leans on his arm; her Poison suddenly his antidote. She wilts and almost wobbles with the realisation a life's dream has morphed. Staring into his incredible blue eyes, her heart flutters. She has intended a discourse but hesitates.

Mathew senses an important moment is at hand; desperate not to miss a chance to augment the enigmatic sensation growing within, he raises an eyebrow in a questioning manner, knowing the first one who talks loses. Heidi turns to gather her rampant emotions, fighting to regain balance and a compelling desire to just blurt out the attraction. She admits her stars and mentors have delivered her perfect man, but her strength succumbs and she goes to water.

'So, Mathew, how long do you remain in Hong Kong?' Still, her eyelids flutter in time with her heartbeat and the chocolates flash.

Mathew recognises conflict and simply replies, 'Thursday night.' He peers intently into her eyes, seeking a flitter, a figment of anything but it isn't necessary.

'Do you have premonitions, Mathew?'

Cautiously, he replies, 'Yes, sometimes.'

'They materialise?'

'Strangely, they do.' He wonders, *Where's this going?*

'In crystal clear clarity?'

'Yes, but not often.'

'Me too.' Heidi pauses; again, Mathew notices the importance of the moment and the premonition bell warns, *Do not rush in.* Instead, he holds her eyes, fascinated by the game, if indeed this is a game.

'In English, you say, between a rock and a hard place, we say, nan pei dun tin, a slight grin seeks confirmation.

Mathew nods, not wanting to speak and spoil the perceived moment.

Heidi halts, looks away again, gathers her strength, and slowly turns back. 'You understand the term honeypot?'

'Yes.'

'I am her.'

'I know.' He grins widely, intent on acknowledging he just gave away the key to the castle.

'Really, you know.' Whilst she smiles to herself, she thinks, *Yes, I am clever. I picked it.* 'Someone tipped you off?'

'Yes.'

'You angry?'

'Of course not. Nothing untoward has happened and I will remain eternally grateful for the opportunity, the privilege and the pleasure, beyond measure, to spend a wonderful evening with a truly beautiful lady.'

Oh my, he's almost poetic, but is he sincere? 'Really you consider me so?'

'Of course.'

The door opens slightly. Be bold, Bite the bullet. 'I hasten back to nan pei dun tin. My chariot has wings. I have no time. You fly home so soon. I need to talk openly, honestly. May I ask a personal question?'

'Yes.'

'Are you a married man, Mathew Allen?' Heidi holds her heart in her mouth, preparing to taste the bitter bile or the sweet, delicate flavour of fortuity.

'I am separated and not by distance but in reality.'

Her heart jumps. *I've bitten the bullet. Lift the lid. Fortune favours the brave. Stuff it. Here goes nothing against the rest of my life.* 'I am a single lady. My heart has always been set on a man to replicate my wonderful father. I spend my life waiting. . . wow, this is difficult.'

'It's all right, Heidi. I am not going to bite. Do you understand the saying, I have big shoulders?'

'Ah, yes, my father used to say that a lot. Indeed, a big man with strong shoulders to lift a heavy load yet at the same time gentle holding me tight so I might cry on them.'

'Exactly.'

Like my beloved father, he has a caring nature, so I'm emboldened, my confidence shored up. Heidi continues, 'I have in my mind my man will be like my father. I hold a fantasy picture in my heart, my man goes with me everywhere as I search him out.'

His ego recognises the thrust of steady pursuit of the matter, promoting the arrogance to admit he knows what she's about to say next.

'Please do not laugh, but he is you.' She maintains a steady gaze resolving whether to float or flounder.

Mathew's arrogance dissipates, acknowledging in his heart the strength garnered, to utter such a statement, after so few hours. 'Do you believe in love at first sight, Heidi?'

'Ah, clever question. In a way, I say yes, whilst in truth I say another way. You have always been in my heart, so it is not really my first sight. You understand?'

Mathew nods and pauses, unsure how to continue without sounding a romantic dork.

Heidi saves the moment. 'How sublime, how subtle, how shrewd the gods play games with our hearts.' She smiles brilliantly. 'You are in my heart. Today you are a reality. Then you fly away. I'm going to make a fool of myself and ask you to come to my flat.'

She knows in that instance of despair she has blighted the moment. Impervious to the sound around them and Christine standing away behind a pillar as if posting guard, gently, he takes her hands, doting on the sudden intimacy. Feeling her warm flesh for the first time, a tingle tarries at his toes. 'Heidi, you are without a doubt the most stunningly beautiful lady I have ever met.'

Without intention, prompted by the tension in her body, she squeezes his hands. He retaliates.

'I have felt myself staring at you tonight, striving to capture your image to my heart, where I might hold you close and know you are there, so how many pixels in the picture?'

Heidi pauses momentarily on the adroitness in the question. 'In my understanding, the more pixels, the finer the quality.'

He offers his most brilliant smile. 'Quite.'

She queries the answer and bursts out laughing. 'You are either a very clever fellow or a unique romantic and I'm not sure which I want you to be.'

'Thank you, Heidi, for telling me your heart. Another time, another place, who knows? I am so truly respectful and grateful you gave me chance to share your feelings, but it's impossible, although like in life, time dictates all.'

For the moment, they were somewhere else – peaceful, perfect. She moves easily, as if by second nature, into his arms. Christine grins and decides it is time not to be seen and heads to the toilets. Mathew holds Heidi close, comforted, she holds him in remorse.

To him, she feels wonderful. He doesn't want to let her go. She cries inside, *So close and yet so far. My gods, you fail me!*

'Shall we return to the others?' he suggests.

The earth starts to spin again. The moment is concluded. But the spell is not broken.

In the private room, conversation ceases; he hears a pin drop. The moment is poignant. All eyes are on them.

Mathew reaches for the fresh stubby, already opened, slowly frothing over the edge. He wonders if Heidi has flashed a signal, a wink, a nod, something that says no. Regardless, as if someone presses Play, the chatting recommences.

Uncle swaps spots with his Miss Hong Kong and communicates with Mathew through Heidi. *He's sobered up in a hurry and maybe this indicates I've past the test.* Mathew glances at Heidi, seeking a clue, finding her forlorn, with her forehead flashing worry lines, readily discernible through the fringe. He suffers pangs of guilt, accepting her recital was reality, not just some soppy story to spring a bewitching trap.

No, that truly came from the heart, yet what can I do? Life is dictated by time and here, it clearly is against me.

Uncle is intent on talking about Milly and her life in Melbourne. Heidi snaps to attention as he thanks Mathew again for entering into their agreement, expounding on its importance to all the people present. The future is endless; great opportunities abound. Uncle refills his glass of brandy and drinks for Mathew, who salutes in return. Then Uncle stands and gestures for Mathew to do the same and they exchange a big man hug, both grinning widely. Uncle shows his badly stained teeth, turns to the others and babbles at length.

Mathew is slightly bemused at the 'under the weather' act, which he deems means, *Don't be silly like me. Stay sober and alert. The clever bugger!*

'The future is endless. Great opportunities abound,' Heidi repeats the words, grasping indeed how propitious it is. *'And I must instruct my spies accordingly.'*

It's the usual bowing and shaking hands as farewells are bid. Mathew does the Aussie thing, kissing the girls and complimenting them on their beauty and manners. Giggling and Chinese chatter follows except with Christine; the handshake, he presumes, is perfectly appropriate. The men, in turn, congratulate him on his property explanation and on his gracious manner with the ladies.

Heidi escorts him to the Princess Hotel. Sitting so close, her hip makes erotic contact. Conversation is strained and engages no substance. They hold hands. To Heidi, a chance in life just passed her by. Mathew grasps it was simply a pipe dream, like the old Chinaman sucking his opium pipe, lost in the cloud of what might have been.

The car stops. She pushes a piece of paper into his hand. He tips the driver and the girl then returns to the rear door, leans in and takes a last intoxicating look. He breathes in her beauty and perfume, which has bewitched his nose all night.

'Heidi, thank you for your brilliant company. You are without a doubt the most beautiful lady I have had the pleasure of meeting. Unfortunately, as I said, another time, another place and who knows?'

And the driver notes every word for later translation.

Mathew shrugs, offers his best smile, turns and without looking back determinedly walks into the hotel, heading directly to reception to check for messages, but no one loves him. He reads Heidi's note, penned in precise petite handwriting. 'Mathew, very nice to meet you. I was paid to be with you tonight, but my offer came from my heart. Might you call me tomorrow?'

The cynic emerges. 'Last try, boys?'

Milly has taken residence in his suite, more specifically in the bed, watching television with the sound muted; the movie is Bollywood with Cantonese subtitles. Hearing the door close, she calls, 'Pop on the coffee pot, please! I'm in the bedroom!'

'What did you do for dinner?' he calls out.

'Went to the fancy dining room. I was approached by several gentlemen imagining I'm on the game. How much do I earn on the job, Mathew?'

'Too much for me!'

'Never too much for you. You are my special gweilo. I never charge you.'

Mathew squats on the bed and admires her beauty, noting she hasn't removed her lipstick nor the faint dash of blush on her high cheekbones highlighting the shape of her eyes. The bed covers by purpose fall to her waist.

'Tell me what happened tonight.'

Mathew responds accordingly, explaining most of the evening discussions, leaving out Heidi's utterances and note, which resides safely in his wallet. 'There you are. I was a particularly good boy by coming home sober.'

'Am I as beautiful as the ladies?'

'More so. That's why I am here and not there.'

'You lovely man, you always say the right things. Now I'll tell you what is happening tomorrow, but firstly, Uncle called to report on the evening. You passed the test. They were impressed by the manner in which you conducted yourself. We are invited to a very private lunch with Mr. Keng at the bank at one o'clock. Uncle suggests we allow maybe two hours. Then we are to go to Star Ferry and a motor junk will take us for an afternoon jaunt around the island and it seems like we'll have dinner on board. Sounds exciting?'

Mathew agrees, but his thoughts are on why he had to explain the night when she already knew. Of the three suits, Keng had been the quietest, not asking a lot of questions and the ones he posed were the most precise, pertinent, to the point, pointing in a specific direction yet not pursued nor delved too deeply, as if saying, *Accept my intelligence by noting my clever questions. In turn, I'll not embarrass you by enquiring and maybe causing loss of face.* Mathew retains the impression that he's the watcher, taking it all in, the inscrutable Keng divulging no emotion.

'Milly, do you know Christine Lam?'

'Certainly. She is a shareholder in the bank, very wealthy, divorced, socially connected, no scandal and has a daughter, Sophie Sunn. Her nickname is SS Titanic. She's in college in Australia. Hmm, Perth, I think. Why do you ask?'

'She was there tonight.'

Milly sits up in a start. 'Really?' Silence prevails. Mathew notes her intensity as she furrows her brow. 'At a dinner like that? Not her type of distraction I'd have thought.'

Milly falls silent, and Mathew understands something's going on and remains hushed. Suddenly, her eyes light up and widen, her nose flares and she exclaims, 'Of course! Silly me, it's you! Obviously, Keng has enticed her to meet you for some reason, or she has invited herself. Maybe she heard you are indeed a handsome man, wealthy, available, interesting. Hey, Mathew, is this exciting your ego? A Hong Kong lady taipan chase after you. Wow!' Her brow furrows again, and she wanders off in pursuit of numerous conspiracy theories.

Mathew interrupts with 'Why SS Titanic?'

'It is said she is the most stunningly beautiful young lady and all the young and old men and all those in between, who have tried to woo her, have been sunk by the iceberg.'

Mathew prepares coffee, talk focuses on the possibilities of the meeting and if the boys will ratify the deal or seek to impose restrictive or prohibitive conditions or delay, by pursuing more information. He probes Milly about Keng's background and notes immediately the shutters go up as she claims little prior knowledge; he's just a man who works at the bank. The jelly doesn't set.

Tiring of the mulberry bush, Mathew concludes, 'As someone once said, I don't give a damn what happens tomorrow, we'll deal with it then. In the meantime, Milly, we have more important matters at hand.'

Heidi lies on the bed, distraught, talking the night out with her roommate and best friend, Sri, who advocates in absolute authority, 'So stupid to expose your heart on a whim, at a one-off meeting with no likelihood you'll ever meet again.'

Heidi hoards the scurrilous statement, unknowing she'll slam it back at Sri one day soon, when she acts on her own capriciousness. Still, factuality fathomed deep in her soul, she cries and is comforted by Sri, who softens the blow by recounting the future foretold. 'Plenty of time, Heidi.'

This inspires hope to gladden her heart but saddens her head, knowing another woman is in his bed. Tomorrow, her second cousin Pixie Poong will discover if they made love. She'll direct the maid changing the room linen to carefully inspect the sheets. *Ha, family and friends, important, yes?* Sri, anxious to change the subject, lies across the couch, resting her head on Heidi's knees and very slowly and softly runs her fingers up her calf muscles on the clear understanding a reaction will arrive.

Christine Lam slithers and almost disappears into the substantial white leather armchair, sipping tea from an exquisitely delicate fine bone china cup; if it is held to the light, one might see right through it. The majestic western escarpment of Victoria Island parades arrogantly across the harbour to Kowloon and extends to the blue blush of Nine

Hills, memorably meeting the midnight black of the night sky at Lei Yue Mun Point and Junk Bay. In harmony with the world, she takes in the spectacle, yet tonight her mind wrangles, over one Mathew Allen. *I love that word, though it's hardly enshrined in my thesaurus and young Heidi, you were not the usual, Miss Coy, Clever and Controlling. Explain please the prolonged eye gazing, hand holding at the bar, statements surrendered, seriously encapsulating intention, gawking even gaping like a school girl. Adulation or just admiration, maybe even adoration, if she suffers an unexpected first crush with the handsome Mister Allen. Ha, and him, how obvious his eyes hid nothing as Cupid perched on his shoulders, then how strange, parting at the hotel, if he was so obviously enamored and Heidi so willing, why?*

She finishes the tea and yawns widely in unladylike fashion. 'I love being Chinese. Whilst anxious to discover, I'll patiently probe and eventually uncover it all.'

Even Christine, in devious contemplations, couldn't possibly fathom the depths of imaginations to glimpse the future.

CHAPTER 21

With time in abundance, Mathew and Milly decide to play tourist, crossing the harbour on a ferry, enmeshed with the manic multitudes. *A shamble of souls*, he thinks. They pass the renowned Mandarin and Hilton Hotels hand in hand; jauntily and joyfully, they steadily climb to the cable car station and ride to the top of the Peak. It's warm, typical Hong Kong, with the eternal haze clinging to the hills, traversing wide valleys; and as if an ancient dragon were breathing murky mist instead of fire and steam, it cascades onto the harbour; emerald, dark, and foreboding.

Milly offers a history lesson. 'The islands were originally called the Pirate Islands, predominately occupied by Cantonese who lived off raiding traders and adventurers who ventured too close to the coast and sustained by farming small holdings and the abundance of fish. Guangzhou, at the head of the Pearl River, was the major trading port for the empire. It was some 2,500 kilometres from Beijing, almost at the far end of the Celestial Empire of the Qing and then the Manchu. Barbarian trade was eventually sanctioned but strictly forbidden to move inland. In the sixteenth century, the area around Macao was established as a trading post for the Portuguese, which developed into an important base for expanding the silk trade from Japan. By the early nineteenth century, the major powers of the day influenced trade, the British most compelling. Winning the Napoleonic wars, bestowed virtual control of the world's major waterways, thus with naval ascendency dominating the international trading scene, conflict was inevitable. Eventually, the chief superintendent of trade, one Charles Elliot, ordered Chinese ships to be sunk by naval gunfire. This erupted into intense political negotiations which lingered until Elliot made the decision to establish a permanent outpost of the British Empire at Hong Kong, including Fragrant Harbour. In January 1841, the British flag was raised at a ceremony attended by Messrs. Jardine and Matheson, as you know major players in the history and expansion of Hong Kong. In 1842, the Treaty of Nanking was signed and the Chinese humiliation complete for 150 years. But, Mathew, in the overall scheme of things, from a Chinese perspective, was it a humiliation or one of history's most perfectly planned and managed reverse takeovers? Who'll ever know? Have you read the novel *Tai-Pan?*'

'You bet. I love his writings. I met Clavell once at a literary lunch in Melbourne. I hold amongst prized possessions a signed copy of *Shogun*, without a doubt my favourite novel. It's bloody breathtaking.'

'Agreed, but I thought the sequel a let-down.'

'We expected too much?'

'Probably. Anyway, I posed the question as *Tai-Pan* was brilliantly descriptive of Hong Kong's early days saga.'

'I've never heard of Elliot. What else do you know about him?'

'Nothing actually.'

'Pity, obviously the man of the hour. How come there are no recognitions or celebrations to his endeavours?' Standing on the Peak, the dragon retires, the mist clears and Mathew closes his eyes, trying to envisage as Elliot saw it. He fails.

They share a pot of fragrant tea and Milly continues the lesson, this time on modern history, but Mathew knows it all. Still, he generously allows her to carry on uninterrupted. Back in the cable car, they take front seats and Mathew exults in excitement. 'The only way to travel down is to sit up front.'

Milly smiles privately as she rates the other side of the man.

Excitedly, they stride down the tired pier at the typhoon shelter, peering expectantly, seeking the distinctive duck egg blue boat, until finally Millie exclaimed, 'Oh golly gosh, my home, it's gone!'

Where home had been another vessel resides. Milly, distraught, makes enquiries and the answer is quite simple. The people moved to the New Territories, occupying a government flat; the boat was sold, and another piece of Milly's personal history vanished. 'Oh, how sad, more of my past disappearing.'

'More motivation to write it down. Pick Uncle's brains. Make notes while he's here.'

They arrive at the bank precisely at one o'clock. Mathew wallows in the classic architecture typical of the salubrious French style of four to six stories, aware it's evident all over the world. On the top floor, Keng conducts warm greetings and conveys them to a corner window meeting room, announcing lunch will be served immediately.

Conversation, as is often the case amongst executives, turns to travel. Keng, a seasoned jet-setter, joins in a lengthy discourse on the wonders of the world, talking at length about his favourite places to holiday and visit for fun, adding Sydney, Melbourne and Perth, where he'd attended banking conferences. Gratuitously, he extends confidence in the great potential of the West, going so far as to say, 'They could cede from federation and become successful as an independent country.'

The insightful comment proposed so casually stirs Mathew to wonder at the depth of his intelligence. *Strewth, even I would never arrive at that hypothesis. However, I'll let it roll around my inbox.*

When discussing Sydney, Keng waffles at length about the fabulous harbour and the vibrant cosmopolitan lifestyle, whereas Melbourne, he recognises, is more conservative, offering great strength for long-term investment. Dipping into his commentary box, he suggests it's the heartbeat of the nation. *Well,* Mathew decided, *I wouldn't go that far.*

After lunch, the guests relocate into gargantuan armchairs. Keng personally pours the coffee. 'I need to have a tête-à-tête about an important matter requiring significant trust, but let me say firstly' – Keng purposely eyes Mathew – 'I have watched you intently. I'm impressed in the manner you have conducted yourself and that has afforded much confidence, in convening this meeting.'

Keng clears his throat, sips the coffee, and proceeds, 'We have access to investment funds of up to twenty-five million in Australian dollars.' He holds Mathew's eyes hard as if seeking a reaction but the man doesn't even blink, yet his heart rate jumps.

'We are desirous of investing in one or two major projects in Australia. Can you arrange this for us?'

Mathew appreciates the box is open ended and pursues the closing of at least one end, sussing out whether it will be a long-term investment or a development.

'To develop, we seek to expand our capital base, so wealth accumulation is the stratagem without being speculative.'

Mathew discerns the tiniest smidge of a smile.

'Well you're talking about a major project and with respect to your confidence, Keng, I might source such an opportunity but to manage same is beyond my talent and scope of expertise.'

'We will pay you 7 per cent of the total investment to source and act as the overall manager. In other words, you appoint the project manager, utilising your current team of consultants and engineers, so you'll be the man from discovery to completion.'

Mathew imagines his knees knocking and his toes tapping out the beat of 'Money, money, money, it's a rich man's world.' Instantly, he wonders what tune Milly might be contemplating and without hesitation, questions, 'And Milly?'

'We will look after Milly.' Keng nods in her direction and, this time, offers a warm smile. 'We have an ongoing relationship for many years. It is her first time to meet me, right, Milly?'

Milly nods, but Mathew reckons there's too much sugar in the jelly; that's why it won't harden. *Something doesn't gel, but strewth, these numbers do, 7 per cent of twenty-five million.*

Bloody hell, one and three-quarter million. Holy shit, if one mil goes to consultancy and management, I'm still $750,000 in front.

After wandering around the issue for some time, Mathew finally suggests, 'With respect, Keng, you might consider this. Why don't you enter into a joint venture with an experienced Aussie group who'll bring a package of funding and explicit expertise and a construction arm that marries a tight relationship with the unions?'

'Precisely, that is exactly the scenario I wanted you to recommend. You have defined our preferred position ideally. Excuse me for going in circles. You had to arrive at our conclusion so we knew we're on the same page.'

Keng pats himself on his back for bringing this foreigner to his way of thinking. Mathew smiles in recognition of the adroit manipulation and Milly basks inwardly, clearly understanding Keng has bestowed recognition of her endeavours. *Yes,* Milly accepts, *it says much about my underlying developing position of power, and it's about bloody time. I admit I'm the glue. It's up to me to build and bond nice and tight and strong.* Her muscles flex in recognition of the strength gathering. Emboldened, Mathew delves deep into their finances, cash flow input, time frames and his management – with whom?

'So, Mathew, you have an association with a company with which we may do business?' Mathew's answer is positive, providing a very short critique on the company who he understands Brian will want to promote, and agrees to instigate negotiations immediately upon his return. The meeting proceeds for another half an hour, travelling in ever-diminishing circles; Mathew appreciates it's a game of clarification; still, it becomes tiresome.

CHAPTER 22

It is indeed a magnificent old junk. Below decks is appointed in the image of a Princess luxury boat; Mathew appreciates the facade is what you'll expect of Hong Kong past. *Majestically historic* is what he thinks best describes it. Not into boats, he incurs a cursory inspection below decks, whereas Milly is fascinated at the luxury and appreciates the full tour. He reclines on the deck, amidst huge pillows and allows his mind free rein, on the revelations of the meeting.

The game plan is obvious. Brian and the boys will be Mathew's number one priority; matters of money and motivation merge. But sourcing a project? Consternation descends like a Hong Kong fog. *Is this beyond me? No, not if I utilise professionals and tightly hold the reins.* Thus, he soldiers on, content, although a smidge of doubt lingers as he reflects on Keng's confident nod when he has referred to Mathew's current consultants. How does he know about them? *Ah, silly me. Of course, Milly has been passing on information.* Then he hesitates. *Let's not jump into a definitive conclusion about*

Milly. Maybe there is another informant intermingled in the mix somewhere.

His contemplations are interrupted. Uncle has been accompanied on board by his Miss Hong Kong and several other beauties. Wei Li offers Mathew a Foster's as Milly remains downstairs with Uncle, leaving him time to appreciate and reflect on the possibility that if this deal comes off, he's made.

Wei Li hovers, but his mind is fixed on business and he misses the signal privacy presents. Then inadvertently, his thoughts switch to the Rhine cruise, assessing if interruption threatens delay or, worse, cancellation. Then for no apparent reason, Heidi is in his head and he senses the perception she's been lying dormant, like a Bogong moth waiting for the right set of circumstances to be set free to flutter and flee. The amazing emptying of her heart gives rise to a strange fit of passion and he considers the question, how many pixels are in the picture, resulting in a brainwave. *If I can paint the project portrait with sufficient BS, be it blue sky or bullshit, to entice Brian to a position of consideration, then he and Keng must meet and isn't that a purler? Obviously, here in Hong Kong, the scene is set, act two with the pixel-perfect Heidi.*

To Milly, Mathew is daydreaming or simply soaking up the sights as they motor up the East Lamma Channel, separating Hong Kong from Lamma Island. Passing Aberdeen with its famous floating restaurants, he fails to notice her appearance, but she notices his tiny grin.

'You seem at peace, Mathew. Pondering pleasant dreams?'

'Thinking of you naked in bed.'

'Ha, funny man. I know you are meditating on the business opportunity presented. You've obviously made a tremendous impression. I knew you would. However, Uncle was worried, believing you'd weaken with the beautiful temptress Heidi Hendrickson, an unusual name for an Asian girl with a remote past.'

Mathew lets the comment go, more intent on urgent matters. 'Our die is cast, Milly. We are going to be involved in important business. I'd like to discuss a commission split before we move too far down the track. Otherwise, it may become messy to finalise. It's like what my mate in the States John would say. "Pay your friends gambling debts quick, then your mates stick."'

'Very wise man. The commission earned with Peter Lee is split half to me and half to Uncle, so with my retainer being non-deductible against commission, I earn around $50,000 a year. This new arrangement, providing we meet the budget, might boost my income to as much as $15,000 a month.'

'I understand, but it doesn't relate to what was proposed today. I'll be blunt. Where do you come in?'

'Simple, one-third of new commissions. Keng estimates my cut could be another $10,000 per month.'

'Considering what I'm to receive, how do you feel?'

'I am laughing. If you close a deal, I'm made. I cannot earn without you and you have to pay the consultants. I bear no risk and you have a little or a lot if you do not manage properly, yes?'

'Good management crucial, I reckon.'

'May we cuddle?'

'You do not care if Uncle sees us?'

'Ha, he knows everything. He is my father, my benefactor, my protector. I hide nothing. That's why he welcomes you so.'

Shortly, Uncle arrives on deck with Wei Li; noticing the cuddling, he smiles inwardly and takes occupancy of another length of built-in couch. Wei Li immediately cuddles Uncle and speaks directly to Milly. 'Uncle asks me to convey to you the name of the various places we are approaching. Up here on the left are Deep Water and Repulse Bays. The peninsula protruding up front hides Stanley, which is tucked around in the bay. He says we will not stop. The ladies may go crazy shopping.' She conveys the add-on comment to Uncle, who nods at Wei Li and they laugh as Milly continues, 'We are heading to Shek O, which faces Tathong Channel. I told you, when I first arrived in Hong Kong as we turned into Victoria Harbour, a jet took off from Kai Tak. I thought it might remove our heads. The noise and the smell of jet fuel was overpowering. Uncle and the crew waved up but they looked at me, sharing my excitement and you know, Mathew, until that day I had never seen or heard such a thing as a jet airplane.'

Milly translates to Uncle. 'He recalls the night. So sad Auntie is not with us. I share his grief. God, what a person. What I have and who I am are all thanks to her.'

Three boys scurry along the dock, seemingly weighed down with food containers, balancing on wooden poles as docking arrangements are secured. Uncle calls below; girls rush on deck, serve and then share, tucking gleefully into the multitude of small delights. Mathew assumes Uncle will control the girls by rod and staff, yet the evening progresses with abundant chatting and giggling. He is often not included; the untranslated Cantonese creates titter and tee-hee. With common sense predominating, he understands he's the reason of the mirth without any snide or spite.

With ancient sails hoisted, they move slowly down the harbour, flanked by a towering sea of light as tall buildings stand bright against the midnight dark blue sky. Boat traffic is hectic; the harbour often in a chop, occasionally dodging and waving at walla-wallas driven by the strength of a lady's arm, not some whacking great diesel. Mathew feels sorrow for their plight, envisaging it's them versus might. Eventually, the sails are lowered, three girls rush to gather and store them. Milly explains it's necessary, in the confines of the harbour to motor.

They dock adjacent to Star Ferry. Uncle and the girls bid them farewell, Mathew, in his fashion, kisses the girls' cheeks but with Wei Li, he simply offers his hand, which she holds for a moment too long and he notices the small but discernible squeeze.

Walking to the hotel, Milly asks, 'You mind some advice?'

'Of course not.'

'You must be careful with a Chinese man's young lady. I noticed Wei Li held your hand far too long, she was sending you a signal. She is interested in you!'

'Yeah, I noticed and a few sly looks but I'd never do anything to upset Uncle, that's why I only shook her hand.'

'You represent opportunity to a young girl. You can take her anywhere, offer her a future, set her up for life. If she is 20 years old and gives you ten or even fifteen years, still, she is only in her early thirties, in her prime, bearing wealth and security, able then to pursue a younger man. The right girl will love and honour you, be committed to you but you must know, there is always another underlying contrivance in

China. How you would say it? Ah, yes, life comes in layers. You understand?'

He is shocked at her forthright comments, yet her utterance resonates. *Layers upon layers of what-if.* 'Milly, I'm not here to upset anyone or commit a wrong. I just want our business, yours and mine, put to bed so we can sleep without worry and I never, for one moment, led her on. She gave me the eye.'

'You are stressing. Settle down. It's okay, I'm just warning you do not pursue her.' She pulls him close. 'Don't become grumpy. You know the saying, don't shoot the messenger.'

Mathew sends an email to Brian seeking an urgent meeting for Friday morning, determining he'll go straight from the airport, but made no indication whether he bore good news or bad. *Make them suffer a little*, he decides with a wry smile.

Thursday has been designated as a free day; accepting it as one of life's little luxuries, Milly takes the opportunity to sleep in. Mathew swims, visits the gym and the other luxuries on offer, then ruins all the right work by woofing down a hearty but unhealthy breakfast, sharing it with the *South China Morning Post* and sugar-laden coffee.

At Stanley, Milly suffers from dysfunctional shopaholic disorder, where it is mandatory to inspect every lingerie outfit in every shop and every pair of sunglasses on each stand. 'Come on, Milly, how many pairs of undies do you have to look at? Haven't you bought enough?'

'No, I want to look great for you.'

'You know the old saying, don't shit a shitter.'

They come across a small eatery attached to the market, Mathew entices her to take a breather amidst the hectic, almost frantic demands of the shoppers to shop, while he admits, mingling in the mayhem is fun. Then with Milly engrossed in another lingerie outlet, Mathew's patience quits and retiring gallantly, he takes the opportunity to make the telling telephone call to Heidi.

'Hello, Heidi, it's Mathew.'

'Ah, Mathew, thank you for calling.' Her voice is particularly bright and bubbly; he imagines the pixels beaming.

'Sorry I couldn't yesterday. It became a day of meetings, concluding with a boat trip around the island.'

'I understand. A pleasant evening?' Heidi knew without reservation there was only one meeting and unhappily, it had been confirmed. the day did not finish with a boat ride. The sheet inspection revealed the truth of the matter, which only led to one question. Is Milly in bed for business or unexpected competition? 'And you return to Melbourne tonight?'

'Yes.'

'Very sad for me. I regret I will not see you again. Might there be possibilities you will return?' Heidi stops smiling, the answer should be obvious after her breakfast and lengthy debate with Uncle.

'Maybe, Heidi, your gods do, in fact, move in mysterious ways. Previously, the answer would have been a simple flat no, yet the meeting yesterday created a possibility, possibly next month.'

Her smile expands as the chocolate boxes beam, 'Ah, very exciting, Mathew. Can you email me at Heidi.h@hotmail.com, explaining your plans, please?'

'I'll do that. Regardless, it will be nice to talk even if electronically. Thanks for looking after me at dinner. I truly enjoyed your company. As I said, another time, another place.'

'You're very kind. Have a safe journey home. Goodbye for now. Oh and, Mathew, how many pixels were in the picture?'

'The maximum.'

Heidi clutches the phone close to her heart and leans against the wall. *So, the attraction sufficient. He telephones me. Now my gods in heaven, bless me with his return. I'll do the rest. In the meantime, I must talk more to Uncle. He must know of my discovery and we may conjure up a conspiratorial scheme to meld Mathew to my heart and soul. But then might I be too optimistic? Could my imbecilic and impracticable ideas just have found a conduit to be realised? Fate is swinging in my favour. My karma is strong. The cards are promising and the tea leaves teasing, tempting the opportunity to utilise my resourceful wisdom and cunning. I'll construct a spellbinding subterfuge that will manifest into something unimaginable. God, how I love a challenge. My first test is, if the pixels are at the maximum, does that mean he is cunning and clever or a real romantic? And, lunch today with Keng should be very interesting. Ooooh I am so excited.*'

Mathew garners a feeling of importance as the Rolls-Royce stops at the front door; he's greeted by the driver while three boys scurry around, busily managing the luggage and opening doors as Mathew hands out American currency in tips. He holds Milly's arm, ushering her into the luxury of the rear seat, noting the light travelling slacks, tight around her rear end. His grin's wistful.

From the suite to the car, one of the boys records every word and innuendo for immediate transference to his superior. And already, the housemaid is inspecting the sheets.

CHAPTER 23

THE COFFEE IS FLAVOURFUL AND the Monte Carlo biscuit sweet. Mathew purposely extenuates, arriving at the big picture, realising in the overall scheme of things, the end result of this meeting, contains a personal ulterior motive. Eventually, recognising exasperation rising in Brian, Mathew poses, 'If the right deal fell on your desk, could you come up with around twenty-five million dollars to participate in a joint venture project?' Carefully, Mathew contemplates the biscuit as if it's a most valuable morsel and gently takes a small nibble.

'Are you serious?' Brian barks.

'Always.'

'Here or overseas?'

'Here.'

'Abso-bloody-lutely yes if the deal's right. What's the skinny?'

Mathew takes another bite of the biscuit. 'I'm envisaging a development encompassing a five- to ten-year life span with a natty twist in this tail, a virtual guarantee to take out at least half the project concurrent with construction.' Mathew smiles; maybe he shouldn't have.

Brian raises his voice and stares sternly. 'You can be a smart-arse prick at times. All right, the fish is on the bloody hook. Let's stop playing, silly buggers. Get to the nitty-gritty.'

Mathew glances at Mandy, who's just as dour; he decides discretion is applicable. *Get to the point.* In emptying his bucket, he explains Keng' s proposal first, concluding with the big meeting, confirmation he's secured commitment to continue, possibly even expand, the sales program.

Brian's mood softens. 'Mandy, take my diary, please, mate. Cancel the meetings scheduled for eleven and lunch, order in sandwiches, brew up more coffee, get back in here fast and ask Sue to field all calls.'

Mandy dashes from the office. Brian reclines and folds his hands behind his head. 'You really are a piece of shit at times, the way you swan in here and set me up. I'm going to get you one day.' The warning comes with a warm smile.

After Mandy returns, so does Mathew for explanations and elaborations, filling in the gaps. Mandy asks about FIRB approval. Brian relates his opinion on the Foreign Investment Review Board, not expecting a problem with a joint venture between a local company and an international identity investing capital, which will be repatriated once the project is completed.

Mathew is unsure about the intention to repatriate and decides to let that cat find its own way out of the bag when the time's appropriate.

Mandy continues, 'If it's a JV, do we put up equal equity or offset against work expenditure?'

Mathew's answer is a simple no.

'Then they'll put in their share in cash?'

'Yes.'

'If it's a development, logically, it must contain a saleable end product capable of returning income with a capital gain potential, so silly question, Mathew, any ideas?' Mandy tilts her head questioningly.

'You're right, silly question.' He smiles. 'And yes, the end product has to provide an investment vehicle for the small players. By that I mean for Milly's people to participate, that's where the virtual 50 per cent takeout comes from.'

Silence prevails as each wanders off into varying directions, until Sue arrives with the sandwiches and the freshly brewed coffee. Brian asks, 'Do they have any preference – where, what type, time frames, construction, financing, et cetera?'

'Basically, no. But Keng is very much of the opinion relationship building is the key, so we agreed, you'll have to meet. We debated where, here or there. He prefers it there.' Mathew elects to push the button upfront; instantaneously, Heidi appears on the back seat of the Rolls. 'I'm not the joint venture partner. I cannot commit to a deal. You guys need to see the colour of his eyes and talk through the issues.'

'When?' Brian looks for a direction.

Mandy continues, 'Before we have a project or afterwards?'

'Before. Why bother sourcing something, doing all the homework, then failing at the last hurdle?'

'A small investment to potentially save a lot of money and heartache', Mandy comments to know one in particular.

'I'm too bloody busy. You'll have to go,' Brian demands of Mandy.

Fortunately, she answers before Mathew would have been forced to say, *No, this is a boys' deal*, reckoning with Mandy in Hong Kong any pursuit of Heidi would be stuffed. And isn't that trite? He placed Heidi before Mandy without hesitation.

'Let's go right back to the start because when the boys ask a curly one, I want to have the answer tied up in one little bow.'

Lunch becomes work time while devouring the delicate sandwiches, together with the delicious contemplation of what may be. 'By the way, am I right in assuming we are set on four sales a month?'

'Locked and loaded, regardless of any further involvement.' Mathew decides now's the best time to raise the matter of the fee and be upfront on top of the good news. 'There is one final matter I must disclose, which I believe is part of the previous commitment and communication with yourself and Horace. Keng has offered me 7 per cent of the dollars invested to source and act as overall manager on their behalf.'

Brian and Mandy look at each other, flabbergasted. 'Fucking hell. Excuse me, Mandy. Bloody hell, Mathew, you have either impressed or conducted the finest snow job of all time.'

'From their perspective, that's my companies' fees to take the project from go to whoa. As you and I understand fees, my fee and all the consultant's fees are added into project cost. Therefore, I'll wax my new fee with you, if you care to come up with a democratic split.'

Mathew left them pondering the plan, thinking it a cunning manoeuvre offsetting surprise against the size of the fee. Today Brian tenders the last surprise. 'Mandy will share some news on the way to the elevator.'

As Mandy pushed the down button, she discloses, 'We closed an agreement to purchase the Murray River project.'

Mathew responds, 'Too bloody bad. If you're busy, I'm kidnapping you, we're going to the coffee shop and you're going to tell all.'

'Ooh, I like a strong man, blow in Jane's ear and I'll follow you anywhere.'

After coffee and her delivering the full rundown on the buyout, Mandy asks, 'Do you fancy takeaway after work, or did those Chinese chicks tire you out?'

Mathew had been mulling over a similar thought and liking the idea of seeing Mandy at close quarters, replied, 'You bet. Bring a pizza and I'll have a ballsy Cab Sav breathing.'

'With the lot?'

'Pardon?'

'The pizza, you moron.'

Mathew runs Mandy through his mind, recognising she's something different, projecting a mystique quality, an air of I'm available to pet and play but that's it. Recognising he can live with that then questions why. However, no answer arrives. *Lost in the layers of the cake,* he determines, but he hasn't grasped that there is an even more important ingredient waiting to be amalgamated.

Mandy arrives with the traditional colourful cardboard box; still, it requires reheating and the microwave works its wonders as Mathew shuffles plates and cutlery while conversation centres on Hong Kong. 'Brian's a bit miffed about the fee. I shouldn't and normally wouldn't talk out of school. You were right in disclosing it. We're grateful for the honesty, motivating trust to motor ahead. However, may I suggest you wouldn't have this opportunity without us?'

'No, I wouldn't have this opportunity without Milly. She approached me with the sales program, I brought it to you guys and I didn't have to. I offered to go to Honkers to meet her contacts and consolidate the deal for both our interests. You guys generously sprung for the trip, Milly and I appreciate that and, Mandy, I'm not bloody silly. That was to protect your interests. The offer of Keng' s I could have taken anywhere. I had loyalty. You received the nod, right?'

'I'm going to nickname you Google. You're always right. Grab the pizza, and let's forget business. I talked out of school. Delete it or I'll be in the shit.'

During lunch at the golf club, Mathew announces the decision to separate. Knowing these are decent blokes happily married where divorce and separation aren't listed on any agenda, there will be anguish for Hope. On the way out to the car park Ian rushes after him, gushing effervescently, 'If it's right for you, good on ya, mate. We're only here once.'

'That's my line, E, but thanks. Appreciate your thoughts.' Mathew expects he will pursue the subject; instead, he just turns and walks away with slumping shoulders and hands thrust deeply into his pants pockets.

Mathew telephones Hope; they converse easily as old friends, choosing Wednesday for the family dinner to discuss the property split. 'I'll bring Chinese, save you cooking.' He offers with a smile.

'You're on. Bring heaps. The kids will tuck in.'

The kids are in contact, welcoming Mathew home. They are aware about Wednesday night, yet no comment is made, either advantageously or prejudicially.

Mathew buys last Friday's and today's *Financial Review*; major projects are often advertised right around Australia. He'd perused the *Age* on Saturday, but it resulted in zilch.

He reclines in his favourite position, dwelling on Mandy's comments regarding the disclosed fee; as Brian hasn't pursued his offer, he decides to resolve the issue. After exercising his pencil, he arrives at a plan to kick back to them 20 per cent directly and to throw in half of the overall net fee into the venture. Estimating an overall project fee of around $1.75 million, he's going to kick back $350,000, plus half of the balance into the project pot.

He peruses the *Financial Review*, but nothing excites. Realisation settles in; it might be a long haul unless he gets lucky.

He emails Heidi, 'Hi, I'm home.' And waffles on about things of little import, then closes his eyes, and surprisingly, her image instead of Min Xie's pops into vision. Slowly, he allows it to revolve around in his grey matter, appreciating the simple assessment of beautiful.

Mathew sends Keng a message. 'Meeting potential partners Tuesday. Will report shortly thereafter.' *I'll pat the dog, whet the appetite, stir the pot, and turn up the gas. Christ, in business, we perpetrate such silly bloody games at times.*

Milly confirms two sales already made for the month and plans next week's placement of investment funds. Mathew has, for some time, held the perception he'd like to elevate her to a position of more trust; it can only help. She could select the projects, the unit numbers and prepare and lodge the FIRB applications monthly, copying to Mandy and himself. On the spur of the moment, he phones Milly and passes on his thoughts, then gives notice of the impending meeting, but Keng is not to know and they must meet next week. The offer gives further credence to Milly's strong belief, her star is assuredly in ascendancy.

Over the next two hours, Mathew diligently contacts major industry players, notifying them of elementary but sufficiently basic essentials relating to his appointment to source a major development project. Several properties are readily suggested, but once the proponents are questioned, the negatives surface. He quits despondently and wanders into the kitchen, reaffirming his previous conclusion that it might take a while.

Meticulously, he peels potatoes, readying them to microwave together with some greens. And after placing the thick porterhouse steak under the grill, he retires to the living room, turns on the television, sprawls on the couch and inadvertently dozes off, until the burning beef sends a signal.

Being creatures of habit, each occupies the same chair. Sue serves coffee, Mathew helps himself to an iced VoVo biscuit and they proceed to play the normal greetings game but not for long. Brucella is all business. 'No time for stuffing around. If you believe this is a goer, these people are serious and you can source an appropriate project, we're in. And the boys concur, I have to see the colour of their eyes. What's the time frame up and back?'

'Save a working day. Fly up Sunday. I'll arrange our first meeting for Monday, set aside Tuesday and Wednesday for follow-up confabs, fly home Wednesday night. You can be in the office Thursday morning.'

'Book it next Sunday, all right?'

'You bet.'

'Any idea for a project?' Brian delves.

'No.' But in that instant, a bell rings in Mathew's brain. 'How about a residential golf course project no more than ninety minutes from Melbourne? Fringe city or town with good medical infrastructure, hospitals, that sort of stuff, preferably with access to a freeway for quick city visits and vice versa and I'd call it Trilogy.'

Brian and Mandy gawk at each other as he continues, 'Baby boomers are the big market. Trilogy is retirement in three stages. One, you retire fit and healthy, so you occupy a townhouse or a villa. Two, you are past being super-active and you require a retirement or care village. Three, you finish up in full care. Enter on any level. I'm thinking as I run. Bear with me, so coming in on level one, in X years, transference to another level is automatic.'

'But how do you sell the end product to investors?'

'What do baby boomers not have?'

'Funds to retire.'

'Too right, so they rent the unit, retaining their existing house equity to retire on, supplemented by pensions. Before receiving rental approval, they'll meet with our financial investment adviser to ensure equity et cetera is properly invested and that should be in collaboration with their existing planner.'

Mathew watches Brian's reaction; involuntarily, he shakes his head and rubs his face like he's having a wash. It's a habit. He runs his fingers through his thin hair and then steeples his fingers. *Bugger, that means something, but it's gone.* Mathew blinks, searching his list of body signals, but it won't come.

'You astound me. Have you run it by a planner?'

'No.'

'Not like you. How long has this little gem been floating around?'

'Just now.'

'Bullshit, just now.'

'You were pushing me, so I thought, what will work in today's and the near future's market?' Mathew recognises he's opened a can of worms.

'Do you have a preferred planner?'

'Not really.'

'We have, down the hall, Paul Fayman has been quite professional in past dealings. Mandy, see if he'll join us to kick the can around.'

Mathew outlines the bones of the concept. Fayman imagines few implementation problems but encourages the idea of potential tenants going before an investment adviser before commitments from both sides. It adds credibility, a sure and safe path for the establishment of 'clients cum tenants' fund management. *Professional opportunity just raised its head, Mathew presumes.*

'The legality of the structure will be the trick. If a buyer in a one-unit requests to move to a two class-of-care unit, how do you do it?' Paul poses.

'Exactly as the villages do now with a rental management plan, it has to be so much simpler and much more cost effective. I can't believe it's not been done before,' Mathew replies.

'Must be a trick . . . I wonder if . . .' Mandy's voice trails off in deep mediation. 'Could it be so simple that it has to do with the return?'

The comment excites Mathew. 'Elaborate, please.'

'Well, normally, total infrastructure costs are proportioned, shared by each property. Therefore, returns are diminished significantly. I'm envisaging a particularly large medical client care facility and trying to write that off in a traditional manner will stuff the return. However, if the medical development expenditure is set up separately, with costs borne by the developer and retired or serviced by client income and likewise, if the golf course stood as a single entity, costs that would normally be applied to the unit owner might be treated quite differently. Thus, returns might be fairer and more equitable.' Mandy holds Mathew's eyes, issuing a perceived challenge.

'And we have what no other developer has, guaranteed investors who'll buy at a lower rate of return as they seek security.'

'Yes', adds Brian. 'And maybe we can be more creative, inventing other income streams, like setting up in the overall management structure, a retired financial planner and the company shares the fees.' The roundabout continues, and when the steam runs out, so does Fayman.

Brian beams. 'I think we are on an absolute winner. Enough came out of that short brainstorm to encourage me to work through the legal aspects. Let's set up one of your round-table meetings, Mathew. Put all the players together, pick the animal dry, see if it smells.'

'Might help if Mathew writes a short briefing paper, each party having insight prior to.'

'Good idea, you'll have it tomorrow with my list of invitees.'

Mandy smiles. 'Milly suggested retirement, meaning the Murray River project. Does it get any better than this? Rent it out now, use it later.'

'But', Brian jumps in, 'what about the poor bloody tenant?'

'Easy. Move him to other equal occupancy standard at the owner's cost.'

Mathew credits the Trilogy concept to John, his friend in the States who'd sent an article snipped from the *Seattle Post Intelligencer* when a company advised intentions to build a staged development outside Seattle. When grappling with 'where's the problem?' he concluded he couldn't find any and neither could he find the article, safely filed but which damn file?

On Wednesday, Mathew phones Milly and enlightens her on the outcome of the meeting, confirming Mandy will invite her to attend the next round table. Then he conveys the details of the impending trip to meet Keng in Hong Kong.

'Did you receive the brief, Mandy?'

'Yeah, it read well, pithy, precise. They'll grasp the intent.'

'We need to meet privately.'

'Tomorrow night's fine.'

'How about a roast?'

'You're on.'

'Beef or chicken?'

'A bird with roast spuds, broccoli and pumpkin. Have it ready around six thirty and I'll bring a nice crisp white.'

The family gathering is particularly effervescent; even the old moggie occupies his lap, purring contently all the way through dinner. Mathew is surprised neither the girls nor Andrew offers any difficulty to motions moved, agreeing readily once appreciating Hope is not to be prejudiced, in any way.

Mathew offers to involve the family accountant to seek input and then laughs inwardly. Max will be blunt. *Mathew, not again!*

After playing Father Christmas in May, Mathew expands on his plans for the impending trip, adding a terse 'No time for shopping'.

Later, alone with Hope, they share a nightcap of hot chocolate. 'You were quiet tonight,' he offers.

'Preferred to allow the kids spell out their thoughts, knowing we can talk through the issues, therefore not seeking to imply influence and retaining Smith's Beach is my priority. We all love it.' Then the smile fades. 'And if you take another woman, do not sleep in our bed and leave the place pristine and perfect.'

'You know that's a given and don't assume a request automatically suggests someone is with me. I might take the golf guys and you know me well enough; it might just be about my time and that applies to you too.'

Hope laughs out loud. 'Come on, can you see me romancing another fella?'

'Why not?'

'Why?' she retorts.

'The why is up to you.'

After arranging the Trilogy meeting, Mathew remains beside the phone; a strange thought enters his head as he wonders about the Labrador at the beach who takes him for the morning run to chase up the seagulls, how lives are interwoven even with animals. Then the next day, no one fronts. Maybe he waits at the gate in excited expectation and then dejectedly returns home.

His thoughts turn to Adderley. *Do I really want to buy there? My fortune is turning rapidly. Why not buy a two-bedder in a building like this with a pool, gym, sauna, or steam room? Hmm, something to start researching with my A-list agents.*

May is his next call; she asks about the Princess Hotel. Mathew endeavours to explain its opulence and service. 'And the bill, May, you wouldn't jump over it and we are going again next Sunday.' He trusts the *we* means Milly. 'So how is Miss Hong Kong? I told Min Xie and the girls at golf I don't think I have seen such a beautiful girl and my god, those legs, they go forever. Hmm!'

'And surprisingly, she owns a great brain.'

'The girls are looking forward to meeting her at my golf day. I've phoned Steve and he is definitely fronting this time. I'll pair you with him. Now another matter, Min Xie will not even talk about you. At golf, when I tell the girls about you and Milly, I see a clear, distinct flash of anger in her eyes.

It remains evident all day and she is playing atrocious golf. What has gone on between you two?'

'Not up to me. Pry it out of her. Is she playing on Thursday?'

'Yes, but I have to shame her. Is it okey-dokey if Janet and I play with you and Steve?'

'That'll be fun. I enjoy her company and anyway how's the family?'

A good call to make. Min Xie is so overcome with angst that it's upsetting her golf. Next Thursday, I'll stir the possum, motivate the dark side, see what skullduggery I might conjure up. I've decided I'm going to play the revenge game.

Chapter 24

Heidi replies to Mathew's hastily sent email. 'Nice surprise. You are coming back so quickly but you did not say you want to see me. Only you will arrive on Sunday night?'

Mathew pushes Reply. 'Airport at ten, Princess Hotel, say, eleven. Would love to share late supper with you.'

Almost instantaneously, the computer bell dings. 'Very best friend runs reception. If it's okay with you, I'll be in your suite and have supper ready and waiting.'

Mathew types furiously. 'Wonderful. Tell very best friend it's all right for you to enter the suite. Looking forward to seeing you.'

Mandy arrives in a fluster, waving the wine. 'I need a drink, mate. Wow what a day. Finally convinced Brian to employ a PA. Any spunk bubble you want to give a job to?'

'My daughter Stephanie, but she's too well entrenched at Sanderson's.'

Mandy removes her bright red jacket, drapes it over a dining room chair, slips out two large wooden hairpins, allowing the blond mass to fall free around her shoulders, not down her back like it used to. Mandy notices Mathew's look of admiration, takes three steps and kisses him, never taking her eyes off his. 'That's better. I hope you are in a cuddly mood. I want to lie on your lovely long couch, take in the lights and be close for hours. How's dinner going? Smells great?'

Resolving to conclude business over dinner, Mathew raises the issue of Keng's proposed fee, suggesting she take the credit by conveying to Brian his new offer.

'When have you told me?'

'Tonight, you silly moo.'

'Doesn't know I'm here, maintaining discretion. It is sufficient the Rhine cruise is in the public domain. Domestic dinners, cuddling on couches are private and personal.'

That's interesting. Mathew chews on the comment and rolls it around, deciding it's nothing special and swallows.

'On the phone, before I come in.'

'That'll work. It will go down well, portraying you've thought it through, seen the other side and thus more respect is enhanced.'

'My agreement with Keng is five payments of $350,000. I'll kick you seventy large each payment and after my wack, slip the balance into the trust account.'

'When are payments starting and finishing?'

'First at contract to purchase, last on project completion, payments in between only resolvable once the nature of the development is determined.'

'Seems logical.'

'Now I have a question. It's a teeny bit delicate. Please take it the right way. I don't know Brian that well. We are travelling to an exotic city with lots of erotic women. I was tested by the bankers, trying to set me up with a lady of the night. I'm sure they will not try again, what I'm getting at, will he want to play?'

'Did you succumb with the offeree, or is it the offeror?'

Mathew smiles broadly. *If I'm readable, she'll appreciate the truth.* 'No.'

'May I ask why not?'

'I might say thinking of you.'

'Could have, but you've stuffed it now.' Mandy laughs lightly. 'Truly don't know. You boys are, after all boys. You'll just have to ask straight out or let him do his own thing.'

'Change the subject then. What's the feeling about Trilogy?'

'Brilliant. Did you really just dream it up on the spot?'

'Well, sort of. A residential golf course project would be my greatest dream. Timing's an issue as the market's a concern, and sooner or later, the RBA will fuck the investment market, spooking mums and dads. It took over fifty years to finally rid ourselves of the fear of depression. Mum never allowed Dad to risk the house, so their greatest investment opportunity she locked up and threw the bloody key away. Now they are underfunded and instead of dropping dead at 70, some will live to be 90 and remain active, but they're broke. We have just survived the longest period of a Labour government since federation and what did they do for Mum and Dad? Bloody nothing, except tax every penny they ever tried to save; rape, pillage and plunder their super and even taxed their bloody saving accounts. Useless bastards. They retire on obscene super-schemes paid for out of our taxes, grant themselves gold travel passes and various bloody lurks and perks. While their comrades are broke, trying to survive on a pathetic pension. Finally, Mum and Dad see the light and start investing, recognising this is truly their last gasp. But trust me, soon the RBA will stuff them up the arse again.'

'My, do we have a radical right-wing liberal here?'

'No and don't start me on them. Malcolm bloody Fraser was given a mandate by the Aussie people to get rid of the excesses of the stupid, ridiculous years of Gough and his comrades. Can you imagine Australians referring to their mates as comrades? And what did Fraser do? Bloody nothing.'

'Are you finished?'

'I love standing on my political soapbox and sprouting forth. In the old days, I'd have been great at Speakers' Corner or down on the Yarra Bank.'

'Yeah, with the commos throwing paper bags full of dog shit at you.' She laughs. 'God, I can see it now.'

'Yeah, you're right. I'd duck for cover and my credibility would be shot.'

'Or you'd really be shot. Bugger this bullshit. What have you conjured up for sweets?'

'Good old-fashioned strawberries and cream?'

'I enjoy cuddling you, I owe you a kiss.'

Mathew becomes hard.

'Don't you ever become horny? No, what I mean is you never demand nor suggest or pursue touching. I've never known a man to be so . . .'

'Patient', he volunteers.

'Exactly. Why? Is it me?'

'Am I upsetting you by not pushing pursuit?'

'Absolutely not.' Mandy looks him directly in the eyes. 'I love it, Mathew. I really love it. I've told you before. I am sick and tired of groping hands on my tits, up my dress, around my arse, home to my place. I'll come to your place or go here or there, book a motel, or screw in the car.'

'Nothing wrong in the car.' Mathew suffers a flash of Min Xie on the back seat under the pine tree with a twinge of remorse.

'Not pissing in your pocket, but I relish being with you. I love your company. You treat me like a lady, not a bloody root. Thanks for being you. Patience will be rewarded. I have some demons requiring to be addressed, so you're perfect. You apply no pressure.'

The couch keeps their company for another two hours, chatting occasionally, finishing the wine, recharging the percolator intermingled with sessions of kissing. It is always her in his arms, occasionally caressing his bare skin. Her adventurous fingers circumnavigate his facial features right into the hairline. His arousal is so complete. Mathew says sorry to his penis.

Mandy has parked in one of his unit's car spaces. Mathew accompanies her to the garage and offers her the gift from Hong Kong, asking her to open it at home and then hands her a garage pass. It is a dangerous move, he decides later.

CHAPTER 25

THE ROLLS-ROYCE IS WAITING. MATHEW recognises the driver, who greets him like an old friend, extending a genuine smile and that pleases him in front of Brian. 'Welcome back, Mr. Allen.'

'You make impressions everywhere, Mathew. Nice touch,' Brian notes.

Reservations hand Mathew two notes – a welcome message from Keng confirming a car will meet them tomorrow and the other from Heidi. At the eleventh-floor suite, the bellhop hesitates, undoubtedly in the knowledge Heidi is in short-term residency.

The room is in semi-darkness. A faint, unmistakable aroma of incense arouses his nose; Heidi appears from the bedroom in a highly decorated and particularly colourful silky and slinky dressing gown tied at the front, with a wide band of matching material. Protruding under the gown are ten tiny toes, each painted a vibrant bright red, peeking or are they ten signs, warning of impending danger?

She bows; Mathew reciprocates, low and long, determined to express ample respect. Heidi battles to hide her surprise; extenuating the greeting act, she tilts her face, kisses him on the lips, short and sharp as intended. Mathew licks his lips to taste the exotic flavour, trusting it's just a sample. 'Particularly pleasant to greet you again in Hong Kong. You look handsome but tired. I have taken the liberty of preparing a bath. You will relax, I will wash you and then supper will be served. I have selected a light omelette with ham, chicken and pork garnished with a small mix of vegetables and a sprinkle of steamed rice.' She smiles sweetly. 'Then a blazing blueberry crepe and finally a pot of brewed coffee waits in the bathroom. I have taken the liberty my girl Sri is meeting your associate, to offer stress-relief bath and massage.' The grin is almost undiscernible but her eyes tell it all, twinkling mischievously.

Deliberations of danger disappear as rapidly as they have materialised. Mathew zones zealously on her stunning beauty and her devious planning and is suitably impressed. But will Brian be?

Mathew stares into her face, accepting the bountiful beauty filling his eyes. He holds out his hands, which are happily accepted and he imagines his knees wobbling, his heart fluttering and his head swimming as his soul is revitalised by Heidi. Her perfume is pervading. Their heads touch gently; he inhales deeply the sweet combination of shampoo and Poison. Squeezing her slightly, he is of the understanding he swoons.

Heidi retreats, holding a hand, simply saying, 'Come.' *I'm portraying Miss Cool, Calm, and Collected, but oh my gods and*

Grandfather in heaven, I love him so. Oh golly, to be in his arms. Oh dear, might I muster the strength for this?

The bathroom has been prepared. Incense burns, the coffee pot brews, the spa bath bubbles. Mathew bows to Heidi, conveying his gratitude for her preparation, delivered with a devilish grin. He transfers his suitcase into the bedroom, removes his toilet bag, licks his lips in expectation and proceeds to the bathroom, noticing the lights have been dimmed. He sets the shaver on a towel, returns to the bedroom, undresses and wraps the second towel around his stomach, walks to the bathroom, sinks into the hot bubbly spa as Heidi enters, who debates one last time, can she carry out the plan.

Unashamedly, she slips off her gown and stands stark naked as Mathew gasps at her beauty as sheens of silk falls down her back. Breasts full with long hard nipples, a distinct waist, a sharp incline to the hips that is more a European trait. Without seeing, he accepts she'll have a beautiful round arse. Inspired by his hard stare, she smiles in a timid manner, tilts her head slightly and poses, 'So, Mathew Allen, how many pixels in this picture?'

'Ah, you are indeed stunningly beautiful. I'm grateful and fortunate you enter my bath. You do me a great honour.' He signals for her to enter.

Heidi sits facing him. 'Coffee?'

'Yes, please, black with three sugars.'

In the motion of passing the cup, she slides her slender fingers along his and he delights at the tingle tripping up his arm. Mathew nods as he sips. 'The coffee is perfect as are you. Thank you for being here tonight and welcoming me.'

Mathew inclines his head, holding her eyes. *Like a chocolate box, wrapped, waiting to be savoured.*

'You extend me a great honour too. Why contact me and not another lady?'

'Because I enjoyed your company and truly, Heidi' – he conveys his best smile – 'the picture captured was peerless. It encapsulated all the pixels.'

'I'm gratified but what does that mean to you?'

Knowing he's trapped, he reaches for an old rabbit. 'I'm of the superstition, what it means to you, is the most important.'

Clever, trying to turn the question around. I can play too. Cop this, Mathew. 'Do not think so. I've told you my heart. I'm on record, one might say . . . but you?'

This is bloody tricky!

She saves the day. 'When enunciating the line about the pixels being perfect, were you being cryptic or charming?'

His grin expands. 'Yeah, well, both actually. I don't know where the thought came from, but I relished it and if you recognise romance, then in the context of just meeting you, I'm happy to say, per the pixels, you are indeed stunningly beautiful, stirring my heart and emotions.'

'Thank you and I tell you the truth. Mr. Keng, Mr. Soo, no one knows I am here.'

The soaping, Mathew deems, is expansive, like the song 'I've Been Everywhere' but not this experience. Mathew muses, *Asian culture, what are we missing out on?*

He tries not to rise to the occasion, but nature inevitably takes its course, promoting the ego when she adds, 'You are very strong. Is it me or the lost lady?'

'Just you, my little chocolate box.' He knows an explanation will be demanded.

Gathering an implement that reminds him of a Swiss Army–type gadget, Heidi explains she's going to clean and cut his nails and attend to his belly button and ears. He suggests a shave is required. 'And I'll do that too.'

Mathew and Heidi enter the living area wearing fluffy hotel robes as two boys prepare supper; they are shuffled gently towards the door by Heidi. Mathew reaches for his wallet but she signals no and to sit. 'Not necessary tonight.'

Heidi doesn't eat, Mathew asks, 'Why?'

'Must look after my shape. You may not enjoy me if I'm fat and bulgy.' She flutters her eyes. 'And would you like to know if Sri stayed with Mr. Bwoosewer?'

Mathew ponders for the few seconds it's required for the brain to grasp the pronunciation; softly, he replies, 'Yes', imagining he's spying.

Heidi grins, 'I will not tell, we must keep secrets but I do this.' She nods.

Mathew wallows in the delight of the massage; her fingers are strong and he wonders how such dainty digits, once onto a tight sinew or tough muscle, bore their way in, often causing a wince. Then he acknowledges the pleasure the little pain brings and he's lost in the hedonistic sensation of her straddling him, working wonders up and down the length of his body.

After the massage, Heidi retires to the shower; Mathew soon hears her singing in Chinese a bouncy, happy tune. Totally relaxed, he almost falls asleep but is sufficiently awake to watch as she crosses to the tall free-standing cupboard that would have looked out of place in any other modern hotel; here, it suits the ambience. Silently, he fascinates, Heidi is dressing. She says nothing then zips up her tall jet-black boots, lays her jacket in the crook of her arm and sits on the bed. Mathew simply stares, readily acknowledging he's dumbfounded.

Her look is one of intent, yet her heart is a jumble of emotions; her face expresses determination and a tiny grin gathers at the corner of her mouth. The chocolate box sparkles, like the sun flashing off the gold paper that wraps the goodies. 'You may be disappointed, but if we are to have a future, as I truly desire, then you must come to me with more than lust in your heart. I am not a cheap woman. Regardless, for you, no amount of money will buy me. So, Mathew Allen, I contend if you want me, you must respect me. In the meantime, you will honour me if I may escort you and Mr. Bwoosewer out on the harbour for a dinner cruise. It will be hot and humid, but I think you will enjoy it.'

'Sounds like fun. Can I confirm by phone and I must demand we pay for the food and the boat?'

Slowly, with her eyes wide open, she leans over and kisses him quickly, allowing time enough for her tongue to lick his lips; and with that, she simply departs without looking back, closing the door almost without a click.

Mathew sinks into the bed and shakes his head. 'What was that all about?' Realisation will arrive slowly.

CHAPTER 26

Looking like a new man, relaxed, clean shaven, bright-eyed and very bushy-tailed, with his usual broad grin spreading right across his face, Brian brushes a hand through his thin hair and asks, 'Did you arrange that? Who else? What a night. I have never been rubbed and bloody tugged like that in all my years. Asian women, bloody hell, where have they been all my life?'

'Let's have breakfast.' They move across the lobby.

'This has to be between us, Mathew. No one must know, especially Mandy.'

'Okay, no problem. Now Heidi has invited us out on the harbour, a dinner cruise. Might be nice on the water. Your call. I have to make contact if we are batting.'

'Tell you what, mate. You pop the pads on and I'll open the bowling.' The laughter regales the room as Brian puts paid to the serenity of the place. 'Bugger, but what if Mr. Ching Chong wants to dine us? We can't refuse.'

'True. Still, we have tomorrow night before we fly out. Then they can have no tests.'

'What do you mean tests?'

Good on ya, Mandy. You just passed the test trap. Would you warn Brian? No. Good, a degree of trust develops.

After an explanation, Brian comments, 'Foxy bastards, but wait, was last night a set-up?'

'Absolutely not, that was all me.' Mathew grins, attacking the hash browns, accepting he'll not be sprung for the little fib.

Moving back into the main lobby, they descend into outrageously deep armchairs, order coffee and proceed to run over the Trilogy concept one more time. 'I remain surprised Hugo fell in line. I know he can be an arrogant son of a bitch, but he's some smart property lawyer, so the trick is simple, stupid. Suss out the right property in the right locale.'

'I think location is relatively easy. Steve and I have already identified three areas of interest. All we have to do is spend time driving with council maps and we'll soon have our property and we can pay above the odds for rural farmland.' Mathew winks.

'And we'll include Milly in the property sourcing. Keng will respect the gesture. Trust runs deep.'

'Should we involve her closer with us?'

'Thought about it. However, for the moment, keep her at arm's length. She is really their girl.' But Mathew is already developing other plans for Milly.

'Mathew, this is as good a time as any for us to have a man to man. Firstly, Mandy comes with a past, not up to me to elaborate. I act as a protector, it's difficult and she's such a stunner, particularly social, wise in business matters, willing to push a boundary, take a risk and be adventurous. She's taken a shine to you. Initially, that grated, you being married but we came to a different conclusion when you separated. We discussed the Rhine trip, giving it to you, trusting you'd take her. She deserves some luck. I respect you as a business person, so can I ask you to be careful with her?'

Mathew nods. 'Of course.' The schoolmaster looks return.

'Secondly, we are surprised you took a different tack with Keng's fee. The boys and I, in a conference call, concluded it is incumbent on me to allay fears that you don't bear any bile in your gut.'

'I've told you before I do not mind putting my hand in my pocket. There is no angst, no anger and I ultimately reckoned it was the right thing to do.'

'It's not the money, more about contribution and attitude.'

With the arrival of more coffee, Mathew shovels in the sugar and Brian contributes to his health awareness note for the day. 'Not good for you, all that sugar!'

'Any third?'

'The third was Milly and we dealt with that. Can we change the subject?'

'Of course.'

'Will Sri join us for dinner?'

'Would you like her to?'

'Bloody oath, mate. God, what a doll. Can I fit a snooze in this arvo?'

'I'll call Heidi.' Mathew pushes the appropriate buttons; she answers immediately as if waiting.

'Hello, Mathew, how are you?' Mathew thinks her voice has a certain lilt like she is smiling either at him for last night or with him, looking forward to the evening.

'Fine, thanks. Enjoying your day?'

'Yes, very good but waiting for you, so can we?'

'Will Sri accompany us?'

'Will he want her to?'

'Yes.'

'Do you remember the small wharf beside Star Ferry?'

'Yes, on the left.'

'Meet us at six. We will enjoy the sunset over Kowloon Hills and watch the lights come out to play. So sorry, I need to ask, will you pay with U.S. dollars, and shall we want the boat for the night?'

'The first answer is yes and the second answer is yes.'

'That is very exciting and Sri will be too.'

'I hope so. Until then, hooroo.'

Mathew turns to confront Brian, only to be met by, 'What was the second yes for?'

'You'd better bring an overnight bag.'

But Mathew's thoughts are suddenly dominated by *How did she know I'd know about the wharf beside the ferry terminal?*

Mathew lies on the couch, reflecting on the last evening. *I must be losing my marbles, fancy feeling happy because a great night of sex walked out the door. Still, it wasn't a knock-back, more a postponement. Therefore, I accept the meaning of the manoeuvre and tonight will be different. Hmm, but why? Of course, women and it's all about romance.* He extracts the mobile phone from his pants pocket.

'Wie.'

'Good morning, beautiful Heidi. How are you?'

'Ah, Mathew, a nice surprise.'

'Are you by yourself?'

'Yes. Anything wrong?'

'No, just want to thank you again for last night, welcoming me in such a wonderful manner. That was a special massage, I went straight to sleep and you are obviously a very considerate person. You know I have another love in my heart but she is gone and if you are not already of the inkling, might I be so bold as to venture, you could replace her.' He shakes his head wondering at the extent of the wank.

'And thanks for your respectful manner when I left last night. I expected you to be all male, angry and frustrated. Now you offer more pleasure by contacting me again and yes, I am excited for the prospects providence holds in her hands.'

'Me too. See you at six o'clock. Hooroo.'

'Yes and oh, Mathew, what is a hooroo?'

In the imposing bank foyer, Mathew carries out the introductions before Keng conducts them to the corner room, welcoming them with a glass of champagne and issues instructions to serve lunch. Brian surprises Mathew, going on the front foot, proactively thanking Keng in a formal and deferential manner for the opportunity. Respectfully, with a smidge of determination, he expands on the salutation. 'My group is desirous for our meeting to be progressive and positive. As such, they'd appreciate it if we part with a resolution to move forward.' He then refers to Milly and Mathew, portraying them as the property experts whom they trust implicitly.

The proceedings therefore commence. For the next hour, it's the traditional backwards and forwards in an amicable, professional business manner. Mathew sits back, letting them go at it and like a slice of sticky date pudding soaks up the sweet sauce, recognising regardless of the outcome, he's the winner. Brian battles to encrypt notes in the midst of nibbling on repetitious appetisers. Keng calls in a young assistant, instructing her to record the gist of the meeting, highlight specific agreements, underline items to be dealt with later, type up the notes and deliver them to the hotel this afternoon. Brian thanks him for the consideration while Mathew records the gesture in his 'nice move' file. Finally, the spotlight focuses on Mathew, offering an opportunity to elucidate and expand on ideas for a project. Assuming correctly that Milly, inspired by the concept, will have forwarded Keng a copy of the brief, comprehension comes readily and that alleviates any need to dwell on Mathew's conceptual imaginations. Mathew confirms with Keng, he, together with Milly and his real estate agent Steve Lowry, will commence immediately to establish a property brief, then the individual property search can be instigated.

Keng simply nods and addresses Brian, pursuing personal comments on the local economy, the current market relating to sales demand, inflationary trends and the current property stock in Sydney and Melbourne. Mathew appreciates the manoeuvre is a deliberate attempt to qualify his previous assertions. *Ho-hum, here we go again.* Brian performs brilliantly, give an accountant the floor with an opportunity to expand on his area of expertise and look out. Mathew wonders if in the end Keng isn't regretting the course pursued. Brian rolls out figure after figure, quoting government and independent sources, offering consummate precise substantiation. Mathew sits back, struggling to control the grin.

After lunch, a gambit of matters are discussed and resolved. The conclusion revolves around the financial structure, payment of deposits, project development funding, banking, joint accounts and general administration. 'Gentlemen, encouraged by your speedy response and Mathew's seemingly creative proposal, we are in and we concur with your opening gambit, we too have confidence in Mathew and Milly.' Sternly, Keng turns his attention to Mathew. 'Find the property, document diligently and I'll be down on the next flight. In the meantime, if I need to be in contact, are you available to meet later?'

Brian apologises, 'So sorry, we have a commitment, but late Tuesday, we'll keep free.' Mathew reckons the answer will only create more questions.

Alone, Keng is immediately on the phone, anxious to discover where they'll be until Tuesday afternoon and more importantly, with whom. *I wonder if . . .* And he smiles broadly.

CHAPTER 27

IT'S INDEED ANOTHER GRAND CABIN. They meld into each other's arms, find each other's eyes and hold the stare. *I'm not in control, I don't understand what's going on and frankly I don't bloody care.* Mathew worries.

Heidi had already arrived at a conclusion. *Opportunity knocked twice. I have to move him on.* She pulls him closer, stands right up on tiptoes and grinds into him.

In a moment of self-righteousness, Mathew displays old-fashioned morals, confronts personal principles and deduces this is all too fast. Confused, he makes an insipid excuse, enters the toilet, squats on the tiny seat and lowers his head into his hands. *What's going on? The most stunningly beautiful girl in the world is out there and I'm in a bloody dunny, confused. She walked out last night, saying all the money in the world won't buy her, yet today she is obvious. Is it me, is it her, is it both of us together?* He's reminded of Milly's words warning him about Wei Li, young girl, and the layers of life. *What do I always say? Time tells all, so let the clock tick. Sooner or later, it will roll out the message, be it another layer, a sliver of the puzzle or the answer to the conundrum of Heidi.*

Heidi is concerned. *I deduced the plan had merit. It was proceeding well. Now this. What is the man's nature? Why retire to the toilet? Might it be a pang of confusion caused by last night or flippant thoughts regarding a future or a lady lost? It may be all compounding. So, what's it all about? Patience, Heidi, patience!*

Back in the cabin, Heidi tentatively moves close and Mathew, without any prior consideration, blurts out, 'Later, my beautiful lady. Let's study the sunset story and scrutinise the stars in their everlasting glory, announcing the evening in the romantic hue of me and you.' Then he relishes a twinge of self-congratulation, hoping the words have conspired to cover the awkward moment.

The utterance surprises Heidi. 'Wow, Mr. Allen, besides being a romantic, a poet perchance, might there be more?' She tilts her head questioningly.

Inspired, Mathew continues, 'The prettiest picture includes you, enhancing the sky blue, the painting rhetoric by your bloom and blush.' He smiles and shakes his shoulders.

Gracious me, I'll have to think about that one. She claps her hands in a gleeful manner. 'Any more?'

Anxious to persevere, Mathew knows he will have to retire to the written word and quickly arrives at what he believes might be appropriate. 'Yes, Fain would I change that note, to which fond love hath charmed me.'

Heidi grasps the wisdom, hesitating to gauge the depth of intelligence to procure such an ingenious line, so adroit, so subtle. *How clever to discover such a cryptic line for such an occasion, how can I respond.* 'My goodness how subtle I recognise the inference to my note, do you know more of that poem?'

Mathew grimaces, suddenly aware he has been sprung. He shakes his head as the smile fades. 'Then allow me to offer you the conclusion of Mr. Hume's poem.

Fair house of joy and bliss
Where truest pleasure is,
I do adore thee:
I know thee what thou art,
I serve thee with my heart,
And fall before thee.'

Heidi nods, serving to confirm the statement conveyed in the poet's lines.

'Now it's my turn to be surprised. I thought I was being particularly smart. Never did I expect you'd know the background of the line offered.'

Heidi holds the grin in, knowing education equals knowledge which acquaints to power, thus ensuring control and doesn't she love it. *And now Mr. Smarty-pants, let this sink in.* 'So come, for me love is the perfect sum of all delight, I have no other choice, either for pen or voice, to sing or write about today tonight.' In a haughty manner, she turns to the stairs. 'Let us therefore venture into the future, wonder at first sunset sighted, understanding it will not for you and me be the last.'

Strewth, Mathew thinks as he climbs the narrow steps. *What have I here?*

Comfortable couches are built into the corners of the deck. Mathew gazes into her eyes, seeing only chocolate balls and similar with Min Xie, farms no perception. If fascination and infatuation count for everything, desperately, he seeks to plumb the depths. *This little chocolate box is a conundrum, the layers of life, the package perfect, the wrapping wickedly wanton, the delight itself delicate and delicious and maybe even bloody dangerous. But what's in the centre – sweet, soft and satisfying or sour and sinful?*

'You thinking of me or lost lady love?'

Mathew surveys the depth of the abyss; suddenly uncertain, he strives to be positive. 'Always you.'

'My eyes tell me to trust you. My soul evaluates your words and challenges my heart to accept them. It does but offers the opinion, fate is at work here. Therefore, in the spirit of romance and working my gods to wheel, I'm content to be on the harbour on a nice boat, on a nice evening with nice people and a nice man. Can you not see, I am a very happy girl?' She cuddles closer.

Mathew contemplates Heidi. *Who is this girl? How can a lady of the night know the lines from such an obscure British poet? What education has endowed her with such literary prowess? How intelligent is her comprehension? Why is she here? Why speak her heart in an almost confessional manner, baring the soul?*

Indeed, she is a mystery. Yet it shouldn't have been.

Inevitably, he bows to the whim of the evening, ready to accept the occasion as presented and in the deepest recess of his mind, appreciates life is all about time.

The evening's indeed warm; a flighty, fluky breeze seemingly swirls around the boat, enticing the waves to dance and display a mystic delight. Heidi wonders if it's her gods smiling. Encouraged, the waves instill an air of excitement, inciting her quest for her man.

Breaking the spell, Mathew poses, 'So, Heidi, what's the game plan?'

Oh dear, maybe he's really not romantic.

'Cruise down the harbour, pass the old airport, Lei Yue Mun and Junk Bay at the end of Tathong Channel.'

Mathew is reminded of Milly's exciting story about her incredible journey's conclusion off the east end of the runway at Kai Tak.

'Where we'll take a hard left and sail up to a village just past Sai Kung. There, we'll stop for dinner and the night, anchoring off the town.'

'I envisaged we'd park somewhere quiet, our own private bay or beach.'

Heidi shakes her head at his romantic inclination. 'No, Mathew, pirates may come to a boat anchored in a quiet spot. Too dangerous. So sorry.'

Mathew thinks, *Pirates, and this is the twenty-first century.*

They cruise for some time before the others arrive on deck. Brian sports a sheepish look. Mathew nods and passes a Foster's extricated from the chilly bin, adding a wink to go with the nod. 'Nearly missed sunset.' He waves to the western hills, over which an orange sun is about to disappear behind a streaky band of cumulus clouds. They stand transfixed, absorbed by nature's altercation, shafts of multicolored hues fighting to extend the day. Finally, the cloud mass and physics win their way, concluding proceedings.

One of the young girls offers finger food. Brian is wary and studiously studies the delights. *Looks like and yep tastes like whitebait. The vinegar dip's bloody tart though.* Gratified, he licks his fingers, wipes them subconsciously on his shorts and when tendered a napkin grins abashedly, acknowledging, 'too late.' Then without skipping a beat, he changes tack. 'You know, Heidi, I've always considered nothing beats Sydney Harbour but this is quite spectacular.'

'I have never been to Sydney, just seen photos and marveled at the New Year's fireworks display featuring the bridge and that mystic sign. I delved into the dictionary to discover its meaning.'

'Eternity.'

'Yes, and I understand the denotation, yet to see it on the bridge on New Year's fascinated, so I went in search of another interpretation but found none.'

'Yes, well . . .' Brain turns to Mathew, seeking to be rescued, only to receive a sympathetic smile and a casual shrug.

'Well, let's see, the word developed an aura in Sydney. There was a poor man, a person whom I understand lived on the streets, so his life was tough, yet he maintained a strong religious faith, epitomised through the word eternity, projecting to everyone, life is part of the whole and goes on forever.'

He glances at Mathew. 'Bloody tough gig mate, next time the brain seeks explanation, can you field it!'

Without hesitation Heidi continues, 'Anyway, Brian, back to the harbour. I perceive the difference is Hong Kong encapsulates the mystery of the East. It has an allure, a charm, a certain something that one is always trying to put their finger on, but it escapes them. You understand me?'

Brian, momentarily lost in her beautiful eyes, wonders at her intelligence. 'Like conjuring up images, whereas Sydney is just the view.' Then he turns to make a comment to Mathew, but he's off on a tangent about the sporting culture of Melbourne with Sri, who is politely attentive. Brian lets it go, admitting he's rapidly coming to the conclusion, Heidi is something else.

During the evening, Brian is particularly social with both girls, who appreciate the interest shown to them as individual and when he arrives at aspirations, Sri renders a fateful statement. 'To live in Melbourne with you.' The determined declaration is articulated with a cheeky smile.

Mathew wonders, *Does it mask insincerity or is she just visa hunting?* Still, he admires her attitude. *It's a Chinese trait.* He surmises.

Sri explains they share a tiny one-bedroom fourth-floor walk-up flat near the end of Moody Road. They'd met at university, where she'd graduated with a degree in business administration and currently works at Kwum Yam Shan High School. Concluding her personal discourse, she says, 'Lucky, hey? Work with brains all day, party with the money all night and save furiously for the future.'

Seemingly in a gold fishbowl, surrounded by towers of steel and glass, they settle into the cushions. Mathew caresses Heidi's arms slowly and softly; she shivers and aware of the indicator, ironically, he asks if she's cold. She pulls his head to her mouth and whispers, 'No, you excite me.' She expresses a special smile, while steadfastly holding eye contact and runs sexual expectations of the night, through her head. *Mathew at last in my company, trapped in my boat web, ensnared and enslaved to my heart as I envisaged. My seduction and clever scheming, good, hey?*

Purposely, Heidi takes Mathew's hand, directing his fingertips to envelope her belly button. The movement captures a mood that rhymes with the throb of engines; Mathew imagines the motor running persistently in tune with Heidi's heartbeat. He visualises the engine under pressure; the accelerator flat to the boards and in a strange fit of passion, transfers the demanding lust and intensity to himself, who senses eroticism erupting. Fervency meshes and merges but is deflated instantly, 'Mathew, please, you're rubbing too hard.'

He opens his eyes and peers off to the horizon for a mesmerising moment, then turns to face the questioning stare. Gently, he smiles and lowers his face, muttering in a minimal murmur, 'Sorry, I was making love in my soul. The passion passed to my hand.'

Unaware he's opened the door; Heidi draws his head to hers and walks right through. 'Was it truly me or a lost love?'

Shrewdly, Mathew senses the portentous opportunity; holding her dense eyes, he disappears into the depths and responds deferentially, 'I promise, honestly, it's you.'

In silent gratitude, she closes her eyes, reaches for his hand, places it on her breast and holds it tight, determined for it not to escape. *Indeed, might my dream be realised with this man, whom I know in my heart I love already. Ah, but what game do I play, so strong up to now? Measuring the will to walk out of his suite nearly killed me, but now I dither, uncertain which tack to take.* Images and ideas of plans conceived, run laps around her head, centering on *Will I, or wont I?*

She manoeuvres her bottom, annoyed by the lumps in the pillows; Mathew takes it the wrong way, imagining mutual passion raising. Deftly, he undoes two buttons on her blouse to caress more bare skin, sliding his hand up under her bra, pushing it off her breasts, seeking to roam freely. A tingle of electricity blasts up his fingers, frazzling the brain; it is a fantastic sensation.

To Heidi, the autumn fog of passion lifts; she visualises her fate and like a soothsayer, the future appears clear and bright. *It's truly love, exactly as envisaged. God, I wish we were in bed.*

The kiss lingers as tongues search and the desperate longing grows, as his fingers move from her breasts to her belly button. His penis throbs, inspired by the erotic sensations his brain tells it to prepare for. Motivated by lust, he searches for the key to the next move, artfully asking, 'How far to go?'

'Maybe an hour.' Her voice is soft and husky.

Brian's head is beneath the blanket; Mathew knows he's not the only one hot and horny. Quietly, he suggests, 'Mate, we dock in an hour. Let's retire, set the alarm, and have dinner on shore.'

'Who'll set the alarm?'

'Heidi.'

'You are a funny man; you don't imagine we'll sleep?' A tiny laugh escapes.

'Come to me, Mathew Allen. Enter the arms of a woman who tells you truly, with her heart open for inspection, I love you. And whilst it may be difficult to purge your lost love from your head and heart, tonight please be with me, not her.'

Her intent is to hammer home the moment, confirming what she's witnessed in his eyes earlier.

In one motion, he moves across the bed, taking her with him, holding her close, peering deeply into the chocolate boxes. Seeing nothing, he sighs. 'Heidi, tonight will be all about you.' He tries, but he's lied and she probably knows it.

It must be nine o'clock; Mathew hears a soft knock as if intending not to disturb. They look at each other in the dimly lit stateroom, smile all-knowingly and kiss quickly. Mathew lingers in silent contemplation; a frightening realisation has hit home. *Was Min Xie really about love or just lust and the pain I'm suffering a severely damaged ego?*

Rampant introspections converge, wrapping around Heidi, the sexual trap and the declaration of her heart, trying to acquaint it with her being on the job, a paid sex employee and the contradiction of when the perfect opportunity arose, she walked out. *It's arithmetic and the numbers don't add up. Now this evening, the foreplay and the lovemaking were wild and uninhibited as she drove incessantly to her climax and then mine. Mathew, you are a silly old bugger. Get it through your head that this is a pro. Well, she might be particularly cute, in fact, stunningly beautiful but damn it, man, a professional doing precisely what one is supposed to! Pity! Why? Because I love little Min Xie and Heidi reminds me of her, although she is more statuesque, more European. Yes, of course, it's bloody East or West again.*

Then Milly's words warning him about Wei Li ring a bell. *It's too fucking obvious. Milly knew Heidi was the temptress, Uncle exposed the plot, and she set out in search of her background and discovered an ambition to escape her circumstances by finding the right European or American or even an Ocker to contrive the opportunity to flit and flee. Well, I'll be buggered. Milly slipped me the information with the clear and undeniable knowledge Heidi would pursue me and she used Wei Li to convey the message.*

Yet Mathew revels in the clear understanding, something special has taken place not just sex for sex's sake or a good holiday root but another particle in the Heidi puzzle, the conundrum of the chocolate box amidst the layers of life.

Heidi is aware Mathew has suffered a moment of turmoil. It is inherent in her nature and understanding of man that she allows him to deal with his demons, whilst she dwells on the most wonderful sexual experience of her life. She kisses him tenderly and vacates the bed, expressing, 'Thank you, it was wonderful, truly special.'

He's suddenly grumpy. Confusion reigns. The bliss of the bed hits home, in a maddening mayhem moment, introspections wreak havoc as Milly's clever warnings resurrect and he wrestles with the loss of Min Xie, separating from Hope, flirting with Mandy, the erotic sex with Milly and now the beautiful Heidi. Indeed, life's an ongoing examination. Still, in time, the story will be told.

The shower is a mini-matchbox, laughable when Heidi squeezes in and cheerily says, 'Fun, hey?' And his anxiety washes down the plughole as she struggles, to soap him all over.

The deck chairs are ancient, hardly fitting the luxurious surroundings. The girls converse in Cantonese as Mathew stares at the pier, looking as if it's been casually tacked on to the edge of the village; all around, boats of varying shapes and sizes lay at anchor.

Well-patronised eateries and bars project boisterous hullabaloo along the tiny waterfront street, invigorating the ancient atmosphere. Mathew strides purposefully on the rough cobblestone pavement, fascinated by the pervading mood of the hamlet, seeking something missing from the norm. No neon signs, maintain the quaintness.

They shuffle in single file through the busy restaurant, packed mainly with Chinese crews, and locals and are ushered into a private room with floor-to-ceiling windows providing a panoramic view over the bay. The floor is crazed stone masterfully laid, the walls and ceiling lined with antediluvian, gnarled and knotted timbers stark and undecorated, yet a sense of life lived seems to reach out and welcome them.

Heidi plays table mother and commences ordering seafood as she scrolls down the single-sheet battered menu. 'We'll start with salty fish and pak choi prawns with egg and bok choy fishcake, lots of rice and a large bowl of green vegetables.'

Brian is in an effusive mood and dominates the evening, like a deprived raconteur suddenly surrounded by a bevy of compliant beauties; when appropriate, he injects a joke that encourages giggling. Often the girls laugh out loud and hide their faces behind tiny hands as if shocked at the merriment. The waitresses are fastidious in attention to Brian's and Mathew's needs, without being overbearing or in your face as restaurant staff can often be, when trying to please.

Back on board, Mathew asks Heidi to ensure the captain moves to a private beach once the sun comes up as his romantic inclination has been rebuffed, by having to park near the village; he's envisaged waking anchored in a quiet lagoon or cove and this might be a nice compromise.

CHAPTER 28

Heidi wakes before dawn; in unintended imitation, she epitomises Min Xie in the dying months of the relationship – insatiable. During the intimacy, the engines stir; the motion changes as the boat has been cast off from its moorings. Like the sex played through his head last evening, the engines rev to full power and the twin diesels steadily throb, reverberating around the stateroom. They make love in rhythm with the waves crashing against the hull of the craft and the motors pulsate like a wild Melanesian Tamore.

Heidi is in love. She has found her man, yet clearly, like the warning light at Lei Yue Mun Point, she must keep him. Tomiko, her tutor, rightly taught her that the way to a man's heart is through his tummy; but equally, if what hangs from it is not inspired, all the food in the world will not save you.

Recognising the change in his motion as the engine roars up, she appreciatively adjusts to the way of his fornicating and he smiles at her perception. Her climax is long, almost violent in her thrusting and groping as she pushes her boundaries to reach the ultimate sensation. He grimaces as her fingernails dig deep into his shoulders, but she is lost in the sexual intoxication, unaware of the pain inflicted.

Heidi lies in his arms; locks of her long black hair fall over his chest and stomach. He strokes it like his old cat now living with Hope. A moment of betrayal beckons, yet like a dog with a bone, he chews around the edges, relishing the sweet meat of memories and discarding that which he cannot gnaw, accepting she'll always have a corner of his heart. Memories flash to the couch in her mother's living room that fateful day of so many years past, and like the dog that appreciates a good bone, he buries it in his heart. Milly's revelations are discarded like a bag of bad bones, incompatible with the romantic inventiveness of Mathew's labyrinth, the layers of Heidi.

'Are you ready to go again?' Her dark eyes flash.

'You're tired. I can wait.'

'No. Do you not have stories that tell you never wait?'

'Yes, come kiss me, sweet and twenty, youth's a stuff will not endure.'

'Sounds like poetry.'

'Shakespeare.'

'Ah yes, the Bard. I took English literature at uni. Tell me, please.'

Damn it, I'm hard, raring to go again, and she's into Shakespeare. Me and my big mouth.

'O mistress mine, where are you roaming?

O stay and hear, you true love's coming

That can sing both high and low;

Trip no further, pretty sweeting,

Journeys end in lovers' meeting,

Every wise man's son doth know.
What is love? 'tis not hereafter;
Present mirth hath present laughter;
What's to come is still unsure:
In delay there lies no plenty,
Then come kiss me, sweet and twenty,
Youth's a stuff will not endure.'

The poem doesn't dampen his ardour; still, she leads the parade. 'Beautiful poem, but you did not reply directly again.'

He allows a small grin to escape and explains, 'Of course. However, when we make love, I want to believe we are pleasing each other. It shouldn't be for you or me, more us together.'

Heidi sits up. 'No, I think not. Sometimes I will be desperate for you but you're too tired. Then you work at helping me achieve my pleasure. Similarly, I'm not in the mood but you are ready, so I should be a considerate, devoted lover and help you to a happy ending. I believe when a man and a woman are together, they must always be of one mind in pleasuring. If not, they'll never be truly happy and in love. When lovers are of the same disposition and desire, with their hearts full of each other, with passion rampant, then wow, making love truly is wonderful, hey?' Heidi embraces the truth of the notion; aware she's just lived the experience.

Mathew digests her comments. How simple. How perfect. If life were only like that. He incurs visions of a sublime life, thinks of Min Xie, and pursues boundaries not measured before. *How perfect could we have been without animals – no dog, no cat, not even a bloody budgie. How do we survive without any meaningful dialogue, no arguing about current affairs, geopolitics and history? God, even a chat about a good book lost all meaning.* He broods about his has age and Heidi; something is happening in his heart. Might it truly be the *L* word?

Silence prevails; conversation ceases. Softly, he says, 'The first time I saw you, I thought physically you were the most beautiful woman I'd ever seen. At the bar, as we talked, I searched your eyes, trying to evaluate the depth of the acquisitiveness. Then inexplicably, you told me your heart, which frankly tickled my ego that one so lovely could see an attraction in an old man. But you were here. I was going there. Fortuitously, the opportunity to return nurtured the spark in my heart. You tempted and teased me. I understand why. Your words emanated from the soul and I recognise, I had to love you to have you. Now you have offered me your body with love. Thank you for being Heidi. You have made me a very happy man.'

'I do truly hope so. I tell you, Mathew Allen, I own a very expensive, particularly rare and ancient kimono. Draped over my shoulders, it engenders the concept of joss. When you held me in your arms after we made love, I captured the spirit of the kimono. I visioned our prospects as you stepped into the Rolls-Royce. Today only strengthens that impression and the future materialises. And like you, I was excited the first time I saw you, a man in control, a gentle person, caring and respectful when I emptied my heart. I never expected to see you again, and isn't life the bearer of such wonderful surprises? You returned. We made love as lovers should, considerate for each and so may I ask a difficult question?'

'Of course.'

'After tonight, will I ever see you again and Sri Brian?'

'Why ask about Sri and Brian?'

'Sri is a very outgoing girl but in matters of the heart a little shy. She worries if he is like all foreign men, come and go.' Her grin widens as the realisation of the comment sinks in. 'Ha, I do not mean it like that.'

'I don't know. She will have to be a big girl and ask him. As to us, I honestly cannot say, may I therefore pose a question to you?'

'As you say, of course.' The reply arrives with a grin.

'Men can be manipulated by a clever woman. Silly old men like me can easily fall in love with a beautiful young lady.' His schoolmaster look is expressive. 'And because it's not true love, it doesn't pass the test of living life together.'

She holds his eyes intently, aware he's on the cusp.

'So, Heidi, let us be honest with each other. You are of the pillow world. I might contend therefore, you harbour a desire to escape your lifestyle. You may yearn to discover a man who will love just you, embellish you with the comforts of life, take care of you and pursue an eternal commitment.'

Wow, he's into the heavy stuff now. I did not expect such a dissertation, such a determined pursuit of my mental position. I will go with the flow. 'Yes.'

'Could I be that man?' Instantaneously, he thinks, *Fucking hell, my brain really does hang between my legs. Why have I rushed into this?*

Heidi thinks, *So the seed has germinated. Life springs forth. Now, clever farmer, nurture and care as you play the game.* 'Would you like to be?'

Mathew spontaneously laughs out loud, recognising the deviously clever answer. *It's like I taught her to sell!*

Heidi takes it the wrong way, not understanding he's coming from Mars. *Now he laughs at me. Why say his heart so succinctly, pose such personal questions, head in the right direction and then laugh? Am I being a silly bugger? Oh well, I am committed to the pursuit. I will wait for his answer, see where it takes us.*

'Too early. I would need to spend time with you away from the pillow.'

'Ha!' Then she laughs, raising her voice in exclamation. 'You think after making magnificent music in bed, we will not pillow? Impossible.'

'I mean, we'd have to live life, not waste it in bed.'

Ah yes, I like that. There is, without a doubt, a lot of life left in this piece of rope, Heidi muses. 'Going shopping, exploring new places, being adventurous, is that what you mean?'

'Precisely. Discover the individual, uncover likes and loves and what excites us like books, poetry, movies, the arts and music.'

'Practising at being together. Do you know the American card game canasta?'

'Matter of fact, I do.'

'What is the term used to signify the start of the game?'

'Melding.'

'Precisely. We might term it canasta, see if we meld, I would enjoy the opportunity but you'll go tomorrow, fly out of my life.' Her eyes are cast down in a look of despair, then she projects that cheeky grin. 'Can I go with you to the airport? We'll have one last kiss and I'll feel your arms around me and like my magic kimono, I'll gather strength.'

'Do you have a man in your life, Heidi?'

'Absolutely no, no man has ever resided romantically in my heart or soul. Do you have a special lady in Melbourne?'

'Not anymore.' He endeavours to convey a serious facade to the brain; which confuses his heart as signals flash, behind the simple answer.

The motion of the boat changes with slowing engines; the bow raises and falls, signifying coming to a full stop. Mathew needs to investigate and removing a robe from the little cupboard, he slips it on, saying, 'Want to see where we are.'

Heidi wraps a towel around her body and follows grinning.

Brian and Sri are eating breakfast at a little table folded down from the side of the saloon. Mathew's breath is taken away, in awe of the magnificent view of the tiny cove. 'Something else, Mathew?'

'Good morning. Yes, what a beautiful place. I envisaged we moored in paradise and here we are.' Slowly, he turns 180 degrees, taking in the bald brown hills acting as a rolling border, to the intense blue of the sky and the water clashing, with the tiny white sand beach. Rocky outcrops at each end, seemingly frame the cover of an exotic novel. The water's clear and inviting; overtaken by a sudden urge, he throws off the robe and dives into the water. Hearing Sri squeal in merriment, he takes one strong breaststroke and exclaims loudly, 'It's bloody warm!'

He looks back at the boat as Brian swallow-dives, hardly making a splash, surfaces nearby, flashing a huge grin.

Heidi calls out, 'We want to swim too, but Sri is not strong. Will Brian assist please?'

'I'll come back closer to the boat.'

The girls move to the edge naked. Heidi dives. Sri jumps and surfacing, thrashes her arms until Brian takes her in his arms. Mathew laughs, saying to himself, *Hey, Bob, wish you could see me now.*

Staff members stand at the bow rail, smiling and waving. Heidi surfaces near Mathew and using several Aussie crawl-style strokes, swims straight into his arms, wraps her legs firmly around his body, kisses him quickly and moves away with her eyes wide open, grinning effusively. 'Naughty old man swimming naked, can I tell you something?'

'Yes, of course.'

'I can love you true, Mathew Allen. I can be anything to you. I can be everything to you. I can make the rest of your life complete. You will understand when I say I am a ball and I'm in your court. Ha, this is so much fun. Thank you, my gods. I love my life.'

Mathew follows determinedly in her wake, thinking, *Am I already the little dog tagging along? Am I ready to grab the ball and run with it?*

Upon reaching the shallows, Heidi calls back, 'Do you mind if Brian sees me naked?'

He hesitates. *Are these Asian sheilas for real? Oh well, it's her body. And if this is how she wishes to express the moment . . .* He shrugs, yet an old-fashioned flash of jealousy stirs deep in his heart. Heidi splashes through the sandy shallows and walks up the beach. Mathew peers back at Brian and Sri, slowly make way; while in the background, a small boat is being lowered into the water. Brian arrives in the shallows just twenty metres away. He pauses, suddenly understanding where he's at. *Bloody hell, I'm naked. What do I do now?* He looks at Mathew seeking a clue, then does a double take realising what he's looking at. The nature of the hilarious moment is such, Brian and Mathew will occasionally laugh in wonder, whilst Mathew again thinks of Bob and what he'd say.

The small boat beaches, bearing robes, towels, a hamper of fruit, juice and coffee in separate containers; the girls wear bikinis with brightly coloured sarongs draped over a shoulder. They giggle hysterically at the bizarre beach scene confronting them. Heidi notices several surreptitious peeks at the male sex on display, and admits, *Why not? Just fun, hey. Pity the water shriveled them up.*

With typical youthful exuberance, once the food has been served, the girls rush into the water, splashing and running around in the shallows like little children on a rare excursion to the sea and it well may be. After some time, Brian suggests he and Mathew take a walk. Slowly, they saunter along the water's edge, splashing as they wade, while behind them Heidi and Sri dash to join in the fun; the sounds of laughing and squealing accompany the boys.

'I need to talk man to man. I have a problem. I'm besotted with Sri. I know I can fly back and see her occasionally but I don't want that. I'd like to put her into a pad in Melbourne as my mistress. Am I crazy?'

'What does she say?'

'Don't know. Too bloody embarrassed to ask. Seems incongruous a middle-aged wanker chasing a beautiful young chick. Bloody stupid, right?'

Mathew blinks, acknowledging the irony. 'I am the bearer of news. Heidi has queried your intentions. Sri is equally besotted.'

Brian's easy big grin spreads; recognition sets in like jelly on a frigid day. 'Wow, really?'

'Yes, wow, really, but you have to do your own dirty work. Tell her how you feel. Tell her your heart and what you propose.'

'Thanks, mate, good news. Now next problem, when do we have to go back? I want to stay the day, stuff the cost.'

'No worries, I'll talk to Heidi and contact the pub in case they panic. Then I'll call Keng and tell him we're on a boat and if he needs anything clarified, I'm mobile.'

Heidi returns to use the boat phone, calls hotel reception, leaving the appropriate message for Keng. With Heidi's reappearance, Brian offers a sly wink and suggests to Sri they go for a walk. Heidi excitedly proclaims, 'Hey, great idea. Let's go too.'

Mathew puts the fire out, only to find she lights another. 'Why do they need privacy?'

'Patience Heidi, soon all will be revealed. Let's go for a swim. Have you been to this place before?'

'No, never. It's called Sheik Wan or Rocky Cove.'

They float around in the water, coming together in the act of cuddling and kissing; she places a hand over his heart. 'Is it me who is in there right now?'

'Yes, Heidi, only you.'

She pulls him close; reciprocating, he stands like a sentinel, tall and strong. Heidi treasures the blissfulness but the moment is shattered by Sri skipping and splashing through the shallows, laughing loudly. Falling into Heidi's arms she delivers an excited monologue in Cantonese. Patiently, Mathew waits; and shortly, the brief translation is conveyed. Brian asked and she accepted. She's going to Australia. Brian sashays casually in a nondescript manner, looking, Mathew reckons, like an old hound dog who just met up with Miss Horny Puppy.

'Might we go for a walk around the cliff and be by ourselves?' Heidi poses in a bewitching manner.

Mathew recalls the old saying about the boy asking the girl to make love on the beach when she asked, 'What's in it for me?' He just answered, 'Sand.'

Heidi notices the smile, and he's forced to explain the silly joke. 'Have you made love on a beach in Melbourne, Mathew?'

'You want the truth?'

'Between us, always.'

'Then the answer is yes.'

'With the lost lady love?'

'No.'

'Good and I have a premonition, we will one day on a beach in Australia.' The grin tell it all!

Amongst the rocks on the water's edge, the ripples play touchy around their toes. Heidi is philosophical and asks the age-old question 'What's it all about, Mathew?'

'What do you mean?'

'Oh, come on, you know, life, living, being here, you, me. You enter my life, you go and return, we make wonderful love, we talk with our hearts, yet you will go again. What's next?'

'I'm no Aristotle. I simply believe in time. Time itself answers all our questions rightly, wrongly, good news, bad news. Time dictates all.'

Heidi seeks clarification in her mind and then says, 'I see your point. However, we have the capability to alter directions and change our lives by the decisions we make.'

'Quite but made in the measure of time.'

'Let me make it personal. At this instance, you have no intention of marrying me. Yet if I asked you directly to marry me and you said yes, therefore, my question changed the direction of our lives.'

'But it happened over time, maybe in that instance quick time but still time. As you say, Heidi, I had no intention of marrying you. Then time passed, you asked a question and I said yes, but it was over a period, so I believe my supposition remains correct. Be patient in life. Time will tell all.'

Hmm, I'm going to have to work on that. Sounds like it has a Chinese connotation. Then she laughs, rolls over, slaps the water and stares him squarely in the eyes. 'What if I posed that question now?'

'I'd answer as before. We need to get to know each other more and for the moment, time is against us.'

'Time will bring us back together.'

'Exactly.'

Heidi lies down and gazes up at the clear blue sky, 'Do you believe in God or a god?'

Before he can answer, she sits up on her elbows; peers at his toes, tapping the water; and proceeds, 'I do. I believe my gods have brought us together. They took you away to strengthen my resolve, test love at first sight, one might say.

Then they enticed you back, we are here and we've made such beautiful love. Ha, and soon you'll go, but I know they'll bring you back again. I have a feeling something wonderful is happening between us.'

'Like a jigsaw?'

'Ah, very succinct.'

'I have brooded and baffled about you, Heidi. I've been reticent to question; might this be another piece of the puzzle?'

Their eyes play canasta; the game begins, horizontally they rollick and roll like the scene in the movie *From Here to Eternity*, surrounded by the rhythmical splash of the tiny waves. Heidi, in a flash, conjures up what in her mind is the perfect line of poetry. *Mathew and me in the South China Sea. My future directed by time, declares he.*

Returning to the boat for lunch, Brian asks Heidi to contact the hotel for messages. As there is none, he ventures forth into the planning for Sri, which encourages Mathew to ask about a visa. 'No worries, mate.' He winks, but Mathew has no idea what it means.

After lunch, they have retired to their respective staterooms. Heidi answers a tiny knock at the door and announces Mathew has a message to telephone Keng.

Keng has only one question: who might the golf course architect be? Mathew enunciates the list of prominent Australian designers, dismissing outright consideration for an overseas contender due to cost for no significantly better result. He vigorously recommends Antony Cashmore and Associates and directs Keng to the corporate website and the sites for the Dunes and Thirteenth Beach, which are keystone projects in their portfolio. Keng allows a grin to escape from his thin lips, imagining the night and the day on the boat, then turns to face Christine and conveys a single yet meaningful nod; she smiles, allowing a meaningful long sigh to escape.

Mathew pivots and is greeted by Heidi and the recognition of where he's at, in the jigsaw, is indelibly imprinted by the beauty confronting him. He gently encourages her to enter an embrace, holding her close as he wants to have this stunning creature in close care. And another bit of the Heidi puzzle, subconsciously falls into place.

In a moment most melancholy, the captain starts the motors and the anchor is weighed; slowly, he wheels around and heads out into the bay. The power transmits to the propellers and the trip back to reality commences with two couples looking back. Sri, in a state of absolute euphoria, struggles to maintain control of her happiness, while committing the memory of Sheik Wan to her store of 'must keep forever', unaware she'll never see the cove again.

Heidi is in a traumatic trance; her few precious moments of bliss are blighted. She's heading to nowhere, a town with no street signs, no directions, no town hall, no planning, no school, no future, no Mathew, no certainty, no hope into which she may insert the key. Suddenly, she doubts if time exists. A tear appears in the corner of her eye; taking a dainty finger, she places it on the tiny blob and transfers it to her mouth, suffering the agony of trying to decipher if it tastes like success or failure.

After docking, the girls accompany them to the hotel and their respective suites. Heidi debates a dangerous decision;

the knowledge that she is returning will sweep through the staff like a raging fire out of control, understanding friends are friends, but gossip is more fun. And as it spreads, it will be elaborated and expanded on.

Mathew expects once in bed, Heidi might consider him vulnerable and it's an appropriate time to pose a question, framed around *us* in light of Brian's plans for Sri. However, the subject isn't raised and for some strange quirk of notion, Mathew can't decide, if that's good or bad.

In the luxury of the silver Phantom, Brian ensures a chilled bottle of Moët accompanies them. 'Great way to celebrate a memorable few day with wonderful people.' Sri leans over and kisses him; Mathew notes tears of happiness, failing to spot Heidi's building behind the wall of determination. At the airport, Brian asks the driver to wait and convey the girls to their home, slipping a handful of American dollars, to consummate the arrangement.

Mathew's farewell with Heidi is particularly emotional; the dam wall fails. 'Sorry, I tried to hold it in and let go when you go. I truly will miss you. This is not pillow talk. This is you and me and the way I feel about you. If only we had that lifestyle time. I want you to know and I say it in front of all my gods, I have never held a man in my heart.'

Mathew is lost for meaningful words, caught in an unusual emotional juxtaposition of wanting to say more, yet fearful of what the future may be and where it can possibly lead, yet as always, he appreciates time will tell and the inkling is about to become an itch.

'Mathew, you are far away.'

'Yes.'
'You all right?'
'Yes, I'm fine.'
'Remember when you quoted Shakespeare?'
'Yes.'
'Do you know "Let me not to the marriage of true minds?'
'Yes, a favourite.'
'Then I have a task for you on the way home. Carefully recall the poem, study its meaning and ask yourself the last two lines. Goodbye, Mathew. Stay safe.' She turns and walks away without looking back.

CHAPTER 29

After the hostess collected the dinner trays, Brian asks quietly, 'Couple of wonderful days. Tell me how you arranged it.'

Mathew explains Heidi was the femme fatale on the previous trip and how he'd declined an opportunity. 'She must have been impressed by the manner of the refusal, agreeing if I returned, we'd meet again.'

'Her name is Indonesian, her mother of Chinese and Indonesian blood, her father from Hong Kong. After the drama of the rule of law of Sukarno – or was it Suharto? – intending to disenfranchise the Chinese, the family moved back to Hong Kong. Interesting are the backgrounds of people when you go searching. What did you discover about Heidi?'

Mathew sits, stunned. 'Nothing.'

'Really? I'm surprised.' He looks purposely at Mathew. 'Not for me to say, but she's in love. Sri and I both noted deep and meaningful looks and how silly, I assumed you'd have gone exploring the soul as well as the heart.

Brian judges he has said enough and returns to his magazine, while Mathew, disturbed and distraught, stirred by the niggle, struggles to wrap his head around the potential women in his life. *Firstly, Milly. And putting it crudely as I've always acknowledged, it's business and sex that works both ways. We'll always have fun, never an item. Then there's Min Xie, who's no longer my Min Xie. Whilst I loved her so, as time moves on, I've had to query my commitment to her. Was it love or ego that's broken my heart or my self-centeredness and self-importance? Or was I just seeking security for her age? In the meantime, she'd have the sex and golf to love. I'm becoming quite cynical, yet look at the ring. Truth be told! How about Mandy, no doubt a special lady? And we'll get it together on the Rhine but what are her demons? If she cannot exercise them, I'm not into long-term therapy. Finally, Heidi. Is the attraction because I implant Min Xie, change one Chinese chick for another? Yet Heidi is of the pillow world. So, what's the difference between having lots of lovers and being previously married? It's only bloody sex after all. Still, the thing that fascinates me is her brain, an unusual intelligence and while I'm at it, let's see if I can rise to meet her challenge.*

Delving into his Shakespeare memory bank, Mathew retrieves the poem and quickly runs the first few lines through his head. 'Let me not to the marriage of true minds / Admit impediments. Love is not love / Which alters when alteration finds / Or bends from remover to remove.' *What is Bill saying? Firstly, marriage must be of true minds, people thus committed to each other, bound by commonality the material binding being love with common interests, meaning they must be true friends. Secondly, there can be no cause to alter the relationship. It cannot change when one is unfaithful.*

Mathew repeats the first four lines; confirming his grasp of the writer's intention and content, he moves on. *'O no! it is an ever-fixed mark / That looks on tempests and is never shaken; / It is the star to every wand'ring bark, / Whose worth's unknown, although his height be taken.* I've known these words for years but analysing them makes me wonder at the true genius who can phrase meanings out of such simple words. Love is like maybe a lighthouse, a beacon in the dark standing strong against any storm and which every sailor can identify and steer by, yes, showing them the way in other words. Seems logical. I like that. But what does the last line mean? 'Whose worth's unknown' taken literally isn't wise when contemplating Shakespeare. Can it simply be that the lighthouse or beacon has no value because it is too important, like some priceless antique? Logical, but 'his height be taken' has lost me.*

Again, Mathew repeats the lines and reassesses his conclusions, resulting in being concerned only about line four and whether he's missed a clue, and there is in fact another answer; if so, he admits he might have failed the test.

Love's not Time's fool, though rosy lips and cheeks / Within his bending sickle's compass come; / Love alters not with his brief hours and weeks, / But bears it out even to the edge of doom. I love the way he uses the words sickles compass come. It's almost bloody majestic, concluding with the power word doom, such a strong word that brings forth all that it encompasses and what we may conjure up doom means to the individual. So again, where are we at? The first line reads like love is not a game, a sport, if you will. Yes, I can accept that, but the rest does not make sense in my brain as I'm damned if I can understand it except it may relate around the use of the word sickle. What is a sickle?

A cutting tool, no more a slashing implement like a scythe but shorter. Anyway, it cuts through those who make love a sport, maybe like cutting them down to size. Hmm, not sure. The rest seems simple. Love lasts longer than hours or weeks and will survive even when tested by the edge of doom or death.

'If this be error and upon me prov'd, / I never writ, nor no man ever lov'd.' Always enjoyed the ending. It's like asking how many grains of sand are there on a beach and then answering with some ridiculous quotation like 20,700,013,474,601 grains. Who's to bloody question the answer? No wonder the man's a genius. 'If this be error and upon me prov'd', you have to love it. And the final line is the icing on his cake.

My answer is this. Love is commonality and friendship binds. It is something to steer by so one becomes lost and finally, it's no game, the key is and I cannot prove what is purported. I know Shakespeare did in fact, write and men have loved and will love in perpetuity – no, in eternity. I like that and she will too. So, if Heidi is contending, we have commonality and friendship, that may be correct. Yet still, we need time. If we can establish the first, the second will keep us on track. Both combined, mean we are not playing a game, it is for keeps and maybe that is the point of Heidi. She wants this to be for keeps.

Then the penny drops. *She is serious. She must be to be so calculating to make me analyse her motives.* Laughing softly, he acknowledges, *this isn't about me at all. It's about her. What a girl!*

Slowly, he sinks back into the luxury of the business-class armchair, brings one shoeless foot under his thigh and dwells on the task, mistakenly assuming it's about him. He shakes his head in admiration, recognising the inventiveness of her brain, trying to reconcile it with her being a working girl of the night.

CHAPTER 30

Steve welcomes Mathew's return with a pot of brewed coffee and cinnamon doughnuts; Mary pops in to say hi, staying to talk briefly about her favourite destination. An unmistakable element of joy pervades the office; contracts have been signed for the sale of two units at Adderley Street. Mathew, inspired, brings Steve up-to-date with the meetings in Hong Kong, telling a small tale by elaborating on 'meetings' as Steve has to know they were working, not romping naked in the South China Sea with two stunning Chinese mermaids. Conceding he's told a fib in Hong Kong, he now discloses to Steve, 'I suggested we'd already selected several suitable towns. Let's get at it before I'm sprung.'

After a general discussion on the proposed project criteria and location preferences, Steve rescues a state map from a cluttered cupboard. Carefully, they circle what is reasonably assumed will be around ninety minutes driving time from the CBD. The advent of freeways, strategically places some towns well outside the circle, making them geographically possible, while some slip out of contention due to the mandated ninety-minute rule. Beach areas are discounted due to the high cost of acreage; clearly, low-cost land a priority. The value of end sale prices must be deemed good value to Mr. and Mrs. Average, who will blend location with medical infrastructure and lifestyle opportunities, all vital, when enticing the end user, to consider relocating to a country town.

Steve advocates freeways allow an extension past Warragul on Highway 1, possibly down to Trafalgar and along the Hume Freeway extending to Euroa or Nagambie up the Goulburn Highway; Mathew questions their medical infrastructure. Heathcote is featured on the list; Mathew's recollections recall momentarily Min Xie's brilliant eighteen holes and his back nine at the local golf club. On the Calder Highway, the line is drawn at Ravenswood, whereas the Ballarat Bypass allows consideration west of the city but Mathew isn't convinced. The city contains great infrastructure and the Creswick redevelopment is only thirteen kilometres north; he weighs up, if it's competition or opportunity. The Geelong freeway offers opportunity to bring Inverleigh and Winchelsea into play, prompting Steve to offer, 'Can't be long before the government will be forced to build the Geelong bypass, so this area has a strong long-term future.'

As a result of the meeting, Mathew calls Milly and arranges for coffee in her apartment. Mathew's next call is to bright and cheery Mandy. 'Brian's positive about the trip. You made the rave review section of dispatches. Did you get him rubbed and tugged the whole few days?' She laughs. Mathew assesses the need to be careful, knowing sooner or later, if Brian proceeds with Sri, Mandy will find out.

Milly's feet are bare, the halter top tight and the simple short floral dress implies casual clothes day. 'No appointments, no need to dress up, not going anywhere and besides, I thought you'd enjoy my long legs.' She lifts the dress to the top of her thighs and Mathew collapses on the couch, laughing loudly.

'I never anticipated you'd wear it like that.'

'I let my imagination run wild and decided you'd appreciate the location.'

'Correct, but originally, I thought it was a classy item for a classy sheila.'

'And I wanted to thank the man in an appropriate manner.' She unties the Hermes scarf, takes two steps and squats on the floor in front of him with her arms out. 'I missed you, Mathew, just for those few days. Did you meet an Asian butterfly?' Before he can reply, she envelopes his lips; whilst he has no intention of offering a reply, the kiss renders it impossible.

Passion is pursued as she licks around his neck and then his weak spot, ears; groaning, he recognises he gives off signals too.

'I need sex. I want to feel it in me.' She sucks his ears as he gasps for breath.

Taking his hand, she heads to the bedroom, where the bed's been folded back and Mathew acknowledges, somewhat whimsically, how easy am I, sorry Heidi.

Milly and May have been communicating; golf day arrangements are made. Mathew realises he's been sprung. May obviously knows Milly did not go back to Hong Kong.

Mathew imposes on Milly to participate in the devious game he intends to play, which has sprung forth like winter grass after an autumn rain. 'I want to make someone jealous.' As he elaborates on the sting up his sleeve.

Milly bangs the bed with her hand and laughs continuously. 'God, who is she, can we pull it off?'

'An ex. I'm being silly. She has a new man who is short, round, not much hair and besides, you are the opposite of her.'

CHAPTER 31

THE GOLF DAY ARRIVES CLEAR but cold; an early winter blast has arrived from the Antarctic. The masochists rug up accordingly to battle the elements, as well as their psyche. The weather is unceasing, unleashing a wild wind which prevents decent scoring, the top just thirty-seven points by Greg Patterson; as such, many egos are bruised. This has become a day in the Chinese community to be seen wagging one's Pekinese tail.

Mathew discretely points out Min Xie, who notices them approaching the pro shop as she heads to the practice fairway. The glance confirms she has stared at Milly, who cuts quite a figure in tight pink slacks matched with a clingy top presenting her breasts for all to see as her lumpy woolen cardigan remains unbuttoned. Mathew notices several other guys and girls admiring or regretting the view, but only Michael Ong and Harry Yao have the balls to invent an excuse to chat her up; Mathew's ego expands as she greets the boys with will and wish. It is only much later, it becomes self-evident, Harry's will successfully met her wanton wish. Beneath the bravado, Mathew's gut churns as he recaptures Min Xie's beauty back onto his eyelid and into his heart as the old saying reverberates. 'Flat arse, small tits and no waist.' Still, in this weather, except for Milly, who knows who has what?

It's like old friends' week – Mathew, Steve and May. Only one person is missing; regardless, the inclusion of Janet does little to dampen their fun and the intention of the pairing, to beat each other up, mercilessly.

Back in the clubhouse, Milly and her friends join them They've had a good day, quite pleased with themselves and likely to win a ball in the competition. Mathew caught Min Xie several times as the crowd ebbs and flows like the tide, but like a wary crab, she scurried to dodge direct confrontation with the circling aggressor. Milly's arm holding incites Janet to wink at May, who in turn surreptitiously shrugs, which encourages a grin from Mathew.

After the presentations, May introduces Dulcy Bright, who represents the charity. Previous golf days have raised considerable amounts of money; today, in total contrast, produces not one donation. However, as Dulcy concludes, Milly brazenly takes to the little stage, commands the microphone, introduces herself and provides a quick, precise explanation on what she does for a living, elaborating on her association with Mathew Allen. Then adds she'll donate to the charity 1 per cent of the value of any investment, in any property and to kick it off, she presents Dulcy with a cheque for $1,000. As Mathew has anticipated, the manoeuvre causes considerable comment; several people seek business cards or confirm the association.

'Might one of these properties suit James and I?'

'Yes, Janet, the Adderley Street project might just be the go.'

'Can I deal directly with you but the charity receives the 1 per cent?'

'Only for you, Janet.'

'Thanks. I'll talk to James again and really, that's all we do, then procrastinate.'

'That's typical. We're all too busy at times to attend to the essentials. If it helps, I'll make a house call after hours.'

'Oh, that'd be great. Time is one of James' enemies.'

'By the way, Janet, I haven't seen Min Xie today.'

'She's here. I'll go find her.'

Mathew winks at Milly. 'I just made you a commission. I'll sell Janet and her husband a unit in Adderley, the deal will go through you and we'll split the commission, which we can argue about later.'

'No, mate, we'll never argue and I've made an appointment of my own for tomorrow with a hottie. Ah, you are so smart to think of this. You are really very clever and I can see your ex coming.' She stands on tiptoes, kicks a leg back and kisses him, infusing the killer grin whilst holding an arm tightly.

Min Xie appears to be in a sour mood and Mathew, not waiting for the niceties, gets stuck right in. 'Didn't play well today, Min Xie? May I introduce Milly Cheong.'

Milly presents her best smile and extends her hand, Min Xie accepts the gesture with a feeble grin. 'I thought, Min Xie, your doctor friend might have volunteered a generous donation. Regrettably, I understand he even fails to pay May the compliment of attending. I recall the glee that overcame you while explaining the man's wealth, all that weekly spendable income.' He intends to kick her in the guts and stick it up the lousy bastard, to make her look so small, she'll have to tell him what's been said, in front of her friends. This is a game Mathew loves; it's called revenge and he plans to be a real prick.

Min Xie appears ready to suffer apoplexy, turning an unhealthy shade of red and Mathew reckons the colour doesn't suit her. Like a fish with communication failure, she opens and shuts her mouth, while Mathew maintains that schoolmaster look of 'no comprehension, Your Honour,' then empties the other barrel.

'We're gratified by Milly's gift. Have you kicked into the pot yet?'

Milly smiles effusively; embarrassed, Min Xie hangs withering on the vine like a missed grape as her friend's gasp at the scene. Turning, she storms out; Mathew follows, they merge at the door and he gives her the planned final shot. 'Tell that miserable little man of yours, if he has a cheque book, I challenge him to bring it in August. Let's assess the size of the person or his inferiority complex, Min Xie.'

Not hesitating nor looking back, she stomps the steps in anger.

He lies blatantly, 'I truly tried, Janet. What did I say to bringing that on? We're best friends, old golfing mates, you heard me? Just stirring the pot. You know the fun we used to have, putting it on each other on the golf course.'

'I have no idea, Mathew. Never seen Min Xie like this. I tell you; she has been quite strange lately. Excuse me, I'll try to catch her at the car.'

Milly, unconcerned at the challenging confrontation, winks and recovers ownership of his arm; she smiles at the milling group, conveying all's well.

Hurrying out to the car park, Janet reflects on how strange the confrontation, she's always been under the impression Mathew is burdened by lust for Min Xie and she for him, particularly after the separation. *I must have a deep and meaningful chat with May. We are of like mind and it doesn't compute. Min Xie was rude, yet Mathew merciless.*

Inside, Dulcy and May join the congregation as Janet reappears, waving her shoulders at Mathew, indicating failure, whereas he understands to the contrary, it was a resounding bloody success. Mathew makes a mental note to call May, ensuring the next golf day is before he heads to Europe. The ulterior motive is undeniable; she'll gossip the news with Min Xie.

CHAPTER 32

Janet telephones Spot on at nine o'clock. 'Morning, Mathew. I enjoyed the game yesterday. James has agreed to meet and while he's hot, I'd like to strike. Any chance you could come over tonight, although the weather forecast is nasty?'

'You're already in the diary. Friends' business is more important than being out in the elements.'

Lunchtime creeps around; he retreats to the kitchen and knocks up a salmon sandwich, adding a lettuce leaf, carrot shavings and beetroot and smothering the lot in mayo. Then he proceeds to annoy the kids, who beg off with recurrently repeated excuses. *Oh well,* he figures, *one day they'll find time for me.* He reflects on the words of the song 'I Want to Be Just Like You Dad' and on his dad but not in a manner he'd particularly want his kids to think of him. Then he regrets the recrimination, against a man who gave his best as he understands it to mean and that people are shaped by their own personal environment. His father came from a different time, a difficult set of diverse circumstances, that evoked a snapshot portrait of his tough life, but Mathew declines the invitation to meditate. The phone rudely interrupts, *We'll catch up soon, Dad... yeah... great.* The voice is professional and precise; Mathew senses Milly is in the presence of her client. 'Is unit eleven at Adderley still available, please?'

Mathew confirms and she replies, 'Thanks. Can you enlighten me about the latest projected completion date?'

He did.

'Perfect. Might I offer a furniture package to an owner occupier?'

'You can.' Mathew appreciates the unseen smile.

'Oh, that's good news. I'd indicated not.'

Mathew smiles and thinks, *Yeah, bullshit, take it away, then give it back equals gaining brownie points.*

'Can you fax the package schedule with the appropriate cost?'

'Now?'

'Yes to 77614099.'

'It's on the way.'

'Hold, please.'

He hears muffled talking in the background.

'Mathew, please hold eleven until the contract is signed tonight.'

Now he smiles. Mathew recalls *'In delay there lies no plenty'* and telephones Mandy, advising of the sale, relating the story of the offer made just yesterday after golf and how she threw in a grand of her own money. Knowing the tale will be immediately transmitted to Brian, he suggests, *Might* be nice to kick back her donation,' then concludes, 'by asking if she fancies a pizza and a beer after work tomorrow night.'

'Too right, chill the beer. See you around six thirty. Hooroo.'

I like this girl – no sex, no pressure, just friends – and will Europe change that? I hope not as I have a warm and fuzzy feeling about our friendship, kind of like the way I feel about Jenny, May and Milly without the rumpy pumpy.

The disc plays a favourite from Andrew Lloyd Webber as David Essex belts out 'Oh What a Circus'. Mathew, as he does with all of Webber's work, marvels at the lyrics. *Writers are like poets with the way they use language to tell the story, in this case the death of Eva Peron.* He whistles along in delight as the car purrs along the main road, the windscreen wipers swishing to the beat while the tyres harmonise on the wet road.

The sale Mathew concludes that night is based purely on trust; his confidence in explaining the project and the specific investment opportunity relate to their individual desires and ambitions, carries the day. James, being the man, he is, left it too Janet as she's driving the strategy and he follows the simple philosophy 'If she's happy, so am I.' And Mathew garners the feeling, this is a marriage made in heaven.

Anxious to convey the news, he calls Mandy first thing in the morning. 'Can you pop a sold sign on unit twelve? I signed the deal last night. It's another Milly sale. I put it together while she attended to unit eleven. I'll give you the contract notes tonight.'

'Have the full deposits been paid?'
'All locked and loaded.'
'Is this another golf sale?'
'Spot on.'
'She just gave them a spiel and in forty-eight hours, two sales in the bag?'
'Bloody good, hey?'
'Too right, I shouldn't have been a doubter.'

CHAPTER 33

If knowledge of Min Xie's reaction had been known, Mathew's arrogance would have accelerated to even dizzier heights. The state of her fury is such she stalks the house and halls in a demented tantrum of temper and torment. Driven by unimpeachable jealousy, she unequivocally admits her eternal love for Mathew and what he's bought to her life. Verbally, she lashes Vincent, venting her selfish spleen, spilling it over him like a bowl of soup in a silly slapstick comedy. Her barrage unceasing, persistent and humiliating, hastily, he inherits her anger, cognisant of Mathew's comments. The vile put-down in front of Min Xie and her friends, coupled with the brutish personal challenge, hits home. He grasps that Mathew has upstaged him, like he after Australia Day; for the first time, they go to bed silent and sulky with each other.

During the next three months, they will argue often over the amount of the planned donation. His anger, like a times table, multiplies. The humbling indignity of the humiliation gnaws infuriatingly at his vanity, replicating an aggressive tumor enlarging and expanding, encompassing daily contemplations of squirreled-away savings being pillaged and plundered. The benefaction a tax deduction isn't pertinent, rather the depletion of cash savings, set aside for any emergency but Min Xie has become the exigency, with maintenance running out of control. The debits cause consternation; the ring worth over $35,000 and the Maurice Lacroix watch, the diamond-studded bracelet and the diamond pendant add another $18,000. Now she's illustrating the notion of a new car, painting by patent purpose the deficiencies in hers, directing his attention to the Audi convertible and 'Ooh, aah, look at that Mercedes!' Without debate, Vincent is cognisant of the simple fact, it's his own fault, splurging in recognition of sex not previously experienced, translating logically into the credit. Lurking in dark recesses of meditations, he is mindful of Min Xie's whorish habits, accepting the truth of the matter about his own little Willy, haunted that the 'Barbarian bastard,' would have proprietary over one more ample to please his Princess. He falls asleep in the totality of the trauma, unsure about her degree of satisfaction.

Milly and Mathew meet at Steve's office and together with Mary, prepare a list of major infrastructure items, priorities to the Trilogy plan. Inventories of towns under consideration are separated by headings 'The Possibles' and 'The Probables'. Mathew fetches the classifications from his cricket years. To play country week cricket, the local association nominated two teams, from which the final squad was selected. He smiled at his youth in crises, not managing the possibles, let alone the probables – another failure in Father's eyes.

Mathew dedicates the day to following up with his consultants, talking through issues in relation to each project and walks away pleased, each problem addressed; clearly, it appears to be all plain sailing, that is, if one can ever say that where projects involving planning and construction are involved. At the same time, he alerts Tony and Nigel he's in the market for several hundred acres of land, within two hours of Melbourne but not in beach areas. He specifies four priorities: close to a town with major infrastructures present, the site relatively flat, the provision of services available or at least able to be provided in one form or another, and finally, if possible, sand a natural soil base.

Surveyors and town planners as well as estate agents remain a resource not to be overlooked, so he faxes his preferred agents and a select group of favoured professionals the priority list. Then recognising to trawl for such a specific catch, he'll be wise to use a shotgun, not a rifle. He refers to his industry diary, loads birdshot and faxes all the surveyors and agents in and around the selected towns.

Settling back into his favourite position, he reads an email from Heidi and receives a wakeup call; she's put out, deliberately referring to Brian's persistent contact with Sri, including loving lengthy telephone calls, whereas she's only received one communication from tardy Mathew. Occurrence hits home, being of the understanding, absence does not make the heart grow fonder; however, twinges of remorse and regret, add comfort to a smidge of betrayal to the honesty she's portrayed. Intent on rectifying the unthinking mistake and accepting the error of his ways, he replies, 'Apologies, Heidi. Went straight from the flight to two appointments and have not stopped since. How are you? I think of you often and would love to spend quality time with you but no news of any trips to Hong Kong unfortunately. Miss seeing you. Please stay safe. By the way, I completed your task and finally grasped it was about you, not me. Very clever, Heidi. I respect your incisive, clever brain and again, accept my apologies for not being in contact. I truly regret my insensitivity.' He pushes Send, acknowledging what a bunch of supercilious crap it is.

But it is her response that shakes him to the core. 'Correct re the task. Yes, I thought you might understand me more if you extricated key elements from the poem. Can you be precise with your thoughts? By the way, you did not say the love word like Brian to Sri. Why? Do you not love me? You need to know more about me? There is much you need to know. From our time together, we have communicated little and I want to know more about you. I am part Vietnamese. I am really not Chinese, only in part, as my grandfather came from a village west of Kunming on the Yuan Chiang River and my father Dutch and my mother half-half, but she died early. I remember he cried and took me to Hong Kong. I am the youngest, an accidental baby. I am going back to Vietnam in July to see my siblings. Can you meet me in Saigon – oops, Ho Chi Minh City? I need to see you, Mathew. I miss you so.'

Mathew rereads the message and thinks about escaping from Melbourne's winter for a few days and without thinking any further, types out his response. A tremor of excitement rushes up his spine; the pixels accumulate and complete the picture in his head. 'Would love to meet you in HCM City. But I have to ensure plans do not clash with Keng's arrival and none are yet in place. Cannot talk of love until we meet again but I can safely say you are the most beautiful lady I have ever met. I love your intelligence and respect the person.' Heidi reminds him he hasn't answered her question re the poem, so Mathew writes it out exactly the way he has completed the task, believing this will give her something to chew on for a while. Wrong! Another email arrives. 'Exactly as you say, but the bit you do not understand is, the star to every wandering bark, refers to the polar star by which sailors once navigated by, therefore, love is a similar guide. His height be taken refers to him taking the high moral ground in the pursuit of love and happiness. I hope you enjoyed the game. We must do it again; it stimulated my fading literature lessons.'

Mathew gazes out to the west, noting nothing in particular, lost in the fantasy forming of the unique and unusual Heidi, who circumnavigates his mental equator and although he's not properly caught on, his heart.

Mandy arrives with dinner in the typical box and consistent with the casual nature of the meal, they half-sit and lie amidst the cushions on the couch with the friendly fire glowing. They play the normal Mathew and Mandy game of kissing, cuddling and caressing. Occasionally, Heidi pops into his head, appearing on his eyelids, extending a warning. *I am watching you.* It stirs notions of being unfaithful; he wonders why, yet declines to pursue the inkling, too nebulous, too fraught with uncertainty about where it may lead. And maybe that's the real problem.

CHAPTER 34

During the next two months, Mathew spends considerable time in the car with either Steve or Milly or both. From their travels, the possibles and the probables are reduced to a team of three, the Heathcote-Seymour-Kyneton triangle, drawing a circle around Warragul and Buninyong south of Ballarat and their immediate environs. These are the number one preference, but confusingly, on the periphery, several other towns incur sufficient pluses, ensuring if a property emerges on the horizon, it will at least rate an inspection. They include Alexandra, the Korumburra/Leongatha line and the Leigh River between Inverleigh and Winchelsea.

Frustration festers. Property investigations are often followed by an inspection, ultimately uncovering sufficient negatives to cease the pursuit. Inspiration comes from Ian, Mathew's golf club mate, who suggests, without impinging on his privacy relationship, a client is grappling with a serious smidge of financial bother. Its resolution may require disposing of a large property-owning frontage to the Latrobe River, just north of Moe. Knowing the town lies equidistant between Warragul and Morwell, which in all intents and purpose meets prime criteria, Mathew's property antenna goes up. The area incorporates an extensive population to draw on for green-fee-paying golfers to assist in the subsidy of the course and is sufficiently close to attract players from the south-east of Melbourne to pay and play. Infrastructure is unrivalled, access to the city ideal, medical facilities first class and the river frontage opportune. Mathew wants to conduct a private reconnoiter, before annoying others; it becomes incumbent on Ian to arrange it with his client.

Barry Lynton guides them around the property in his four-wheel drive. It's hardly necessary; Mathew is enamored as they crest a small rise and Ian points out, 'That's it from the major corner post' – he indicates off to the right – 'way out to the line of trees flanking the river and north to that pretty little ridge.'

Mathew is blown away by the beauty of the place – the gentle rolling slopes and the imposing stands of gums, make dramatic statements in select paddocks, then stringing off to join another copse, forming wind breaks and natural subdivisions. Even the name instils inspiration, Lynton Lea. Mathew imagines it spread across a marketing brochure featuring a photo of a giant ghost gum and a stunning Cootamundra wattle, whilst the grass is glossy green and the sky a brilliant blue, heightening the contrast so typically Australian. Along the river, a proliferation of various native tree types harbour a variety of birdlife, particularly amidst one extensive area of native bush, extending from the river towards the road to the north.

'My contribution to the way it was.' Barry explains. The remnant vegetation of some fifteen hectares remains home to a small mob of wallabies, a family of wombats, lots of bushy-tailed possums and all the native indigenous trees owning home to this environment. And at least twice, sometimes three times, a year, it is visited by the odd koala. 'You'll note lots of manna gums. I've kept planting them to encourage the furry little beauties.'

'Yeah and pity our useless Council's don't plant them, anyway how about birdlife varieties?'

'When I was a kid, my dad kept records, written down in a tattered old exercise book. Fifty-eight different sightings, but today we are missing snipe, quail and the robin redbreasts. I loved to see them on a cold, crisp winter morn lining the fence. It was as if they warmed my heart. The skylarks have also disappeared whilst the ground larks are becoming scarce, together with the bronzewing's. Even the starlings that used to flock up like huge black clouds now number dozens, not thousands. The world's changing, bit bloody crook mate. I think we've cocked it up.'

Mathew's into planning mode, envisaging green grassy fairways sweeping around the bush, running adjacent to the magnificent gums that stands out in the paddocks, serving as preservation nodes and along the riverfront, to buffer the banks. He's enraptured; it is difficult to contain his excitement as he's already determined, if an application for Trilogy can be successfully prosecuted, the result will create a profitable project.

Driving back to the city, part one of the journey revolves invariably around the property and Ian conveys vital news; Barry's given permission to disclose his fiscal position if it moves Mathew towards a decision. Ian unveils the story which comes out like an Irish rug. 'He's under pressure, but he isn't.'

Mathew reckons Ian is unrolling the rug in chapters like a granny's colourful patchwork quilt, so he goes in search of clarification and Ian replies, 'It isn't critical.' Recognising the Irish, Mathew pushes for more elaboration and Ian complies, without breaking client privilege; the prime option at Barry's disposal, a deal involving Mathew, will bring more dollars to his customer's poor box, rather than one conducted in the open market. Conversation ranges and Ian perceives Mathew isn't going to say too much, so he decides it's time to change the subject as he has always sought to. 'How did you arrive at the decision to split, from what appeared to us, to be a happy marriage?'

'Wasn't easy, but I'll tell you and only you, sex became the motivation rightly or wrongly. Hope and I enjoyed a steady, comfortable relationship without any physical closeness, then I had an affair and came to the conclusion, I wanted more from my life.'

Ian is jolted by the casual manner in which his friend tells it so openly, yet it's the affair that shakes him. 'Hope took it well?'

'The affair she knew nothing about. Separation came as a surprise, but it wasn't, if can you grasp the contradiction. We'd talked about separation before but I didn't pursue it. Finally, I realised time is running out, my life clock ticking furiously and as I'm all right financially, I can leave her comfortable and secure, so I went.'

'I want to split too, but I haven't the courage.' He let it hang; so did Mathew. Eventually, Ian asks, 'What do I do first?'

'Are you totally committed?'

'Yes.'

'Another woman?'

Ian looks at Mathew and laughs. 'Don't be silly, mate. I'd not be that lucky.'

'How will the kids take it?' Private previous conflicts reignite. Mathew knows the questions to ask, the buttons to push and as the kilometres mount, so does Ian's resolution.

'I'll do it like you, find a pad and rent while the dust settles. Can you not mention this at the club?'

Steve and Milly agree to accompany Mathew to Moe on Friday. The week progresses slowly; anxiety prevails as the concept rolls around in his head, together with amateurish project planning. He is overridden by fears of being gazumped, as he understands the property and the position, are indeed perfect. Concern mounts, all the green lights flicker in his brain and the neon light blinks boldly. 'This is it!'

Mathew elects not to make comment, seeking instead their reaction without influence or duress; he bites his tongue as they turn into the long driveway, highlighted by a white painted fence surrounding a line of trees, one evergreen, one deciduous at the moment, bare and stark; he notices the grass under the trees has been neatly cut. Upon capturing first sight of the old Australiana house, Milly exclaims, 'Isn't this terrific? Can you imagine the driveway in spring? Do you realise they are flowering pears?'

'Quite, and can you imagine it in autumn?'

After the tour, guided by Barry, they return to the house; Barry's lady friend Emily is in the kitchen. The aroma reminds Mathew of his mum's and grandmother's bakehouse. 'We miss so much these days. Poor, bloody kids living life without ever taking in the aroma of a nana's kitchen.'

'I've knocked up scones. Have a cuppa before you go?'

They readily agree, recognising a demanding lady when they hear one. However, like the book and the cover, Emily not only turns out to be a great cook but also comes enshrouded with a vibrant personality. Within the elapsed time to drink the tea and devour two cheese scones, they have heard her life story. 'Born and bred in Hinnomunjie.' And when queried where's that, the reply is as if you should know. 'Just north of Omeo, mate.' The story encapsulates school in the bush, high school in Omeo, the tough life and the disastrous bushfires that drove her dad off the land and into Dandenong to find work in the car industry. She married a bastard who'd get pissed and bash her and the two kids, so she disappeared firstly up to Wandiligong and then down to Poowong, finding work in the cheese factory, eventually meeting Barry at the local show.

'I have a weak spot for fairy floss. Guess who was making it.' Barry expresses the moment with a bright smile, winking deliberately at Emily, who rightly winks back.

Steve offers purposely, 'That's it, mates. You happy, Milly?'

'Love it, but you, Mathew, you've been like Steve. Very private?'

'Reckoned it was right the moment I drove in the gate and as Barry drove us around, the more it stirred my imagination. I can hardly contain my excitement and I venture Cashmore will love it too.'

A game plan develops. Mathew is to suss out more information about the financial set-up and construct an offer sufficient to wet Barry's dry pocket. Once an acquisition plan is established, it will be incumbent on Mathew to conduct Brian and maybe Mandy to the property. Mathew worries about his car's doing so many k's. Should he trade it? No, silly move. He loves it too much, so he ponders buying a runabout, one of those awful four-wheel-drive truck things with bull bars so he can be aggressive, but the notion slips straight into the too-hard basket.

Mathew forwards a pertinent, straight-to-the-point email to Keng. 'We are finally investigating a property which meets priorities. More information to follow.' He knows Milly will be in contact, so he doesn't see any merit in repeating what she'll undoubtedly pass on, particularly as her digital camera was active throughout the tour.

At golf on Wednesday, Mathew unloads part of his strategy on a need-to-know basis, confirming details are to remain in house, not conveyed to Barry, and Ian confirms the asking price is $2.8 million. Mathew, anxious to move this deal acts creatively and suggests three million, subject to a permit within six months, figuring time is marginally more important than price. After a short consideration period encompassing four golf holes, Ian offers a compromise engendering an interesting twist, proposing the additional two hundred thousand be paid directly to Barry and two holes later adds, 'I'm not talking about out of school, Shifty. My client's in a bit of bother and a personal friend's pursuing a property and I'd like to help them both. The two hundred thousand will allow him to contain the financial pressure whilst you proceed the application. It's hurt money but if your planners are up to the job, they should be able to determine, whether council will support the application. Barry's immediate need is cash, not a huge sale price. You know as well as we do, if he chases a sale in the marketplace, a buyer will burn him to obtain a short settlement. So the compromise might be for you guys to punt the cash, plus the costs, in lieu of a price reduction of say $400,000, which acquaints to a real reduction of $200,000 and to me, that's a win-win as you secure the time to plan and run the application.'

To Mathew, this suggests an element of accountancy ingenuity, but he appreciates he'd best be on strong ground before pushing that barrow; the loss of two hundred large, plus costs, will not sit well in many a lap. Although he retains a notion up his slippery sleeve, the final negotiating chip might be to extend part of the payment, even if for twelve months, knowing it will massage the money; in the immediate future, planning becomes the foundation. After much deliberation, Mathew decides to tackle the hurt money issue upfront, rather than inciting excitement and then dropping the hammer. To his surprise, Brian reckons it's a great idea, providing Mathew establishes a direction from the planners and Barry agrees to leave half a million secured by second mortgage, for twelve months interest-free.

By the time Mathew collects Brian and Mandy, he's received no news from Nigel, so he proceeds according to plan, trusting the call will arrive during drive time. Mathew has assumed Brian will sit up front, so before leaving home, he adjusts the rear-vision mirror so he can glance at Mandy; and as if playing the game to perfection, she settles with the short dress shuffled halfway up her thighs. After several sly peeks, Mathew visualises a slight opening of her legs, leaving the aspect more exciting, the thrill of seeing but not quite. *Like a massage*, Mathew reminds himself, *sex when you're not having sex*. At the next glance, she catches his eye and winks and then wrinkles her nose. *She's on to me and it's all a big tease.*

Nigel telephones, full of apologies. Hugh, the chief planner, hasn't been available due to the pressure of debates regarding a controversial commercial rezoning in the town. He's just spoken at length by conference call and the snapshot is, council has expressed a semblance of support, tinged with a brush of dubiety, until an appraisal of the overall concept can be carried out. It will depend, purely on the conceptualisation and planning required to meet standard council policy and that shouldn't be too difficult. Nigel confirms he had a ring around, checking on Hugh and all reports were, he's a straight shooter.

Mathew conducts Brian and Mandy around the property as best as he can; fortunately, it hasn't rained, so he reaches the sections of interest without asking the city folk to walk too far. The tour highlights the river frontage, the copse of trees and of course the bush where Mandy is surprised, sighting several bush wallabies out on the pasture, nibbling peacefully, the fresh winter grass. At the same time, kookaburras sing in the treetops and magpies warble merrily; faintly in the distance, bellbirds tinkle their message, extolling the beauty of the place.

Mandy comments, contrary to her plan, 'It's beautiful, the consummate Australian scene to enrich our appreciation. How lucky are we to have this at our back door?'

Mathew is unable to maintain self-control. 'Like the vision splendid, it's there, yet few notices it.'

Back at the house, taking cursory investigation of the shedding, they walk the perimeter of the rambling Australiana; Mandy spies the group of old rocking chairs on the veranda. 'I can see you, Mathew.'

'Yeah, but can you see who's with me?'

Brian arches an eyebrow and Mathew's unsure if it's in agreement or not, with the flippant comment. Regardless, Mandy doesn't reply. Moving around the corner, with Brian acting as chief Indian and Mandy trailing along at the rear, Mathew discovers two hands rubbing his bum. Pushing into him, she whispers, 'I loved you perving on me.'

Before he can reply, she says, 'Look at the size of this daphne. Must be something else in full bloom.'

On the veranda, they shuffle the rocking chairs, talk about the project plan, consider the price, move the planning forward and debate the consultancy team. 'I'll need to approach Keng in regard to the hurt money but bugger it, for the sake of the punt, we'll commit ourselves if necessary.'

Brian addresses Mandy with a toss of his head. 'You've not said much. Do you have a feel for the place? Anything rattling around in your bones?'

Mathew thinks he made her sound like a witch doctor.

'I intended to play hardball, be Miss Negative, pick the bone, be difficult if you like but I have to tell you I'm blown away. It is just wonderful and as we walked around, with Mathew offering insight into his planning ideas, I visualised the future.'

CHAPTER 35

MATHEW RECEIVES ANOTHER EMAIL FROM Heidi. 'I found this Robert Burns poem. It is how I'd like you to think of me. Am I being over-optimistic?

> O my Love is like a red, red rose
> That's newly sprung in June;
> O my Love is like the melody
> That's sweetly played in tune.
> So fair art thou, my bonnie lass,
> So deep in love am I;
> And I will love thee still, my dear,
> Till a' the seas gang dry.
> Till a' the seas gang dry, my dear,
> And the rocks melt wi' the sun;
> And I will love thee still, my dear,
> While the sands o' life shall run.

And fare thee weel, my only love!
And fare thee weel awhile!
And I will come again, my love,
Though it were ten thousand mile.'

Mathew replies, 'Ironic this is June. You know, I cannot say how deep in love I am but take heart from the notion of your poem and I will come again, yet it will not be ten thousand miles to Ho Chi Minh City.'

Heidi recycles the words twice as is her manner, ensuring to grasp the real intent of the message. *How clever to respond using the text of the poem, and perhaps I'm wrong. Possibly, he does indeed possess a streak of romance coursing through those lustful old veins.*

Mathew maintains the pursuit of properties, recognising additional strings to his bow, will supplement an opportunity if Moe falls over and he's resolute, Keng will acknowledge his diligence, in investigating other opportunities. Then he vacillates, wondering if he's taking the wrong attitude; if Keng believes each week another potential piece of dirt erects a For Sale sign, might he be more difficult to close on Lynton Lea?

Mandy parks regularly in the second slot under his building, delivering dinner in a box or being waited on by 'Chef' Allen. They split a ballsy red, a crisp chardonnay or top a frothy or four, cuddling and kissing but no more. She never asks nor seeks to stay the night. It is, Mathew reckons, an anomalous yet invigorating relationship, extending to gross sensuality as her underlying wantonness and erotic allure at times of close intimate contact, encourages Svengali-type overtones of good, contrasted by dark and evil sexual intent.

Diminishing daylight is not conducive to golf after office hours; time constraints drive Mathew and Mandy to play on Sunday at the Dunes. The wind is at naught, perfect for golf in the Cups Country at Rye and that holds until the fifteenth. They notice the wind picking up and by the time they're heading up the seventeenth, it buffets their clothes, lashing directly in their faces like a gale. 'Bloody hell, where did this come from?'

'Antarctica.'

'Yeah, thought I recognised the waddle from somewhere.'

Later, they share a jumbo-sized mixed seafood platter, peering through the restaurant's streaked windows at the white tops out on the bay, whereas in the Mornington boat harbour, it remains relatively at peace, except for the rain, slashing and sheeting across the dreary wintry scene.

CHAPTER 36

It's the first week of July. In continual electronic contact with Heidi, Mathew appreciates an understanding is developing; he is gratified as it doesn't revolve around sex. It has more to do with relationship building. They discuss poetry, philosophy, current affairs and he arrives at the conclusion, she owns superior intelligence – quick, incisive, able to delve and discern inner truths to casual statements. And that leads him to be circumspect, paying scrupulous attention to the dialogue committed to the electronic paper, as Heidi obviously analyses each email to its core. Often, she'll reply cryptically; and once deciphered, he finds she's analysed his heart and his soul, and that offers pulse to the purpose, making his heart rate beat faster, as he shuffles the pieces in the puzzle.

'I'll meet you in HCM City on the twenty-sixth of July, but I only have seven days. The planning is up to you.' Not fussed or caring about the agenda or itinerary, he only wants to spend time with this fascinating girl.

In the meantime, Milly maintains the sales rate. To celebrate a record month, Mathew decides to escape for a weekend, suggesting, 'It's a surprise. Bring your clubs, bikini and some warm clothes.' She considers the instructions incongruous but agrees to the proposal.

Milly had purchased an apartment, or sub-penthouse as she refers to it, in St Kilda East. It offers an extensive south-westerly view, containing one spacious bedroom with a dining room created by demolishing the stud wall which originally formed the second bedroom; clever Milly instituted an alcove partitioned with Chinese screens, creating the illusion of a separate office. Being an exceptionally neat and tidy person, it works. Mathew knows it wouldn't for him.

At Tullamarine, they catch a Saab turboprop flight to Mildura, collect a rental car and motor to the accommodation units located on the golf course. They play by themselves on Friday and Saturday and on Sunday join in the mixed club competitions. Milly, now owning a handicap at her home club, Eagle Ridge, is anxious to be competitive.

Saturday evening is dark and dreary; Mathew appreciates it will be particularly cold out, so a hot buffet dinner is the way to go with a bottle of Wynns Coonawarra red. Milly has played well and that gives Mathew license to suggest, 'If you're going to take the game seriously, change your club.'

'Where do you suggest?'

'With the holiday house at Rye, you really only have the choice of Sorrento, Portsea, the Dunes or Moonah Links. And if you intend on walking twice a week, in my opinion, they're just too bloody hilly and St Andrews is pay to play and they don't have a clubhouse, so I reckon for you guys have a gander at Rosebud Country Club – two eighteens, nicely undulating, easy to walk, fully licensed, has pokies. It's a fun club which, knowing you and your friends, you'll love. Let's have a hit one day.'

'You're on, but May is on to me to join her friends at Woodlands.'

'Now you're talking. Play twice a week, plus twilight, during daylight savings. And if you want to go to Tootga-bloody-rook, play Saturday morning in the comp and then drive down for R & R. You could even come home Monday morning and have a hit on the way. It's not as if you have office hours anymore.'

Back in Melbourne, Brian works with Mathew to finalise the itinerary for the Rhine trip. Plans are set in place to fly to Vienna for two nights at the end of August and then by bus or train, possibly changing at Linz and onto Regensburg for a one-night stop, boarding the boat the next day to Amsterdam, where only one night is spent before flying out.

Mandy visits for dinner. Mathew grills two salmon steaks with baked spuds in the jacket while the coloured veggies go into the microwave. Dinner is shared with a very cold, crisp Mornington Peninsula white, the balance of which accompanies them to the long couch opposite the fire.

'Getting close, Mathew. I'm excited, only fifty-seven days.'

'Too right, but we have Keng to deal with first. I was surprised he sprung for the hurt money. He must be hot to trot.'

'And business is flying, Milly is incredible, every month four sales on the nose and yesterday she bragged next month, sales will increase to five and they might stay at that rate.

Plus, she's now bought in five sales from the golf day. The two referrals helped though. I thought we were very generous paying her the bonus commission but I saw your point of view.'

Necessity, being the mother of invention, drives Mathew to meet Tony Cashmore for lunch. He selects the Provincial Hotel in Brunswick Street, where without preamble he empties his bucket on the Trilogy concept at Moe. But he soon notices Tony isn't with him and wonders if he's waffled on too much, so he waits and then asks, 'Are you with me?'

Tony smiles broadly. 'No, mate, I'm way bloody ahead of you. What I'm about to tell you must remain in house, okay?'

Mathew readily agrees, unsure of what it might have to do with a major project.

'I have been commissioned to plan, design, construct and market a substantial project in Shenzhen China. I have full license to control the whole shooting works. And my client is close to another project outside Shanghai and I'm in the midst of negotiating another deal, fringe Hanoi. That's the good news. The bad is, what do I do with my team? All my projects locally are complete, so what happens to Warren and Alex? I can't leave them to be snipped by Thomson Wolveridge, my main competitors.'

Mathew soaks it all in, then asks, 'Does this mean you'll move to China?'

'Too right, this is huge for me.'

'What about the language problem?'

'None at all. I have been reading and writing Mandarin for six months, and I'm nearly literate.'

'Are they aware of your plans?'

'Yes, both have been very much involved in the Chinese project and assisted in the draft muddy for Hanoi. The big picture is, I need to be able to use them if anything comes up, on any Aussie projects. Just between us, Warren after his divorce, does not have the money to keep Alex, even part time, while he finishes uni. But if you took them on with your project, we could have a nice trade-off and you know Warren's expertise and they both know Nigel.'

Mathew takes another sip on his red to give his mind a minute to grasp the opportunity, then asks, 'I'll appoint Warren, but I need you to break the ice with council and once we are cosy, Warren can be introduced to run the design etc. with your input.'

'What are you doing after lunch?'

'Going to Preston and Brunswick, assessing two possible development sites.'

'Can you then call into my office? I'll nick back and have a meeting with the boys and be ready for you in, say, an hour and a half?'

'Perfect.'

Tony phones his office and confirms both Warren and Alex will be available to meet; then they elaborate on the business plan including office space, timing, an on-site property inspection and meeting council officers.

'This a lifesaver for me, Mathew. I'd be all sorts of shit if they were snipped by any other design company.'

Wandering around the suburbs gives Mathew time to confirm his spur-of-the-moment decision; he concludes it might be a godsend as Warren comes wrapped in professionalism and great contacts and by all accounts, is easy to work with. Tony has always spoken highly of Alex and the way he combines his role, while completing his university course.

'Moe Mathew, is the purchase incentive a pair of moccasins?'

Mathew appreciates the comment but lets it go as Tony chuckles on and reaches for his glass of red.

'Beautiful Shiraz, must be South Australian?'

'Yeah, direct from Langhorne Creek.'

'Ah, then it's a Bleasdale.'

The red disappears with the sensational porterhouse steaks. 'Great mushy sauce.' Tony licks his lips, Mathew unsure if it suggests relishing the food or the friendly shillyshallying backwards and forwards. 'So, Mathew, we are not here to talk about footy with my mob on the bottom, although with your boys in contention maybe you should pay for lunch!' The grin says it all.

CHAPTER 37

Mathew elects not to annoy Barry with another conducted tour; instead, he acts as a guide walking Nigel and Tony Cashmore around the pertinent bits which he assumes a creative architect will want to savour. After just twenty minutes, Mathew can tell Tony is enraptured, whereas Nigel remains the unemotional professional.

Hugh Martin, council's head planner, introduces his offsider, Jocelyn Brown, a Miss Prim and Bloody Proper, Mathew imagines. Nigel commences the proceedings, elucidating in technical, conceptual terms on the overall proposal, allowing discussions to move in several directions around planning philosophies and general guidelines, which within reason Mathew accepts are resolvable, except for the river and the attendant conservation issues. As planned, this opens the door for Cashmore to ease gently through, espousing and enlightening on his extensive experience at the Heritage project, where he's completing the second course around the

Yarra River. He shoots down nicely and professionally every objection floated by Miss Brown, utilising the Heritage and most particularly the Henly course and the Yarra River interface in nearly every example, throwing in on occasion, as pertinacity dictated, reference to the sand dune preservation program at Thirteenth Beach. His final comment tickles Mathew's sense of Tony's capacity to think outside the square; he offers to conduct both of them over the Henly course, especially the river margins. Agreement is concluded; all preliminary plans are to be run through Hugh directly for comment, which pleases Mathew, eliminating interference by junior planners wanting to stick their inexperienced bibs in. However, it comes with a downside; the scope of the project, Hugh confirms, has to be advertised and that's not negotiable. Mathew stews; advertising increases the scope for objection, allowing individual input or, worse, interference by an organised committee or legal representation and an advantage to promote scare tactics by militant anti-development groups, to muster and motivate forces and by blame and bluster, to divide the community and worse still, the council. In conclusion, Mathew speaks as the proponent, elaborating on what a $50 million development will do for the image and prestige of Hugh's department and the council in general. He demands a time frame and council's unwritten support. He's upfront and adamant. 'We'll simply move to a comparable district and seek another property.' He determines, *I'll not be stuffed around.* Hugh, experienced at the tactics and tantrums of cowboy developers, realises Mathew presents a façade; still, he isn't to be bullied by bluff. Therefore, in a professional manner, he allows the waffle to pass uncontested through to the keeper.

Tony and Nigel commit to meet on the weekend to rough up preliminary mud plans. Mathew calls in on Sunday to offer support and to make the coffee.

'Did you bring any nice iced doughnuts, young Mathew?'

'No, but I take it if I intend to keep you working, I'd best go find some.'

'North up Lygon Street, left-hand side, you can't miss the bakery.'

Mathew returns with a dozen mixed doughnuts and double-shot lattes all round.

Monday's meeting brings conclusion to discussions on the rough first draft master plan sufficient for the purpose of Keng's visit and that leads Mathew to plan the site tour. *Who do I take? Brian yes, Nigel obviously, Tony key, Milly must, Mandy up to Brian. How to transport them as they won't fit into one vehicle unless I hire a minibus? Perfect, another problem solved.*

After meeting Keng at his hotel, Brian and Mathew escort him to a Chinatown dinner, democratically inviting Milly as she remains Miss Vital in the overall relationship. Dinner turns out to be a jovial event; the prospect of this particular property's opportunity encapsulates conversation and Milly proves a worthy choice of companion, interposing interplay, cleverly opening doors into the group and their activities.

Milly goes home by cab, whereas Brian and Mathew drop Keng at the hotel, where politely, Mathew thinks, they walk him into the foyer. Typical of Mathew, if the girls are attractive, he'll spot them; Keng strolls towards the elevator and the two stunners he's noticed, stand seemingly to follow. Brian comments, 'Good girls.'

'Pardon?' Mathew blinks, unsure of what's to come.

'The Hickey twins from the Gold Coast, they'll do anything for a large each. Keng is going to have the time of his life, my son.'

As the cold air of night embraces them, Brian let's go of one of his belly laughs and Mathew joins in. 'You sneaky bastard!'

Keng and Milly meet in the first-floor restaurant for breakfast to confirm the information passed on and for her to provide personal due diligence checks, including details on the Cashmore–Warren Hastings deal that Mathew asked her to explain, again adding to her importance in the overall. Keng acknowledges gratitude for her attention to detail and willingness, to take the often long hard road of discovery. After breakfast, he excuses himself and returns to the suite; it stirs Milly's fertile imagination about why, when they are ready to leave.

Keng sets out to pick their brains on the drive down. However, upon returning, he's more on the predatory prowl, into everyone's ear, seeking clarification or more detailed information, motivated by purpose as once the inspection has been completed, he's inspired at the potential. He pushes the consultants' barrows, ensuing he's as much at the pointy end as they are. Mathew reckons he's taking the opportunity to exert professional intent, letting them know he'll be up their individual noses, ensuring diligence, discovery and oversight, are maintained. In fact, Keng is driven by another aspiration – to impress a young lady whose beauty staggers him to his bachelor's jockeys.

Tony Cashmore proves again he's the key to the lock as he professionally reflects on the environmental issues, town planning aspects, and integration of various nodes of the residential components – all in relation to the golf course layout, the walking tracks and the preservation of Barry's Bush. Keng asks to visit one of Cashmore's projects and this inspires a gambit to pull off a scintillating ploy.

'Oh, Hugh, Tony Cashmore here. Apologies for the very short notice, but I have an international guest I'm taking to the Heritage courses tomorrow. Might you and Miss Brown be available to lunch and tour?' The quick yes signifies more than a chance and Cashmore grasps the significance, Hugh is determination to push the project, rather than a meeting of Browns cows. Realising what he's just said, he glances at Mathew and laughs at the faux pas and then endeavours to explain to Keng the meaning relating to Hugh's assistant. After one try, he quits, but Milly finds the handle and conveys it in their common language.

Mandy arrives late at the apartment for dinner. 'Save the red, mate. Been busy. Shouldn't have wasted the day taking the tour again. I need an early night.' During the quick meal, Mandy pursues all manners of questions relating to the project; Mathew assumes she is just trying to keep up with the goings-on, unapparent she's being clever and cunning, manipulating the conversation. It may well have been Mandy's intent for early night; the message on her phone promotes enquiry, which leads to an offer that she cleverly refused, appreciating the offeree had a determined resolve.

Brian had confided to Mandy, Keng has his own plans for the evening. 'Do you know the Hickey twins, Mathew?'

'No, mate, new to me.'

'Oh. Brian said Keng was going out with the twins as if you would know what that meant.'

Mathew shrugs; regardless, she decides to pop it away in the pending file.

Mathew emails Heidi, confirming his flight on Vietnam Airlines and hotel reservations at the Majestic, an Old-World pub built in the French tradition back in the twenties, which features a rooftop bar overlooking the Sai Gon River. In her instantaneous reply, she seeks to change the reservation to one night and Mathew realises, Heidi has plans.

Tony Cashmore reports, 'Mate, I'm brilliant. What a day. Hugh and Missy respected the design and construct work carried out along the riverbanks. As long as the plan meets their residential guidelines, I can't see any problems, unless a red ragger or an anti-development movement instigates objection trouble.'

Driven by the pressure of time, Cashmore moves his master planning meeting forward and the consultants gather at his office. The agenda is simple – throw enough shit on the wall and some will stick. Attendees are invited to trawl the depths of their imaginations and come up with ideas. Initially, trepidation restricts the banter; confidence soon emerges, often tinged with some hilarity as Nigel, in an innocent manner, suggests a massage centre, meaning therapeutic but

Milly takes it the wrong way and retorts, 'What are you proposing, popping Viagra in the old bloke's porn flakes?' The list soon congests the white board with so much fat flowing that they revert to hunters and aggressively attack each item. The pruned checklist includes matters ranging from the location of residential nodes and the sizes thereof, to ratios relating to the various 'levels' of entry. One debate involves the retention of the old farmhouse and its future use. Milly comes up with the idea of turning it into a local museum, highlighting the pioneering and pastoral past; they take it on board but elect initially to use it as the site office. Mathew determines to lock up the master bedroom and use it as his farm-type getaway; later, in privacy, he throws the thought at Tony, adding, 'I'm practising to get some shit on my boots.' It goes right over his head.

The community centre developed into a multipurpose self-service coffee shop, meeting place, a card and board game area with a small business centre, via bifolding doors, the gym doubled as a floor exercise area, whose flexibility is to be utilised for line and ballroom dancing.

Towards the end of proceedings, Milly laughs. 'You know, once the word of this place gets out, Melbourne will become deserted. All the oldies will be here, having a ball.' She pauses and then suggests, 'This is such beautiful grazing land and from all I've gathered, usage is only going to encompass some 40 to 50 per cent and we have determined some 15 per cent will be set aside for conservation. So as we are developing a haven for oldies, why not establish farm-style accommodation and use rural activities to supplement income, offering city kids the thrill of staying on the land while visiting grandparents and opening accommodation for anyone to stay and play golf, while the kids have a farm-style adventure?'

Nigel shakes his head. 'Bugger it, Milly, I'm the planner. Bloody great idea.'

Brian handles the legal aspects of the purchase, instructing Hugo Swisser, his property solicitor. Mathew slots Ian into the fee structure of 1 per cent under the loose heading 'Consultancy'. When conveyed the news, like that kid and the new toy, Ian says, 'As there is no agent involved, plus I sprung the 200 large that saved Barry's bacon, he loves me and I'm in for 2 per cent.'

'And I love you too, E. Take the bickies and use them for your first overseas sojourn when free and single.'

'We could go together.'

'Why not? Take our clubbies.'

'Another personal question, Mathew. On the weekend we spent with the girls down the Bellarine Peninsula, I was attracted to May. Am I right in recalling she's a widower?'

'Yes, and still single. Want to meet at golf next month?'

'You can spring it?'

Mathew notes, 'Of course.' Then he smiles, thinking May might appreciate E's on the hunt.

'Pull it off and keep the twenty-six large.'

'No, you keep the pin, take May overseas, escape somewhere exciting and discover each other.'

'Really?'

'You have to start thinking differently, take your accountants hat off and forget about bloody debits and credits. Life isn't a balance sheet.'

May answers his telephone call at the first ring.

'Good morning, May. Easy to see you're not busy, picked the phone up too quickly.'

'Ha, you funny man and, how are you?'

Chatting to and fro, deliberately dodging reference to Min Xie, Mathew says, 'Keep your eye on Milly at the presentations. She'll have a donation for the charity.'

May files the information in her golf day memory box and then reckons she's held back sufficiently to engender good manners and empties her bucket. 'And, Mathew, have you heard the scandal Min Xie has bought on herself, stealing Winnie's man? How could she do that to her best friend? I tell you; we are shocked and saddened. Now she brings him to play in our golf day. I ask, who do I partner them with?'

Might my balls be big enough? No, silly move. 'Have you selected a partner for yourself, May?'

'Not really.'

'Do you remember Ian, who played with us at the Bellarine?'

'Yes, very nice man.'

'He'd like to play with you.'

'But he's a married man.'

Mathew stirs the pot. 'No, May, golf!'

The pause is pivotal; she giggles. 'You naughty man, I not take it that way.'

'Maybe you should.'

'You men really are from somewhere else at times. Explanation, please.'

'He's in the process of separating, here's an opportunity for a smart young lady, honourable, professional, comfortable and with a cash flow. Nice catch for the right lady.'

'Hooley dooly, you mean he's attracted to me?'

He grins at the colloquialism. 'Obviously. He asked specifically to be partnered with you.'

'Separating, you say? So, he wants to golf or play?'

'You know the way of the world between man and woman. Man hunts and asks, whether to play is your call.'

There's a momentary pause before the tack changes. 'You and Milly are playing with a Chinese lawyer and his wife. I tell you, Mathew, being a friend to me, he asked to play with you. More than golf, hey, my tip to you.'

CHAPTER 38

After meeting Hugh and Miss Brown to discuss the second mud map, Nigel telephones Mathew. 'That went well, particularly the way Tony explained the proposed work around the river and the preservation of Barry's Bush.'

'What about the farm stay idea?'

'Left it on the back burner. Frankly, I haven't had time to nut it out and I'd like to discuss it with Barry and then project costs, against income.'

'Maybe for a dollar he'd consult?'

'Yes, good idea but a local resident might be more advantageous down the track.'

'Yeah, I like that, Johnny-on-the-spot.'

'We must start crunching numbers to design the Trilogy accommodation mix. If it's not right, we'll be in the shit big time. Why don't you throw it at Brian and the accountancy department?'

Mathew keeps the news in motion, passing the request to Mandy and then asks how she found Keng. The question is casual, a matter of chit-chat; the answer unforeseen. 'He asked me to accompany him to Hong Kong and Tokyo first class. Bloody nice offer. I'm undecided between the Rhine and the wine or the realm of Bushido amidst the cherry blossoms. The ideal bachelor, obviously wealthy, tall, dark and married to the mystique of the Orient.' In the perplexing procedure, Mandy floors him with the flippancy of her prose.

A day trip to the Murray is required. Mathew feels obliged to stay abreast of construction completion so, when necessary, he can talk authoritatively from first-hand experience. It's the reverse of 'Bullshit baffles brains.' Ian has accompanied him and, on the way, Mathew says, 'Extract your diary. Slot in Thursday, the eleventh of August. You have a golf date.'

'You beauty Mathew, I owe you one.'

'Bout bloody time someone did.'

Mathew lies on the couch amongst promising pillows and cuddly cushions; contemplations invoke a headache. It is a future fraught with perils and either Heidi or Mandy burnt beyond redemption. Finally, he relents and advises the latter, he's going to Vietnam on Sunday. It's unrelated business and he'll return refreshed for the Rhine.

'Oh, that's nice. Ah, the brochures we need to plan the day trips? I've prioritised everything as suggested.'

Flabbergasted at Mandy's lackadaisical manner of uninterested narration, a worry bug squirrels away in his gut.

CHAPTER 39

Under direction, he packs lightly, carrying only hand luggage, ensuring on arrival there's no delay in passing the bureaucratic essentials of international travel. First out of the security area, he sights Heidi, unmistakably tall and elegant, dressed in a traditional white Vietnamese gown, standing with an attractive lady, but he only has eyes for one. 'Wow, how stunningly beautiful is this girl?' She rushes into his arms openly, expressing happiness and holds him close. Then remembering they have company, she introduces the travel arranger, Pinh Lhoung, who greets him with 'Xin chao'.

He replies, 'Xin chao, ten toi la Mathew.'

'Ah, very good. Have you visited before?'

'No, first time, but I toi kong noi.'

'Well, you wouldn't know it. Have you been teaching him, Heidi?'

'Have not. He surprises me too.' Heidi turns directly to Mathew. 'Explain please where did you learned Vietnamese.'

'The Lonely Planet Asian Phrasebook. Picked out a few basics and worked on them. San tot, hey?' Heidi and Pinh both laughs.

'Come, I have a car waiting.'

Pinh directs the driver to the hotel, asking, 'How did you select such an excellent hotel?'

'Reading travel brochures, it conveyed romance – Old World French with Juliet balconies overlooking the river. It just read right.'

Merging from the airport precinct, the traffic built rapidly, increasing dramatically as they closed on downtown. Within minutes, it's almost gridlock, the street's a mass of push and motorbikes; yet surprisingly, the traffic moves. Mathew is fascinated at the complete trust and understanding the riders and drivers appear to operate under; seemingly no traffic rules operate or at least are adhered to. He counts as many as four people on one bike – no helmets, no support for kids tucked in between adults or standing, holding on to whomever or whatever happens to be in front.

The hotel reception is highlighted by intricate leadlight work running the length of the desk. On the back wall six antique French clocks are set to various world times. Heidi attends to check in; Pinh Lhoung waits with Mathew and notices him studying the lead lights.

'The foyer is quite beautiful at night. These columns feature rows of tiny lights. You'll find them impressive.'

Heidi signals for help. 'As we are not married, please confirm to the manager I'm your guest and you are responsible for the room account and any item I sign for.'

Mathew grates eyes severely with the manager. 'I am of the understanding this is an international standard hotel. What rubbish is this? Heidi has as much right as myself to account to the bill. I'll give you my credit card, impress it now to secure the account.'

The manager gasps at Heidi; speaking quickly and expressively, he turns to Mathew. 'You must understand we do this for your protection. This is a country where, often, ladies pursue men, obtain entry to their room and walk out with cash and other valuables. I have offered apologies to Miss Heidi for any misunderstanding as I do you, Mr. Allen.' He waves for the bellboy, hands over a small wallet containing two smart cards and two breakfast vouchers. 'May I enquire what time you require to be checked out in the morning?'

'Tam goi.'

'If you call reception when leaving the room, we'll have your bill ready. I trust you'll both enjoy the stay and if I may be of further assistance, please contact my office direct.'

The view from the balcony spreads out like the gentle curve of the Sai Gon River. 'Like the bloody Yarra', Mathew muses and Heidi poses a questioning look. 'Flows upside down.'

Leaving her with the challenge of discovery, he notices four large showboats at what he learns later is the Bach Dang Pier. They are readying to take tourists for a lunchtime cruise. He takes in aspects up the river, noting a frantic crossing where several ferries ply non-stop, carrying masses of bikes and foot traffic. The sound of the street reverberates. 'Do they all have to toot at the same bloody time? Let's go in.'

Taking his hand, Heidi steers him to the bed, removing without comment his shoes and socks and pushes him onto his back. Heidi returns with a hot towel, washes each foot and massages them with strong fingers; he winces on several occasions. 'It may hurt a little now, but your feet will thank me tomorrow.'

He's learnt a short phrase; in the peace and tranquility of the moment, Mathew holds her close, measures the depths of her eyes and discovers something in the chocolate boxes that adds more meaning to the dissertation. 'You are em bep lam.'

Heidi laughs softly from deep in her throat, captivated at the simple pleasure of being in Vietnam with Mathew. 'Almost perfect pronunciation. I appreciate you telling me I'm beautiful and as long as you believe it, I will see it in your eyes and I'll rejoice for eternity.'

Located on the first floor, the pool is enclosed with no aspect to the sun, Mathew wonders if that's the common sense in the architect's plan. *Who needs to be in full sun in this weather?*

They relax on timber sun lounges, sipping delicious freshly squeezed fruit juices; it's time to discuss the evening. 'So, Miss Tour Conductor, what do you have in mind for tonight?'

The chocolate drops flash, her grin incredibly cheeky. 'Are you for real?'

He laughs. 'Before that.'

'Ah, let's wander up the street, find a restaurant and enjoy some real Vietnamese food. Then we'll head home to bed and I'll give you a nice massage to make you sleep.' The grin is cheeky.

On Dong Khoi Street, with the humidity swirling amidst the pandemonium of the traffic, they arrive at the first cross street. Heidi provides theory and practice on how a pedestrian crosses a road. 'The trick is just walk. Neither bike nor car will run you over but under no circumstance must you hesitate. Then the rider has no idea what's in your mind, so you walk straight and they drive accordingly. Good system, hey?' Mathew surveys the scene. The traffic is terrorising; a mass of bikes bears down, intent on his demise. With Heidi holding his hand like a security bond, he nervously paces out as instructed and marvels at how easy it is but recognises the importance of adhering to the unbreakable rule – do not hesitate.

Many shops remain open, particularly the touristy types dealing in antiques, clothes, craft and gift opportunities. Some have families out front, squatting or sitting on broken, uneven slabs of concrete around a tiny portable gas ring, boiling rice or stirring a fry. Some stare openly but most smile as Mathew extends, 'Xin chao'.

Several banter with Heidi, who fields a comment and interprets for Mathew, who ruffles a youngster's hair, asking, 'Ten ong la gi? Ten toi la Mathew.' He sends the little boy scurrying to his mother, seeking safety. Everyone laughs, an old man points at Mathew in shock and his cigarette falls out of his mouth; calmly, he reaches down, picks it up and gazes as if assessing its worth. Accepting it has value, he pops it between his lips and sucks vigorously.

'They are surprised a Yankee would take the trouble to learn their language.'

'Oh bugger, I can't have people thinking I'm a bloody Yank. Next time, I'll make sure I add Uc Dai Loi so they know I'm from Oz.'

'Then just your luck, you find a clever person who will assume your name is Dorothy.'

It took a moment for her observation to sink in. Then he adds, 'But I don't have red shoes.'

At another crossroad, Heidi looks left and spies a restaurant with a neon sign flashing an erratic welcome. 'The Lemongrass, sounds traditional. Want to take a chance?' The shop is narrow gutted with battered linoleum floors; each table is occupied. A sour-faced girl approaches and points up the stairs; normally, Mathew will have suggested, 'Get stuffed' and walk out but Heidi is already on the move. The next level is also full, so they go up again and luck upon a window table, but it offers no view, just the noise of the city and a tiny breeze.

Mathew suggests to Heidi she order on one condition. 'Mot ba xin.' As instructed, Heidi signals the waitress and asks what is fresh and the cook's recommendations for the night. Once appraised, she orders accordingly, together with a beer for Mathew.

'We have many beers – Tiger, 333 – but I have ordered one called appropriately Saigon. I hope you enjoy my selection.'

Dinner includes prawn and pork rolls in sheer rice paper, followed by a large steamed combination with crispy noodles and a separate dish of green vegetables. To Mathew's palate, there are many hints of varying spices mingling, with subtlety obviously the intent.

Heidi collects the bill and diligently checks the arithmetic. 'Expensive, Mathew. Including two beers, my tea and the tip, fourteen Aussie dollars.'

He shakes his head. 'I'll pay with dong, okay?'

The Caravelle Hotel, Heidi suggests, has a nice bar called Saigon Saigon. On the eleventh floor, they elect to sit on the little balcony with their 'juicy, fruity' drinks, watching the maddening traffic and listening without option to the commotion. The piano bar is in full swing, surrounded by a smoky blue haze. Mathew wonders, *Is it the piano or the smell of the smoke that attracts?* Many males of European extraction sit or lounge around, most in company with attractive Vietnamese ladies dressed appropriately in national style.

'Beautiful girls, Mathew?'

'It's the dress. Makes you girls look so erotic, extenuating the exotic, yet it's not nearly a sexy outfit as the cheongsam.'

'The ao dai suits the stature more.' Heidi leans forwards. 'They are professional girls, trying to meet a man for the night or preferably for life.'

'Yes', Mathew muses. 'And they probably think the same about you and me.'

Slowly, in keeping with the heat of the night, they wander along Hai Ba Trung. 'Let's have tea, Mathew and watch the world go by.' Perched on little timber chairs, resting the tea on a rickety table, the rest of the world seems to ride by. Mathew is attuned to his personal excitement, aroused by the unceasing action taking place on the street, the consummation of the exotic food and the realisation, he's in company with a lady, stunningly beautiful and singularly special.

The hot, steamy night without warning gives way to rain, a typical tropical deluge, which catches them several blocks from the hotel; within moments, they're drowned by the torrents. Hugging and laughing in a fit of lunacy, Heidi will recall it later as a 'special wet moment'.

Outside, the humidity hangs suspended in the still of the night; inside, the air conditioning is set at eighteen degrees, thus separated by a pane of glass, they are in another world. The lovemaking lasts for hours; he is unable to get enough of her and she of him. Mathew struggles not to say the *L* word, yet he is of the understanding he stores a reservoir of pent-up love which desperately wants out into someone else's heart, someone who'll care and cherish him. He dwells on the Heidi puzzle, trying to decide if all the bits are in place and his heart pounds out an emphatic yes.

At a time, undiscerned during the night, they face each other in the semi-darkened room and she starts to talk. 'Do you know Martin Luther King?'

'Yes.'

'You know his speech at the reflecting pool in Washington DC, I Have a Dream? I think it's one of the most powerful speeches ever made, articulated with such dignity and pride, controlled yet evoking undeniable passion, brave without being audacious. I love those words, Mathew. I have a dream.'

He hears her breathing, mindful of the faint intake, aware she's preparing to proceed. 'I have a dream of my own, Mathew Allen, never narrated, locked in my heart. Firstly, my past. I'm a late baby. My brother already 12 and my sister 10. Then Mother passed on to meet her gods when I was 6.

But my father unable to survive, so sad. Vietnam too difficult without her, so he took a contracting job in Hong Kong with Royal Dutch Shell Company. An uncle agreed to foster the older children and father took me with him, leaving money to educate Tek and Weng. Tek went to uni and became a lawyer. With Weng, it was the same but she became a doctor. Father sent me to uni in Hong Kong and I studied law. Ah, so sad. Then my father died and I was left alone. Brother begged me to come back and work with him in his little law firm but I think it was not fair. He was just being a good brother, so I decided I needed to make money quickly.'

He notices that her breathing is shallower, in sync with talking faster, wound up, intent on spilling her beans.

'A friend at university explained she paid her way by entering the pillow world and enticed me to try. Ha, the very first man I went with bought my contract and transformed me into a first-class, very expensive lady of the night by introducing me to a Japanese couple, who trained me for one year in the ways of pleasuring and caring for men. So, I specialised in the Nippon way, learning to play the samisen, taking singing lessons and because I am expensive, I am not in big demand, sometimes going a long time with no man client. Men respect me as a lady. I have never been badly treated. Lucky, hey?' Mathew nods and she continues, 'So for many years, I am an exclusive lady of the night. I earn very big money, paid by my boss man and together with tips, I save really hard. So that is my past. It's only fair you know it all. Now my dream. I save so I can return to Vietnam. I have this very historic, very beautiful town with lovely beaches in my heart. I desire to take the special man who will be my man for life to my town. I'll take you tomorrow because I have my heart set on you.' She touches his lips. 'Say nothing, please. I know what you intend to express. You an older man but that does not worry me as you treat me as a real person, we have fun and laugh together and you stimulate my intelligence. I love the way we interact with our email, talking about the arts and life. So, I ask, why can't I have my way? Men have their way in life. I want my way. I worked, scrimped and saved hard for my future.' Her stunning smile shines through the soft darkness. 'And I want you to be my future, so I entice you here to enjoy the country of my birth, where we can discover each other and you can see if you detect me in your heart, enough to say the love word, and if you love me enough to live in Vietnam for six months and Melbourne six months. Can we at least try? If you love our making love, why can't we live like this for all the days our gods grant us? Truly, I believe between you and me there is more than just wonderful sex. Our life encompasses a more mystic meaning.'

Mathew's emotions churn. *What do you say? Her thinking is so deep, set on making commitments. Do I want to live here for six months of the year? Strewth, do I want this or that?* 'An offer no other man may refuse, and I'm not refusing. I need this week, and we'll talk then.'

Mathew strokes steadily up and down inside the odd-shaped pool, taking a turn to the left to lengthen the effort, reaching one end, suddenly, two legs drop in front of him. Heidi appears under the water, pushes off the wall, kisses him and breaks the surface, laughing.

'Fun, hey.' Then she swims away in a slow crawl as Mathew offers, 'She's even elegant in the pool.'

Mathew chops into the crunchy hash brown, mixing it with his runny egg, shoveling it into his mouth he looks at Heidi, who is hoeing into a huge bowl of fresh fruit and muesli. 'Fun, hey,' he's intent on imitating. Casually, he gazes up the river, taking in the scene, looking both north and east. He notices again the frenetic, frantic ferry crossing gearing up for another hectic, demanding day. It's hot yet not overpowering. Overhead on timed occasions, fine mist squirts into the air, creating much giggling and comment from often startled guests.

The drive to the airport again fascinates Mathew; the seemingly impossible traffic mixes and merges. Drivers dodge and dart yet move coolly and calmly. The driver explains there are seven million people and three million motorbikes, Mathew reckons, they're all out today.

Heidi snuggles into his arm during the flight to Danang. 'I am very excited, Mathew, to see my birth town again, to recall the snippets of my childhood, see my wonderful brother and his lovely wife, enhanced by the joy you bring. It means much and who knows? It may become meaningful to you too.'

'Time will tell. Let's enjoy the experience, store the memories in our hearts and see where, as you say, your gods take us.'

'Yes, and always in life, the final decision is the man's discretion.' Without waiting for a comment, she says, 'We are going to Hoi An.'

'I know Hoi An. It's a very ancient town, if I recall occupied by the Chinese and the Japanese in the old days as a port and trading station and then lost in the mist of wars. A backwater until 1993, when a man on a motorbike road into town and told a travel book about the amazing architecture, the beach and life along the rivers.'

'Yes, but when you say, old days, it's only back to the sixteenth and eighteenth centuries. It retains great heritage, being once a very rich, successful port city and famous today for tailoring skills. That's why I suggest you travel light. We'll make you new clothes and may I ask, how do you know the name Hoi An?'

'Only because I study geography, investigating maps and travel brochures, seeking off-the-beaten-track experiences.'

'You have travelled a lot?'

'Yes, extensively.'

'With wife?'

'No, she's a homebody tied to hospital and house. I ventured alone.'

'How strange, a lonely man on a lonely planet.'

Mathew asks Heidi if the eighteenth of August in terms of recent Vietnam history means anything. 'No, so sorry. Remember, I'm a child of Hong Kong. Vietnam is my heritage but not my understanding.'

'Yeah, well, thirty-eight years ago a very important battle in Australian Army history was fought in a rubber plantation at a place called Long Tan in Nui Dat Province, just east of Saigon – oops, Ho Chi Min City.'

Heidi butts in, 'It's okay. Most people from the south still call it Saigon. Vietnam was separated for many years. In the south, the people could work and prosper, whereas in the north the communists ruled harshly but they won the war, earning the right to change the name to honour Ho. Sorry, you were saying?'

'I think exactly 108 Aussie diggers backed up by New Zealand artillery fought off 3,000 North Vietnamese regular soldiers' intent on wiping out the base.'

'Never heard of it.'

'Not to worry, not many Aussies know of it either. And unfortunately, consecutive Australian governments have treated the vets like shit. Still, it tickles me why, all of a sudden, this skirmish is suddenly promoted as the battle to celebrate in relation to this conflict. For some reason, it's incorrectly portrayed, mostly by uneducated and uncaring journalists anxious to be seen to be fostering it as the big battle of the war, which is totally untrue. Long Tan lasted for the duration of one single afternoon, whereas the Battle of Coral lasted twenty-six days in May and June 1968 just north of Saigon, where the boys – and many were just boys – the subject of conscription. You understand, Heidi?'

'Yes, and you know, I often asked my father about the war but he would just look at me quite sadly and say, one day, my dear, not now and that was it. So sorry, please tell me more.'

'Well, before Coral, the boys fought a war of patrol and ambush. But here, they faced an enemy who virtually owned the territory and came looking for a fight. This battle put the diggers in the big league, it was the largest unit battle we participated in, in that terrible wasteful war.'

'So, Mathew, what is Coral?'

'The name of a fire support base located immediately north of Tan Uyen in Bien Hoa Province, which borders north on the Song Be River and the other fire base involved, was called Balmoral.'

'And who won the battle?'

'Well, it's interesting. The Paris peace talks were under way and Hanoi was throwing everything at Saigon, to improve their bargaining position. The Aussies' disruption and defeat of the attacks on Saigon, was considered, not only a military victory but also a political one, as Saigon was no longer under threat.'

'I need to study Vietnamese history more. From my schooling and uni in Hong Kong, I know more European history than my own, so I have just given myself a new task – learn more about my birth country.'

'The American war may not be a good place to start.'

'Still, it appears, from what little I know, Vietnam has always been at war.'

Mathew nods. 'Yes, sad, hey. However, let's take the positive attitude the country and its people, can only progress, in one purposeful direction now.'

Pinh Lhoung has arranged for a driver to take them into China Beach, where they stop to take a short walk on the historic white sand; Mathew notices small waves, breaking sufficiently close in, to provide a small ride.

On the way down the coast, Heidi explains the river in Hoi An silted up and closed as a commercial shipping harbour back in the eighteenth century, so ships of any size sailed in and out of Danang thereafter; and for a time, commercially, Hoi An died. 'Maybe it's a good thing, Mathew, as it remains quite faithful to its past, retaining lots of heritage and history.'

'Still would, except for that silly bugger on his bike.'

The road is busy. Large Korean- and Japanese-made trucks exercise their air horns regularly; many drivers of small vans and cars seem to drive with a hand permanently placed on the horn button. Motorbikes, more often than not, carry people or stock and trade, battling the traffic, whereas the pushbike riders appear most serene, riding along almost oblivious to the mayhem around them, with the girls dressed in ao dai, always riding with its length held and gathered usually in the left hand. Mathew is immediately in rapture, pleasantly surprised at the distinct character and quaintness of the ancient town.

'It gets better. The inner part of town has little traffic access. One can only walk it, so we'll have fun, hey?' Heidi says. Mathew asks the driver for a map as he quickly becomes confused by the many rivers – the Hoi An, the De Vong and the Thu Bon.

'Pinh Lhoung has recommended the Hoi An Hotel. She tells me it's not the most luxurious, but it's right in the heart of town and brother and I, thought it important for you to be in the action. And besides, it has a great pool, a bar, a restaurant and a coffee shop, all wrapped up in wonderful service.' She smiles. 'And the only other thing you need is me.'

Settling into the charming room, Heidi reminds Mathew her brother is a very smart man, a well-connected lawyer. 'If you get into trouble, call him and he'll get you out of jail.'

Together, they marvel at the incredible town, the streets narrow but straight, planned in grid fashion. Mathew wonders at the history of the settlement as they stroll past interconnecting alleys full of shops, appreciating for the tourist, this will be another shop-till-you-drop experience. Imagining Milly, he thinks, *Wrong, she'd drive me crazy.*

Time in abundance encourages mingling with the crowd and tourists like them, falling in love with the cute and the quaint, the old and historic moss-covered buildings of mainly two storeys in a spectrum of colours. Heidi decides to telephone her brother and arrange introductions to the right tailors and shoemakers for a shopping spree. However, in accord with her plan, Mathew is the centerpiece of her scheme; thus, the desire to visit family is intensified.

The discovery tour leads them to a tiny riverside restaurant on the Hoai River. Romance pervades the sensual hot air as Mathew continually gazes at the beauty sitting opposite him. Occasionally, a small breeze rises off the river and then dies; suddenly, another zephyr wafts across the water, bringing relief for a moment, disappearing as quickly as it materialised. Mathew is fascinated at her delicate hand movements as she handles her food deftly. Her mannerisms and little facial features add comically to the moment – arching an eyebrow, furrowing the brow, turning up the corner of her mouth. But always, it's the eyes – those deep chocolate pools that without hesitation smile, sparkle and bless the moment he relishes. A bare foot caresses his calf; she wrinkles her nose with eyes flashing and a smile commences on her lips and spreads across her face. 'Fun, hey?' She's intent on shuffling the last of the crabmeat onto her folk, while his instant introspection imparts much musing, this isn't about lust; he's not hard nor horny. This is simply her, Heidi, the whole sum of the symmetry, the puzzle pixels perfect.

And finally, he admits, *Christ, I'm in love!*

His thought is interrupted. 'May we dine with my brother and his wife tomorrow night?' She holds the napkin to caress her lips, dabbing daintily the corner of her mouth and suddenly grasps the look on his face. *Wow, what is this? He is here, but he's somewhere else. Is this about her? Strike while the iron's hot.* 'You are not here. Who are you visiting?'

A blink accompanies the softly spoken words. 'Visiting your soul, em dep lam Heidi. And silly question, of course, I'd love to meet your family. What do you have in mind during the day?'

'Shop in the morning, drive out to Cua Dai Beach, have a swim and then relax at the hotel during the afternoon heat. Wednesday, we might take a private car tour down to Tam Ky and out to My Son and visit the Cham ruins. I understand they are something else, but the American bombing during the war, did awful damage I'm told.'

Mathew wakes early and slips downstairs for a swim. Then watches the staff set up for the day, shuffling furniture, sweeping with wicker brooms, making tidy to an already spick and span environment. A young man waters the plants and then opens the bar area. Mathew wanders over, greeting, 'Xin chao.' The boy is surprised but reacts quickly, responding in kind.

Mathew asks, 'Ten ong la gi?'

The boy smiles widely. 'Phan, sir.'

'Cam sir. Ten ong la Mathew. Nong, hey.'

Phan nods in respect and replies in excellent English, 'You speak Vietnamese well. Where you from?'

'Uc Dai Loi.'

'Ah, we have many Australian guests. May I bring you coffee or tea?'

'Black coffee and a tall fresh pineapple juice on room number 307. Okay, gam on.'

To stimulate business, Mathew projects onto his eyelids his current ventures and scrolls through them, seeking to identify foreseeable obstacles. Sensing company, he opens his eyes and finds Heidi removing a robe, revealing the tiniest bright blue bikini. She shakes her head and her long black hair cascades down her back and over her shoulders, shimmering, shining like satin. 'Trying to tempt me?'

'For you, my love, I'm always ready.' She grins, turns and dives into the pool. Mathew follows and gathers her into his arms; Heidi searches his eyes. 'Such a beautiful blue.'

'What do you see?'

'You, your soul, your life, our future and what do you see?'

'Nothing.'

Shocked, Heidi pulls away. 'You serious? You see nothing?'

'It's like trying to measure the depth of a pool of dark brown chocolate.'

'So sad, you cannot visit my heart, not able to discover the truth waiting therein.'

'You detect the truth in my eyes?' he queries.

'That is why I know you are a good man. I see who you are. I see it so clearly and can say I love you. In Viet, you say, toi yeu em and may I ask a personal question?'

'Of course.'

'Tell me the story of your ring. I admire it so.'

'A gift from a lost lady love.'

'Ah yes, so that is why you peer at it constantly.' Her face, just for an instant, reflects a sad smile.

Breakfast consists of mixed fruits and stunning light, fluffy croissants lashed with real New Zealand butter and pineapple jam, Mathew wonders why he has never seen it at home.

With purposeful determination, they follow the descriptive directions and readily find the shirt and shoemaker amidst the 517 shops comprising the ancient town. The shirt shop is on Tran Phu Street. Mathew orders six golf-style silk shirts and two pairs of walk shorts made out of easy-care microfibre at a total cost of ninety-five Australian dollars. He suggests to Mr. Chan, 'Very best quality and I'll pay an even hundred.' The old man grins widely, exposing an orphaned tooth; his tongue protrudes at an odd angle, while he scribbles adjusting the docket.

Mr. Shoes is really Mr. Slick, with jet-black hair, glued down with a part set equidistant from his ears; a pure white shirt with long sleeves culminating in French cuffs, featuring large multicoloured stones, set in gold. His slacks are black with sharp faultless creases, flaring slightly, sitting perfectly over immaculate black and white brogues. Mr. Shoes diligently catalogues the order of four pairs of shoes, including one pair of two-tone, brown and white golf shoes, copied out of a Footjoy catalogue.

In the small crowded streets and the tiny shops, the heat and humidity becomes oppressive; still, Mathew appreciates the quaintness, and that's coupled with the excitement of accompanying Heidi and the bliss of no noisy motors, no blaring beeping horns. Heidi is expressive in expanding on its history, discussing the architecture, pointing out remnants of monumental floods, elaborating on some of the timbers used in construction, now rare, some extinct. Mathew wonders at her intelligence.

At one particular house, they admire the lacquered decorating panels, some engraved in foreign characters. 'What does this Vietnamese writing say, Heidi?'

'It is actually Chinese explaining what type of produce was sold here in olden times.'

'Antique marketing?'

'Quite.'

Farther on, they arrive at a small temple. 'Wow, this is cute,' Heidi exclaims in excitement.

Mathew, looking past the temple, says, 'Talk about wow, how about this bridge with a pair of dog statues. Let's walk across.' At the other end, Heidi spies a pair of monkey statues and Mathew decides, here is a question for her brother at dinner.

A piece of paradise on pure white sand dotted with round leaf-clad rotunda sun covers expands away both north and south before his eyes. Underneath each shade cover resides two sun lounges, one on each side of a small square timber-top table in a hexagonal pattern. 'What's this beach called?'

'Cau Dai.'

'Is that Vietnamese for paradise?' he asks, but there's no answer as Heidi has disappeared into a small wave.

Sprawled out on the lounges, conversation drifts to Sri, and Heidi confirms, after much promising, the visa application has arrived and mailed back the same day. Mathew nods, then heads off in pursuit of more personal matters, about her past life and asks if she has regrets.

'No, but I'd rather arrive as a virgin, symbolic in pure white. Still, I trust you see my heart is chaste. Besides, the world has changed, young ladies' countenance different attitudes. Sex is everywhere, even at home, all over the TV. Girls prefer to marry later as, often, they pursue a career and morality is not the same, so what's the waiting for? By the time a girl is 25, saving virginity for ten years, she marries a man who might already have shared twenty or a hundred experiences. Where's the logic?'

CHAPTER 40

Evening settles; they venture out to confront the humidity and her relatives, at another riverfront restaurant. A contrasting couple stand waiting in the foyer. Heidi rushes up the steps in obvious glee to greet her brother and sister-in-law. Mathew, in proper manner, is introduced to Heidi's brother, Tek Te and his wife, Thanh, the tall and the petite.

Tek hasn't ventured out of Vietnam, yet he controls a resourceful mind retaining totally what it takes in, enabling him to converse readily and steadily on local and international matters. Diminutive Thanh comes in an attractive shape and a pleasant round face framed by the quintessential short haircut with the perennial fringe. Thanh's English is not of Tek's standard; still, she communicates freely, addressing clarifications to either Tek or Heidi then presents an engaging warm smile, extending a comforting feeling of welcoming and acceptance, as a friend. Over the course of the evening, Mathew deduces she's quite intelligent, her background typical of many girls. Assistant of her father in his business has given her a bookkeeping education; now employing home-honed skills, she's the financial brains in her husband's law firm and secretary cum accountant, to the local town's residence committee, a lady of influence. Inquisitively, Tek asks Mathew to elaborate on his business and he assumes that's because, in a communist state, the way of the entrepreneur is difficult to comprehend and land ownership, an old concept, lost in the takeover. Mathew, confused, tries to imagine the old philosophies of Marx and Lenin prevailing in Vietnam. Heidi, without appearing overbearing or pushing any particular points, encourages wide-ranging discussions, always in the sphere of property development. Thus, the door opens for Mathew to explain his role in the bringing together a Hong Kong company with an Australian group, forming a joint venture, involving a combination retirement village and golf course project, east of Melbourne. Nudged by Heidi, Tek stalks elaboration and Mathew expands into a summation of the site purchasing process; the utilisation of the various professional consultants, including Tony Cashmore, the golf course architect; the process of arranging a development permit; and planning involving governmental instrumentalities. Heidi deftly and deliberately injects pertinent one-liners, opening windows in Tek's cerebral psyche, spurring Mathew to augment explanation. Not anticipating he'd be in a symposium, he espouses his love of property development, relishing the opportunity and soldiers on until grasping he's been waffling. Ceasing abruptly, he turns to Heidi, who greets him with a smile, which he takes the wrong way. 'Gee, sorry, folks. I've been waffling.' And with that comes an expression of loss of face, but Tek responds without hesitation.

'No, Mathew, so sorry. You are wrong. I am thoroughly enjoying your elucidations. I would appreciate it if you continue.'

Breathing a sigh of relief, Heidi pushes Mathew into the realm of project financing while severely admonishes herself for the slip with the smile. *'But it's going perfectly, hey, just as planned, ha, who has all the brains around here.'* Self-consciously, Heidi shrugs, grins openly and faces Thanh, ready to answer the next question while Mathew precedes doing that, which Heidi perceived, he'll do so well. Mathew is mindful Thanh and Heidi are in close communication. Thanh querying quotations and comments, sifting the information, broadening her comprehension, undaunted by the relentless business intercourse. An opportunity to participate, even indirectly, offers an amazing chance to learn from this man, with whom, she has quickly gathered a degree of comfort and trust and whom, she recognises, her sister-in-law is besotted over. That realisation shepherds Thanh to be more attentive to the way Heidi and Mathew interrelate, at the same time appraising his background and experience, understanding her husband is engrossed and thus pillow talk, will revolve around Mathew Allen, his property expertise and the beautiful Heidi.

As is the way with men, eventually, the subject turns to sports. Tek explains at length his long love affair with football. 'I was, right from my first street games, a goalie. My height dictated my position and it continued right through university, onto playing provincial representative games.'

'And', Thanh adds, 'what Tek does not say is he was emergency goalkeeper for the national Olympics team, making us very proud.' She leans and touches his hand; Mathew recognises the love that flows from the simple act and the fleeting glance of adoration Tek conveys in acknowledgement. Heidi notices it too and peers longingly at Mathew.

In a casual farewell, Tek asks Heidi, 'Still playing golf?'

'Occasionally but lost in the mist of incentive and you?'

'Not often, too far to Danang.'

Instinctively, as planned, when the chance arises, she hits like a starving fish with a huge worm dangling temptingly. 'You need a new course along the coast road, ready for the booming tourist trade you say is coming.'

The comment goes straight over Mathew's head as he is waiting to seek the reason for the statues on the bridge and once posed, Tek looks at Thanh. 'You're the historian.'

Thanh smiles, gratified at the opportunity to explain. 'Well, that bridge is called the Japanese Bridge. It was built in the 1590s.'

Mathew shakes his head. 'Really, that old?'

'Yes, that old. The French altered it to make road traffic possible in 1986. The original purpose was to gain access for the Japanese community to commute with the Chinese on the other side. The reason for the two animals is unclear but we have two guesses. One relates to Japanese emperors born in the years of the dog and monkey but I like this one. The bridge started in the year of the dog and finished in the year of the monkey.'

'Very good, Thanh. Now any exciting history on the old temple opposite the bridge?' Mathew asks.

Thanh looks at Tek as if seeking approval; when he nods, Thanh smiles. 'Well, it's a local thing.' Her smile broadens. 'It was originally home to Cu.'

'Who?' Heidi blinks.

'Cu was a giant monster.'

Heidi mouth falls open.

'Yes, a giant monster with its head in India, its tail in Japan and its body in Vietnam but they built the bridge and killed it.'

Tek continues, 'The locals felt sorry for Cu, so they built the temple to honour the monster.'

They all nod and grin, and Thanh concludes by telling them, there is much preserved history and she would love to take them for a history tour one day, to which they both jump at the offer.

The hotel is a fair distance at the other side of the town; the walk takes in a slight hill. Regardless, Mathew suggests they walk, rather than be whisked away in a cyclo. Heidi says he's being fatuous and frivolous, depriving people of earning a living. 'We must contribute to the local economy.' She grins and takes his hand, ushering him towards the hotel. 'Just trying to be helpful. not sure you'll manage the walk, old man.' By placing his arm around Heidi, he encourages the closeness, inadvertently injecting a surge of passion as their hips bump and her firm breast harasses in a demanding manner. Often, they encounter blank stares – one a foreigner, one Viet. Many of the older brigade are mortified as resentment from the war remains. Fraternisation with Americans is related directly to the number of orphans, left by uncaring soldiers, not willing to take an Asian bride home, particularly to the South.

CHAPTER 41

Wednesday is dedicated to driving; fortunately, the air conditioning in the Toyota extracts the rank heat out of contention and along the coast, a breeze saves the day. My Son is a highlight; the intriguingly historic place enthuses and inspires their combined search for Vietnamese history and culture. Originally, this extraordinary area contained over seventy stupas and temples, built from the fourth century but it sunk into decline, eventually disappearing into the jungle, until rediscovered by a forgotten French archaeologist in 1898. Now after the U.S. bombing, just twenty stupas remain, which encourages Mathew to petition why.

'I understand the Vietcong or the North Vietnamese army, used the area as a hiding or staging area to attack Danang, trusting the Americans would respect the heritage of the area.'

'Ha, fat chance. Nothing against the Yanks but it was war and trust is categorically, a word not used often in that particular conflict,' Mathew asserts forcefully.

As they drive out of the remote jungle valley that is My Son, Mathew raises the subject of golf.

'There is much about me you have not discovered and, is not that the purpose of this week?'

'You're right, so tell me about golf.'

'I was influenced by my master, who believed all serious ladies of the pillow world, should be able to enjoy a man's pastimes, sharing in the excitement of his sporting pleasure. He arranged for me to learn how to golf, to swim, to play lawn bowls, to grasp the intensity in a rugged game of football and the gentleman's game of cricket. And ha, what a funny game that is, played over many days and no one may win.'

'Yes,' butts in Mathew. 'What you do not understand, is the horrific, sledging, that often takes place out on the pitch. Cricket is no game for gentlemen.'

Heidi nods; still, he isn't sure she grasps the inference to the verbal jousting. 'But I did learn the finesse and tension, a tight game, with its twists and turns, can engender. But I love horse racing best, standing on the rails, hearing the thunder of hooves shaking the very ground, the jostling and jousting, calling and cussing of the jockeys – god, the spectacular spectacle of the cacophonous crowd, as colourful and brilliant as the race itself. Amongst the bookies, in the betting ring, the sponsors' tents and the luxurious grandstand – ah, the people milling around, massing in happiness or woe.'

Articulating by mood and manner being somewhere else, Heidi immerses in a memory culminating in delight, pleasuring her inner soul and dwelling momentarily in memories sublime, until finally she says, 'I only hit balls at the range, maintaining rhythm just in case.'

'I golf.'

'Really, Mathew? I didn't know. Let's have a hit in Ho Chi Minh City. We can hire clubs and how clever, having a pair of golf shoes made and how silly I am, the brain bell not ringing, something else we have in common.'

'Yeah, good, hey.' Mathew is suddenly lost in a moment of mystery, pondering a tantalising yet disturbing thought unable to be grasped, a weird contemplation, striving to scratch the surface, of the strange theory rattling around in his brain. Grasping the handle, he discovers a conspiracy theory underscored by a hidden agenda, leading to the conclusion, *something is not kosher here.*

While Heidi reads, Mathew broods over the earlier observations, trying to sift chafe from the wheat, searching for the needle amidst the confusion of her bold statements, of love and life. The conclusions are unrewarding, except her respectful command of the English language, her inimitable articulation and her intelligent insight, analogous to the poetry task. He concedes if the apple reaches maturity and falls to the ground, he'll probably pick it up, as he recalls the saying Chinese ladies have, about apples. The finest reside at the pinnacle of the tree, but man is lazy and often intimidated to reach for the ripest, taking instead that which is easy, even if it means picking one that has fallen. Whilst the quality waits patiently at the top, for the right man, to appreciate their beauty and take the chance, to score one for himself. The L word looms large in reassessing her qualities; like a fussy car buyer, he ticks off priorities, before making the commitment to purchase and after all that, fails to appreciate the apple story and where he perceives Heidi is, on the tree.

Heidi disturbs his thoughts, 'You seem to command a strong general knowledge of the American war. May I ask why?'

'My time, I suppose, my part of living history with the other youth of the day. We were traumatised by the death of Jack Kennedy. You might say, Heidi, he was to the young people of the day, the beacon or polar star in Shakespeare's poem, a guiding light, a star pointing and leading the way. When we lost Jack and Camelot collapsed, we fell over with it, lost our way and that ushered in flower power, the hippy generation, the dropouts and those seeking any excuse to be bums. I hate to admit it now, but I fully supported the war. Unfortunately, like the great majority, I was conned by the Gulf of Tonkin incident, the CIA and the warmongers in the American government, tricked us all.'

'I never liked Kennedy.'

'I know why.'

'Ah, Mr. Extrasensory Perception, explanation, please.'

'Because he wasn't of your time, you weren't part of the excitement of such a handsome young man, with a stunningly beautiful wife and cute kids, running the world and running around in The White House. We loved his speeches, his manner and demeanour. It was as if he truly represented us, the youth of the free world. However, you saw the real side of the man, the drinking, the women, sex in the White House, the mysterious death of Marilyn Monroe, the dereliction of duty at times, the scheming and politicking with the CIA and other clandestine groups. The rush to support the piss-weak French, covertly becoming embroiled in Southeast Asia. But getting back to your original question, I have a great passion for modern history, mid-seventeenth century sort of thing. It fascinates me and so, Heidi, what is your infatuation?'

'Firstly, to conclude Kennedy, he had nothing to do with Marilyn's death. That was Robert and his close contacts.' The nod and the grin tell Mathew to shut up. 'So hmm, let's see, my passion and purpose? Life itself. I love people. I'm bound to talk to strangers, seek out someone who appears lonely and try to add something to their day. I truly am frightened at times by my mother's early death and then shattered, by my father's. I look at life similarly to many young people. In reality, life acquaints to work, work, struggle, struggle, maybe lucky enough to amass sufficient wealth to enjoy the fruits. But you become ill, catch a nasty disease and die. I want it all now, happy to die poor, desperate to live life to the fullest, while I can.'

She takes possession of his eyes. 'That's why I want you, to have and to hold, to love vigorously with vitality yet compassionately and caring.' He detects a tear in the corner of her eye, taking a fingertip he captures and conveys it to his mouth. 'Part of you.' He kisses her eyes and lips while the driver adjusts his mirror to capture the scene. *'Oh, my golly gosh, what a story to tell at dinner tonight.'*

Heidi retires to the air conditioning, Mathew to the pool but eventually he's beaten by the humidity and retreats to the suite, taking a cold juice for the girl, whom he discovers asleep; he undresses, lies on his side, and soaks up her sensual beauty. *A gem, a polished stone shaped and set in perfection. Still, the sands of time are running out. Only a few days to make a decision.*

He laughs softly. *Silly bugger, then what? Go home and probably make love to Milly whilst preparing for Europe with Mandy?*

Mathew revels in the protracted caressing, absorbed at the exciting pleasure of an Asian woman with skin like silk, aroused simply by touching the scintillating flesh. *It is about time – the time I take to extract the sanguine wantonness, winding her passion to another level. I'm going to drive her crazy.*

Glistening sweat gathers on her top lip, chest shimmering as if a thin veil of dew has descended. Unable to resist, he's driven to fiddle and fondle her breasts, retaining the lustre of lust around the nipples; across the cleavage, he proceeds to lick, motivated by passion, unrelenting in demanding momentum. Her chocolate eyes open and flash in the dark, reflecting off the moon that has snuck quietly into the room, steadily spreading illuminance light by stealth, like a spotlight steadily moving towards an undiscerned target. Incapable of fathoming that which is shrouded in the deep dark pools and as if comprehending his disadvantage, Heidi whispers in his ear, 'I love you, Mathew Allen. I want you for myself for as long as we are part of this earth.'

Overcome or simply caught up in the tick and tock of time, his heart relents to the brain's demands and he blurts out, 'I love you too.' Then he wonders where the thoughts suddenly materialised and recalls at the cricket club, his mate Al used to say, 'God gave man a penis and a brain but not enough blood to service both at the same time.' Then he compounds it with 'I want you out of the pillow world.'

Silence prevails.

'Really? Truly? That demand will change my life.' Her voice is faint and frail, frightened to pursue definition.

'Without redemption.' He nods and frowns.

Wow, this is so unexpected. Stop my heart from beating. He must not detect the exhilaration. Quickly! What's my best course of action? Steeling her nerves, the preamble commences. 'I'm bound by contract until the end of the year. When my previous agreement expired, an adversarial trait reasoned and reminded me of my age. Therefore, I decided to contract my services, at a guaranteed amount, to ensure and protect my dream. I'm bound till the thirty-first of December.' *Ah, very good. Now flutter my eye, raise one eyebrow, pout and hammer the nail.* 'Unless you buy out the contract.' Mathew sits dumbfounded, aware of the situation he's put himself in. *Christ, now I've torn it. I don't want to ask the question as failing to act will inflict huge loss of face. I might lose her. Silly bugger, now I'm in a bind!*

Ha, come on, girl, be bold. Account for the unanswered question and his commitment will be guaranteed. 'Thirty-five thousand American dollars', Heidi orates and holds her breath.

Strewth, what's that, fifty thousand Aussie dollars? Mathew calculates and charges forwards. 'For you, Heidi, I'd pay anything.'

She jumps on top of him, crushing his lips with hers, then sits up, laughing, 'You really do this for me?'

'Yes.'

'You must love me so.' Her face remains lit.

'Yes, I do.'

'Allow me to make the arrangements in Hong Kong. I obviously cannot until I return. You must wait. So sorry.'

'You recently said no amount of money would buy you. Did I just become a purchaser?'

'I meant for just one night. Now you want me for life.'

The kiss melds and molds the moment. Heidi is lost, not in the kiss but in something of more significance. *I love him so, but he will die and leave me in my middle years. Still, I'll be beautiful. I'll find another man and not grow old lonely. How exciting. He has committed to buy the contract. How intuitive of me to devise and design the way to determine his love, by proposing the compact as if it, in fact, a reality. Shall I speak the truth or retain the money for future security? Ha, no need to rush. I have time to ponder and the cash will be safe and sound in my secret U.S. dollar account. Ah, I am so clever.*

Heidi almost giggles, elated at the success of her strategy and schemes. *If my other machinations might be as fruitful, only time will tell but my karma is strong and taking after my maternal grandfather, who farms the land, prepares the ground, ploughs it, plants the seed, tends the crop with love and care, reaping that which he has sown. Indeed, as I'm truly a tiller of the mind, Grandfather in heaven, pay me respect. I'm going to be a very successful farmer.*

The phone purrs vibrantly; she glances at Mathew, who silently by nodding confirms, *Answer it.*

'Xin chao.' She listens for a moment and turns. 'Tek and Thanh invite us for dinner.'

The night is a repetition of the previous, except the ice has been broken; the manner of the meeting, more reminiscent of old friends, convening. Mathew enjoys their company. *Bright and bubbly with an air of excited exuberance dances around Tek's eyes and mouth, shrewd yet open and engaging, a man's man*, Mathew appreciates. *And given the right circumstances, I could become close to this man and his woman.*

He studies Tek, trying to discover some Heidi in him. Unable, he admits, he's as handsome as she's beautiful.

Thanh changes the subject. 'One of our passions is golf, what do you play off, Mathew?'

Heidi volunteers, 'Seventeen.'

'Would you care to join us at Danang tomorrow? I can arrange to hire clubs from our professional.'

Back in the room, Heidi comments, 'Thanh paid you a compliment, for an Anglo, you are quite handsome and we make an alluring couple. She suggested I try to trap you as my man. Can I tell her tomorrow, we have committed to each other but it is love, not I trapped you?' Heidi swallows the truth of the matter. *But of course, I did!*

'Sure, why not? But now I have you out of the pillow world, I don't know what I'm going to do with you.' He is indeed serious.

'Should we talk about our future, Mathew?'

After two cups of coffee, Mathew resolves not to resolve the tomorrows. Suddenly, a thought crosses his mind. 'I'll buy out your contract and the money will go to your boss man. What are you going to live on, until say next year, when we have, us, resolved?'

'I'm so sorry. I must not have explained, apologies I assumed you'd know the way of the pillow world. Fifteen per cent of my contract comes to me, so seven thousand odd hundred Aussie dollars is my fee. In Hong Kong, the way I live, it will last me and maybe I'll have more leftover, if I replace Sri, to share my flat. Then I want to live with you, or share with Sri, in Melbourne or we can live in Hoi An?'

'That has merit. However, Brian will not have you at Sri's apartment, encroaching on his paid-for space. He'll seek to visit her day and night, so he'll not appreciate you hanging around.'

'Thought so, but I had to clarify.'

'We are not going to be easy to arrange. I'm involved in the acquisition and design of a residential retirement golf course project out of Melbourne. It's going to keep me busy for some time. In fact, my life is very busy. I work particularly hard; I have a multitude of projects I am working on.'

Heidi conveys sadly, 'I understand. I will be patient and true.'

Yes. Mathew worries. *May well you might, but I won't. The Rhine cruise is going to be a nexus, another conundrum to bond or break relations with Mandy and you. What a bloody mess, I have cleverly managed, to manoeuvre myself into.*

Heidi wakes early.

'Why do we to drive to Danang, come back to sleep, then drive back again the next day? Let's change hotels. I'll arrange for the driver, to take us sightseeing, on the way.'

'I'm easy, but we must collect my shirts and shoes.'

The golf game christens his new golf shoes, which fit like that proverbial glove. Mathew is appreciative of travelling the course in a motorised cart, the temperature has sat at thirty-two degrees, with the humidity oppressive. For an amateur with an average swing, diagnostic Mathew analyses their practice swings, deciding they've been taught by a professional. Tek won the day being eleven over par, but no one is counting.

Tek, takes every advantage, to pursue the accumulation of more information, about the golf course project, Mathew has alluded to. *He's conveying more than average interest. I wonder why.* Tek asks why, he has chosen a golf course designer, he's frankly never heard of. Mathew reminds him to look at Cashmore's website, sets him a task and wonders what he'll see.

After the obligatory showering and changing into fresh clothes, Tek excuses himself but soon returns, shaking his head and suggests politely to the girls, have another iced tea, while he conducts Mathew into an office, takes a seat behind the computer, finds his search engine and enters firstly 'The Dunes', asking Mathew to explain each picture as it displays. Mathew is unable to recall each hole, but he does know a little of Cashmore's philosophy, so in layman golf terms he expresses, to the best of his ability, what Tony is trying to achieve with each hole. Discussion progresses adequately, until they arrive at the notorious six bunkers, fronting the fifteenth green.

'Thanh will not like this hole.' He laughs.

Mathew answers tritely, 'Not many of us do.'

'But what is he trying to achieve?'

'A definitive statement hole, one which a player will not only be wary of but also quickly recollect, when that course is talked about.'

'Ah yes, of course, like we are now, because of the intense group of bunkers.'

'And because, in Australia, we buy beer in six packs.'

The knowing smile tells it all.

Returning to the girls, Tek speaks very fast in his own language, appearing to Mathew to carry an edge that inspires excitement. In translation, Tek is thankful for Mathew's successful explanation of the philosophy behind the designs. This makes Mathew wonder why, such an interpretation, should engender such excitement.

Regardless, he concedes golf course design, construction management, and final shaping are an extremely complex, all-encompassing business. Anyone can draw lines on paper, converting those lines into a course that people appreciate, 'I like this course and I'll come back' is the key. Today too many designers make the courses impossibly difficult, by tricking them up, being over-imaginative and instead of working with the basic land characteristics, let loose a bulldozer, not sticking to the tenets of the game's philosophy. The real players, are the amateurs, who have an average handicap of eighteen and who are too often severely compromised. Tony's philosophy is 'You have to make the course enjoyable and, on their day, the player can beat it. That's the challenge in good golf course design.'

Their suite at the Furama Resort opens directly onto Non Nuoc, otherwise known to the world as China Beach. 'Oh, Mathew, this is beautiful. Let's go swim in the sea. I'll race you.'

They change in frantic fashion, wildly discarding clothes, finding and dressing in their swimsuits, charging to the beach, dropping their possessions and plunging in, coming up like kids, splashing and thrashing in a frenzy of pure delight. Heidi giggles and squeals as Mathew stumbles. She jumps on his back and drives him under the water, laughing as he emerges.

'You look like cho, caught in the monsoon rain.'

'I'll show you cho. I'm a bigger stronger dog than you.' Laughing, he sets off in determined pursuit.

Abruptly, they cease the game. She probes his eyes, tilts her head slightly and poses, 'Is it true, Mathew Allen, you will take me for life?'

Time, as he always knew it will, arrives. The significance of the truth peers intently. The final decision is nigh. An emotional thrill shudders through his being. *Yes, I'm ready. It's her I want.*

He extends his arms, 'To you, Heidi Hendrickson. I'm prepared to envelope you into my life, entwine you with my family, stand strong together as we meet our friends and foe. If you are prepared to accept my spit and polish with my foibles and follies, then move into my arms on the clear, understanding, you will never move away again.'

Oblivious to the world making haste, time stands still; without faltering, she takes the stride that will transform her life, gazing resolutely into his eyes. Holding them with the sheer will of her being and purposely, she searches their depths. *Yes, it is there, the love in his heart, only for me and how romantic the way he asks me.*

'I accept, Mathew Allen and I tell you, I will love you true. I will stand by you and support you and will always be there for you. You have given me, what my heart and soul have searched for unceasingly, since I was old enough to understand, what a man and a woman together means. Come, kiss your love, understanding this is the kiss of life.'

Neither the people on the beach, or on the decks and balconies of the resort hotels, nor the flock of seagulls resting on the sandbank, are au courant of the momentous public, yet private occasion, performed in front of them. The kiss is ongoing and as if bored, the gulls move out past the sandbar; snubbing the lovers, they disperse in silence.

Mathew shows Heidi how to set, wait and push off with the wave, add two quick strokes, and allow the water to impart the impetus. Heidi catches on quickly. 'Wow, this is fun, hey.'

'One day in Australia, I'll take you to a beach with real waves. Then you'll discover the absolute thrill, of body surfing.'

'Sounds exciting. I can be quite adventurous.'

'Yes', he agrees, 'I can imagine.'

At water's edge, little spent waves make play with their toes and the sun retreats to the west. *It's perfect*, Mathew admits in the solitude of his mind. *I love this part of Vietnam. I could return to historic Hoi An as long as she is with me.*

And as if in harmony, Heidi offers, 'I am enjoying this so, Mathew. Have I told you today, I love you?'

Like old-fashioned newly-weds, experiencing the first thrill, when uninhibited sex allows free rein to lust and passion, they tour the resort's wet areas, swimming in the pool, lounging on the steps, delighting in the sauna. Yet they loved the steam room most and Mathew reflects back to the episode in Shepparton, with the king-sized bed. 'Will you find me?' resonates and unable to control the impulse, he advocates, 'You'll have to find me in the steam.'

Lying in the Jacuzzi, grinning like little kids who'd just stolen their first apple off the neighbour's prized tree, discovering the sweet juicy texture of permanence, Heidi encourages her brightly painted toes, to become persistent little explorers.

Mathew's inbuilt alarm clock wakes them at sparrow fart. 'Let's go watch the sun come up?'

The sea is a magic sheet of glass converging with the sky; the magician casts huge orange and red hues, brilliant, bold and fiery, declaring a warning of the heat to come. On the cool sand, they observe in mutual awe the atomic cataclysm, exploding life on the planet. Irresistibly ascending out of the ocean, it squats momentarily above the horizon as the vividness dissipates; and finally, the celestial and sea blues fuse, secede and send a clear message. 'We are not one.'

'Wow, that was something special. I understand why in Japan they worship and cherish the rising sun, so exemplified on their distinctive flag. Not many nations disclose their soul on their flag, hey?'

Wow, he reaffirms, *she really has a brain or twenty-seven*. 'Very perceptive, Heidi. I like that proposition. Shall we make a game? Who can list most countries whose flag portrays their nation's heart or soul?'

'Hey, that's good, Mathew. When is time up?'

'Tomorrow night.' He thinks, *what a dumb idea, I can't, in the first instant, think of one.*

Heidi worries, *Bugger, he must have some up his sleeve. At the moment, I can't think of any.*

Mathew suddenly laughs.

'So?'

'I was just thinking of the Hollywood movie about the Vietnam War. The title escapes me. Anyway, the closing scene is the sun setting on a beach, so which beach, Heidi?'

She appreciates that the test must be a trick, but what? *War movie offers no clue – closing scene no clue, sun setting no clue and which beach no clue. Stupid bloody question! But wait couple the words together see what I can deduce, war movie closing scene, no clue and the sun setting on which beach hey hold on?* She looks around at the hills to the west. *The sun sets in the west. Which beach?* And she bursts out laughing. 'I love you, Mathew Allen. You make my brain work. It cannot be a Vietnamese beach as none faces west, yes?'

'Very perceptive but there may be one exception. Thinking cap back on.'

'Don't think I love you anymore!' A pout arrives with the grin.

Mathew, patient, anxious to espouse the answer before Heidi arrives at the right conclusion, declares, 'Time's up.'

'No, one more minute.' Heidi wrinkles her nose and shakes her head as if trying to pries it loose. 'I've failed the test.'

'How about an island?'

'Of course, so logical.'

'Isn't everything when you know the answer, but this one. Where is the coldest place on the equator?'

'Ha, you truly are a bugger. Let's see. I'll manage this one. Start at, say, Singapore. Go east, Borneo, very hot jungle. Micronesia, or is it Melanesia? Regardless, too hot. Across the Pacific to Panama? No, much too hot. Across the bottom of the Caribbean? Now fly the Atlantic. Maybe it has something to do with the water flow up from the Antarctic. No, it can't be. So, Africa? Landfall where? Bugger, I can't remember, but I know the Congo and Kenya are very hot with all the wild animals and the jungle. No. Now cross the Indian Ocean, but there's nothing there. Oops, sorry, Sumatra, no resolution either. She wrinkles her nose again like Tabitha but no magic appears. Got me again, you'll suffer for this.'

'How about on top of a mountain high.'

'But where?'

'How about Mount Kenya? Will that do?'

'Ha, you clever man, come cuddle. God, I love this, Mathew. We will have fun all our lives and if we lived six months of the year here, we could do this every day,' Heidi comments, patting the water affectionately.

'My business is such, I can't see myself being able to do that.'

'We have time. You must retire one day.' Heidi rolls onto her back. 'When I was a little girl, mother and I occasionally would go out at night, lie on our backs and wonder at the stars in the sky. Sometimes towards the horizon, we'd sight a falling star. It would excite us so, yet Mother would say, 'But it talks to us only on its deathbed.' Sometimes, we'd lie in the shade during the day and Mother would debate why life is so tough, so remorseless in its difficulty to just survive. Once she admitted, when expressing her soul, she only had three things to be thankful for, her parents, her kids and her man.' She wiggles her toes and sighs deeply. 'It is quite ironical. I sought you so long yet always in mortal fear that, once found, my maternal instincts would run rampant through my body. Already, I have the passion and paroxysm to make life, to bring forth a future, to share my genes, my hopes, my dreams. We would make beautiful babies, Mathew?'

She rolls towards him; tears streak her cheeks and dribble onto her lips. Mathew kisses her gently and tenderly as he whispers, 'I love you, Heidi. It's sufficient you bring life to me.'

She bursts out crying.

In the privacy of the shower, Heidi resolves to be happy. Mathew stretches out on the bed, listening to her singing a favourite from Andrew Lloyd Webber, 'Love Changes Everything' in Cantonese, or is it Vietnamese? He never can tell. His mind wanders. *She talks so positively about the future. I'm suffering pangs of conscience, concerned about the Rhine and Mandy. Can I unravel the trip, unzip the unalterable, escape the maze of life? Simple answer – no. Therefore, I foresee traumatic, troublesome complications, consequences too terrible to contemplate as the drama of my life, descends to disaster. I should be happy, elated at my luck in life. Now I'm confused by the perilous premonitions of doom and bloody gloom.*

Chapter 42

Approaching Hai Van Pass, a waterfall appears on the left, 'created', Mathew imagines, by the construction of the six-kilometre-long multi-lane tunnel. 'How incongruous,' he reckons. 'A nation of bloody bikes but none allowed to use the tunnel.' Heidi is unsure whether it's a question or a statement and taking the easy way out, continues to read *Cloud of Sparrows*.

'Who's the author?'

'Takashi Matsuoka, his debut novel.'

'Good?'

'Typical of the genre, lots of intrigue, samurai lore, geisha love, the life of the time explained comprehensively, clever and well written.'

'Hue, the original imperial capital, was ruled by the Nguyen kings and then the first capital, when the country was firstly called Vietnam, in 1802, after the end of the war, between the Trinhs in the north and the Nguyens in the south. Do you know if this area was originally settled by Chinese? For some reason, I have an inkling that's right.'

Heidi hesitates. 'I think so. The sixth century comes to mind but do not hold me to it. But you know, Mathew, it is considered to be one of the most important areas in the country, for its ancient history and famous, historical sites.'

In haste to discover the ancient heritage, they visit the tombs of Tu Duc and Khai Dinh and then boat up the famed Perfume River to visit the Thien Mu Pagoda. Heidi comments, 'I can't believe how they built such places, to last over the centuries. It's like Angkor Wat, which I have a strong desire to visit one day. Ancient places fascinate me.'

'You'd love Turkey.'

'Another Mathew Allen adventure, I suppose?'

'A long time ago. A fascinating diverse country with an incredible ancient history and the ruins are something to behold.'

'I'll put it on my list of must-dos.'

'Is it a long list?'

Excitedly, she exclaims yes and notes a distinct air of mourn about him as he answers, 'Pity, I imagined so.' As he wonders, if he'll have the time, to share her adventures.

The Saigon Morin Hotel is situated in the heart of town, occupying a prominent corner position fronting the Huong River. The building is over 100 years old, recently redecorated to retain its French style and charm, another indication to Mathew, tourism is a burgeoning industry.

Discovering, as tourists tend to, by accident, a quaint restaurant in Vo Thi Sau Street the An Binh has an interior dominated by heavy timber beams in the vertical and horizontal planes, while two huge chandeliers appear out of place. Large windows, extend the outside in and a pink painted wall, framed by lattice and lanai, colours the scene. Still, Mathew discerns an anachronism sits on a wall. 'Heidi, I've spied something that doesn't seem to fit the ambience. What might it be?'

Her search is painstakingly patient but she fails the examination. 'The more I fail, the more you'll suffer, so tell me.'

'A cuckoo clock in a Vietnamese eatery, so what might such a clock say, Heidi?'

'Coo-coo, you silly male chimp.'

Magnanimous, Mathew shouts Heidi a private massage but she switches venue to their suite, as he concludes, *How considerate. I can now enjoy the magic rub with my magic girl.*

Mathew is surprised at the attractiveness of the two girls, who immediately have them naked on their stomachs. He's even more startled, when the towel is removed; however, nothing untoward, twigs or twitches any bells, as he stretches out on the king bed, side by side to Heidi, yet he'd admit later, it seemed a little strange for his prudish upbringing.

They face each other, occasionally opening their eyes, gazing deeply into the depths of brown and blue. 'Your girl is Tih and mine Minh Vy,' Heidi offers. Their chatting is non-stop; to Mathew, it sounds like they are having fun, their voices tinkle musically as the tone key, moves up and down, the range modulation, like the massaging.

The giggling intensifies. Heidi joins in. Mathew wonders why. 'They are discussing your manhood, debating if you will be hard and how large it might be.'

Mathew mutters, 'How weird.'

The massage, as is custom, traverses the back, around the legs and as is often the case, a relaxing prelude, to the eventuality of rolling over. Mathew notes, Heidi virtually stares, as he carries out the manoeuvre and she poses, 'For me or Tih?'

'You're funny, Heidi.' He salutes the crowd.

The girls giggle and smile, chatting and nodding at Heidi. 'They are saying you are not overly huge. However, you stand proud and obviously very hard. Minh Vy thinks you'd be a good lover and you stand for a long time.'

Mathew turns his head to watch Minh Vy oil and massage Heidi's breasts, fascinated at her tree tops, popping up between tiny fingers, working erotic wonder. The girls move in between, he loses visual contact with proceedings but assumes correctly, Minh Vy is massaging her tummy. He looks intently at Tih, catching her eye; she winks and smiles and nods at his penis. His ego is excited, blood flow is stimulated; seemingly, he hardens as eye contact is retained. She massages up his thighs, reaching tantalisingly close to the family jewels.

Smiling, the girls yak in chitter-chatter. *Like a chime, a little Vietnamese bellbird tinkling.*

'What's being said, Heidi?'

'That you're waving like a palm tree in a wind, they wonder if the coconuts might fall off.'

'Tell them absolutely no. They are securely attached.'

Heidi translates, both girls laugh and the pleasuring continues, unabated.

'This is quite erotic, Heidi. I would have imagined, I'd be slightly embarrassed, such a wanton display of sexuality carried out by two girls.'

'Why?'

Christ, how do you answer that? 'Conservative upbringing. This is not something done in reality.'

'Don't you have a massage, with beautiful young ladies in Melbourne?'

'No, never.'

Heidi bursts out laughing and explains the reason to the girls, who stare unabashedly, imagining he'd just arrived from Mars. 'Is it true you never did this before?'

'Cross my heart.'

'No wonder you are feeling excited. I'm happy you are with me for your first time. I truly trust your enjoy it. But to appreciate it, you must let yourself go. Revel in the spirit of the moment, Mathew. Funny, hey, this was to be my massage, now it's all about you.'

Mathew watches Minh Vy touch Heidi very lightly in her groins, across the top of her pussy and back around the inner thighs. Tih moves slightly down the bed and commences exactly the same with her hands running up under his bum and then with one finger running down his crack, meeting the other gently at his balls. 'Nice?' Heidi poses in a husky voice. Mathew turns and notices her body arch up as Minh Vy moves to her lower stomach, caressing slowly and then one hand shifts back to Heidi's breasts, where he discerns, she rubs and squeezes a little harder. 'Yes, for you too, I see.'

'You can tell I'm climbing the ladder?'

'You're not Yuri Gagarin.'

'Ingenious summation, but you are already off the planet, in another place and it's exciting you?' Mathew feels his bum moving in motion with Tih's hands as Heidi continues, 'And when the girls depart, I'll make magic love to you, Mathew. You know I love you so. Anh yeu em. Toi yeu em.' The girls giggle and wink at each other, sharing happy wide smiles.

'What did you say?'

'I told them I love you.'

'Anh yeu em, em dup lum.'

Both girls nearly fell off the bed, laughing and chatting at the same time with Heidi. 'You surprise the girls, you speak such good Vietnamese and you said in front of them, you love me and consider me a beautiful person. Such openness is rare in front of strangers. From me, I say thank you.'

Mathew is incapable of controlling the smile. *How bloody stupid. I'm naked with three women, and they giggle because it's not custom to display love and appreciation of beauty, in front of other people.*

Silence prevails except for the sloshing, swishing, gentle slapping and chopping of oily hands on slippery skin. Mathew alternates looking at the simple attractiveness of Tih and back to Heidi, who with each glance seems to writhe more on the bed. Minh Vy slides off and shifts to the other side, retaining full view of the action.

Heidi's eyes are shut. Mathew notices her toes curl up. Minh Vy spreads her legs slightly. Smiling, she raises her eyebrows and deliberately drips oil onto Heidi's pussy, places one hand completely on it and commences to make tiny circular motions, with Heidi moving in tune to the action, groaning, 'Oh god, this is wonderful. Are you watching,

Mathew? Yes, of course, you are. This is a lesson. One day I want you to do this to me, massaging as you love me. Can you?'

'How about tonight?'

'Thank you, but tonight will be a waste. You will not have to do much to inspire my sexuality.' She opens an eye and emits a small laugh while her grin epitomises mischief.

The girls' chattering ceases. Heidi's breathing increases and her toes tap dance. Mathew recognises, subconsciously, his bum is moving in time with the stroking and he accepts Heidi's advice, go with the flow. He looks at Heidi; her chocolates are closed. She's somewhere else; he wonders where.

The girls stand and head to the bathroom, where shortly the shower blasts on. Heidi and Mathew hold the stare, until he slides over and the kiss is like a combination soup, all ingredients present and accounted for. The flavour bursts forth in frenetic frenzy, rolling frantically until Heidi finishes on top and asks quietly almost in a whisper, 'Have you been like this before?'

'Never, this is unbelievable!'

Heidi smiles. 'Be patient wait for the girls to go and you can let your emotions, your lust, your pent-up hidden desires go. Be Asian, be erotic, be adventurous. This is for you.'

Mathew slips off the bed and keys in the security numbers into the room safe, extracts $300 and places it on their carry bags.

'Too much you spoil them.'

'No, worth every penny!'

'Oooh, then how much for me?'

'After they go and we finish, might be the appropriate time to negotiate.'

'No Mathew, making love is one thing we will never never debate.'

The girls return, find the money and become very excited smiling, giggling expressing, 'Chao ahn cam on.'

As soon as the door shuts Heidi jumps on top of him, 'Quickly, Mathew, put your hand between my legs, feel the pleasure waiting for you.' She finds his lips; the kiss is long and hard, as he commences softly and gently touching her. She moans and groans, thrashing her body to meet the dancing digits and researching Mathew's eyes deeply, as if in search of the Holy Grail and maybe she is. 'Are you truly enjoying it? Is it me in your head, or your lost lady love?'

'God knows it's you, Heidi and you know it's you. The rest of our lives, always you.'

Heidi climaxes again. Mathew notices the tension of her body, culminating with rapid gasping, breathing and tiny grunting. Then she relaxes as the demand for air diminishes. Mathew loses control and turns his smile into a loud laugh. *I'd like to shake my head and make sure this isn't a dream, but then in a way it is. It's a sexual fantasy, one of amazing sensuality, heightened by the fact, I'm with Heidi. Asian women, who can understand their eroticism and who bloody wants to?*

In a state of minor inner turmoil, surprised by the sex, unsure what to say, Mathew mutters, 'That was simply sensational.' And then chooses to be more open, in what he assumes, is the Asian way. 'I've truly not experienced, anything quite like that before. Are all the girls so sensual? I didn't ask for special girls. I just ordered a massage.'

'I was pleased you ordered a massage just for me, so I decided to change the girls and have hot, sexy ones to pleasure us both. You see, Mathew, I'm normal too. I become hot and lust overcomes me when I'm with you, so it was erotic for me as well.' She laughs softly. 'I must be very naughty, but I did enjoy it so and you felt my come. Huge, hey?'

'Same same', he comments while in thought. *Now I'm becoming Vietnamese.*

In the peace of her mind, with Mathew sleeping deeply, Heidi recalls the sex and meditates thoughtfully on the evening's carnal display, of sexuality. *How exciting involving the man in my heart, unburdened by pecuniary interest, nor paid to participate in a pretend circumstance. My gods, what an assignation. Even in my wildest imaginations, nothing might match the excitement so extreme, from the feel of her hands, knowing his eyes were fixedly glued to the erotic performance, portrayed perfectly by Minh Vy at my direction. Ha, how wonderfully well the girls met my instructions and how it pleasured me, to my inner soul. Yes, we have to do it again.*

In urgent contemplation, her hands go to her breasts and gently caress the nipples innovatively in expedition, intoxicated in expectation of the fantasy, to be performed again and now stirred, the fancy unwinds. *Shall I wake him?*

White pearls flash in the dark, caressing her lips with an inclined tongue, tasting the sex in her mouth. A hand leaves a flinty nipple and reaches under the sheet.

CHAPTER 43

Ho Chi Minh City greets in a humid manner, stifling, steamy and oppressive. The manager welcomes them back with a smidge of over-the-top graciousness, which arrives with a complimentary dinner at the seventh-floor restaurant, and Mathew accepts with equally engineered grace, thinking, *Well, that ensures future business if opportunity arises.*

Heidi walks to the Lucky Plaza Trade Centre Arcade, intending to shop for Sri, but it's too touristy and tatty; something different is desired. At the end of the arcade, she arrives at busy Nguyen Hue Street and for no apparent reason, turns left and shortly arrives at an emporium. The premises appear more upmarket; the front-page photo entices her to enter the book. Inside, she peers down one side of the store, featuring huge tapestries and rugs in a multitude of colours and exciting designs that stir delight, but she recognises, *Can't be for Sri.* Sauntering slowly, she is taken by some stunning bright red dinner sets but decides in the negative, then picks up a highly glazed, ancient Vietnamese pottery lady, supporting the quintessential timber carrying beam, with two baskets, neatly balanced at each end. Heidi studies the stooped figure and is suddenly lost in a moment of remorse; she concedes, *This, could be my grandmother.* A salesperson approaches and Heidi snaps back to reality.

Heidi stands in front of the mirror in the huge tiled marble bathroom; Mathew steps out from the American-style shower and proceeds to dry off, waiting for her to look at the sex on display. 'We are to have no secrets?' poses Heidi as she strives diligently, to secure her hair, balancing precariously on the top of her head.

Mathew seeks a reason behind the question; finding none, he replies, 'True.'

'Then I am exceptionally horny. I really enjoyed the two girls.' Giggling, she loses concentration and her hair collapses. 'Bugger, I tell you truly I never shared that experience either.' Heidi dithers, indicating intent to continue, doubtful and dubious of the impending reaction. 'So, can we do it again tonight?'

Mathew wakes at sparrow fart. The memory of the night's romantic dinner floods back, wrapped in an element of sexual tension. The table is allocated perfectly, offering a long, wide view of the river. To the south, a white cruise ship lay moored; the activity on the dock takes precedence in the viewing selection.

'Are they making ready to sail, Mathew?'

'Probably. Most cruise ships arrive at their destination in the morning, so the tourists can tour during the day and then at night, off they go. And in many instances, arrive the next morning, at the next port.'

As it turns out, he's wrong. A layover in Ho Chi Minh City means at least a two-night stop; there's much to see – the city itself, the Mekong Delta, a fast hydrofoil trip down the Sai Gon River to Vung Tau or the Cu Chi Tunnels, which are not far out of town. And there is an opportunity for those inclined to golf at Song Be or the twin-course complex at the Vietnam Golf facility or to journey farther to hilly Dong Nai.

Dinner is concluded to rave reviews. The cooking is French in influence. The fish fillet entrée 'petite,' yet makes up for it, by the delicate flavour and is complimented by the generous portion of pork chops, delivered with a distinctive sauce containing, he recognised, a faint splash of Cointreau. The contradiction concludes with baked ice cream and that, really tickles his imaginations and his taste buds.

Peering into the mirror, the man gazes back, smiles broadly and declares, 'I love this.'

Mathew replies in normal voice, 'Me too.'

He cleans his teeth, swirls mouthwash and returns to the bed, only to be asked, 'Who were you talking to?'

'Myself.'

'About last night?'

'Something like that.'

'You enjoyed the girls?'

'Yes.'

'I particularly reveled in watching you enjoy the massage. You obviously love the experience.'

The word *tranquility* pops into Mathew's mind, confirming, *My heart truly is at peace, in a state of utter tranquility.*

Heidi sits up. 'Hey, we forgot the test.'

'No bloody wonder. At least we had our priorities in the right order.'

She dives off the bed, reaches into her purse and removes the list. 'I'm ready. You?'

Mathew retrieves his wallet. 'Ladies first.'

'Canada.'

'Yep, me too. That's a good one, the maple leaf truly representative, although I'm not sure the French in Quebec would agree.'

'USSR.'

'No, it doesn't exist anymore, just democratic Russia.'

'Was a good one, though, the hammer and sickle typical, hey. And you know North Vietnam before unification had the same symbol on their flag and what did you call Russia?'

'Democratic. Times have changed, no more KGB.'

'Are you kidding me?'

'No, why should I?'

'Then you're serious. You believe Russia is democratic?'

'Yes.'

'You've been listening to Bush too much. Tell me who the FSB are.'

'Crikey, I don't know.'

'They took over from the KGB. Nothing has changed as their members dominate the duma. and as to democracy, ask the human rights advocates in Russia and the people of Chechnya. Mathew, your ignorance appalls me. If you're a modern history buff, what did Chamberlain say about Hitler? Because that's what Bush said about Putin, 'trustworthy'. Frankly, I don't think Bush has got anything right.'

'Well, you're a little gold mine of knowledge. Modern might have to become a subject of choice, and as to current Russia, let's chat one day as you obviously know more than me.' Then presenting a straight face, he says, 'But we deviated off the test. What about the Banana Republic?'

Noticing the hesitation, he adds, 'You know, a yellow banana circled in a small green leaf on a white field.' He struggles to maintain composure, but the grin emanates from his eyes and gives him away.

'Oh, you silly bugger.' She punches his arm. 'You had me going for a minute. However, I have one for you. This is a beauty. You ready? The Boxing Kangaroo.' Heidi falls over on the bed, laughing and slapping the pillow in obvious delight. 'I bet you didn't get that one.'

Mathew just grins, wallowing in her incisive sense of humour. 'Okay, you got me. I like it, very clever. Any others?'

'Of course. How about Israel? The Star of David appeared on a flag, way back in the fourteenth century.'

'Oh, very good, Heidi, I missed that one and I liked the history lesson. You have any more?'

She says no.

'Then I have one more that put the fear of God into many a man, woman, and child, the pirate flag.'

'Ah, beauty, Mathew, that's clever. How about the UN? I just thought of it.'

'Abso-bloody-lutely not.'

'Why?'

'Because it should be called the Ununited Nations, and the map should be all the countries fragmented. Christ, to think of the money the wealthy nations of the world waste on that disorganized organisation, I cringe. No, sorry, can't have that one, so I declare the game's a tie.' Yet neither notices Heidi actually won.

On Saturday, their last day to play tourist, Mathew conducts a quick reconnoiter of the brochures and calls out, 'How about the full-day Mekong River tour? The pickup is at nine o'clock. Can we make it?'

Heidi, in one motion, vacates the bed. 'I bet you a personal massage I'll beat you to the lobby.' Heidi wins; regardless, Mathew knows he'll be the winner.

The Mercedes bus includes a mix of Aussies, Kiwis and a few Yanks. After a two-hour drive through the countryside, they arrive at My Tho, an interesting town. 'Orderly', Mathew offers as they park opposite the river and the tour guide points in the direction of the restrooms. Mathew takes one whiff and decides, no one should rest here.

Heidi comes rushing out, wrinkling her nose. 'Wow, not very nice. Change the town name to My Po on the Mepong.'

Mathew gazes up and down. 'Yes, this is a river. The Murray is a creek in comparison.'

A commercial ferry conveys them to the other side, where they walk a short distance and catch another boat, that takes them downstream, whilst angling across the waterway at the same time, eventually alighting, on what they discover later, is an island. Here, they take a jungle walk and meet a huge python where the adventurous drape it around their neck for the obligatory photo opportunity. 'Come on, Mathew,' encourages Heidi.

'No bloody way', he objects and backs away.

'Chicken. Take the camera.'

With that, one of the local boys drapes the snake over her slender shoulders. 'Wow, it's heavy. Quick, take the photo while I'm still grinning.'

Under an umbrella of tall trees, accompanied by the songbirds, heard yet not sighted, they arrive at a bee farm. The tour guide keeps moving them along to watch coconut lollies being made; they swallow a sample of pineapple grappa and chew on a juicy native pear. Then they unexpectedly arrive at a little rickety wharf, which appears quite by magic in the middle of an orchard. In groups of four, they squat on tiny seats, in wooden dugout canoes and are paddled, by two Vietnamese ladies, through the jungle on tiny natural canals. Occasionally, small heads bob up amongst the reeds as the local kids cool off in the muddy water. Two matronly American ladies pass by as one boy rises sufficiently for just his hand to rise above the level of the boat; Mathew thinks the screaming might be heard in Ho Chi Minh City.

A beautiful botanic park hosts them for lunch. It contains a spectacular, high and long aviary. Mathew is disturbed at a small enclosure, containing several types of monkeys, springing and jumping in the cage as if stressed and in a form of panic. He expresses serious comment to the tour guide. Westerners do not appreciate seeing animals so enclosed and encourages the tour operators, to point this out to the park administrators and then he threatens to report the incident, to Australian authorities. Heidi listens and adds a comment in Vietnamese on Mathew's behalf, while wondering at his bizarre anxiety about a couple of monkeys, when millions of people in Vietnam struggle, each single day to survive.

Lunch is a whole deep-fried fish with the curious name elephant ears. 'Funny name for a fish, Heidi, and clever the way the chef sits it on the fins.'

'Almost too good to eat.' Heidi wrinkles her nose. 'But I'll try.'

The waitress, strips off chunks of the firm white flesh, wraps it in a small lettuce-type leaf with a combination of fresh vegetables and tops it off using a battered old wooden spoon, ladling on the dense, tangy dark sauce.

Heidi is enraptured in the day's adventure and when time is opportune, comments, 'First time I see so much of my birth country and visit historical places. I have to thank you, Mathew. I am surprised you know so much of Vietnam, so thank you from the bottom of my heart for being here and expressing your sentiments, about our future.'

They pause at an antique-type shop. To Mathew, it's a mass of old junk, some in a dreadful state of repair; however, amidst the trash, Heidi discovers a treasure, a hand-decorated old pottery teapot and admires it at length. Mathew, perceiving her attraction, commences into mirthful negotiations, resulting in Heidi, coming into possession with a piece of the past. Tears decorate her eyes as he makes the presentation. 'It is very old, Mathew. How I'd love to know its history. Maybe over time, it will talk to me of its past.'

Heidi considers her man, both honest and true and worries about having foxed him, something savagely, over her contract. *But what can I do? It's too late to say other. He will lose trust in me, so I will keep the money. If he becomes my man in perpetuity, then I will give it back as a gift, from my savings, which is true, yes? Yes, of course, it is, then he will be lucky Mathew.*

On their last night, aimlessly in the stifling humidity, they wander without intent on a destination. At an attractive little restaurant called the Mandarin Cathay, Mathew orders duck and Heidi plays it safe and chooses sautéed chicken and pork, with half a dick as he terms limp noodles.

Satiated, wrapped in each other's arms, conversation ceases as the realisation of the moment, sinks in. Time drifts by, accompanied only by the hum of the air conditioner and the maddening beep of vehicles' warning devices. In a small voice, in pronunciation and resignation, tonight's it, Mathew laments it is their last night.

'Yes, I am very melancholy. However, Mathew Allen, I only have one matter left to ask. Are you ready?'

'I've already told you. Anh yeu em.'

'I like to hear it, but do you truly? Will I be yours and you mine to love and hold like this forever? My heart is pure. You are my first love. If I reside in your heart, treat me gently and I'll never waver.' She gazes deeply into his eyes. 'The wandering bark is just for you.'

It takes Mathew a moment to grasp the line.

The last day commences with breakfast, at the rooftop restaurant. Mathew eats healthily and sips unsugared tea, not coffee, which surprises Mr. Coffee and Tea, who's previously watched in fascination, Mathew shoveling the sugar.

Mathew has two issues to deal with and they ruffle his self-assuredness. 'I have two totally unrelated matters to discuss. The first is I'm going to Europe on business next month, just for two weeks. I'll keep in touch regularly, so nothing to worry about. And secondly, you must post-haste arrange for me to pay out your contract. From today, you are finished with the pillow world.'

She grins outwardly but not inwardly. 'Yes, I'm committed and thank you for my contract. I'm a free woman and can return to uni., to complete the last part of my law extension course, full time. I'll be finished by Christmas so I can work on my golf game so next time, I might beat you. Pity we did not have time, there are many good courses around Saigon, I'm told.'

Mathew encourages Heidi not to travel to the airport, but she insists as does Pinh Lhoung, who has another tour group to meet. 'Another group of Aussies, mate.' She laughs, adjusting the little gold kangaroo some friendly tourist has given as a memento. 'It brings me good luck and the Aussies always laugh, when I greet them by saying, G'day, mates.' Shaking their hand, she extends her thanks and good wishes. Pinh turns abruptly and directs her attention to the next challenge.

Mathew and Heidi sit talking until the last desperate minute when there's no choice, he has to go. At the last parting embrace, she hands him a note. 'Open it on the plane, please.'

Without hesitation, he passes into the security area, taking one last longing and loving glimpse, which lingers.

Heidi retreats to the nearest seat, remorseful as she isn't comfortable, with the way, he has almost flippantly told her about the Europe trip. *Why didn't he ask me to go? Why did he wait till the last minute to tell me? What business would he have in Europe? Doesn't gel. I'll instruct my spies to seek further information. Apart from that'* – she brightens – 'all went according to Hoyle. *I am indeed a good farmer. I tilled the ground, planted the seed and watered it. I'm confident it will sprout, but most importantly, I won his heart. I think he shocked himself when he first blurted it out. I saw the moment of confusion. My heart nearly died, but he revived it and what surprises me most, he is, in fact, quite romantic. Ha, fun, hey.*

She brushes down her ao dai, swishes her hair and strides briskly and confidently to the taxi rank, oblivious to the stares she commands as, like Pinh Lhoung, she is already preparing for the new challenge – to meet her sister.

Mathew uses his diary, to list matters, requiring attention before Europe. He's in no hurry; it's a long flight. Deliberately and carefully, he rechecks the information, together with the notes attached thereto, to ensure no slip-ups. The work in progress offers intent to pass time before dinner, so as not to dwell in a state of regret over Heidi and the pangs of conscience, offering sustenance, to the worm of worry, nibbling away in his head and heart.

After dinner, willing the sleeping tablet to work, he lets the lovely Heidi wander through his brain; and then remembering the note, he opens it and laughs quietly. 'One more flag, Ireland. Good one, hey.' Like the dawn, realisation pops over the horizon and the rays of understanding warm his heart. *I've loved her since I first settled into the back seat of the Rolls.* And, he thinks, *how weird. It was love at first sight. I never would have believed it possible and this time, I won't stuff it up.*

Was it Min Xie who said once that life is about karma, like the song 'Que Sera Sera'? Maybe the writing was always on the wall. Min Xie and I were not meant to be, because the gods knew, Heidi is the ultimate part of the plan for Mathew Allen.

Chapter 44

At Steve's office, conversation progresses firstly and rightly to business, concentrating specifically on marketing strategies. The market's holding, sales are strong and the office bubbly and buoyant.

Unannounced, Mathew proceeds directly to Brian's office; Mandy beams her welcome and introduces her new PA, Sue. 'Brian is interstate. Shall we go out for coffee?'

Over a cup, Mandy acknowledges, 'Business progresses without any hiccups. Your people are so bloody professional. Anyway, can we have dinner one night? I need to go over the Rhine day tours again.'

'Friday?'

Mandy nods, continuing, 'Have you seen Milly's sale list for last month?'

Without waiting for a yea or a nay, she enlightens him. 'Five Hong Kong sales, allocating one to Preston, so with the two agent sales, we only have two remaining. I can tell you the boys are rapt. Then there are two hotel suite sales, due to the price point and two units in Sydney, and then, Mathew, cop this. She rolls in two more Adderley sales from the golf day. Can you believe this girl?'

'Lucky she isn't going to Europe. We'd go broke. So, Mandy, what is her gross sales volume out of the golf day?'

'I know it off by heart, seven sales with a total of $2.646 million.'

'Christ, that's worth $26,460 to the charity.' He thinks, *My god how bloody marvelous.* He smiles. *And Milly can take all the limelight.*

At Cashmore's office, Mathew discovers he's out, which is of no concern, all he needs do is peruse the first draft print.

'There's an unrolled copy on the boardroom table. Would you like a coffee?'

'Thanks, Kate. Can I go peek?'

'You peek. I'll coffee.'

The plan appears sensational at first glance; however, it's the detail he needs to check. And while devouring two coffees, he completes the scrutiny and suggests to Kate, 'Tell Tony, apart from some of the densities on the golf villa unit precincts, which I don't believe meet council requirements, I'm happy. When can I have copies?'

'Looks good, hey?'

'Yes, his work is outstanding and quick, but that's between you and me Kate. Otherwise, he'll get a big head and increase his fee.' He winks.

'I hope so. I need a pay raise.' She winks back.

Mathew trundles out the sales and commission ledger and brings it up-to-date by including Milly's latest creations which, she's emailed while he was away. With no suspect sales in the books, he emails his friendly business banker and asks him to approve an overseas transfer of $US35,000 and in a substantiated manner, faxes the commission statement, knowing he'll be blown away.

His final call is to May; they chat about family and then his trip and the next one coming up quickly. She confirms everyone is set for the golf day. 'I relented and invited Min Xie and that bastard Vincent to play with Ian and I.' He knows she is smiling.

'Why are you smiling, May?'

'Because Ian asked me out. We had dinner last Saturday night.' Now she is really smiling. 'Yes, very nice night. And hey, changing the subject, I have to ask because Janet and I talked about Min Xie storming out last time. She's nearly always angry and grumpy, what did you do to upset her?'

'Nothing. Ask Janet. Maybe she's having problems with her new man.'

'Janet said you stirred Min Xie about him not attending the golf day, nor making a donation. Maybe this time, he'll be okey-dokey.'

May's phone rings immediately as she hangs up. 'Hey, Mayla, its Min Xie, just confirming Thursday and to tell you Vincent is going to make a big donation to surprise everyone, so can you give him a good welcome and invite to the podium?'

May agrees, knowing clearly, who Min Xie means, by 'everyone'.

Min Xie doesn't disclose, Vincent had only agreed to the final donation, after she spent most of Sunday afternoon, trying to get his willy up and active, even if it had been, brief.

Afterwards, her recollections, contrary to the chilly winds, brought warm thoughts of Warrnambool, Shepparton, and Kyneton. *If Mathew only knew, I have him in my heart.*

A coffee cup greets Mathew at Tony Cashmore's office. 'I'm too bloody smart for you, Mathew. Do you know why I had several wrong densities in the planning? Because I want Hugh to have a win and pick me up on the odd point and that'll give him gratification and recognition, before Missy.' They move to the boardroom table, where Tony adds, 'Remember, in planning, everyone needs to win, young man.'

'Hey, hold the bloody phone. I'm older than you.'

'Yes, but you look so much younger. It's all that hair.'

They proceed to walk the course with steepled fingers. Mathew appreciates, Tony has used Barry's Bush, to allow the animals to access the fairways, so as not to interrupt, current habits. He regrets, the bush is unavailable for the locals to enjoy; still, the rights of the animals, in this instance, come first. The riverbank protection is created, by utilising golf course fairways as setbacks and the bush adds the bonus in width.

'Pity we have to set back so far,' Mathew throws in.

'Yes, but it allows us to utilise the circular walking path, to go right along the bank, with several designated contemplation places, which I believe are worth the trade-off, particularly this one.' Tony points at the most distant contemplation spot. 'On my last visit, I spent a lot of time, trying to discover exactly, where the bellbirds gather and this is it.'

Mathew can only nod, wondering at the genius and the extra mile Tony has taken, just to make a specific part of the project, something special. Tony walks his finger to the facility centre. 'How is this going to work in the Trilogy concept?'

'For the first-stage clients, it has no effect as they are out in the residential nodes and the walking paths traverse the precincts, so you have covered that well. The key is stages two and three, which have to be adjacent and you've incorporated that as planned, with the clever use of the combined kitchen service area.'

'Maybe not. What happens if one area comes down with an infectious disease or gastro, something that makes one area quarantined for a period?'

'Yes, that's a bloody good point.' Mathew scratches his head in sympathy with the observation. 'That one I'll leave with council to nut out. Maybe they can work with VicHealth.'

'True, but you know me. I like to have it right. I'll work on it.'

Mathew's last thought is, 'Is the community centre too isolated?'

'No, I don't think so. Still, like everything else, it's open to comment. I elected to set it away a little as it allows for some after-hour functions, community parties, dances, private functions, even hire it out for a wedding or other function. The income will help supplement costs.'

'Point taken, but it doesn't work well, being separated from the kitchen. And you're right, income is a priority. That's all from me, Your Honour.'

'I'll contact Hugh and set up my next appointment. I think, as the "official" proponent, you should be there, even if for no other reason than to wave the flag and express any concern. We'll play good cop, bad cop. That way, I keep my nose clean with Hugh and staff. And by the way, a small second kitchen is easy to include.'

CHAPTER 45

Arriving at the golf club, Mathew makes his way to the pro shop, where he pays the green fee and checks out the new range of golf bags. He finds Milly on the putting green and kisses her on the cheek; she kisses him squarely on the mouth. 'Not trying to be forward, but your ex is watching. Do not turn around.'

'Thanks, I'm actually fired up to play well today. I gave myself a five-minute talking-to in the car.'

'With an ulterior motive, your old lover and her new man are here and you'd like to stick it up them, something fierce.'

'Spot on. By the way, did you work out the donation payment? I assume Brian sprung for it.'

'Too right, he invited me into the office to meet and greet. I know Mandy, of course and I met her PA as well. Nice girl. We had coffee and cakes and calculated the donation to be $26,460.'

'I concur.'

'Mandy presented me with the cheque, made out to the charity. I'm a bit nervous, Mathew. What will I say?'

'You know better than me. I gave you the idea. You put it into words at the last golf day. Who could have imagined it would bring in so many sales? You've been brilliant. May and Dulcy will love you forever.'

'Pity, you did not include yourself. Still, I know we are only for straight sex, when the spirit inspires us and isn't it wonderful? No complications, no demands and no jealousy.' Smiling, she adds, 'And I'm going to ensure the fervor motivates us often. I love sex and I need it regularly.' She let the contemplation drift around her erogenous zones.

Ian arrives all bouncy and chirpy, 'Hey Shifty, want $10 on the game and where did you find Milly? Even with slacks on, I can imagine her legs go forever.'

'Milly and I are business associates and you're on with the bet. Have you seen May?'

'She's in the pro shop. Do you know we are playing with Min Xie and the new bloke?'

'Yes, and by the way, a little birdie told me someone, took someone out for dinner, last Saturday night. How did you wangle that?'

'Lots happened while you were away. Life changed. I'll talk later.' He grins like a little kid with an ice cream.

Mathew answers, 'Yes, for me too. We really do need to swap some stories.'

'See you later and good golfing, if you can concentrate.' Ian shakes his shoulders, laughing.

Mathew indeed has one of those days and Miss Golf Luck played with him, but he plays match play with Vincent all around the course. Min Xie is there too, watching in the murky depths of his despair.

Ian rushes into the clubhouse, all smiles. 'I like this course, Mathew and it liked me. How does thirty-eight sound?'

'Just give me the ten and I will not embarrass you.'

'Oh, come on Shifty, what have you done now? I played brilliantly.'

'Sorry, mate, forty-one but still, you had a good day?'

'Yes and, you remember Min Xie down the Bellarine, bright chirpy little thing? Well, today – Christ, mate, Miss Frosty and her bloke, what an arrogant arsehole who played like a dog. Can you believe twenty-one points and only eight coming home?' Ian laughs out loud. 'It was a classic. I said to May at one stage, couldn't happen to a nicer prick.'

May said a quick hi and asked Mathew to look after E as she's busy. He caught the use of the nickname and thought, that didn't take long.

Janet and her group join in as does Mr. and Mrs. Chang, whom May and Mathew played with previously. More introductions are required as they brought their guests along, to join the big circle. Mrs. Chang shuffles up beside Mathew, saying, 'Mr. and Mrs. Zhou will make a small donation today. You know, Mathew, I think it's a wonderful charity.' She grins. 'Maybe because we all worry about our old age.'

People come and go; the crowd is like a tide, in and out, always changing, except for Min Xie and Vincent. Mathew tries not to be obvious, ducking and weaving, trying to grasp a glimpse, with his gut churning, endeavouring to fathom whether it's anxiety or jealousy, or does his ego reside in his stomach?

Mrs. Chang returns and asks for a private conversation. They move to a relatively private corner, and Harry Yao makes a determined play for Milly, but it's Mrs. Chang who has Mathew's attention. 'We are very private people. My husband and I hold matters entre nous. We have decided, to buy an upmarket unit for our children to use whilst at university, one that we can turn into an investment or part of a retirement plan, but we do not want anyone to know. Often, people become jealous and envy overtakes common sense.'

'Which uni?'

'Why, Melbourne, of course.'

'Yes', he thinks, 'who's up who here?'

'We will pay up to $750,000, but it must be off the plan, so we save all the abominable stamp duty and it must have a view and of course, excellent transport.' Mathew extracts a business card and writes the address of the Adderley Street project, saying, 'Have a look. I can do a great deal for a one-level penthouse. If you have an interest, I'll deliver the plans and specifications.'

Mathew wonders if Brian might appreciate tucking some cash overseas and that it may be worth a discount and besides, the Changs will have to declare the money, if they bring it into Australia.

May calls for attention and introduces Dulcy and the club captain, asking them to make the presentations. 'When May first started this charity golf day, she gave my association the opportunity to join you. On behalf of my committee and all the Alzheimer's sufferers, I extend thanks for your support. Those who attended the first day will remember, this man made the first donation and I think it is most appropriate,

I announce, Mathew Allen has won the day, with forty-one points. The crowd parts as if by magic and Min Xie stands almost in isolation and to Mathew's surprise, she flashes a smidge of a smile and a nod of recognition. Unable to contain himself, he grins and feels it spread across his face. He thanks his playing group for their support, commiserating with the runners-up. 'Been there, done that.' And he continues to smile as he congratulates May and her committee, on the great work they do and how much, is taken for granted.

Mathew is unaware Min Xie stirred Vincent after the last golf occasion, and the purpose of today is to knock everyone's socks off with his large donation. In conclusion, he says, 'And shortly, Milly will make a donation to the charity.' He notices the look of surprise, Min Xie passes to Vincent; her smile vanishes, replaced by an expression, depicting the coming of the next ice age. May repossesses the podium and with a sweeping gesture, recommences proceedings.

'My dear friend Min Xie is here again today, accompanied by her golfing partner.' *Hmm*, May thinks, *I did that well.* And she carries on. 'Dr Vincent Woo has asked to address you, so please welcome Vincent.'

On his way to the speaker's stand, Vincent is suddenly overcome in a manner of trepidation, like a buyer negotiating for a hot property. *I'm going to be gazumped.* The premonition sticks in his craw and that causes his attitude, to swing from Mr. Confident to Mr. Weary. He freezes on the dais and feels the sweat gathering on his forehead and under his arms. 'This', he mutters, 'isn't the way I'd planned it.' The cheque is momentarily lost in his wallet.

A wag who knows him, calls out, 'The moth's not willing to let go, Vinny.' Min Xie blushes openly in embarrassment.

In a quiet, almost timid voice, he commences, 'Min Xie has been to all these events and encouraged me to be here today and may I offer thanks, for the welcome?'

'What bloody welcome?' Mathew sneers amidst rising anger at seeing this particular man, on what he arrogantly perceives, is his turf.

'As a doctor, I understand the other side of this disease. And as such, I present to Mrs. Bright and her charity a cheque for $15,000.'

Min Xie blinks. 'What happened to my recognition?'

Vincent beams as the crowd erupts, his chest protrudes and his ego expands; accordingly. Mathew's antagonism proliferates, in Holy Communion with his gut. Min Xie sidesteps a guest, affording a clear view and eyeballing Mathew, who taunts him as if to say, Up your arse! But all he sees, is her unmistakable beauty and how stunning she looks.

Two corporate guests make a donation, the entertainment ceases and Vincent retires from his brief moment of joy. To all intents and purposes, the day's over. The crowd senses it. Guests drift towards the exit.

Mathew reckons she's leaving it a bit late. Milly recognises the terrific timing and makes her move. Like a Massey Ferguson tractor out of control in the farmyard, she scatters guests like chickens, jumps onto the podium and like last time, patiently demands complete attention as Mathew muses, how brilliantly she takes command, without uttering a single word. Crowd noise diminishes; a sensing of something important about to occur simmers. Several people glance around, aspiring to ascertain what's going on. 'Last golf day, I made a short statement about the investment property business Mathew Allen and I are involved in, and I offered a percentage of each sales made to or via you will be donated to Dulcy's charity.' She stops purposely to heighten the tension. 'It is my pleasure now to acquaint you with exciting news.' The pause is almost insensitive as people ponder the revelation. Her grin widens and looking with purpose at Vincent, announces, 'Seven members, friends and associates have invested with us.' She directs her attention to Mathew, winks and without hesitation adds, 'I have here a cheque' – she flourishes it almost arrogantly, waving it vigorously – 'made out to the charity and I'd like Mathew to come forwards and help me present it. I wouldn't be here, without him.'

Mathew searches out Min Xie, winks cheekily, and raises his eyebrows. *And up your cute arse too.* He glances at Vincent and wags his shoulders as if to say, *Got you this time.* Milly extends the cheque to Mathew, who motions for Dulcy to join them. 'A cheque for $26,460, we know you will use it well.'

Milly takes Mathew's head in her hands and kisses him hard on the lips, they embrace and the crowd goes crazy, as all the pent-up tension dissipates; it's like a football grand final day. Milly completes the handball and Mathew kicks the winning goal. The crowd cheers as the members and guests mill around; Mathew discovers late, it was Steve and Ian who started 'For He's a Jolly Good Fellow'. Mathew reckons every time he hears that song; he thinks of silly bloody Neville Chamberlain waving his worthless note.

Celebrations are abruptly cancelled as the worry worm makes nuisance in his gut. *Is my Munich approaching?* He shuts his eyes and Heidi appears. She does not look happy.

Reality resumes. Milly is on a high. 'If you support us, we will support the charity. We'll be here next November with another cheque.' Adroitly, she drops the bomb. 'And maybe if you visit Dr Woo, he'll come back with another cheque too.' Then she directs a wicked grin at Min Xie and Vincent. The crowd is totally unaware of the meaning of her barb, takes it as a great joke and laughs continuously.

Mathew's day is made, yet the worm churns. Milly strides past him, saying out of the corner of her mouth, 'I'm so fucking pumped up after that. I need to go to bed with a great man. What are you doing later, great man?'

Remorse and anxiety mix with melancholy and loneliness as he ponders Heidi and her commitment. *I'll never waver. The wandering bark just for you.* He confronts his personal demon and offers privately, *'Love alters not with his brief hours and weeks, but bears it out even to edge of doom.'*

'I'm going to confront the past, Milly. Don't go too far away. I need to talk to you.'

He finds Min Xie on the far edge of the crowd and can tell she's fuming as her little cheeks, glow red like traffic lights. Vincent is verbalising her aggressively. Mathew notices the veins jumping out of his skin and wonders, if that's smoke coming out of his ears and how frigid it might be at home tonight. Vincent stomps out with shoulders slumped. Min Xie scans the ceiling. Inexplicably feeling sorry for her, alone in the midst of such merriment, Mathew excuses himself to no one in particular and trudges towards the triumph, which has turned into a tacky, tardy mess. Min Xie spots him coming and bores into his eyes her face full of anger and hate. *Bad move, Mathew*, he concludes.

Min Xie unloads her bucket of bile, whispering, 'You bastard, you and your bitch, you deliberately upstaged Vincent and me. He lost much face and I lose face too. It's your fiendish plot to embarrass us, you horrid man. I hope I never see you again. Vincent has gone in shame, because he lost control as you upstaged him.'

Tough, Mathew thinks, suffering no compunction to be sorry. He did, however, recall a wonderful trick learnt many years ago. When someone tips a bucket on you, just smile and ask them to repeat it. Imparting his best smile, he says, 'Sorry, I must have missed something. Can you repeat, please?'

Min Xie, confused by his tack, is suddenly indecisive. Instead, she bursts out laughing. 'I always said, watch out for, Mathew, he is the best salesman. You turn my anger, you clever old bugger.'

'Maybe it wasn't real anger?'

'Yes, it was.' She stomps her foot, shaping to go.

'Check with May. There's no way Milly or I could have been privy to your plans.' He extends his best smile. 'Regardless, it was nice to see you smile. Tell Mr. Woo, I personally challenge him, man to man to bring his cheque book in November and match Milly and me.' Powerless in victory to control his arrogance, it bursts forth as he laughs stridently at his superciliousness and downright impertinence, that will be regretted later, but for now, he inserts the knife again. 'You may not have appreciated seeing me, but I enjoyed looking into your black pools. You are, as ever, my beautiful little hotchew chick.' He looks at the ring. 'Beautiful and symbolic?' She stares at his finger; Mathew understands she will recognise the game as she turns at the door, smiles and offers a little wave. *In defeat, or has she surrendered? Will she telephone tomorrow and most importantly, what might I say?*

Appearing at his side, Milly demands, 'Did it work?'

'If you mean reconciliation, no, won't happen. Possibly, friendship may return one day but never the way we were. You did great tonight. I'm pleased you received due recognition and thanks from me. I appreciate it.' They hug closely as the friends, they truly in time, will become.

Milly changes the subject, 'No contacts today, maybe we have stripped all the fruit, from this garden.'

'One door shut. Another opens.'

'Meaning?'

'Referrals, if they work, there's the answer.' He reckons her brain is in calculation mode and gives support. 'We need an override system.'

'Mathew, you are as foxy as all get out.'

'Sometimes. Anyhow, how are things in Hong Kong? Everyone happy?'

'All good except Uncle. He's suffering from arthritis, claiming his time on the sea is nearly up.'

'Would you bring him to Australia?'

'Ah yes, I tried that, but he said he's too old to change his woman.'

Mathew and Milly share the company of Sheridan and Christine Ho, who after the game utilise time to catch up with friends. However, as Mathew prepares to leave, they approach him with a very quick, simple proposal revolving around a commitment to purchase two properties, one for straight investment, the other a holiday rental, mixed with private purposes. The codicil attached, includes the condition the Ho's retain a commissionable right, to arrange sales via contacts in Shanghai, on the basis of half commission upfront, balance on settlement. Catching Mathew at the death of the day, offers restricted time to negotiate, so he explains the facts of life, suggesting 3 per cent with one paid upfront and two on completion and sweetens the pot by taking the bit in his teeth, suggesting buyers may qualify for a discount, by paying 10 per cent of the price, using either U.S. dollars or British pounds overseas and 10 per cent in yuan as long as the currency is already domicile in Hong Kong. Soon the Ho's will be additionally rewarded as the referral plan, already germinating in Mathew's sales pyxis, will considerably enhance their commission account.

Walking away, Christine Ho, without even turning sideways to address her husband, comments, 'An abrupt type of fellow at business. Acceptable terms, though and I think my friend Florence will have oodles of referrals for 1 per cent.'

CHAPTER 46

It is only later, via May, Mathew learns indeed, the ice age arrived at Min Xie's house. Fiery, spiteful Vincent attacked with a foul mouth. 'I told you when we agreed on our arrangement, you must never see him again and you must never talk. How come the bastard knew of our plan? He set me up to take my money and to chat you up. You still have the bloody hots for him. I saw the wink. Are you bastards in clandestine contact!' A small bit of spittle gathers at the corner of his mouth. Min Xie imagines it bubbling with his blood pressure. But her own fury is fired by his elucidation in the extreme, so slowly and deliberately, she lays it out for him, word for bitter word the challenge Mathew dangled. Vincent goes ballistic at Mathew's arrogance to issue such a challenge, which he gathers is like pouring sour cream on top of Milly's rotten cake. In payback mode, for the personal bucketing he's heaped on her, Min Xie concludes, 'You're so bloody smart. Tell me, how he'd know?' Vincent stomps up the stairs as Min Xie watches with a sense of doom descending. She makes a cup of tea and sits on the couch. *I see you, Mathew, on my couch, cuddling, having coffee, dunking my doughnuts, chit-chatting about our golf, being in love. You are in my heart. My loins ache for you. Ah and to have your kiss. Wow, our kiss drove you crazy. Yes, you silly old man, it drove me crazy too. I miss you so. Should I call you? What would I say? What would you say? But I have manufactured my bed. I must therefore continue the repose.* Gently, she places the cup on the table and takes each step with painful purpose as if carrying a heavy load. Approaching the bedroom, stops and peers at the threshold, smiles resolutely, shakes her shoulders in resignation and crosses over, to another world.

Mathew is in reflective mode. *Golf is often the stuff that binds and the girls are bonding like the house and the fire and my personal relationship with Ian is developing. I need a close mate, someone to communicate with.* He dwells on his mental anguish over the split with Min Xie, heightened by not having anyone close to share the highs and lows. Then he meditates on the recent escapades in Asia, the day on the boat, the beach, sex in Vietnam, all about Heidi, someone to talk to and he cottons on to the fact, that's the trick – Heidi to talk to, to have and to hold. *Wow I really do miss her.*

On the way to Milly's apartment, he breaks the news. 'I consider you a friend, whom with May I wish to remain close to.'

Mathew pauses as Milly pushes the boundary.

'Remember, going to the Murray River project, I sussed out your moments of silence. Is this another one of those?'

'I'm in love with a young Vietnamese girl from Hong Kong. I met her on the first trip."

'Bloody hell!' Milly exclaims in excitement. 'Heidi Hendrickson, ah, you men are so silly. I told you they'd test you and you confirmed the temptress attended the dinner. Then Uncle tells me, he recognised unusual verbal and physical body language at play. I asked him to discover more. I don't know how, but after your next visit, he said you'd spent a night with her on a boat. Ah, how delicious. Why did you go to Vietnam? Of course, to see Heidi.' She takes a more serious pose. 'Uncle is adamant, she is the most beautiful lady he ever met and that is some statement, coming from him, so tell me all.'

At Milly's front door, they hear the phone ringing incessantly; she rushes in, listens intently then says, 'Yes, he's here. No, we've been at the charity golf day. Did you forget?' She turns to Mathew. 'It's Brian. Bad news.'

'Yes, mate, it's Mathew.'

'Mandy has been run over! It appears she tripped or stumbled outside the office and fell into the path of a cab. She's in St Vincent, critical.

'Where are you?'

'Home. Nothing I could do, just been on the phone.'

'I'll go in. Does she have family in town?'

'No, just us.'

What does that mean? But then this is not the time to ask, Mathew decides. 'Any change, shall I ring the house number?'

'Call anytime.' Brian hangs up before he can say hooroo.

'How weird our lives are. We share a wonderful day while someone close to us is at death's door."

'Shall I come with you?'

'Thanks, nice offer but if she's critical, nothing to do. I'd just like to be there for Brian. He's really cut up by the sound of his voice.'

'And I'm here too if you need me.'

Mathew looks at his mobile phone, knowing he deliberately left it off during golf presentations and dinner, forgetting to turn it back on, which he now does, thinking, *It's a bit bloody late, mate.*

Because he isn't family, Mathew, is starved of meaningful information. Patience his constant companion, forced to wait, stoically sipping the stale, sour coffee, traipsing the tired hallways, thumbing through trashy tattered magazines of ancient vintage, annoying the staff in pursuit of updates. Stretching self-restraint, he twiddles his thumbs for almost three hours and slowly arrives at the conclusion, he is becoming accustomed to the coffee. Then Dr Edmondson appears and elaborates, 'She has internal damage and has undergone surgery and technically, she's not critical. We have managed the internal damage including a bleeding spleen. Also, she broke a leg, a nice clean break that should mend without complication. There are severe facial and body abrasions and they will heal with time. Her vitals are strong, so we are quoting stable. You might be able to visit after ten o'clock, but contact the nursing station prior too.'

Mathew provides the latest update, and after a short backwards and forwards, Brian asks, 'What will you do about the Rhine tour?'

'Haven't even thought about it.'

'With respect, may I suggest you take Heidi? I have a premo you're closer to her, than you'll ever be to Mandy. This is Father Brian talking.'

Mathew stops at an all-night cafe, purchases a double-shot latte, loads it with sugar and returns to the car to contemplate Heidi, Europe, Mandy and Brian's suggestion. *As much the accident is a personal disaster, it finally resolves, I truly want to be with Heidi and I just dodged my own personal Munich crisis and Winston would have been disappointed.* He laughs at his perceived smart comment, swallows the last dregs of the coffee, goes back into the shop and suggests, 'Wanna swap cups?'

The old bloke emits a grunt. 'You're on for another two bucks.'

It's a two-hour time change to Hong Kong and Mathew decides it's not too late

'Xin chao, Heidi. I've not woken you?'

'No, I'm watching a late movie. Wait, I'll shut the TV off, so how are you? This is a nice surprise.'

'Yeah, good, thanks. I had a great day on the golf course, won a competition.'

'Congratulations. I've been practising and working tirelessly on my university course.'

'Good for you. Look, Heidi, a situation has arisen with my European trip. My associate can't go and we've had to cancel meetings. However, I've booked and paid for a Rhine cruise it's non-negotiable, not refundable. So, if I change my flights via Hong Kong, this could be something very special for us to do together, so I'm asking very earnestly, will you join me?'

'Is this about us, a life together? You really want me to go?'

'Silly moo, of course.'

'Then no question, I'm in. Explain more, please.'

'Oh, that's great, we can have more of that special time together. Tomorrow I'll email all the relevant information. You might have to book there. Anyway, I'll talk to Qantas in the morning. And by the way, I still haven't received the contract payout.'

'So sorry, been negotiating a lessor sum. I'll chase it up tomorrow. Good night, I love you and thank you, Mathew.'

'Yeah, love you too. Night.'

Heidi hangs up the phone and calls out in excitement to Sri. 'Wake up! The gods indeed are smiling on me and this time, I'll be in Melbourne. I guarantee it!' But deep down, she worries about a two-week cruise and how it fits in, with a series of business meetings; it doesn't sound right.

Mathew breathes a sigh of relief. 'I can complete the pursuit without paddling or piddling, muddying the water.'

Milly is curled up in bed, watching a video movie, her mind on the one that got away.

Mandy wakes to find Brian holding her hand. Always the patient, caring father figure and concerned, he gathers the strength to convey the truth, recognising the bad timing but she has to know. Now alone, in slight physical discomfort, the bitter taste of the pain pill is sweetened immeasurably, by the dozen red roses that must have appeared in the wee hours. Aggravation is abated further, by a surprise phone call from Hong Kong, a message left at the nursing station.

Chapter 47

Mandy is tied to a movable post containing a drip, morphine pump and antibiotic drip, together with an oxygen supply obtrusively stuck under her nose. Mathew settles into the usual hospital talk. 'How are you? Are you in pain? What's the time frame?'

'My surgeon is visiting later this morning so all will be revealed, I assume.'

The nurse reappears and suggests politely, 'It's time.'

'Sorry about Europe, Mathew. I wanted to do that special trip with you, but life has ordained differently. I'll think of you, send a card to home, come give an old crock a kiss. Just don't lean on the bed, I'm a bit tender.'

'I'll see you before I go. Take care. Steve and Milly send regards, she enjoys your company, hook up when you're on the road again.' Mathew notices the roses as he walks out.

'Hello, Mathew. I love you. Now you say it. Thank you. I know you'll be happy I negotiated my contract down to $US30,000. Therefore, send to account Ngay Mai Ngan

Hang Company, bank number 07 066 0467, account number 555 976 006. The answers to your questions are listed below. I understand, Qantas will send confirmation to the airport office and I'll collect the ticket on the day. I will see you on the plane, as you'll be in transit. Please send more info re what I should take. I like to travel light. I'm so excited. Are you too, my love? Love you.'

At the coffee shop downstairs from Brian's office, Mathew ponders the news about Horace. *Eighteen months for perjury, over a really minor infringement, relating to the Wood enquiry, and I reckon he's been nailed, to the cross of opportunity.*

The family dinner begins stiffly but eventually comes together and towards the end of the night, Mathew delves carefully into the subject of the settlements and how they should proceed. Andrew takes control. 'As far as the girls and I'm concerned, you do what you think is right. We're going to mutually benefit in one way or another. Just keep us in the loop.'

That's all very well. I appreciated their confidence, but they are being naive. What if I decide to marry again? Mathew lets it go, deciding now isn't the time. Hope has been relatively quiet and now pipes up, 'I'm happy to retain this house unencumbered and the beach house. Smith's is for all of us to use as previously discussed, Mathew. I have a good super scheme, but worst-case scenario, I'll sell Smith's, or you buy it to keep in the family.' Mathew blanches; this wasn't part of the agreement and without any personal debate suggests, 'Why don't we just change the title to Tenants in Common in equal shares, instead of Joint Tenants?'

'What does that mean?'

Andrew bobs up with the explanation and concludes, 'That seems fair. Mathew hardly uses the place, yet we're receiving the benefit.' With all eyes focused on her, Hope perceives the duress and complies unhappily.

'Thank you, my son, nicely done.' Mathew recognises he has just dodged a dangerous bullet and pleased at the outcome, changes the subject and discusses his trips including the Rhine tour, which is rapidly approaching.

'You're amazing how you travel by yourself,' Hope quips.

Mathew couldn't contain himself. 'Yeah, well, at least I go.'

After golf, Mathew visits Mandy and notices four bunches of flowers arranged neatly. 'My, you are being spoilt.'

'Yes, and bloody none from you, mate.'

'Mine will be here today. The nursery has to grow them as my instructions were explicit. They must be particularly remarkable blooms.'

The effort to laugh promotes a grimace. 'You're full of it, bugger. I can't even laugh properly.'

'Who are the best friends?'

'Starting from the left, Milly, Steve and Brian.' Mandy pauses purposely, intending to add mystery to the moment.

'And the dozen reds?'

'Keng.'

'Then his invite to Hong Kong and Tokyo was for real.'

'You didn't believe me?'

'Oh yes, I believed, just never considered it further. You certainly made a big impression. Anyway, how are you feeling today?'

'Oh, Mathew, you can be such an arrogant prick, never considered it further indeed.' She is angered. 'I'm good, no pain, sat at the window in the sun for a while. The heat on my body is a wonderful feeling. The doc is happy. The op went well. He envisages no complications. Tomorrow they'll start disconnecting me from all this.' She waves at the mobile post supporting the paraphernalia. 'I'll be out in a week. I snuck a peek at my body this morning. God, you should see the bruises and the abrasions. I'm so lucky.'

'How did it actually happen?'

'Well, I was walking towards the road – you know, outside our office. There's no parking as the cars use that lane to do their left-hand turn into Rathdowne Street. Silly me, I tripped. I remember stumbling, trying to keep my balance, worst thing I could have done. I fell onto the road, and – bang! – that was it. If I'd taken the fall, the accident wouldn't have happened.'

'Trying to stop grazing your legs.'

'Exactly. Ego is a terrible scourge and look at them now. Will you be first to sign my plaster?'

Scribbling a note, he asks, 'Who will look after you at home?'

'Brian will arrange someone. I'll be okay. Go to Europe and enjoy and have a nice Riesling or twenty-seven for me.'

Mathew rushes home to prepare for his first official dinner party. He's decided to prepare an entrée of King George fillets on soft mash with a thin slice of carrot and a couple of long beans to add some colour. *Mains*, he reckons, *will be a real bloody surprise.* It is to be followed by simple fresh fruit salad topped with cream or ice cream. *I'll percolate coffee and serve after-dinner mints.*

He has previously prevailed on Ian to bring Milly as she's on the way. When the bells rings, he's wearing a tuxedo jacket, a white tea towel drapes over an arm and imitating an up-your-nose British accent welcomes them with. 'Welcome to the Allen residence. Please, to enter the drawing room, Mr. Allen will join you shortly.'

'You're a silly bugger, Shifty,' Ian concludes in typical laconic fashion as he sets off in exploration of the accommodation and the office. 'How do you work with that view?'

'Not easy at times.'

'I don't want to be rude but this must cost you a bomb,' May questions.

'It doesn't actually, did a deal with a business-related company, that owns it fully furnished and we adjusted rent, against my commission account.'

'Creative accounting. Your numbers man must love it.'

A Krondorf chardonnay is passed around while they discuss the golf day. Retiring to the kitchen, Mathew reheats the mash; with the veggies and fish prepared, he asks the guests to be seated. Conversation arrives at his most recent travels, including Hong Kong with Milly, Vietnam and then the impending Rhine River sojourn. 'Something I always wanted to do.'

'But by yourself?' May poses pointedly and worries. *A man like Mathew does not go on a river cruise by himself. He takes a lovely young thing on his arm, so the fun begins. Who is the filly, because it's not Milly, it's not Mandy nor me and it certainly isn't Min Xie? Hmm, all Ms. What does that mean?*

Dinner is placed on a large serving tray, covered with an oval-shaped lid, discovered in the bowels of the bifold corner cabinet. Comments concerning the delight about to behold are many, amidst great expectations and extravagant flourish, Mathew lifts the lid, exposing four Big Macs. Silence prevails for a moment, until the funny side tickles the right bone and they burst out laughing.

'You bloody idiot, Shifty. What a classic.' Ian laughs.

'Oh, come on, Mathew, what happened to the roast you promised?'

'That's next week, Milly.'

During the evening, Mathew catches silent glances, secret peeks and peeps between May and Ian. *See, doesn't matter how you try to hide it. Someone catches on.*

Later, in front of the fire, Mathew suffers more pangs of conscience that are stirred by his failure, to stop the situation until Milly saves the day. 'Mathew, may we speak as friends?'

'Of course, always between you and me.'

'I love our sex, but it's more important we are always true business friends and my associates are of common thought. Trust and respect are developing. I'm urged, therefore, to protect our business relationship and I tell you truly, we are like the moon, starting as a sliver, a fingernail cutting. But as time moves on, it grows bigger and bolder until it is full and bright. Do you know the American saying about a harvest moon?' Without waiting for an answer, she says, 'We are going to have a bumper crop.'

'What are you saying?'

'Sex must not disrupt business. It's for fun, our mutual satisfaction but not for love.'

Mathew pulls her close. 'Deal but know in your heart, Milly, you'll always be close.'

'Thank you. Now let's go to bed.'

A bell rings in his head; one peal is for Heidi and one for business. Suddenly circumspect, Mathew says, 'No, not yet. An idea is rattling around.' He pauses in final debate, offering Milly the instant to ponder as she wonders, *Crickey, what's this all about?* And sex falls off the page. 'You recall the eleven-golf course frontage lots at the river?'

'Yes, great sites.'

'I've offered to buy them.'

Milly squirms, desperate to know the nitty-gritty but grasps this is Mathew's time and he'll control the telling.

'Each lot will be subdivided; I'll design site-specific condos on each lot and apply for planning and building permits contemporaneously.' He stands and paces as ideas rage. 'During the process, I'll sell each lot to an investor client from my databank. Then I'll contract with one builder, ensuring a construction scale of economy is maintained.' He smiles. 'As you might say, a win-win.'

Excitement escalates as Milly wonders if an offer is forthcoming.

'Each unit will be locked into the project's rental management plan, first year guaranteeing a 6.6 per cent gross return. Investors who hold, will find the rental yield providing succour and security, while the project beds down. The upshot is a profit will be made from on selling the lot, a fee from the client to cover the cost of the permits, plus, say, a flat fee of five to ten thousand, depending on the construction profit projections and a 3 per cent commission from the seller, when on sold to the end investor. The key, Milly, is the first investor will be a very happy chappie and will be automatically locked into a databank, ready to go again.'

Milly anxiously debates that, like the season, there's a reason. *They are not my clients, so what's the cunning bastard up to? Ian is right in calling him Shifty. He could, in fact, be a shifty, slippery little shit!*

Mathew pauses, deciding how to pose the offer. For Milly, the wait adds tension to the tremor in her tummy. 'This is probably a three-year deal. In out, done and dusted, no downside, no risk.' Milly wonders if she should comment and decides to go for it. 'Sounds like a great deal and typical of you, all the round pegs in the right holes.' She grins, wondering if he'll pick up on the inference.

'I like you, Milly. I love your attitude to business, so in accord with my beliefs and in recognition of sealing a great relationship, would you consider doing a partnership deal with me?' As he has imagined, there is a degree of silence. The opportunity is sublime as he is fascinated at the numerous ways her mouth moves; her eyes circle, open and shut; her nose flare and he even thought her ears wag. He grins. She grins. 'I reckon we can make a quarter of a million minimum each.'

For Milly, reality finds an office and the business chip clicks into place. 'So how much did we offer?'

'One million five hundred and forty thousand dollars.'

'Seventy a lot.'

'Exactly.'

'Will it buy it?'

'Not sure but it'll be close, as it's really $77,000 gross, if you add on commission, interest and marketing.'

'And the deposit?'

'Standard 10 per cent, $154,000.'

'And how do you propose to fund the balance, equity or debt?'

'That will depend on you.' He smiles.

'Why?'

'Because I want you in and I'll make it as easy as I can.'

'Thanks, but the more we borrow, the more interest we pay.' She holds his eyes. 'I can come up with $270,000. Can you cover it?'

'Yep.'

'Then you have a deal partner, but I think you're wrong. We'll not make that much. You're close but not quite.'

'Really?' He sits forwards and she explains.

When finished, he knows it is time. 'Let's go to bed?'

'But just for sex, Mathew. If it's going to be you and Heidi and we are partners, this will be the last time for us. No hassles and no angst, deal?'

And it is.

CHAPTER 48

On Sunday, Mathew drives his mother to Mordialloc for lunch on the pier. The specialty's an old favourite, flattie tails with lots of salted chips washed in fresh lemon squeezed by hand. His mother rejoices at the opportunity, to talk of the old days, when the family gathered on the adjacent beach, playing cricket. 'Anyone around could join in.' She laughed. 'If the sheila's a good-looking sort, then the boys'd argue over whose side she'd be on, until the giant of a husband would turn up and the boys, duck for cover.' Laughing brightly, she recalls the day Charlie panics the swimmers. 'He spots several sharks, heading towards the beach, running up and down, screaming, "Shark! Bloody shark!" Everyone joined in as the throng rushed out of the water and turned back, in safety, to look at the evil menace, only to find a pod of dolphins cruising past.' She hesitated and then added, 'The highlight at the carnival was a long highly polished bumpy timber slide. The rider sat on an old wheat bag and went flying down the slippery dip, often coming a gutser on a bump. The smart blokes gathered at the bottom, the uninitiated girls would normally lose control and find their dress over their head, with the boys copping an eyeful. Bit of a bugger, son. Us girls never had a chance to have a good perve, not like the blokes.'

At his last visit with Mandy, Mathew wants to ensure the wheels are oiled and if the PA will be up to it. 'Don't worry, she will be a gem. I'll be lucky to get my job back. I might return as her PA.'

'Yeah, pigs might fly.'

Ian phones and asks if he can pop in and say g'day. Then Mrs. Chang phones to confirm they like the position and to question the quality of completion, will it meet their standards. Trusting it can, he commits and agrees to deliver the additional information required.

Ian and his wife have agreed to split; he's at home in the little third bedroom, until he finds a new abode. 'Are you under pressure to move?'

'No, but it's coming. This is one corner I can see around.'

'Any plans?'

'Yes and no.'

'Fucking hell, Ian, tell me the way it is, not that twaddle.'

'Well, I think I've fallen for May. Can you fall in love so quickly?'

'Have you slept with her?'

'Yes, first bloody night, went home to her place. Strewth Asian sheilas, I've never in all my years had sex like it.'

He is grinning but Mathew wonders if May is trying him out. 'Did you last night?'

'Yes, her place again. It was just as sensational. She is so loving and caring and grateful. Bloody hell grateful. I should be on my bloody knees, thanking her.'

'Could it just be about lust?' he asks.

'I guess so, but I really like her. I love looking at her, I love touching her, I love it all. You know, she got up this morning after we did it again, made coffee, and bought it to bed with something called Chinese doughnuts, you have to try them, dunked in coffee. Would you believe?'

'Does May know your situation with Jan?'

'Yep, told her my life story, held back nothing.'

'What would you do – and think carefully – if she asked you tomorrow, to move in with her?'

'No hesitation, I'd go. I wouldn't want to leave a chance, for someone to come along and steal her away from me.'

Mathew's gut churns automatically. *Hello, anyone home?* 'If the pressure mounts, come and live here. I have a spare room. It might be perfect. In fact, why don't you just do it? Use the pad to woo May, although it sounds like the wooing has been done. Bring her home here, turn the heater on, put all the cushions and pillows on the floor, kick back and relax with a bottle, and go for it.'

'Oh, Mathew, that would be great, but I couldn't stay forever.'

'No, you can't, but it's a start.'

The week disappears. He speaks daily to Heidi by email or phone. Her tickets are confirmed by Qantas Hong Kong. 'Mathew, you did not tell me we're going business class. We are in seats 6A and B. You are spoiling me.'

Tuesday is Tony and Mathew with Hugh and Missy. They still haven't picked up on the wrong densities. 'But they will, mate.'

The meeting progresses in an orderly, professional manner, following the traditional town planning, sparring and negotiating, pushing the boundaries, measuring the perimeter and then pulling the extremities back to an acceptable reality. Hugh gives support, although it comes with nothing definitive, so they know the number of objections, will dictate the future.

Mathew meets Brian for a final general chat as he needs to ensure absolutely all projects are on line and as they are parting, Mathew exclaims, 'I've done a deal with Sheridan and Christine Ho for sales out of Shanghai. You'd better hear the deal I've concocted.' Mathew proceeds in explanation, which they both realise arrives at the right time. 'We might need some new blood, mate.'

Brian concedes. 'No hassles, just try to work out the foreign currency bit and interpose Milly if you have to.'

Only after Brian's approval does Mathew tell him they have agreed to buy two units.

'You are a shifty shit. Which project?'

'Rye. It's perfect because the permit has been approved, two sales straight upfront.'

Mathew has elected to use the same architect who has designed Preston; he appreciates the two-storey town houses, conceived for that site, will suit ideally and apart from some tweaking, it works. The facade instructions have been simple, face brick and weatherboard with some stone features keeping it beachy modern. The final plan, finishes up, comprising four two-bedroom units, each with en suites and three single bedroom units, with a small multipurpose area extending from the living area. To Mathew, it is the usable fifteen-square-metre decks, Calvin has designed, that add much to the functionality of the entertaining area, particularly due to the northerly elevations, escalating the holiday environment over the bay.

He's asked Calvin to proceed immediately to working drawings and apply for the building permit at the same time, keeping the specifications standard, the same as Preston and finally suggests he'll receive a call from Milly, seeking copies of all the plans. Then, Mathew raises the issue of the Changs and an Adderley Street penthouse.

'Mate, try locking it in with a 5 per cent discount, as long as 20 per cent of the contract is paid overseas and we'll pay you out of that. If it's a goer, refer to Sue and she'll make the fund arrangements.'

Mathew visits Mandy three more times during the week and, on each occasion, debates, *Is it sorrow, regret, or absolute bloody delight that the windmill turned at the right time?* He notes no improvement except her facial abrasions have turned to scabs.

'My scabs are ugly and itchy.'

He reminds her about the ugly duckling and in appreciation, she tries to smile.

His last visit is the most difficult as he realises he's going to pursue a dream, whilst her dream, is simply to make a full recovery and it seems strange Mandy has declined to pursue, what has happened to the other ticket. Departing, he notes the flower count, has risen by another dozen red roses.

Ian moves in. Mathew hands over the key he's extracted, by agreement, from Mandy's purse. The boys have invited the girls over for pizza and beer. Ian and Mathew are bonding as are the girls. The night is one of merriment and lots of casual banter. Business banished backstage until late in the event, when Ian confirms he's been paid, his 'first pat the dog' fee. He elucidates on Mathew, mentioning he should use it to go away golfing; he grins at May and asks, 'Are you in, somewhere overseas?'

As there is no hesitation from that quarter, he concludes by posing, 'And are you guys in?' Mathew tries to play a straight bat but Milly's right out there in her enthusiasm, so he is forced to go along with it. Yet they both know deep down this is one plan they'll fail to consummate; still, the trip will eventuate and they'll tour Vietnam. Only Mathew and Milly will be accompanied by other partners.

Mathew and Ian ride together to golf. Mathew debates discussing the trip but decides not now and instead, he takes the opportunity to talk about new cars. 'I've been thinking but no action.' The chat resolves, he'll buy a Subaru Outback or something of that ilk and retain the Jag. Being an accountant, Ian queries, 'Why new? Go to the auctions, go second hand with up to six or eight thousand K's and you'll save at least eight, maybe ten large.'

His last meeting is with Milly. They shake hands. Mathew is surprised. Milly laughs. 'Isn't that the way partners greet partners?'

'Yeah, good one. Come here and give me a proper cuddle.'

She pulls away. 'Come, we have a lot to do and I have to be at Brian's office. Make me a coffee while I set myself up on the dining room table.'

'You talk while I make ready.'

'Okay this is what I've done, Colin Hargraves plucked a company off the shelf and we need to impart our own name and I'll send it to the bank and Brian's Solicitor. Then I visited Stuart at the ANZ and delivered a copy of the draft contract, the feasibility study, the estate plans, and original copies of the permits. Stuart's comfy with the lend up to 65 per cent, plus an overdraft to cover the costs of the plans and permits, on the understanding each marginal profit from the first sales cover the costs and we've calculated that accordingly. I went to see Bruce Bruce-Smith. I love his name. Clever parents, hey?'

'Or twisted.'

'But he's too upmarket for us, so I'm happy to go with Calvin, but I'm going to have trouble with their names, Frantonelli and Georgeopolous.' She grins.

'Just call 'em F and P like we all do. It's a great combination, Italian and Greek.'

'Yeah and all they need now is for the next partner to be a Turk.'

'Yeah, I like that, so where are you at with Calvin?'

'He's committed to have all twenty-two plans ready for your return.'

'Great, but keep the pressure on to complete the working drawings and the building permit application. And, Milly, I trust you on this. Why don't you just run with it? You know our priorities. We've agreed on style. All he has to do is switch them around. The floor plans are easy, the inclusions we've agreed on and if you're not sure, go and have a natter to Steve.'

'And you'd like me to have them built and all sold by the time your home.'

'Of course. Want another coffee?'

CHAPTER 49

He holds the glass to the plane window, studying the brilliant translucent red of the West Australian Cabernet Sauvignon. Today he's indulged in two glasses of this particularly fine wine as it combines perfectly with the prime fillet of beef.

Mathew invoiced Keng before he left home for the first $250,000 fee, arranging with the bank to send a confirmation email to his Hotmail, reckoning he'll find a computer somewhere to confirm its arrival; and in turn, instructions are provided for the bank, to transfer $110,000 to Brian's general business account. He encourages various sundries to run riot through his brain, which leads to recalling Brian's comments on Mandy and the Rhine and him suggesting that Heidi take the trip. *Where did that come from? So bloody obvious, you idiot. Who does he talk to each day? Who is he bringing to Melbourne? Of course, Sri. So, is he sucking her for information, or is she freely emptying her bucket of knowledge gained by her friendship with Heidi? Then again, maybe Heidi's feeding the information to Sri, knowing she'll pass it on.* Then later, he thinks, *yet is Heidi foxy enough? The answer has to be yes.* Mathew understands all the Asian girls he's met have, in their own way, been sharp as a tack and maybe even a little tricky. He ponders on his own infidelity, his affair with Min Xie, Milly in Hong Kong and Melbourne, his preparedness to take Mandy to Europe, knowing fully the sexual implication thereof and now Heidi, who he readily admits is the girl he wants to spend his life with, yet he was prepared to turn his back on her, to ride down the Rhine with Mandy. He knows, the new business deal with Milly will change their sexual relationship and Mandy, one might say, has missed the boat, but someone is in pursuit. The red roses flash green. He confirms his contrived plan, offering Milly a partnership in the eleven lots, reduces profit but it equally diminishes risk. He appreciates, she'll work her bum off to entice initial investors and then, sell the investment package. In the end, it will lead them onto another project. 'Yes', he admits, 'a good deal.'

Finally, the flight is called. Mathew assumes transit will be ushered on first, so he loiters as long as possible before going on board, where he waits just a few minutes, before she arrives.

He's shocked by how beautiful she looks. Nothing's said except *xin chao* as he folds her into his arms; without any hesitation, she kisses him hard. A hostie walks past and winks at Mathew. 'You make a beautiful couple. May I enquire if this is a special occasion?' Heidi takes over and virtually explains their life story. Mathew thinks she's lucky to escape as Heidi is all revved up. Mathew sinks into the depths of her black pools. 'I love you Heidi, you look so beautiful. I am so happy you are here and we are taking another step in our discovery.'

She peers back into his eyes. 'Anh yeu em. You remember, yes?'

'Yes, em dep lum.'

Heidi, being in 6A, has the premium seat to admire and marvel at the sparkling, twinkling view as they take off to the north. The panorama over the harbour and the city is amazing until, finally, they bank steeply to the left, climb into the clouds and seek coordinates to track to Rome. The engines remain on full power, quickly pushing them above the clouds, onto the ceiling for the flight.

Heidi is dressed in denim, complemented with a fine traditional pale blue street shirt, unbuttoned to show off the small swell of her breasts and the white lacy bra flashes seductively and her hair hangs naturally, like the lyrics from the song, streaming, flaxen, waken. 'You're looking so intently. Are you pleased?'

'You have no idea.'

'You can tell me in bed. We can caress each other, arouse the passion and lust that will drive us to our mutual pleasure, so are you aroused?' She looks down at his crotch. 'Later, when they turn the lights off, I'll find out. Can you tell I have missed you?' she whispers.

'You'll drive me crazy?' he suggests quietly.

'You have no idea.' She smiles 'Can you see in my eyes, Mathew Allen?'

'No.'

'Pity because you would see my love. It is there. Seek it with truth and love in your heart.' She relaxes back in the seat and gazes at the fluffy layer of clouds far below, completely understanding, *Now I have you. I'm going to drive you sexually crazy as I know how to please a man and you will never, for one moment, have the energy to look at another woman, let alone consider taking her to bed. You are mine; Mathew Allen and I intend on keeping you.*

'As you have tempted me with this wonderful trip. I've been busy reading the history of all the major cities we are going to visit. I thought maybe we can play games and test each other like in Vietnam.'

In Rome, it's hot, humid and uncomfortable. The airport is grubby, the service people surly, and the small shopping outlets rude and uncivil. *'Typical,'* Mathew muses, *'what's changed?'* Then waits like a coiled cobra for someone to give Heidi a hard time or make even the slightest innuendo about race or colour and he'll explode. 'It's a pity,' he complains. 'We have to wait three hours in this dump, to catch the onward flight to Vienna.'

They pass the time drinking coffee, which at least is strong and full of flavour, even though it costs seven dollars a cup. Conversation continues unabated about their lives, the past and the future. Then Heidi asks, 'Hong Kong has nine hills. How many in Rome?'

'Bad luck, Heidi, I know that one. Seven, so my first question to you is – and I'll give you one as a factor of argument – how many seas touch mainland Italy?'

'Good one, Mathew, so the Adriatic, the Ionian, and the Tyrrhenian, but is there one more, or is it just called the Gulf of Genoa? Hmm, if it has another name, I'm stumped, so I'll say three, plus the Med.'

'Very clever. I thought the Mediterranean might confuse and the gulf does have another name as it really forms part of the Ligurian Sea.'

'Here, try this one. It should be easy. Turkey is the only country residing in two continents. On which part does the Gallipoli Peninsula lay?'

'Ah, yes, canny question for an Aussie. I have to think, from Istanbul did I cross the bridge travelling east or west, before I turned south and then back to Ephesus, Troy, Canakale and crossed the Dardanelles. So in Europe.'

'Made you think though.' She wrinkled her nose.

The flight to Vienna is uneventful, but it's overcast with a slight drizzle, but it does nothing to stay Heidi's excitement, as the hotel bus conveys them to the Hilton Vienna Plaza located on the Ringstrasse. The sauna and the whirlpool seem appropriate as the most sensible places to start. Heidi carries with her a handful of tour brochures, to plan tomorrow's adventure.

Changing into street gear, they set out to find a cab as a busload of Aussie tourists arrive into the hotel drop-off area; they are boisterous and obviously having fun. One bloke assumes Mathew is a local and acknowledges him, as he walks past, with 'G'day.'

Before Mathew can reply, quick as a whip, Heidi says, 'Good on ya, mate. Beaut day.' And keeps walking as Mathew turns to the bloke and winks. He suddenly laughs, seeing the funny side of his blooper and being replied to by an Asian sheila, so he heads off excitedly to repeat the story.

The cab drives them through the bustling streets to the Sudbahnhof, passing the Belvedere Palace and its spectacular gardens. Heidi carries a small map, so it becomes the driver of the cultural tour, which includes a walk along Prinz-Eugen-Strasse, where upon reaching Schubertring they turn right. History is part of the beauty of old Vienna, intermingled with the arts and architecture; recognition of the visual culture adds appreciation to their very long walk, through the old days long gone. Heidi offers as a simple matter of conversation. 'Isn't that what you come to Europe for?'

The drizzle stops. It isn't particularly cold for Mathew, but Heidi shivers occasionally. They pass several restaurants and eventually, driven by the ravages of grumbling, hungry stomachs, they settle on one featuring little flower boxes out the front, with red and white check curtains, adorning traditional, colonial-style windows. Inside, the greeter is a man in lederhosen, and Heidi remarks, 'He is very cute and traditional.' The waitress is dressed in a white blouse, a traditional full dress with a red and white check apron. 'What shall I order, Mathew?' Fortunately, the menu is printed in German and English, which Heidi considers, a particularly smart way, to please the tourists.

'Up to you, mate. Anything that tickle your fancy?' Mathew asks for a pot of tea to start and the waitress hesitates. He nods and she wanders off, shaking her head.

'Maybe the beef schnitzel sounds good?'

'Entrée?'

'No thanks. I save up for Bavarian apple pie and a traditional Austrian coffee. I love apple pies.'

'With real thick cream.'

She grins. 'Or ice cream. I don't care.'

They resolve to walk dinner off, but it becomes too cold for Heidi. She doesn't complain; still, Mathew grasps she may well be uncomfortable and she's being stoic.

Reception, seems the logical place, where Mathew can pursue access to a computer. 'On the first floor up the stairs, turn right or left out of the elevator.' Settling at a workstation in the business centre, Heidi assists Mathew as he battles to start the computer and discover the way, into the Hotmail address.

'Bloody modern technology, you know it won't last, Heidi,' he states in an authoritarian manner.

She giggles, replying, 'You silly bugger, you open it like this.'

Achieving success, he discovers one solitary email from the bank. It reads, 'Mathew, you can now enjoy the trip knowing you have the $ to pay off the credit card! Currency transfer from HK confirmed, transfer out completed. Enjoy. Have a stein or 27 for me! Stuart Cross.'

Heidi doesn't ask him what it means, but she reads it, giggles internally and silently thanks Mathew for this holiday, knowing the Aussie forty-odd thousand dollars now reside, safely, in her overseas account.

The awakening is different. Heidi has risen early and filled the spa; the fresh, rich aroma of coffee tantalised his nostrils, but shortly, the doorbell rings and Heidi rushes to open it, ushering in the waiter, who places a tray on the small table, departing as he acknowledges the tip with a German accented, 'Your've velncome.'

Heidi calls out, 'Close your eyes, Mathew.'

He feels the tray being placed on his knees.

'Open.'

Surprise spreads. 'How did you know, one of my favourites?'

'Just luck, hey. You enjoy while I check if the tub is nice and hot and bubbly.'

Mathew munches greedily into the large crispy apple Danish as he hears Heidi singing merrily in the bathroom. Contentment reigns supreme.

She returns to the bed, removes the tray and kisses him hard on the lips; he tastes fresh toothpaste. 'I love you, Mathew. Xin chao. Come quickly. The bath is ready.'

After cleaning his teeth and using the tiny complimentary mouthwash, he finds residence in the spa. Heidi waits on him, pouring the coffee and adds three sugars. 'I spoil you today, but really, two are enough and one day you will not have any.' She pouts, grins and stamps her foot as if adding confirmation, to the determination.

She slips the flimsy robe off and stands naked beside the bath. 'And what do you say to me after you look at me?'

He smiles. 'Yes, I love you, Heidi.'

Making the bus tour should have been easy. It left at nine thirty and Heidi woke him at seven thirty; it was a busy two hours.

Mathew has visited Austria previously as part of his tour with Bob; he recalls the spectacular country scenery, particularly the train trip from Vienna to Schladming, Bischefshofen, Innsbruck and Solbad Hall, which he remembers as a stunningly beautiful town as it was seemingly trapped in a valley, surrounded by towering snow-covered peaks and where vaulted archways, cover the footpaths. But he's forgotten most of Vienna, probably because he was hungover from Munich.

Heidi comes prepared with a brand-new Minolta digital camera and she isn't shy, asking people to take their photos, in front of all the sights and then offers to reciprocate. Mathew notices her propensity, to readily and without encouragement, slip easily into conversation with fellow travelers. She even tries it with the driver, but his broad, thick accent makes life difficult.

The tour does not include lunch, so rather than return to the hotel, they disembark in the city centre, deciding to walk with Heidi's little tour map as their guide. 'We'll become Marco Polo's true explorers, Mathew.'

'Then we're in trouble.'

'How come?'

'Think about it.'

'Ah yes, another test, so we're in Europe and he went to Asia. Ah, you silly man, you mean we are indeed lost?'

Unintentionally, they find themselves in Prater Park and Heidi notices a huge Ferris wheel. 'Can we ride it, Mathew?'

When Asian girls become excited, their whole face beams and their eyes twinkle and flash. He's seen the look on Min Xie's face many times and here is Heidi, glowing in eager anticipation. The view is spectacular, but to Mathew, it's the image of Heidi's delight, that will always be the epitome, of the visit to Vienna.

'This is fun. I like Vienna. Can I ask one thing?'

He nods, understanding if it was Min Xie, she'd probably have wanted to make love on the wheel. He couldn't help himself; he laughs, which prompts her to ask, 'You seem very happy.'

'Yes, Heidi, I'm suddenly very happy.'

He envelopes her and holds her close. 'I do love you, Heidi.'

She wiggles her bum and snuggles close – in excitement, he assumes. 'I'd like to see the Danube River. Is it blue, Mathew?'

'Is this a quiz question?'

She thumps his arm, laughing. 'No, you silly man. I just love the waltz and I envisage the blue water.'

'My golf pro told me to swing to the beat.'

'And do you?'

'You've seen my swing.'

'Yeah, it's more Germanic, swinininmissinhittinslicin searchinhuntinfindin.'

'Ha, you silly man, no wonder I love you. I'm going to learn that.'

Under his breath, he admits, 'They all say that.'

A cab driver, after some difficult translation moments, realises the destination, after Heidi waves the map under his angular ancient nose and drives them to a park with a quaint old bridge. On the way, he chats away furiously in German under the misapprehension, they understand what he's saying.

As Mathew pays the bill, he acknowledges the driver with 'Ja dunka bitta.' He rightly motors away, wondering why more tourists don't bother to learn his language before visiting.

'Oh, the water isn't blue.' Heidi pouts. 'God, I'm so disappointed. I wonder at the almost mystical mystery this river has held in my psyche, since I was a small girl at my open-air school and I stand here today, only to discover this.'

She throws out her arms as Mathew adds, 'You won't then be disappointed when you see Melbourne's Yarra River.'

'Ha, it must be muddy as you've told me that before.'

'Yeah, sorry, hate to be repetitive. It's like the opposite of having Alzheimer's.'

'And that's okay. They say as long as you can think about it, you don't have it.'

He debates the comment momentarily, shakes his head, and wonders if it's Heidism.

As the park isn't particularly exciting, they elect to walk back, following her handy little map. Inadvertently, they come across an ugly war memorial. 'Wow what's that?'

'Test question?' she poses.

He shakes his head as, grinning, she scrambles for her little book and completes the puzzle. 'Ah, a memorial to the Russian Army who liberated Vienna in 1945.'

Mathew couldn't help himself. 'Must be about time the Austrian's blew the bloody thing up, in the name of saving their reputation as a beautiful city.'

It was around four o'clock. 'What do you want to do, Heidi? This is as much your holiday as mine.'

'I'm happy to go back. Maybe we can have a sauna and a spa. I really enjoyed it yesterday. We can soak, have coffee and some little cakes and then tonight, I'd like to eat out again.'

'You're on. Let's go. If we follow this road and connect here' – he pointed to the map – 'we can see St Stephen's and we'll catch a cab back, all right?'

'So, Mathew, tell me again, what is the plan tomorrow?'

He swallows the last piece of plaice. 'God, that was good, so sweet.' He licks his mouth and then, using the napkin, dabs it as if stabbing tiny morsels of recalcitrant crumbs. 'Yes, well, we need to find the bus or train station and that could mean the Sudbahnhof or the Westbarnhof. I should have checked with the hotel. Remind me when we go back.'

She nods, thinking, *Forgetfulness, part of becoming old. Maybe I shouldn't have joshed him about Alzheimer's.*

'We need to take a bus or train to Linz. Perhaps the train is best, whatever is quickest. We have to be in Regensburg tomorrow night, sightseeing the next day before we embark on the boat at three in the arvo.'

Returning to the Hilton, Mathew needs no reminder to seek information about travelling to Regensburg. 'No trouble, sir. Train to Linz on a Eurostar and then change for the regular train to Regensburg arriving at four in the late afternoon. Do you have onward bookings, Mr. Allen?'

'No, can you recommend a hotel? Maybe in the town centre as we only have until three in the afternoon, when we need to be at the dock.'

'Yes, leave it all to me. I'll make train bookings all the way through. Do you want a private cabin on the Eurostar?'

Mathew seeks affirmation from Heidi, who shrugs, so he decides, 'Why not?'

'I'll book your hotel and a transfer to the dock. I assume you're taking the Viking Sun to Amsterdam. Do you have bookings there?'

'Yes, one night at the Sofitel.'

'I'll confirm that for you as well. Please have breakfast early and be here at eight for checkout and we'll transfer you to the station. The train will leave at nine sharp and shall I include the costs, onto your Visa card?'

'Yes, and I thank you for your wonderful service. Goodnight.'

Mathew sits up in bed, saying to Heidi, who's trying to solve the mystery of the on button for the television, 'Can you believe that service?'

'Yes, I can. And in the morning, I expect you to say the same to me.' She laughs. 'I had a lovely day, Mathew. May I ask why you come all this way and not book at certain places?'

'Yes, it's a bit silly, but I enjoy an adventure. Otherwise, it's all wrapped up in plastic.'

She offers no reply, understanding in the future she'll ensure there will be loopholes, in any travel arrangements.

Chapter 50

The Austrian scenery rockets past at a shattering speed. Mathew has forgotten how the Eurostar's zip along. Eventually, a waiter delivers coffee and sweet, sticky pastries. As he departs, Heidi locks the door. 'We did not make love this morning. I'm sure if you caress me, I'll become aroused as I know you will and we can make love on a train.' She removes her brightly printed blouse and lacy bra, lifts her free-flowing summer dress, removes her panties and lies across the seat, with her head on his lap. To Mathew, a rear seat of a car comes to mind and it all happens as she suggested.

'You know, Mathew, in Hue, I had never done that before. I was hesitant, but once the massage started and I saw her rubbing your back, then talked about your little man and we rolled over, wow, I became so hot.'

He smiles. 'It was special to me too, something new, erotic and exciting, and my sexuality and passion, for you, took over.'

'You were very strong that day. Your little man was so hard. I noted the same in Ho Chi Minh City. Would you do it again?'

Mathew concedes this is close to the bone. *What does she want me to say? When in doubt, answer a question with a question. No, bugger it, I'll wing it.* 'For an old man like me, to have sex in front of beautiful ladies was indeed something special. However, if you and I are going to be together, then I only want to love and enjoy you. Your body and your mind is enough for me as long as you can love me and enjoy me equally.'

She came up from lying on his lap to kiss. It was one of those never-ending ones which Mathew loves as he appreciates arousal soon follows.

They don't see much of the Austrian scenery between Vienna and Linz. However, the train to Regensburg is a real train; it is a trip back to reality as the motor is diesel electric while the passenger cars quite ancient yet clean and tidy. They find themselves sharing a compartment with two young English backpackers; it is difficult to tell which one is the boy and which is the girl. The other couple are locals who speak no English and offer no effort to communicate.

The kids are intrigued by Heidi and Mathew. 'But Heidi is Dutch and you are Chinese?'

'No, not quite. My father was Dutch, my mother Vietnamese with a Chinese connection, so half-half. However, I've lived nearly all my life in Hong Kong. In fact, Mathew and I just ventured back to my birth country to visit my elder brother, his wife and my sister.'

'Are you married?'

'No, just lovers.' Mathew stirs the pot.

'Are you blokes going to Regensburg?'

'Just for tonight. Tomorrow afternoon, we'll catch the cruise boat to Amsterdam.'

The kids help them pass the time as they are seasoned off-the-beaten-track travelers, a bit of what Mathew thinks of as 'I've been everywhere, mate.'

The hotel is perfect, very old, very much in the boutique mold with a touch of class. The rooms are spacious, loaded with all the modern conveniences, bright and airy. 'Someone has spent buckets on the upgrade,' he acknowledges to no one.

With daylight saving, it remains quite light; so donning their walking shoes, they set off in pursuit of an adventure. They hold hands, often arm in arm, oblivious to the world. They exchange a quick kiss, hesitate and then exchange a meaningful glance and Heidi invariably will grin, suggesting, 'Fun, hey.'

Dinner eventuates, in the dining room, of an even quainter hotel. Heidi brings her little map and tourist book out to conduct an examination. 'Do you know who founded this town?'

'No, but I'd venture a Roman.'

'Correct, but which one? I'll give you a clue. He was very, very famous.'

'Ah, has to be Caesar.'

'Logical, but it was Marcus Aurelius. The history can be traced back over 2,000 years. It is said to be the oldest city on the river and do you know this, smarty-pants? Why is it so well preserved?'

'I can only assume, because the Second World War passed it by, like Prague.'

She smiles. 'Clever bugger.' She wrinkles her nose and winks.

As the evening remains warm and with the continued blessings of the soft light, they proceed to walk the wonderful old town, where every corner is truly a postcard photo opportunity. Heidi is compelling, smiling brilliantly when asking anyone passing by, to take their photographs.

Indeed, the cock crows up the dawn. Mathew always understands it's a sparrow. Heidi lies in peace; he listens to her deep, rhythmical breathing, essentially moving in and out, whilst he identifies with the word *spent* as he's too tired even to brush the annoying hair that hangs over his face and he accepts the notion, 'she's going to kill me'. He opens his eyes and looks at the black strands of hair falling over his chest, retaining, the faint aroma of shampoo. As usual, he's on his back with Heidi partly over, her mound firmly implanted on his thigh while his left arm reaches down her back, caressing ever so lightly. She stirs. He speaks almost relevantly, conveying a secret. 'Xin chao. I love you, Heidi. Just to lie here with you is paradise.'

Her left hand reaches out, accepting his right into her soft grasp. She kisses his nipples. 'Can we always be safe and happy like this?'

'That's surely up to us. Our fate is in our hands and our hearts and you know, I thought recently of the word tranquility. It applies, yes?'

'Yes, it is a beautiful word and in my eternal soul. Mathew, I love you so.'

'Thank you.'

By the time he wakes again, Heidi is sitting on the couch, fully dressed. 'Xin chao. I was just about to wake you. We have a stunningly perfect day. Let's go exploring. Can I trust you to move and I'll meet you, in the breakfast room?'

Regensburg is truly a beautiful medieval city, with every street and turn exuding the history, in an almost brazen display, of how an ancient town should appear. Heidi utilises her little history book, continually offering the story on every building in town, until finally they reached St Peter's Cathedral, where they rest to take it all in and catch their breath.

Today, however, whilst the exploring is of significance, there's one appointment neither intends being late for, and it's deemed appropriate therefore that, as conscientious travelers, they'll arrive early to board the ship. Cabin 212 is located on the upper deck, it's pleasantly decorated in light, bright tones with comfortable appointments, including a double bed, two-tub-style chairs, a small writing or dressing table and a TV. Heidi finds the bathroom hidden behind the entrance door. 'Hmm, I like the tiny shower, Mathew. Will be fun, hey?'

Once the cabin door closes, a new phase in their relationship opens. Now they are locked together on a ship – and a small one at that.

Chapter 51

The window furnishings are open, to encourage the moon, to share the moment and for them to look down the harbour, at the incredible view. Mathew understands, sometimes dreams live up to expectations and Brian was right, Heidi is the girl to share it with as they bond and grow as one day drifts idyllically into the next, equally blissful one. Yet they've not been reclusive or singular of mind but instead seek to mix and mingle with the diverse guests on the ship, electing to sit at any table so at each meal time they meet people from various countries, with different ways of life, all sharing the same sense of adventure, the pursuit of a dream. The cities and towns they visit, turn the trip into one of walking, living history, watching the locals go about their business, while the tourist's mass around.

Heidi proves to be a fanatic shopper, loving as most women and some men the intense inclination to burrow into a shop, delving, discovering and seeking that elusive gem, or perceived bargain. Heidi becomes Peter Rabbit, finding a delicate jade necklace set in finely beaten silver. Even Mathew considers it an outstanding piece, but she declines it because of the cost. Mathew recognises she loves it as a slice of mystic unknown history, something she could dwell on and fantasise about, so he slips back later, deciding it is the perfect parting gift, once back in Hong Kong.

Mathew remembers Nuremburg as the philosophical centre of Nazism, yet the history far surpasses the short interlude of those terrifying years as it is a city dominated by wonderful Gothic churches, dating back to the thirteenth century. To gain access to the city, they motor a short way up the Pegnitz River.

Heidi rejoices at the brief visit to the Durer Museum. 'Oh, Mathew, I remember him from university art lectures. I completely forgot this is his home. What a surprise.' Mathew doesn't take to his work at all; it is too dark and somber.

'You know, Mathew, he pioneered the classicism of Italian Renaissance, introducing it to northern Europe.' For all Mathew's interest, he thinks, *He could have left it in bloody Italy.*

At Rudesheim, they ride the famous mini train. Heidi suffers the embarrassment of her hat flying off and falls over a culvert-type bridge into a muddy drain. She exclaims without thought, 'Oh bugger!' Mathew is the only person around who laughs.

Bamberg, a World Heritage site, tickles Heidi's fancy as she comments, 'Like Hoi An.' Then she questions the ancient heritage of her town going back to the sixth century, whereas Bamberg traces its history past the Romans.

Mathew loves the majesty of Cologne, where the magnificent cathedral seems to overpower all from the outside; inside, it totally dominates the conscious mind, struggling to come to grips with the intricate amazing detail of the design and exquisite decoration. He sits for ages, endeavouring to capture the creative genius and spirit of the architecture, until Heidi rouses him to move on.

The river towns add image to the history and beauty of the Rhine Valley, through which they traverse. Whilst the weather is perfect, some early mornings and late afternoons, when a breeze rises off the river, heightened by the influence of the valley's geography, they obtain large rugs to snuggle under, sitting out in the fresh air, sipping morning tea or an afternoon white wine. Invariably, Heidi will comment and Mathew becomes attuned, to when she might say, 'Fun, hey.'

Mathew continues the geography and history tests they set each other. One evening approaching Cologne, he asks, 'So, Heidi, next test, how many rivers have we travelled on?'

She thinks long and finally says, 'You're going to trick me like that silly equator question. The obvious answer is one, the Rhine. But at Nuremburg, we went up that other river with the funny name, so the answer is two.'

She grins in expectation of the teacher saying, *Good, girl Heidi, go to the top of the class.*

Instead, the teacher says, 'No, wrong.'

She sits up, almost spilling her Moselle, 'Really, I am wrong?'

'Yeah, sorry, mate. We actually have sailed on the Danube as that is where we started at Regensburg, then the Main

River and finally at Mainz we connected into the Rhine, plus the Pegnitz.'

The surprise at the conclusion of the trip is the inclusion of an ongoing cruise through Amsterdam. To facilitate the negotiation of the canals, they transfer to a glass-topped boat specifically designed to take the shallow, narrow waterways and to navigate under the bridges. It is one of the highlights of the trip and so unexpected.

However, Mathew recognises, without hesitation or contradiction in his heart, the real highlight of the trip is simply Heidi. They revel in each other's company, both willing to compromise, see the other's point of view, go where sometimes, they'd have elected to take the other tour, if they were by themselves. No angst, no impatience, no pushing, no urging on, no arguments. It is as one old Kiwi lady has said. 'You are the nicest young people, always so happy and chatty to each other. I hope you have a long happy life together and God bless you with lots of children.' Mathew wonders if the old chook is blind. Later, in the peace of a cold Riesling, he understands her comments as it is exactly the manner in which they act. Whereas Heidi appreciates her comments come from the heart as they truly work hard at being obliging to each other. She also understands, the children comment reinforces her commitment to an older man; since her accident, she knows a young and healthy man might, for some time, love her for her body and her mind. Inevitably, one day the paternal instinct will drive them apart. With Mathew, she is safe.

Heidi appreciates the weather; being summer, it is hot with clear, sunny days around twenty-eight to thirty degrees along the river, with tranquil warm nights, after the afternoon breeze dies. Primarily, each night a sheet suffices; occasionally in the morning, one or the other pulls the doona up.

One of Heidi's fondest memories will be the evening dinners onshore, where they'll stroll casually around a town, electing to dine outside a restaurant with a table on the footpath or quay, most often with favoured shipboard guests, whom they've taken a quick affinity to. Mathew recognises the guests have warmed to them as a couple, because of Heidi's influence, not his.

The pool becomes a centre of enjoyment as they join the other sun worshippers, lying around and delighting in the magic of the scenery as it cruises past. Heidi, in her many moments of tranquility, ponders regularly. *Can it be any better than this? Thank you, my gods. How lucky am I.* If she'd asked her gods instead of just thanking them, they might have surprised her. As her joss continues, the planted seed germinates and seeks to create a life for itself, on the other side of the globe.

Mathew has, by now, totally fallen in love with Heidi. A word he uses often comes to mind, *besotted*, when he thinks of her and their relationship. He's prepared to make a commitment, with the clear intention, her past, is in fact, her past; thus, he dismisses it from any part of his mind. As far as he's concerned, the matter will never be raised as not only is the chapter completed but, indeed, the volume has closed and locked away in the book cupboard. The future, however, is difficult to calculate and quantify. During his last night at the Marco Polo Hong Kong Hotel, he determines to resolve final issues with Heidi.

He glances longingly at her, stretched out, fast asleep. A tiny purr escapes from her mouth. Instinctively, the male urge comes on him to reach over and kiss knowing she'll not object.

It's one in the morning; they're sitting up in bed, looking down the harbour after finishing the late supper. 'Heidi, I have a gift for you.' He goes to his jacket and removes the valued and treasured piece of jewellery, wrapped only in soft paper and hands it to her. She recognises it without seeing it. 'Oh, Mathew, what a man to have gone back to buy this for me. I have often thought, how silly, missing the opportunity to buy something, I fell in love with.' She reaches over and kisses him. 'I fell in love with you, Mathew, like I fell in love with this necklace. It was love at first sight as you stepped into the Rolls-Royce, at the Peninsula. My heart leapt with joy. I knew in that instant; you were going to be my man.' In his nakedness, he slides from under the sheet, rolls off the bed, kneels on the floor and looks up at her. 'I believe you love me. I love you too and to signify my love, I want to commit to you and ask you to marry me. I understand in your tradition, as in mine, it is the appropriate time, for me to offer you a ring. I don't have one.'

He turns his hands up in the international sign of empty. 'But if you accept, we will go shopping in the morning, to find you a ring you will love forever. So, Heidi, I want you to be my lady for life, if you will have me.' The hesitation nearly kills him. Suddenly, she jumps across the bed, pushing him backwards onto the floor. All he can see is a lovely naked bum and long legs falling over him. Her lips find company and they roll over the carpet. 'So, Mathew, you found the way to see into my pools, to discover what lies therein, only you?'

'Yes, Heidi, I can see the secrets in your heart and soul.'

'They tell you of my love, my sincerity, my commitment to love you until you die and leave me. It is written, Mathew. You will go first and leave me, but no one will ever replace you in my heart.' He's heard that before too, but this is different. He's, without reservation, going to marry this one and keep her to himself forever. *This one will not slip away.*

They struggle back onto the bed. 'I don't need a ring or a symbol. What counts is what's in our hearts. Come kiss me again.' But he knows the Asian in her will demand a quality investment, so she can wave her hand around, to display her man's love and commitment.

Next morning is drizzly, yet still humid as they start late up Nathan Road, to find the perfect ornamentation for her petite finger. Heidi utilises contacts, who have recommended them, to three wholesalers, where they'll be buying at the right price. In reality, they only manage it to the first store, where Mrs. Wang treats them as if royalty is visiting as she has been warned of their impending arrival. Mathew believes her, when she says, 'Now, Heidi, when you arrive in Australia, go to a reputable diamond man and have this magnificent piece valued for insurance purposes. If the valuation is not 40 per cent more, than what Mathew has paid, you send me the valuation and I'll pay you the difference.'

To celebrate the ring, they lunch in a street side cheapie. 'Least I can do is save you money after this.' She waves her hand with the ring attached. 'My contacts saved you heaps, yes?'

He concurs, 'Yes, it was a win-win, but they also saved you money, Heidi, as from now on what is mine is yours.'

'Ha, you are sounding Asian now.' She laughs. 'But god, look at it, Mathew. The diamonds sparkle just like my heart.' Still, Heidi doesn't miss his comment; and to herself, she just acknowledges, *Yes, Mathew, same, same.* And she chuckles secretly.

Mathew, when paying for the ring, clearly understands he is using someone else's money. He's set aside the full value of her contract, yet he has saved thousands, thanks to her negotiating skill. Therefore, the cost of the ring at $A12,000 is really only a part and he couldn't wait to have her in Australia, to introduce her to Lindsay and Terry, to have the value verified.

Heidi enjoys a solarium delight, including a massage with the works yet not like Hue and Ho Chi Minh City, Mathew assumes. Whilst Heidi luxuriates, he takes the opportunity of meeting the Hong Kong connections. They greet him with respect and what he believes is a joyful reception as they delight at the progress of the project. They quickly display plans Tony has sent electronically. Mathew marvels at modern technology, not truly understanding the how. Going immediately to the heart of the matter, they manage to conjure up questions, which lead into general conversations, relating to time frames, the ongoing legal and financial structure of how the end sales and leasebacks, will work.

They apologise for not arranging a dinner. Mathew assures them no apologies are necessary, in too late last night and out tonight. They promise next time.

Back at the hotel, Heidi is beaming. 'Oh, Mathew, I loved the pampering so. Come, let me pamper you before we have to part.'

Heidi is massaging his back, straddling him naked. He could feel her bone pushing and rubbing on his bum and his thighs. 'It's hard to concentrate, Heidi.'

'But fun, hey.'

He turns over. 'Heidi, we need to make plans, I don't want you living here, while I'm there. If we are going to be together, then let's be that way. Do you know, how far Brian has managed to pursue Sri's application, for the visa?'

'Yes, he will be ready to receive her around mid-December.'

'Three more months, I can't live that long without you. I'll talk to Brian first. I'll email you ASAP. Maybe you have to come down on a tourist visa to start. Oh shit, what about the law extension you're completing?'

'I have thought about that. I handled the work easily while I travelled. I don't see why I can't complete electronically or by mailed correspondence.'

He recalls her daily thirty to sixty minutes on the computer via her Hotmail address, linking into the university course. At one stage, she returns to him on the sun deck, exclaiming to all and sundry, 'My mental therapy completed for another day.'

'Then forget my time frames for the minute. What are yours? If I said jump on a plane, how quick can you settle your affairs and leave?'

'Well, I'm free as a bird. I can fly anytime.' She smiles. 'You know, Mathew, I have to pinch myself in Europe. It was so wonderful every day an adventure. Now today I pinch myself as my life forward, will be another adventure, and I am so excited to experience Melbourne. Plus, can you imagine Sri and her excitement, we will be best friends in our new home city?' She pauses in obvious contemplation of whether to pursue the question. 'Mathew, will I live with you, or are you thinking of me living with Sri?'

'No, silly moo, you will live with me. As I've said, Brian will not have you living with her.'

Her smile spreads. 'What will I do with myself?'

'Bloody good question. I have a spare bedroom for you.'

'You what? I'm not sleeping with you?'

'No, we have a law in Australia. You cannot sleep with me until we are married.'

Heidi looks aghast, but finally, the penny drops and as is their way, they just laugh.

'Anyway, back to your question. My office is in our apartment and as you are a very smart chick, I thought of us working together. I'll introduce you to my consultants. You can attend meetings, meet my business associates and clients. You know Brian, the Hong Kong connections from our dinner, so it seems reasonable, I involve you in my work.'

'Oh, that would be wonderful. Give me something meaningful in my life, besides you, of course. Yes, that would be terrific. Wow, I'm now really excited. Maybe my legal studies can be put to work.'

Mathew didn't think to question that.

CHAPTER 52

Mathew arrives at his apartment and finds Ian working from his new home; they greet each other like long-lost friends with man hugs and huge grins. 'Oh, mate, you look great. Must have been top weather. Look at your colour, so tell me all.'

Where do you start? Mathew poses privately. 'But firstly, tell me about you and May.'

'You can be the first to offer congratulations. We are going to become one as soon as I become officially single again.'

Mathew does what Heidi has taught him – look into the eyes deeply to see the heart and the soul, acknowledging he is indeed serious. Mathew hugs him. 'You're a good man, E and I think May is a gem. You know I wish you well. How about a double wedding?'

It's quite strange seeing a man dumbstruck, totally and absolutely blank across the face. Mathew smiles and turns to reach the coffee cups.

'What are you trying to tell me?'

'Make me a coffee, please. Is the computer on?'

'Yes.'

Mathew connects his digital camera via the USB box to the computer and screens one of Heidi's best poses as Ian enters and places the cups on the desk. Mathew moves away from the computer. 'This is Heidi. We are engaged.'

'But that's Miss World. What game are you playing?'

He flashes up shots in Vienna, with the backpackers in Regensburg, on the ship with fellow travelers around the pool and a raunchy bedroom shot. 'That's enough. The lovely Miss World and I are an item. I love her and funny thing is I really believe, she loves me too.'

Like two teenagers talking about their first love, they sit on the floor and discuss their new lives, the plans in place and those to be implemented to make it legal.

Ian is aware he'll have to front Jan. Mathew understands he needs to do the same with Hope, knowing the property settlement has been agreed, he knows Max will be moving things along for him.

May has invited Ian to live with her. Mathew warns him not to until he's sorted out Jan.

'Yeah, you're right, but would you believe she's set up the spare bedroom, wired and made ready for my new office? I can't believe it, mate. You know I had the hots for May the first time I met her at Barwon Heads. You guys joshed me, about her asking me to stay the night, with her in Geelong. Well, I told May all this and would you believe the girls talked about us? And how weird. May reckons she imagined me as her lover and she admits, she regretted I was married as she wanted me to pursue her. Life is so strange and do you know what? All the girls told Min Xie; you had the hots for her. They said you were so obvious. So, Mathew, any comment?' He grins.

Mathew doesn't. 'No, mate, that's another life. It's past me. Maybe one day I'll tell all.'

After that comment, Ian couldn't wait to see May as her pillow talk has been right. Min Xie and Mathew have a past no one knows about and now, he has Miss Hong Kong. 'May thinks Milly is a stunner. Wait till she meets this one.'

Mathew phones Brian, asking firstly about Mandy. 'At home, doing nicely, working towards returning to the office part time to see how she goes.'

Whilst there isn't much to discuss, he does raise meeting the boys in Honkers, where he thinks he's successfully patted the dog. He also confirms Tony and Nigel are working in tandem on the application; the report should be ready next week. Finally, he gulps and asks, 'I need a favour.'

'The short answer is Heidi can come on a tourist visa anytime she wants, maximum six months. In the meantime, we'll engineer the application for her migration, which may take that long and three large. With a bit of luck, she may not have to go back. So, congratulations are in order. I heard from a little bird and without being boring, I told you so.'

'Yeah, a little Hong Kong nightingale, I assume and yes, you were spot on. The bug was there before the trip.'

'You were very obvious, Mathew. Even I saw it. Before Sri suggested you had the hots for Heidi, I think she is some smart, attractive cookie. I'm happy for you and I have explained the situation to Mandy, she's sweet, so don't sweat it, but you need to see her and say hi, I want you two to stay close.'

Mandy greets Mathew at the door with a huge grin, balancing neatly on her crutches. 'Oh hello, traveler, so nice to see you. It just costs one small kiss to enter, and thanks for the cards. It was really nice of you. I did appreciate them.'

As he passes her, they kiss on the cheeks. 'You look a million from last time, how's the leg?'

'Yeah, good, all's fine, it's just time now.'

He presents her with a small jewellery box. 'For your leg when it mends, and I found this Thai silk scarf, in Honkers. I thought it was you.'

'Oh, wow that is beautiful. I don't have an ankle chain and the silk is wonderful, all the colours of Mandy. It will go with the Hermes.'

'Exactly, so Brian tells me, you're going to start doing some part time. You're not rushing it too quick?'

'No, next week or so, see how I go. Talking of Brian, he tells me you have huge news. Where did this come from?'

He tells her the full story, figuring she'll find out eventually.

'Yes, you're right, it does sound like a fairy tale, yet Brian tells me she is indeed a beautiful princess. You know, I wondered about your trip to Nam. It just didn't fit, so are you truly happy, Mathew?'

'Yes, I love her dearly.'

'Come give me a cuddle. Congratulations. Now tell me about the trip because I'm going one day.'

As he walks away from the lift, something worries him. It's hiding in plain sight, he sees it but it doesn't register, yet the dozen red roses, sit bold and beautiful on the mantelpiece.

Mathew thinks he hears music in his heart, Heidi singing as he types out the email. 'Give me two weeks to prepare the spare bedroom and you can fly, little bird. You don't need a visa. Still, be safe. Check with the travel agent when you book. Love you. Miss you. PS: Can you drive a car? If not, take some lessons. How did you get on with uni?'

She replies, 'I look at my ring each day and love you more. Sri is beside herself with joy as we are going to live, in the same city. Realistically, I'm maybe a month away. The travel agent confirms I do not need a visa but cannot stay longer than six months, unless a permanent one is put in place. No, I cannot drive, no reason too here and regarding uni, I can complete it electronically. Love you so. Miss you. Be with you soon. Can you believe it is forever? PS: Regards to Brian.'

He sits in his contemplative position. Ian has left for an appointment down at Mt Eliza. 'I'll be late, going to May's for dinner.' Mathew knows he will not come home. It seems strange to be alone and he isn't sure he enjoys it. He stares at the view but doesn't see it. He is thinking of Min Xie and how quickly and ardently he pursued her. She'd been compliant and willing in the pursuit and the seduction. They shared a relationship that revolved around golf; one passion led to the other, sex. In reality, they have had little else – the movies twice, the beach once, the hills twice. What else did they do? The bed and the back seat of the car are featured. But she discouraged introducing a married man to girl friends and family, discretion prevailed and that curtailed any socialising.

Does Min Xie ever ponder the promises and commitments on that fateful day when, in spirit, she married me? How bloody weird, when one looks back, on the dirty water. Mathew determines, he'll mix Heidi into his group of friends and business associates immediately. Ian and May will become key and if Heidi and May click, maybe Heidi can replace Min Xie in the girls' golf group. And that notion stirs his dark side, imagining his fiancée replacing Min Xie.

Heidi commits to arrive on Thursday, the twelfth of October. Mathew's bank, under instructions, transfers the business-class airfare. Mathew arranges for May and Ian to put Friday the thirteenth in their diary, to meet Heidi and for May to include her, in their next golf day.

Mathew and Hope meet at her favourite Chinese restaurant and he thinks, *how ironic*, as he spills the beans about Heidi. Hope immediately tinges the conversation with a smidge of colourful angst, suggesting she's the reason for the split. The anger expands, her thin lips tighten, her nose flares, and her eyes flash as she accuses him of lying about no other woman being involved. Patiently and calmly, he settles the bile; still, it becomes apparent Hope couldn't come to grips with it. If he hadn't even met her, how can this have transgressed so speedily? General conversation progresses more civilly, she advises Mathew that Max, their accountant, invited her into his office, to discuss the separation schedule and the procedure forwards. 'He was very considerate and fair and thoroughly appreciated my situation and our agreement, so I signed the preliminary documents. He's preparing the final, so soon you can apply, to make the divorce final.'

On a lighter note, Hope explains the kids had been using the beach house during the winter months. 'They have discovered your love of the open fire, but Andrew gets cheesed off, he cuts the wood, sets the fire ready for next time, but next time is girl's time and they don't reciprocate.' She grins.

'I'll want to take Heidi. Is it still okay?'

'As long as you stick to our agreement, I'm not your enemy. I think we have both handled this split very adult like. We have lots of history. Let's keep it, not destroy it. Besides, I'd like to meet her one day.'

'Thanks, Hope. You and the kids have been great. You know I appreciate that and I'll never do a wrong thing, by any of you.'

On the drive home from the restaurant, it occurs to him what a nice dinner that has been, how friendly, how civilised after a rocky start, how even now, when they are about to be totally separated, they still hang together, yet he knows in his heart, what a deceptive, unfaithful bastard he's been and within his heart and soul, it diminishes, the way he thinks of himself.

The time leading up to Heidi's arrival is maddeningly slow in passing. Mathew strives to pursue business opportunities, working diligently and thoroughly, following up the current projects and that adds purpose to the plans, multiplying and formulating in his inventive mind, which he trusts, will sire and spawn the new Heidi. Heidi, as if by transcendental engineering yet in a contrasting manner, sets out to close down a huge part of her life. To facilitate the break, it is often undertaken in solitude but more likely with Sri as she visits old haunts, places of important remembrance and old friends. It's complementary and similar to Mathew's pursuit of business, a conduit to the passing of time.

On several occasions, she visits Masaki and Tomiko, who have been her guardian angels, training and directing her, in her early formative pillow years. In typical Japanese fashion, they take tea, adopting the art of chanoyu; and Heidi, in respect, dresses in her valuable kimono, which she has never bothered to have appraised as this is a gown representing that which cannot be measured. Still, she understands, the value far exceeds US$20,000 as it is ancient and spun with gold; and once draped on her slender shoulders, she believes she inherits the strength of a samurai, the concept of joss and the intellectual intelligence of wei ch'i. During the tea ceremony, as is their personal tradition, only the language of Nippon is spoken.

The last meeting is difficult. Heidi undertakes to possess great mental strength of character, committing not to weep nor wail, yammer, or yowl as she seeks to express gratitude that can never be conveyed correctly. But then they, being of similar character, comprehend her dilemma and extend empathy as they realise before she, her future will persist and prevail, inexorably and irresistibly, tied as part of Hong Kong. It is not to them a sad day, more a promising and propitious occasion, as Tomiko notes the tidings in the tea leaves.

Privately, Heidi forages the future, diligently pursuing Mathew's comments in relation to her involvement in his business and she grins. It's like Vietnam, a unification of the parts and that's a substantial bonus in her planning, as it melds perfectly to the symmetry of the flower, having sprouted, now growing so many miles away. She wiggles her toes and bum, excited at the prospects, but immediately demands patience. Still, she thinks of having Sri close, the adventure of meeting

May and Ian and Mathew's associates and reassociating with Brian, whom she understands may well stand as a rock to lean on in any nasty eventuality; however, also recognising she will have to be particularly careful, as she recalls the fire and lust in his eyes, as they stood naked on the beach, in Sheik Wan Cove. She determines to forge a harmonious relationship with Mathew's children; then suffers trepidations, recalling her favourite TV show, *Big Brother*. Now she is the interloper, the unwanted intruder.

Finally, she cringes at her bank account, swollen by Mathew's money, clocking up interest. She giggles. 'I was so naughty but oh so clever and so, Grandfather in heaven, can I do this? Can I make this huge move in my life? Wow it is all so difficult, so many problems, everyone will know I am a lady of the night. Who will trust me? What if one, or all Mathew's children, turn against me. His ex will hate me, for who I am and what I have done. Imagine the family get togethers, no I'd rather not! Mathew speaks so highly of his consultants but what if one makes a sexual move on me, wow imagine the ramifications? And Grandfather, I have to consider his age. I have no idea of his real health, silly me why didn't I suggest he have a test, maybe I still can, stir the health pot in a funny manner. But time is against me and remember, I still have all that money, squirreled away in my very secret accounts, so in reality I could just disappear. But, is that the meaning of my life, be safe or take a very distressing risk? What a conundrum I have made for myself?'

THE END

**THE EPITOME OF HEIDI IS ON THE WAY
LOOK OUT FOR WHAT HAPPENS
TO HEIDI'S CONUNDRUM.**

CPSIA information can be obtained
at www.ICGtesting.com
Printed in the USA
LVHW041503240723
752991LV00010B/316/J